Lost and Found in Prague

"Dramatic and disturbing echoes of Prague's Velvet Revolution and of personal loss and redemption reverberate through this inspired murder mystery. Many layered, intelligent and atmospheric, with an unusual cast of characters, this is addictive stuff from Kelly Jones."

—Elizabeth Cooke, author of *Rutherford Park*

"Kelly Jones brings the ancient city of Prague alive for the reader in this captivating novel of political and religious intrigue. *Lost and Found in Prague* captures the reader with a complex plot and engaging characters as it explores the interrelationships of good and evil, of faith and doubt."

—Donna Fletcher Crow, author of *A Newly Crimsoned Reliquary*

The Woman Who Heard Color

"A moving and dangerous journey of a remarkable woman who risks her life to preserve what she loves under the rising shadow of Hitler. You will not be able to put down this extraordinary story of condemned art, unshakable family loyalty, and secret passion in a time gone mad."

—Stephanie Cowell, author of *Claude & Camille*

"[An] intense and richly detailed novel . . . A wonderfully imaginative spin on art and history."   —*Publishers Weekly*

"Shifting the story back and forth between the past and the present, Jones fashions a narrative about love and war, mothers and daughters, painting and history, courage and sacrifice, which is itself a work of art."   —*Chicago Tribune*

continued . . .

"This novel holds great historical background and will appeal to lovers of history and art . . . Jones manages to put a human face on otherwise unpleasant past events." —*RT Book Reviews*

"This well-crafted story offers a nuanced portrait of life between wars, then behind Nazi lines, and is based on true stories of people who risked everything to keep the German culture of the time from perishing forever." —*Historical Novel Society*

"Moving . . . Reminiscent of Ian McEwan's *Atonement* . . . As a story about art and love, it's beautiful." —*The Literary Gothamite*

"Filled with history, art, mystery, suspense; it is beautifully written and filled with heart-palpitating moments. I was captivated." —*A Novel Review*

"Jones has a knack for telling a good, suspenseful story . . . If you're interested in art, Nazi looting, or just a well-told, human story, *The Woman Who Heard Color* is an amazing novel to pick up. Jones creates her characters with such care, and her story is so rich and vibrant, even in the worst of circumstances." —*S. Krishna's Books*

PRAISE FOR

Kelly Jones

"One of those rare reading experiences; page-turning and insightful, it explores the human condition in a way that few novels do. Kelly Jones is a wonderful writer, and definitely one to watch." —Nicholas Sparks

"Fans of . . . *Girl with a Pearl Earring* will love Jones's well-imagined romantic saga." —*Idaho Statesman*

LOST AND
FOUND
IN PRAGUE

Kelly Jones

BERKLEY BOOKS, NEW YORK

THE BERKLEY PUBLISHING GROUP
Published by the Penguin Group
Penguin Group (USA) LLC
375 Hudson Street, New York, New York 10014

USA • Canada • UK • Ireland • Australia • New Zealand • India • South Africa • China

penguin.com

A Penguin Random House Company

This book is an original publication of The Berkley Publishing Group.

Library of Congress Cataloging-in-Publication Data

Jones, Kelly, 1948–
Lost and found in Prague / Kelly Jones.—Berkley trade paperback edition.
    pages; cm
ISBN 978-0-425-27670-9 (softcover)
1. Prague (Czech Republic)—Fiction.   I. Title.
PS3610.O6264L67   2015
    813'.6—dc23
    2014036558

PUBLISHING HISTORY
Berkley trade paperback edition / January 2015

PRINTED IN THE UNITED STATES OF AMERICA

10 9 8 7 6 5 4 3 2 1

Front cover photograph: Czech Republic, Prague,
View over Vltava River © Henryk Sadura/Getty Images.
Back cover photogaphs: View of Charles Bridge and Prague Castle © f9photos/Shutterstock.
Cobblestones © Bruno D'Andrea/Shutterstock.
Cover design by Danielle Abbiate.

ACKNOWLEDGMENTS

Thank you to writing group friends who offered suggestions on very early drafts of the story: Linda Kahn, Susan Richards, and Pat Koleini. For faithful readers, Paul Van Dam, Judy Frederick, and Coston Frederick, I express my gratitude. And to my husband, Jim, who read more versions than either of us can count, please know that you are truly appreciated. Many thanks to my Berkley editor, Kate Seaver, and also Katherine Pelz and Erin Galloway who continue to support me through the process of making a story a book and introducing it to you, my readers, for whom I am always grateful.

· 1 ·

The quiet woke her as it did each morning when the dreams faded. Claire lay, taking in a deep breath, aware that she had been given another day, forcing herself to be grateful for this. She rose, her knees creaking as she grasped the edge of the bed and lowered herself to the hard, cold floor for her morning offering. "O my God, my sweet Infant Savior, I offer thee my prayers, works, and sufferings," she began.

After a silent *Amen*, she crossed herself, slowly unfolded her aging joints as she stood, and stepped to the narrow closet. Laboriously she tugged the night garment over her head, slipped on the dark brown tunic, the panels of the scapular, followed by white wimple and black veil, a ritual she had performed each morning for the past seventy-six years. She smoothed the covers on her small bed and sat, rubbing her feet together to encourage the circulation. The Barefoot Order of the Carmelites, she mused, though sandals had always been part of her habit. Today she would need a good pair of stockings to protect her toes from the early-morning chill. She worked the warm wool over her feet, pulling the socks up around her plump calves, and then nudged the sandals from beneath her bed and slipped them on, bending to secure the straps, a simple task that had become more and more difficult. Before leaving her room, she wrapped a frayed knit shawl around her shoulders.

In the darkness, she shuffled down the hall, through the kitchen, past the pantry. After retrieving the keys from the box near the door, she dipped her fingers into the dove-shaped holy water font that hung on the wall, offering her day for a second time to the Infant Savior.

Silently, she crept down the stairs, counting each step with an aspiration—*my God*—step—*and my all*—step—*my God*—step—*and my all*. Sixteen total. Making her way along the hall, she disturbed no one. She unbolted the heavy wooden door, pulled it open slowly, crossed the small courtyard, unlatched the iron gate, and stepped out onto the square. April's dampness hung in the air, intensified by the silence, the absence of others. Sister Claire wrapped the shawl tighter and reached for her rosary. She knew exactly how long it would take to walk the short distance to Our Lady Victorious. One rosary. Twenty-five aspirations. As she grasped the small crucifix fixed to the beads, touched it to her head and heart, left, then right, she realized she wasn't sure what day it was. This happened often now, and her greatest concern this morning was her uncertainty over which mysteries to contemplate. She decided on the Joyful to combat the feelings that had invaded her for the past weeks and months. The Joyful Mysteries were designated for Mondays and Thursdays, and she thought it was Thursday.

She encountered no one as she walked. The first light of morning had yet to rise over the golden-tipped spires of Prague. The bakers, whose delicious scents would soon fill the pastry shops in the neighborhoods of the Malá Strana, had just begun to rub sleep from their eyes, and it would be hours before the vendors, whose wooden wagons bumped early each morning with an uneven rhythm over the cobblestones, would offer fresh fruits and vegetables from the stalls at the open market.

Claire felt an energy in her prayers as if with each step, each word, she was nudging a soul closer toward heaven. She finished her rosary and kissed the cool metal of the cross, her lips pressed against the ridge of the nail piercing Christ's feet. "Forgive me, Father, for I have sinned," she whispered.

She had no permission to walk alone from the convent to the Church of Our Lady Victorious, though she was sure the prioress knew she often rose and moved about in the darkness, unable to sleep more than a few hours each night.

Later, she would return to her cell as she did each morning, then emerge once more in timely fashion, joining the other nuns in the chapter room for their silent procession into the convent chapel.

She recited the twenty-five aspirations, counting them off on two and a half decades of rosary beads—four more years' indulgences. At times she thought she could feel and see the souls being lifted heavenward, greeted by the Father. She chided herself for such pride, thinking that she, a humble servant, could be an instrument in delivering these waiting souls to their eternal reward.

With the last aspiration, she arrived at her destination and in the darkness her fingers searched for the lock on the door. She slid the key in and entered. Immediately she sensed a foreign presence had infused the interior of the church. A faint vibration pulsed along the floor, and the glass chandelier above quivered with the slightest tremor. Yet, such movements were not unusual in themselves. The church was over four hundred years old; often she sensed spirits from the past still lingered, lurking in the crypt below, hovering in the attic above.

Inhaling, she wondered if the scent that clung to the air, a smell she knew but could not name nor retrieve from the proper pocket of her mind, was the source of this uneasiness and confusion. Memories, like pennies stored in a pouch riddled with holes, slipped out so easily now. Despite her misgivings, she approached the main altar and bowed—no longer able to lower herself for a proper genuflection—then continued to the sacristy where the cleaning supplies were stored, determined to complete the task for which she had come. She checked the altar alarm and found it had been turned off. Had she done this the day before? Forgotten to reset it? She gathered the plastic pail, inserted the whisk broom and dustpan, gripped the shears, and stepped back into the church, realizing with a touch of relief that the perplexing, yet familiar, smell was that of incense. A remnant of the previous evening's services, it perfumed the air, mingling with the aroma perpetually clinging to the marble altars and ancient stone. But this relief coupled with the recognition of a recurring uncertainty. What was happening to her mind that she could not remember from day to day what had come and gone the day before? Today wasn't Thursday. Yesterday had been Thursday. Holy Thursday. Today was Good Friday. There were no flowers to refresh, no dried blossoms to pinch or stray vines to clip. The altars were bare. How had she made such a terrible mistake? Today she should have contemplated on the Sorrowful Mysteries, meditating on the Passion of Christ. Today was the day Christ died for the sins of all mankind.

Again she felt a presence. A voice. "Accomplished with ease." Was this merely her mind playing with her once more?

Then another, far away, near the door, the words carried on the air of a familiar melody, a distinct timbre. "A well-played plan. My reasoning correct. He is with us, guiding the way, as surely this would not have been so accomplished without."

Then words, unspoken, a familiar voice, spinning about her, yet only within. The melody, the verse she'd often heard and pondered:

Under the wing of peace we march in gentle revolution
to claim our cherished life and freedom
The salvation of the world
to be found in the human heart

She stood, hands trembling, tightening her grasp on the shears. Lingering in the shadow of the altar of Saints Joachim and Anne, she listened. A click of the door? Nothing now. The voices had stilled. The church was quiet. Claire heard only her own breathing.

Moments later, deciding that the voices—which, together with the thieves of memory, had become her personal cross—were only imagined, she made her way down the side aisle. Again, she stopped and listened. Nothing. She was alone in the church.

She proceeded on quiet feet to the altar of the Pražské Jezulátko.

At one time she had been allowed to dress the Infant, but this task has been handed over to the younger nuns, Sister Agnes, Sister Ludmila, and Sister Eurosia. Claire knew she could still do it without difficulty. Her mind and hands had memorized every curve of the precious little body. She knew how to enclose the small figure in the metal shell for protection. She was aware of the scent and texture of every garment, the history of each. Tomorrow the younger nuns would remove the Infant from his position high on the altar and prepare him for the glorious day, dressing the little King in the colors of the Resurrection.

She bowed before the Infant, suddenly aware of another scent, similar, though distinct from the spicy smell of incense. The voices could deceive her, but this smell, layered upon stone and incense, she easily identified as the residue of tobacco. No plumes curled in the air, nor invaded her nostrils, yet she knew someone had been here, and she knew the odor, a scent that would cling to a body, leaving a distinct trail long after the flame had been extinguished. She did not imagine this. Someone had been in the church.

Instinctively, she tilted her head up toward the altar. A knot tightened in her chest. For the briefest moment she felt something— a swish of warm air against her face. Then a sensation of empty air. A void. Something missing. Gone. The sharpness circling her heart increased, the weight of her body pulling her down as a deep sting cut into her cheek, warm and wet. The clatter of her plastic pail dropping to the floor, dustpan and whisk broom rattling out. Another voice gently calling. "It is time, my faithful servant."

Claire's own voice, humble, but strong, "Not yet, my Lord."

· 2 ·

Two weeks, two days before Easter

The streetlamp provided scant light; he used the flashlight beam as he traced along the outline of the form, bulky as a grizzly bear in winter. A bullet hole pierced the side of the head. Twisted beneath the tower of the old town hall at the Staroměstské náměsti, the man's body lay as if placed on the bull's-eye of a target, centered in a circle constructed of dark stones alternating with light stones, a sidewalk mosaic. The astronomical clock hovered above, marking time, tracking the movement of sun and moon. If it had been summer or fall, the tourists might be gathering now, though the chimes would not sound for another two hours. It was too early, too cold, too dark.

Chief Investigator Dal Damek of the Czech Republic Police Force and the Městská policie Praha officer who'd made the call stood conversing in low whispers. The young officer, part of the city police force, had heard the shot rip through the quiet morning and claimed to have seen a quick flash from the roof of a building—he pointed across the square toward the Grand Hotel Praha.

A tilt of the head from Damek sent Detective Kristof Sokol and

the team off toward the hotel, the eager young rookie leading the
way. *Charging,* Damek thought, with the barely tested enthusiasm of
a novice.

"There." The Městská policie Praha officer's voice trembled, as did
his still-extended arm, and Damek guessed he was new to the local
force, an officer whose duties normally consisted of overseeing traffic
and animal control, attending to the tourists. Damek himself was
well seasoned, seven years now in homicide. Seven days as chief investigator.

A cool wind whipped through the square, tumbling a paper cup
along the cobbles, catching against the wheel of the forensics van. Tiny
sparkling flakes, dust motes, danced in the glow of the streetlight.
Damek pulled a kerchief out of his pocket to catch a sneeze. Too early
in the season for pollen, but something had invaded the morning air.
Once more he surveyed the scene, then folded the square into his jacket
and knelt down on the hard, cold stone.

The victim, a man with broad shoulders and thick legs, wore
expensive, finely polished leather shoes, a heavy winter coat, soft black
fur around the collar. Little more than a week into spring, mornings
had yet to welcome the season. The last snowfall had come in early
March.

"I didn't touch anything," the Městská officer assured him. His
voice quivered with nerves and Damek knew the man hadn't
approached the body. The location and appearance of the entry
wound, the lack of blood, indicated it wouldn't have mattered; death
had come quickly. Once more the investigator scanned the square,
his eyes settling on the hotel where faces pressed against the windows.

Branislov Černý, "the old Commie," as some of the younger officers called him, stooped to examine the metal door at the base of the
clock tower. The photographer, other technicians, and officers scur-

ried about, recording details, taking measurements. Damek could not see an exit wound, just the small hole in the dead man's head. Gauging the distance to the hotel, the way the body had fallen, it was likely the fatal shot had originated from the roof, just as the young officer had said.

Černý approached, his left leg slowing him down in the cold. Something perhaps overlooked during his last physical as he neared retirement. The senior detective stood beside the chief investigator, staring down. Damek knew the expression that had settled on the man's craggy face even before he glanced back. An expression that some would call no expression at all. They said Detective Černý had been doing this too long—he was a holdover, one of the few, from the old days. He operated mostly on gut instinct. Passed over too many times for promotion. Now just biding his time. Over the years, Damek had come to know the man well, and he knew exactly what the old detective was thinking—this was not the work of an amateur. One bullet to the head. This was an execution, a professional.

A small crowd gathered, standing at a distance, held back by the bright yellow crime scene tape. Curious, hushed voices. Others were cordoned off, being questioned now, anyone who might have seen or heard anything. Two of the officers were turning the body, face fully visible now, tongue protruding from a distorted mouth, a thin drool jelling on the gaping lower lip. A pair of pale blue eyes stared up at Damek, wide with astonishment. The man's dark hair was peppered with silver.

A cell phone rang. The uniformed officer meticulously bagging the victim's belongings glanced at Damek, who nodded. The officer handed him the dead man's phone. Nothing to identify the caller on the screen—the number officially blocked. Damek hit answer.

A rough voice, quick and impatient. "I wish to continue our discussion.

Ten. Same place." Damek said nothing. He heard only the caller's shallow breathing, then dead air.

The officer handed the man's ID to Černý, who in turn pressed it into Dal's hand without a word. Damek glanced down at the official government-issued ID, then at the body, matching the victim's face with the photo of a jowly middle-aged man, aware of how easily one could be stripped of power, control, and dignity. Again his eyes met Černý's, and once more he read the old detective's thoughts.

Seven days in, and Damek had been handed his first high-profile case as chief of homicide. Once more, he scanned the square, then stared up at the clock, the signs of the zodiac on the face of the tower. He'd come here to the Staroměstské náměsti, the Old Town Square, often with Karla when they were young, after the revolution, then with Petr, particularly for the holidays. During the Christmas season and again for Easter, the square overflowed with vendors and festivities. Easter, just two weeks away. The traditional beginning of the tourist season.

The unseen apostles remained silent and still, high in the tower, enclosed within the intricacies of the ancient mechanical device, hidden behind the star-dappled doors, as if they were the gates to paradise. Damek knew how it would all begin. The knell to mark each hour. The sliding doors opening to reveal the turning figures, the apostles' procession. Below this parade of saints, four figures of stone stood without motion, poised for what was to come. Vanity held a mirror. Greed grasped a bag of gold. Death stood to the right, along with Sloth, two more figures for symmetry. Death, a form devoid of flesh and heart. Mere bones. In the left hand he grasped a rope, prepared to pull; in the right hand, the hourglass ready to turn. The sand would slip slowly, each sifting grain a reminder of time running out.

In myths and legends, Death stalked at midnight. Damek looked to the east, spires of the city visible in the early pink glow of dawn. In Prague, Death danced with delight after daybreak, performing each hour for tourists and visitors gathered in the square. This morning the esteemed Senator Jaroslav Zajic had been invited to join the show.

· 3 ·

Two days after Easter

She traveled alone. Unnoticed. A woman, neither young nor old. Neither beautiful nor plain. Perhaps a woman with a secret, something hidden. Yet, if one were to look deeply, sorrow, rather than secrets, might be revealed. A grief she wished to share with no one. And so, each year, she left, arranging her schedule around the Easter holiday, leaving behind laptop, cell phone, any thread of connection to home, choosing destinations where she was unlikely to encounter anyone she knew. Dana Pierson wished to be alone, to disappear into the crowds.

She gazed out the airplane window at a vast expanse, wishing for a moment she could become part of it, then stared down at the open novel on her lap, realizing she'd read a full page, unaware of a single word. It wasn't the type of book she'd normally pick up at home—an improbable mystery requiring little thought, silly and complicated at the same time, a book she may or may not finish and would probably leave in the hotel room for the next guest.

She'd spent a week in Rome and was now flying to Prague where she planned to visit her cousin, an exception to the solitude of her spring escape, though by virtue of Caroline's life choice the two women would have little time together. Dana heard her brother Ben admonishing her, "Better with those who love you. You must know we are here for you."

Caroline hadn't been there. She'd sent a letter. Filled with words, attempting comfort. Dana hadn't seen her in years. At one time they were very close. Then something changed, and Caroline had made a momentous decision that Dana had never understood.

Her thoughts turned to a gloomy November almost twenty years earlier, a youthful journey, an introduction to Prague. Dark clouds cast a shadow over this unknown world, and Dana had wondered, as she looked out the train window, how she had conceived such a notion, why she hadn't listened to Caroline's protests about the dangers of entering a Communist country. Caroline, generally open to possibility, always game for a little adventure, perpetually seeing the good in everyone, was, in fact, afraid of godless Communists, and it had taken some cajoling on Dana's part to convince her to agree to the excursion. The wall in Berlin had just fallen and figurative walls were crumbling all over Europe: The Iron Curtain had been rent. They had heard from others along the way about groups of young, hopeful students organizing in Prague and throughout Czechoslovakia to demonstrate for justice and freedom. As an aspiring journalist, Dana wanted to witness history. Caroline did not share her enthusiasm.

"We could see the Holy Infant of Prague," Dana had offered, and this turned out to be the shining lure—the opportunity for Caroline, a young woman who believed in angels and saints and divine intervention, to see the small, revered sixteenth-century religious icon.

They were twenty-two at the time, just graduated from college. Both from Boston University, Dana in journalism, Caroline in art history.

The trip was a gift from their parents, the great adventure before settling down to enter the real world of employment and grown-up responsibilities. Originally intended for a month-long adventure, a summer trip, it had now extended into the fall, and now as winter took hold.

Dana recalled clearly the noisy locomotive coming to an abrupt halt at the Austria-Czechoslovakia border, the mismatched pair of armed guards muscling their way onto the train, thumbing through passports, checking for visas, glancing up at every turn of the page. The younger officer, short and compact, eyed the Americans suspiciously. The larger and older, square-shouldered with thick dark brows and tight-set mouth, took his time examining papers as if viewing every foreigner as a potential threat. The girls exchanged guarded looks and Dana guessed that Caroline was praying they might be sent back to Austria, fearing that, if allowed to enter, they would be arrested immediately and thrown into a rat-infested prison, their parents not even aware of where they were.

Two hours later, the train huffed and snorted and continued on. When they finally arrived at the outskirts of Prague, they were greeted by a scene more dour than Dana had imagined. Slowing, they rolled past filthy building facades, tile roofs caked with soot, a winter sky clogged with black puffs billowing from dirty brick chimneys. The train jerked to a stop at an ancient-looking station.

A slap of frigid air greeted them as they filed out with other passengers. Lifting backpacks to shoulders, they started through the city, Caroline clutching her coat tighter and tighter around her throat, throwing her cousin one look of concern after another. Breathing air that was barely breathable and reeking with smoke, they walked past boxy Communist-constructed apartments, people bundled up in colorless clothes—few making eye contact—then more dark, filthy structures. With each step, Dana wondered if this had been a terrible mistake.

Eventually, they found a student hostel and, after they'd checked in and surrendered their passports, a plump matronly woman in a gray sacklike dress, clipboard in hand, led them silently down a narrow hall, past walls of peeling paint, over a speckled linoleum floor buckling beneath them. The girls' dorm, lined with lumpy beds blanketed with itchy-looking wool, smelled of cold stone, overripe fruit, and wet socks and overflowed with the noisy chatter of young women. Mostly students, Dana guessed, all speaking in languages she did not understand. She glanced around, a few girls throwing furtive looks their way, no one offering a smile or welcome. Laundry—dingy underclothes—hung on makeshift clotheslines. Dana pressed her fingers along the side of her head, attempting to thwart the headache she felt coming, and then collapsed on her assigned bed.

Caroline threw her backpack on the adjacent bed, unzipped a pocket, and rummaged around, glancing at Dana with another one of *those* looks. Dana didn't want to tell her cousin she was now having her own doubts.

Caroline took off down the hall to shower and wash her hair. A natural beauty, without conceit or arrogance, she had one vanity— her lovely, thick, long blond tresses. Dana, who often hopped out of bed and quickly ran a comb through her lank brown hair, frequently teased Caroline about her time-consuming ritual of washing, drying, combing, fluffing. Yet Dana could not deny that a girl with lovely, long blond hair, especially one as attractive as Caroline, caught the attention of the fellows. A definite plus when hanging out with her cousin. Boys sometimes told Dana she was cute, but Caroline far surpassed cute. She turned heads.

A thin girl, speaking in broken English, approached and attempted to bum a cigarette, which Dana didn't have, and then invited her to join a march the following day to commemorate International Student Day.

Caroline returned to the room, shivering, her damp head still spotted with dabs of shampoo suds. Glaring at Dana, she shrieked, "The goddamned water just went off!"

Dana felt her lips splitting into a smile at the memory, particularly in light of what Caroline was now doing in Prague. *No swearing. No hair problems.* And then, like an unexpected hiccup, a quick high-pitched laugh escaped. She cleared her throat and glanced quickly at the man sitting next to her. He looked up from his newspaper with a faint smile of amusement.

"Good book?" he asked. He spoke in the deep, roughly textured voice of a smoker. Late sixties to early seventies, she guessed, with noticeable fatigue in his eyes, which were mapped with fine red threads. About her father's age, if he were still alive. The man wore a dark suit with a nicely pressed white shirt, open collar, no tie. His black hair, little more than a neatly trimmed fringe set below a balding pate, was touched with a hint of gray. A large man, the bulk of his round body pressed against the armrest dividing their seats. Yet there was something rather refined about him—a man who had perhaps overindulged in the better things of life. He, too, appeared to be traveling alone.

Dana stared down at her book cover, feeling a blush of embarrassment over the shiny gold-embossed title, the woman in shapely silhouette holding a smoking gun. "Good book?" she replied. "Not really." The man tilted his head as if waiting for her to explain the smile, as if she might owe him an explanation.

"I was thinking," she said, "of an earlier visit to Prague." As soon as she spoke, she wished she hadn't. She could have nodded a yes and returned to her reading.

He folded his paper and stuffed it in the seat pocket, eager and ready to engage in conversation. She noticed his hands, carefully manicured, soft as if he'd never engaged in a day of hard, physical work.

"You are on holiday?" he asked with interest, and she nodded, realizing she'd randomly drawn the seat next to a talker. A person who actually enjoyed engaging with strangers. "You spent time in Rome?" He spoke with a slight accent. Italian, she guessed.

"Six days," she answered.

"You enjoyed it?" Something in his voice told her Rome was home, that he was proud of his city. "A lovely place to enjoy the Easter holidays."

"Yes, I did enjoy the city." She'd done the regular tourist things: the Colosseum, the Vatican, St. Peter's. But Easter Sunday, the five-year anniversary, as well as the day before Easter—the cruelty of a moveable holiday requiring she relive it twice every year—she'd done nothing but wander the streets, purposely placing herself in the busiest squares, the areas with the most pedestrian traffic, in order to be alone, and yet among others. To be unnoticed. To become a no one among so many.

"Rome is a beautiful city with much history. As is Prague." His tone was friendly. "What brings you back to the Czech Republic?" he asked.

"I'm visiting a friend, my cousin, actually," she said. He seemed a nice enough man, and the flight wasn't long enough to get bogged down in a lengthy, unwelcome conversation.

"She lives in Prague?"

Dana nodded.

"It's been some time since you've visited?" he asked.

"About twenty years."

"On holiday then, too?"

"Well, yes, though ..." She stopped. Why was she sharing this with a complete stranger?

He raised an inviting brow as if to say, *Do tell me, I'm interested.* "Prague twenty years ago?" he asked. "What brought you to the city back *then*?"

"A revolution," she replied, wondering if this would shock him terribly.

"A revolution." He repeated the words slowly. He was pensive, rather than surprised. "*Sametová revoluce,* a velvet revolution." The word *velvet* rolled off his tongue devoid of any roughness, imbued with a softness the word itself deserved.

Dana nodded, acknowledging his familiarity with the history of Prague.

"Prague, they say, has become the new Paris," he told her. "Much changed since the Communists." He tilted his head as if offering this last statement as a subject of discussion.

"You're also on holiday?" Dana asked, using the European word, which sounded more fun than *vacation* or *break*, like a true celebration.

"I'm not sure," he said with a laugh that had a rough, raspy tone, as if it came from deep within, rattling up through his lungs. "I'm visiting a dear friend. Like you." He held out his hands, palms up, then turned them back to himself, as if he and Dana shared something in common. "Though I have not been apprised of the details, I believe I've been called upon to exercise the skills I've developed in the course of my work, in positions I've held through the past several decades." This was pronounced with a combination of pride, authority, and something that might have been described as a tease—a tease in the sense of *My work is so important that I'm not at liberty to discuss it with you.* "Not an official assignment," he added.

She offered a curious smile. The man's face held a hint of the same, the possibility quickly aborted with an agitated glance around as if searching for something or someone.

"This dry air," he said, bringing a closed fist to his mouth and clearing his throat. "I would certainly enjoy a drink." He gazed down the aisle at the smiling flight attendant pushing the refreshment cart, slowly making her way toward them.

He'd aroused Dana's natural curiosity. She felt tested to draw out more, as if he were challenging her to do just that.

"You work for a business here in . . ." she said, motioning back with her head to imply where they'd come from, rather than where they were going. "Italy?"

He stared at her for a moment, as if determining her need to know. "Yes," he conceded. He leaned closer as if they were about to share a secret. She smelled the liquor on his breath, as well as his spicy cologne or aftershave, along with a scent that confirmed he was a smoker. "I work for a large organization based in Italy," he said softly, and she was sure she detected a taunting twinkle in his eye. The Italian Mafia, she thought with an inner laugh, edged with a small portion of self-warning. Was she sitting here with the Godfather?

"My work, in some aspects similar to yours," he added.

"Mine?" she asked, the single word coming out slow and tentative. "My work?" He'd caught her off guard and now she felt more irritated than inquisitive. Did he know her? Had he read something she'd written? She was about to ask if they'd met before when he called to the flight attendant, chatting with the passenger in front of them.

"Per favore, signorina." He spoke rapidly, urgently, in Italian. Dana sat back in her seat and gazed out the window, feeling as if her space—if such a thing existed in the narrow confines of an airplane—had been invaded. Though she'd certainly opened herself up for conversation.

"You, miss?" The flight attendant leaned in and asked, "Would you like something to drink?"

Dana looked up at the smiling face, the perfectly applied mauve lipstick and white teeth. "No, thank you."

"A journalist?" she asked the man as the attendant poured him a whiskey. "You're a journalist?" She prided herself in being observant, but she couldn't place him.

"Like you, my work often involves gathering facts, analyzing, and recording my findings. Though, no, I'm not a journalist, not published traditionally as you." The attendant handed him his drink and moved down the aisle.

"You've visited Boston?" Dana asked. They stared at each other for a long moment, and she sensed that he was playing with her, that he was enjoying this.

"My work often involves travel."

"And your work, or pleasure, now takes you to Prague."

"Not officially ... yet, as a favor to a friend. Like you ..." He tipped his head. "On holiday, visiting a friend."

"I see," she replied, waiting for more.

He raised his glass in a toast. "To friends and holidays."

"Salute," she replied, using an Italian toast.

"Salute."

He leaned back, closing his eyes, and took a slow, obviously pleasurable, drink. *Conversation over,* he seemed to say.

She opened her book. She was done with him, too—he'd started this, then cut her off. She refused to play his game, though that ever-present curiosity pried about in her head as she attempted to retrieve a memory of this man who seemed to know her. She dismissed the impulse to ask and gave her glasses a little nudge to keep them from slipping on her nose. She glanced over at the man, napping now, breathing heavily, clutching his empty plastic glass as it rose and fell rhythmically on the perch of his large belly.

After the flight attendant had gathered empty cups, napkins, and snack wrappers—plucking the empty cup from the still-slumbering man as she shot Dana a smile—a deep voice announced their descent into the Ruzyně Airport.

Awakened by the broadcast but still heavy lidded and groggy, the man pulled a black briefcase up from the floor space in front of his feet, unzipped a side pocket, and inserted his newspaper. Dana slid her book into her bag.

He turned to her again and said, "It's been a pleasure visiting with you." He'd released his seat belt, though the light was still on. He wasn't a man used to playing by the rules, she guessed.

"We've met before?" she asked, unable to end the flight with the question unanswered.

"Oh, no, but I do know your work."

The flight attendant glided down the aisle, head bobbing from side to side, checking to make sure those in her care were secure, kindly reminding the man to fasten his seat belt, gesturing toward the lit sign.

He let off an indignant *humph*, but he complied, and they soon hit the runway.

"You're familiar with my work?" Dana asked.

"Yes," he replied, but offered no more.

When the seat belt light dimmed, he stood abruptly and made his way to the front of the plane with a sense of entitlement. He had no overhead luggage, just the briefcase.

She watched him, and there was something about the way he moved, the grace with which he carried that excessive weight.

After gathering her own carry-on, it dawned on her in an unexpected flash. They had never met, but she had seen him briefly—from the back as he slid into a shiny black Town Car. She'd attempted to find him when he came to Boston. An elusive ghost of a man.

Ah, yes, she thought as she started down the aisle, that organization based in Italy—much older than and often as mysterious as the Mafia. Those perfectly manicured hands? A man who held the body of Christ would keep his hands as pristine as a newly baptized baby's soul.

· 4 ·

Father Giovanni Borelli hated to fly. He did not enjoy the bustle of airports, the queues for boarding, and then the dreadful, confined, cramped quarters of an aircraft. He loved his work, which often, at least in the past, required that he travel—wherever the miracles, the apparitions, the transgressions might take him. But he liked to be in the middle of things, not going there or coming back.

Yet he often met interesting people in his travels. He had enjoyed speaking with the woman from Boston. Years ago, they'd played a little game of cat and mouse. He recalled watching her then—he peering through the blinds in the bishop's study, she stepping off the front porch, glancing back, and then hurrying down the sidewalk with a quick, agitated gait. When he found his seat on the plane, he easily recognized her, though there was nothing that would make her stand out in a crowd. She looked to be perhaps in her late thirties, though he knew she had to be at least forty if she'd been traipsing about Europe during the time of the revolution in Czechoslovakia. Her frame, slight. Her hair, an ordinary brown. He guessed with a little makeup and perhaps a more flattering hairstyle—hers hung limply to her shoulders—she might have turned a head. Her style of dress—jeans and T-shirt—certainly did nothing to enhance her figure. Borelli remembered when women used to take care with their appearance, dress like women. Gia had always attired herself as a proper, refined lady. He found this trend of casual dress, surely started by the Americans, inappropriate.

But he'd been unkind, and he'd have to confess. He'd engaged in a verbal game as if they were opponents, which they were not. They'd both arrived at the same conclusion in Boston.

He knew it was that old, yet familiar, sin of pride—he liked to have the upper hand and had quite enjoyed their conversation, she having no idea who he was. He should have walked off the plane with her, introduced himself, told her how fairly he believed she'd covered the events in Boston. But, damn, he had to get to the terminal and find the restroom. And he needed a cigarette.

He'd probably never see her again. Prague was a city of over a million and this time of year, with the advent of spring, it often appeared as if the population had doubled. One could practically walk across the Charles Bridge, the Karlův most, without lifting a foot, the tourist traffic so heavy a person might be carried along in the stream of flowing bodies.

After using the men's room, he made his way out of the terminal, along with other travelers hefting, dragging, and wheeling an assortment of baggage. Father Borelli had but his briefcase, preferring the ease of traveling sans luggage. His wardrobe was limited, though he took pride in a neatly pressed suit and a fresh cassock being available at all times. He always packed a box and sent it ahead to his hotel with instructions to have the garments pressed and waiting in his room when he checked in. This assured he'd have a presentable wardrobe for the duration of his stay, though he was concerned since the urgency of this trip required he send the box special delivery. With the holiday weekend he was aware it might not arrive until several days into his stay. The thought irritated him, though the shipping company guaranteed his package would arrive within a day, and his hotel was always good about seeing to his requests. Fortunately he'd called ahead and been assured a room would be available for him, even on such short notice.

At least a dozen passengers waited in line at the cab stop, though he noted not a single cab in sight. Tourists everywhere. He reached into his pocket, grateful he had time for a smoke. He inserted a cigarette in his silver holder—he hated cigarette stains on fingers—lit up and drew in a comforting drag. He was content to stand and wait, though if he'd been wearing his collar he would most likely be invited to go ahead. People in Europe still respected the collar.

He tapped his cigarette ash into a receptacle by the cab stand and noticed a wrinkle in the leg of his trousers. Another reason he hated the confinement of an airplane. He gave it a quick, firm brush with his wide hand, pressing the crease with his fingers. By the time he finished his smoke, he'd moved to the front of the line. His cab arrived and he gave the driver the address of his hotel.

As they drove into the center of Prague, he wondered what Ms. Pierson would think coming back after an absence of almost twenty years. It was now a vibrant, commercial city with modern shops and galleries, cafés and theaters, combined in a charming way with the centuries-old buildings, cobbled streets, medieval churches, and ancient castles. Little physical damage had been done to the old city during the war. Most of the historical center had been spared, and he found it one of the loveliest in Eastern Europe. He'd once heard Prague described as the finest Italian city outside of Italy. Yet, during the forty years of the Communist regime, there was no pride in ownership and buildings had fallen into disrepair. The privatization and commercialism after the revolution had done much for the city. A visitor, such as the American woman, returning after a long absence would find the city quite delightful.

His first encounter with Ms. Dana Pierson had been seven years ago now, though the offenses that brought him to Boston had gone back decades, the sins of betrayal, the perhaps equally great sins of denial and cover-up. All had contributed to a terrible time in the history of the Church. When he reported back to Rome, it was with a heavy heart.

The trip to Boston had been one of many sporadic assignments after the dissolution of the office of Promoter of the Faith and then Father Borelli's resignation from his position at the university in Rome. He had a reputation for being fair and thorough, though many of his efforts received little recognition. Much of his work was done "unofficially," on special assignment. Now he found himself in Prague, though not officially. Not even unofficially. He had come simply because Giuseppe Ruffino—Beppe—had called. Over the past several years he had often visited his friend, who had been appointed the prior of Our Lady Victorious by the Holy Father shortly after a new government had been established in the early nineties. He'd give Beppe a call as soon as he got to the hotel. Saint Giuseppe, he often called him. They had been best friends since childhood, growing up in a little village south of Florence, one of the prettiest places on earth with its lovely vineyards and rolling hills, an area well-known for its fine wine production.

His cab arrived at the hotel and he tipped the driver generously, as he always did, though he had but the one small briefcase, which he carried in himself. He picked up his keys, inquiring if his package had been delivered. It had not. He'd packed a clean set of underwear in his briefcase, along with his toiletries and breviary, but he should not have trusted that the delivery and pressing would be done, particularly with the holiday. He took the elevator up to his third-floor room, miffed that he had nothing to wear other than what was on his back. Aware that he should be climbing stairs if just for a little exercise, he excused himself by the fact that he'd had a long day. As he stepped off the small elevator, he felt a familiar cramp knotting in his left leg. He also needed to pee. Again. This getting old did not agree with him.

In his room, he used the bathroom, then opened his briefcase, pulled out a bottle, fixed himself a drink, got out his cigarettes, flipped on the TV, and settled down. As a vintner, he enjoyed a nice bottle of wine with dinner. But for a good numbing jolt, he preferred a fine whiskey. How did the Americans say it, *liquor is quicker*? There was something to be said for both distillation and fermentation. He took another satisfying drink.

He would call Beppe tomorrow, when he had a pressed suit and cassock hanging in his closet.

After gathering her checked bag, Dana went out to find a cab. She hadn't noticed her traveling companion waiting at the carousel, and wondered, *Who travels with so little?* Then realized a man in his line of work would not require an extensive wardrobe. If he wanted to look official, he could slip on a clerical collar. As she waited, she pulled a tourist guidebook out of her carry-on. She'd have plenty of free time in Prague. Caroline had explained in a letter that she'd have no more than one free hour each day. She'd invited Dana for lunch tomorrow.

Grilled lunch—you on one side of the grille, me on the other, Caroline had written.

Her cousin had always had a sense of humor, though often now the words in her letters were wrapped in such a serious tone, as if the convent had stripped her of her wit. This was obviously a joke, as Dana knew the order wasn't cloistered in the truest sense. Caroline had explained that the nuns lived a monastic life, meaning they lived in a closed convent and adhered to a strict schedule, with much time dedicated to prayer, meditation, and solitude, though they did venture into the world to work. The small and intimate community of Discalced Carmelites consisted of fewer than a dozen nuns. From the Latin *dis*, meaning "not," and *calceatus*, "shod." Dana envisioned her free-spirited cousin, dancing joyfully *unshod* about the ancient convent, her toes wiggling without restraint. Perhaps her feet were the only part of her to experience such freedom.

Caroline, Sister Agnes now, had written that among the nuns' duties were caring for the altars and the priests' vestments and attending to the Holy Infant at the Church of Our Lady Victorious. She'd also lamented that the church was beginning to take on the trappings of just that—a tourist trap. Tourists coming in and out with all their disruptive paraphernalia, cameras and guidebooks, and noisy disrespectful chatter.

Her cab arrived and the driver helped Dana with her luggage. Easter Monday as well as Easter Sunday was a holiday throughout most of Europe, and it seemed the activity had not subsided even today as she witnessed a continuing celebration, more secular than religious, as they drove toward the city center. Throngs of people scurried about, carrying bags and backpacks. Children slurped ice cream cones, and parents snapped away, tiny cameras recording the festivities.

The driver chatted in English, offering bits of tourist information as Dana gazed out the window. The weather could not have been more different from the damp, dark November of her first visit. The sky was a lovely clear blue, the sun highlighting the fairy-tale village with gothic spires, romantic bridges spanning the Vltava River, and narrow cobbled passages and alleyways. Years ago this had seemed mysterious in an almost sinister way, but it now appeared as if everything had been spruced up to welcome the many visitors. What had the priest said—that Prague was the new Paris?

The cab came to an abrupt halt. A wide ditch stretched the length of the street, which was obviously being dug up—new water or sewer system, Dana guessed. This, along with restoration of one of the medieval buildings covered with plastic sheets and flanked with scaffolds, made the street impassable for a motor vehicle, other than perhaps a small motorcycle, as evidenced by one haphazardly zipping around them right now. The cabdriver turned and motioned outward.

"No drive to hotel," he said, shaking his head.

"Road construction?"

"Yes, you walk."

"How far?" she asked, realizing this was the end of the road.

"Not far, just there," he said, pointing. He jumped out, opened her door gallantly, then hustled around and pulled her bag from the trunk. "No parking," he said with another wide gesture.

Dana paid, giving him a tip that could have been larger had he actually dropped her at her hotel. Flipping the handle up on her wheeled luggage, she settled her small carry-on on top, hiked her handbag on her shoulder, adjusting it for balance, and started down the narrow street, maneuvering around the scaffolding and stepping carefully on the wooden planks set out for pedestrians to get around the construction. Narrow, pastel-colored structures lined the street, many of them sporting the old names and symbols used before the buildings were numbered. U červeného orla, the Red Eagle, with its

faded painting of just that; U tři housliček, the Three Fiddles, identified by a relief created to designate the home of three generations of
an eighteenth-century family of violin makers; U červeného lva, the
Red Lion. Tiled roofs had been scrubbed since her last visit, and
stone buildings sandblasted, all pristine and sootless.

She smiled as she continued down the street toward her hotel, her
wheeled bag bumping along the cobbles with an even rhythm. The
sunshine stroked her face like a warm hand, and she felt a sense of
being in a good place. The heat sent a spark of energy through her,
coupled with a sense of excitement verging on happiness, something
she had not felt in a very long time. She was looking forward to getting together with Caroline. Suddenly she was young and adventurous. It would be a good week.

· 5 ·

"He expected you sooner," Pavla Bártová told Chief Investigator
Damek and Detective Kristof Sokol as she led them into her uncle's
study. A thin woman, wearing a skirt and sweater set, she appeared to
be about thirty with the demeanor of an academic or librarian, which
she was, according to the information recently gathered by Detective
Sokol. She worked at the city library in the village of Kutná Hora in
Southern Bohemia about seventy kilometers east of Prague. It was
just 9:00 A.M., they had no appointment, but the woman's face had
registered little surprise as she opened the door. Even before the two
men introduced themselves and produced identification, it seemed
she was expecting them.

Dal, too, had hoped for *sooner*. Working nonstop, assigning extra
officers, they seemed to be making little progress toward resolution
in their investigation of Senator Zajic's murder, and they were getting
pressure from above, the chief of criminal investigations, who he was
sure was also getting an earful from the independent prosecutor who
oversaw all police proceedings.

Professor Josef Kovář was one of many on a list of those who might
desire to see Senator Jaroslav Zajic dead, among them the senator's

wife as well as myriad political and personal foes. The professor might have been placed nearer the top of the list had they known his where-abouts sooner. He had left his position in the history department of the University of Prague more than seventeen years before and, though he had gone but a short distance, it had taken over two weeks to discover his whereabouts.

"He's doing well," Pavla said as she glanced back at Investigator Damek and Detective Sokol. "It's sometimes difficult to understand him. His speech has been affected by the stroke, though his mind is still crystal clear, which I'm sure you understand leads to some frustration." They entered the room, dimly lit by a single lamp. The niece went immediately to the blinds. The snap seemed to rouse the man sitting nestled in a blanket wrapped around his legs and lower body, head hung as if he'd momentarily dozed off while reading the newspaper held limply in his lap. A thin, blackened log smoldered in the fireplace.

Quickly, Dal cast his eyes about the room. Seeing a small cot with a rumpled quilt wedged against one wall, he guessed that the study, as the niece had called it, also served as the man's sleeping quarters. The scent of the log along with a medicinal smell permeated the air. Bookcases filled with hardbound books threw in a hint of dust and mold and history, creating a mix of scents that sat heavily in the stuffy room. Dal took in a deep breath, wishing for fresher air. Wishing the niece would lift the window as well as the shade.

"Uncle Josef." The woman spoke softly to the man, then turned to the detectives. "Detectives Damek and Sokol, from the Republic Police in Prague."

The professor nodded, one side of his mouth lifting slowly in a knowing smile.

"Coffee for our guests," he told his niece in a low voice. The words, as carefully formed as his smile, seemed to emanate from just one side of his mouth. He appeared to be much older than late sixties, barely recognizable as the man in the academic photos in his file. He whispered to the niece, who immediately left the room.

The professor studied his visitors for several moments before speaking again. "Please," he said, lifting a finger to indicate the chair near the opposite side of the fireplace, identical to the one in which he sat, then toward a small sofa facing the mantel. "You are here about the senator." His speech was slurred but understandable.

"Thank you for seeing us," Dal replied. "We'd like to ask you a few questions." He lowered himself to the chair. Kristof perched eagerly on the edge of the sofa.

"Yes, yes . . ." The professor reached with shaky hand into the pocket of his robe, pulled out a tissue, and carefully wiped the corner of his mouth. "I can tell you little . . . as I have been confined for some time. A stroke," he said, repeating what the niece had already told them.

"You've had no recent contact with the senator?" Dal asked.

"No," he said, paused, then added, "I have never personally met the man. But, yes, you are correct, I am not unhappy at his demise." Each word came forth with great effort.

Professor Josef Kovář had been one of the first victims of a lustration program set up in 1991. Zajic, not yet a senator, had chaired the independent commission formed by the Civic Forum. Its purpose— to remove from office or ban from academic, judicial, military, and high-level civil service positions, those who had been involved as spies or informants or otherwise active in the StB, the Communist secret police. The commission had labored until 2000, sifting through and studying millions of documents relating to the Communist reign, which lasted from 1948 until the Velvet Revolution of

1989. Even after his removal, the professor had continued to write scathing articles, most recently concerning the corrupt state of the Czech Republic and specifically Senator Zajic, though these had been published in liberal media with little if any circulation.

"Do you know of anyone who might want to harm the senator?" Investigator Damek asked.

Professor Kovář laughed, then nodded. "With all the commotion made by the commission, fewer than one hundred were removed. Not a particularly worthwhile project." His lips quivered, emitting a hissing sound that Dal thought might turn into a word. Again he wiped his lips with the tissue clutched in his hand.

Dal waited several moments before asking, "You are aware of others who were removed?" Dal knew that many had since died, the professor being one of the few left.

"The Communists were seen as the saviors," the professor began again, speaking now as if he stood before a classroom lectern. He looked directly at the younger detective, sensing a captive audience. Boyishly handsome and always attentive, Kristof Sokol looked several years younger than his twenty-nine and could have passed for a student. His pale blond hair was a shade normally seen only on children.

"Coming after the Nazis," the professor continued, "they were a welcome sight. But as each new government takes hold, the powers shift. Communism in its truest, purest form will tend to its citizens." The words were slow, laborious, but Dal sat quietly as the professor continued. Perhaps he would catch himself in a net of his own arduously placed words. "Few of the idealists are left. Czechoslovakia," he said, using the former name of the two countries, the Czech Republic and Slovakia, "now sits in the quagmire of its own corruption." The man's hand lifted from the blanket wrapped around his lap as the newspaper slid in slow motion to the floor. Dal glanced down, but did not retrieve the paper as the professor waved him off.

The headline read: **PARTY LEADER ACCUSED OF GRAFT.**

"Look at your beloved democracy," he said directly and dismissively to Dal, as if this democracy truly belonged to the police investigator.

The niece entered with a tray bearing two cups, one sturdy-looking mug, sugar bowl, and creamer. She asked the young detective if he would like cream or sugar as she placed the tray on the table in front of him. He replied, "No coffee, but thank you."

Dal lifted a cup from the tray with a *please*, a nod.

The woman added cream and sugar to the professor's and set it on the table next to his chair, lifting several books to make way for the mug. She stepped to the bookcase and began replacing them on the shelves.

"Yes, yes . . ." The professor started in again. "I might have reason to wish the senator gone. But we were not Nazis. We were not killing the Jews. Do I look capable of killing the senator?" He laughed, the resonance oddly strong as if it had emerged from the half of his body not ravaged by the recent stroke. He held up his hand, forming a gun with his fingers. "Shot in the head? I would wish to see his eyes as he fell. The morning of the murder, I was here . . ." His uneven gaze wandered around the room, settling on Pavla. "Ask my niece. I go nowhere. I speak with few. Surely not an assassin. I communicate by writing. The pen: mightier than the sword. No guns. You may search." The man's arm waved over the room. He breathed heavily now. Pavla approached her uncle, protectively placing her thin hand on the man's shoulder.

"I believe my uncle has told you all he knows. It is no secret that he despised the senator, but as you can see he is incapable of committing such a crime. And my uncle is not known to pass such important tasks on to others." She smiled wryly.

Dal nodded to Kristof, who rose.

"Thank you, Professor Kovář, Miss Bártová. If you can think of anything that might help with our investigation . . ." He handed the man his card. "Thank you." Pavla motioned and the two detectives started out of the room.

"The young actor, Filip Kula," Professor Kovář said, and Dal turned. "Killed recently in Prague at the feet of St. Wenceslas on Václavské náměsti. Oh, not so young anymore," he said, words unhurried and reflective. "Stabbed through the heart . . . this case has been solved? Very quickly, as I understand. Your predecessor, Tomáš Malý, perhaps, Investigator Damek, he is much better at this than you." The man smiled again. And this time it appeared as if he had engaged his entire face in the effort.

Dal didn't reply. The case had officially been closed, a Romany man sitting in jail at the moment, accused. *Murder of film star solved,* the headlines read just days before Malý's retirement. Certainly adding dramatic flair to the finale. The case still lingered in Dal's mind, taunting him not with jealousy at his predecessor's glory in such a quick resolution, but with the so obvious lack of resolution. Now, the professor brought up this case, perhaps to goad Dal. Or perhaps to alert him to the fact that he, too, doubted this case had been solved.

"As a professor of history," Kovář added slowly, "I often advise my students to look to the past. Always good advice in seeking a solution. But perhaps the answers are in the future."

· 6 ·

Father Giuseppe Ruffino and Father Giovanni Borelli sat in the garden, enjoying a midmorning coffee and Italian breads prepared by the monastery's new cook, Brother Gabriele, a young Carmelite monk recently arrived from Arenzano. The spring weather, along with the just-out-of-the-oven bread mingling with the scent of newly mowed grass bordering the orderly beds of herbs and vegetables, made for a pleasant morning respite, tempering the agitation Father Borelli had felt that morning upon learning his suit and cassock had yet to arrive. Fortunately he had the clean underwear he'd slipped into his briefcase, or he'd still be sitting in his hotel room in day-old undershorts. The desk clerk assured him they'd contacted the shipping company and he would have his clothing, pressed and hanging, by noon.

Giovanni Borelli had not visited for several months now, though the two priests corresponded frequently, the old-fashioned way, through handwritten letters, exchanging ideas on theology and politics, personal thoughts, and old family stories. The man was like a brother to him.

Spreading a second buttery roll with homemade apricot *marmellata*, Father Borelli attempted to look at his friend in an objective way. In his mind, he always pictured Beppe as the young boy he had been, yet his hair had long ago turned silver, unlike Giovanni's, which had all but disappeared.

"How do you do it, my friend?" Giovanni took a bite of the fresh bread. "If I had joined a monastery with such daily offerings, I would be twice my size." He licked his fingers, then patted his ample belly. "How do you remain so fit?"

"Blessed be those with good metabolism," Beppe replied. "I get my exercise. Each morning I walk as I read the Divine Office." He waved toward the covered, columned path of the cloister just as Brother Gabriele returned with the coffeepot to refill their cups. With his halo of golden curls, he looked more like the archangel from whom he'd taken his moniker than an Italian monk.

"*Grazie*, Brother Gabriele," Beppe said. "You have made our distinguished guest from Rome feel very welcome."

"Indeed," Father Borelli concurred. "*Grazie.*"

The young monk smiled humbly, tilting his head in appreciation before retreating back into the interior of the monastery.

Father Borelli lit a cigarette. Beppe had found a receptacle for his ashes, a tin can large enough to hold sufficient beans or vegetables to feed a monastery of hungry men. He didn't scold, but Giovanni knew his friend did not approve of this harmful habit.

Gazing about the garden, Father Borelli took in a comforting drag and reflected on what an agreeable setting Father Ruffino found himself in. Years ago, when Beppe wrote that he was being uprooted from the Carmelite community in Italy to care for Our Lady Victorious in Prague, Giovanni knew his true wish was to return to his mission in the Central African Republic, where he felt his services were truly needed. But, an obedient servant, Giuseppe Ruffino had accepted with grace. The position as prior of the Church of Our Lady

Victorious had been vacant for some time, the Carmelites having been driven from the city over two hundred years before. The church had fallen into disrepair. If anyone could revive the church and nurture the devotion to the Holy Infant, it was Father Ruffino. He had settled down in Prague, accepted this calling with an open heart.

Giuseppe Ruffino was that rare gifted soul who seemed to have come into this world with an abundance of blessings—a superb athlete, a scholar, a handsome lad. He could have done anything with his life, but everyone knew that Beppe would be a priest. He was a good, compassionate man. He had been a good, compassionate boy.

Giovanni himself had come to the priesthood in a more roundabout way, and even now after over thirty-five years, he wondered if it had been a true calling. He had never experienced a spiritual summons as if the Holy Spirit had invaded his soul with a message to "come follow."

Yet he felt he had served his Church well. He was no saint, but he liked to think that in his own way he had made a contribution, particularly in his work as an officer of the Sacred Congregation of Rites. After his appointment as Promoter of the Faith, known also as Advocatus Diaboli, he often teased his friend about the power he now wielded.

"You are aware, Beppe," he'd said, "after you're gone, I will have to approve your canonization."

"With all your bad habits," Beppe had immediately come back, "you surely don't expect to outlast me?"

Giovanni often laughed at the memory of his friend's response. Perhaps more truth than humor, unless there was validity to the old adage *the good die young*. He surely couldn't expect to outlast a healthy man who treated his body like a temple. Now as they both approached seventy, Giovanni Borelli acknowledged that they were not only well beyond their youth, they had passed right over middle age and were entering the twilight of their years. At times, he looked in the mirror and couldn't believe that fat, old, balding man squinting out at him was the once-handsome, slender Gianni Borelli.

Beppe had yet to bring up the reason for this requested visit. They had just relived a particularly exciting soccer match in which the two men, mere boys then, played heroically to bring a championship trophy to the village where they both attended school. Yet, even in this familiar and often repeated discourse, Giovanni sensed something was not right, that Beppe was merely attempting to gather the courage to speak of a matter of great importance, that this chatter was merely a prelude.

"Another form of exercise," Beppe went on, piling another stone of avoidance upon a stack that Giovanni sensed was about to tumble, "getting down in the garden, down on my knees." His laugh was sliced with nervousness. "As if I don't spend enough time on my knees, begging the good Lord to watch over us, to keep our little community in his graces. I pray he does not see me as the beggar I am, that I do not become too much of a nuisance. But the good Lord has entrusted me to look after this little church, after the Holy Infant, and I must do what is necessary…"

Beppe often wrote of the commercialism in the city, how the tiny church of Our Lady Victorious had been swept up in the growth of the tourist trade.

"We need to keep up with repairs, our museum and gift shop, to attract the tourists," he said, "yet maintain the dignity of the church and a respectful devotion to the Infant. I'm afraid it may become a circus. The circus of the Infant of Prague." His words carried a hint of sadness, accompanied by a dismissive shake of the head. "The assignment has its challenges, but I have truly been blessed."

Now Beppe adjusted himself in his chair, his eyes flashing briefly toward the door into the monastery where Brother Gabriele had disappeared just minutes before. Father Borelli knew a half dozen other Carmelites, both priests and brothers, lived in the monastery, but the morning air carried no telltale signs of activity.

"The reason for my call..." Beppe's voice was low as he leaned in, his eyes still darting about. "There was a...an incident in the church."

Giovanni took a final, quick draw on his cigarette, snuffed it.

"Friday morning," Beppe said.

"Good Friday?"

Beppe nodded. "I always arrive early before my servers to open the church. That morning I found it unlocked, which gave me a scare in itself. I did a quick search of the church, starting in the sacristy where we keep the gold chalices, ciboriums, and monstrances, then on to the museum and altars. We have a collection of valuable paintings and statuary."

Valuable statuary, indeed, Giovanni thought. The world-famous Infant of Prague, here in this tiny church in the Czech Republic.

"When I approached the Infant's altar, there she lay." Visible sweat beaded on the man's brow.

"Who?"

"Sister Claire." He pressed his fingers to his forehead. "She was ninety-two. She accepted her vocation at an early age. She knew no life other than one of service to the Church, to our Lord."

As you, my friend, Giovanni thought, but said nothing to interrupt.

"I was unaware," Beppe continued, "though the prioress knew she often rose in the night. I'm not sure she knew...well, until...that at times she might have left the convent. Sister Claire was always in attendance for early-morning chapel. She tended the altars. I learned recently that this might have transpired at odd hours. I play no role in overseeing these duties. I leave it to the prioress to set the schedule and supervise the nuns."

"Were the altars not stripped for Good Friday?"

"She suffered from the ailments of age . . . her memory. Often confused." Again his hand rose to his head, a tap to indicate the demented workings of the old woman's mind.

"You found her in the church? Lying at the altar? Dead?"

Beppe took in a deep breath, eyes closed. "Sister Claire passed in the church." His eyes shot open and met Giovanni's. "The circumstances of her death are suspect."

"You called the authorities?"

"Why, yes, of course." The priest's eyes narrowed.

"The circumstances of her death?" Giovanni asked, repeating Beppe's words.

"A gash, a cut across her face."

"Murdered?" Was this why his friend had called? Did he wish Giovanni to investigate a murder? His heart pounded at the thought. He had substantial investigative experience, but he had never been called upon to investigate a murder.

"She was still alive, though barely. I suspect she was waiting for me. For a last anointing. She passed in my arms, took her last breath as I prayed to the sweet Infant Savior."

"There was nothing missing from the church?" Giovanni asked. "Is this correct?"

"The investigator went through the church with me to make sure nothing was taken." His voice grew quiet.

"Any damage?"

"No damage," Beppe replied tentatively. He stared down at the table and then looked up. Giovanni noticed a twitch in his friend's eye, a blink. His hand trembled as he placed it flat on the table. He covered it with his other hand, perhaps attempting to quiet the tremor.

"Is there anyone who would have motive to murder this elderly nun?"

"She had no enemies," Father Ruffino replied. "Few acquaintances other than the nuns with whom she lived. No remaining family."

"There is an ongoing investigation? Why have you called me?"

Father Ruffino ran his fingers through his thick hair. "Because of your investigative skills, I . . ."

"The police?"

Beppe shook his head dismissively. "The Czech police . . ."

"She was stabbed? A knife?"

"The weapon, perhaps her own garden shears. We keep them here in the church for the nuns to tend to the altar arrangements."

"When you arrived did *you* see anything unusual?" Father Borelli asked.

Father Ruffino shook his head.

"Nothing on the surveillance cameras? The alarms?"

"The alarms had been turned off. By whom I'm not sure." Father Ruffino's voice quivered, and Giovanni sensed he might carry a burden of guilt upon his own trembling shoulders over the nun's death. "The cameras . . . we are hoping to set up a new digital system. The equipment is old. Not trustworthy." He shook his head, and Giovanni understood there was nothing recorded to help with the investigation.

Giovanni placed his hand on the arm of his fellow priest. This normally calm man, who had always put his fate in the hands of the Lord, was shivering, running his fingers along the edge of the table now.

"As I've said, Sister Claire was ... Well"—Beppe hesitated as if gathering his thoughts—"she was still alive when I arrived. And ... she was dying. I'm sure she was aware of that. I'm not sure how clear her mind was." Beppe smiled faintly. "The prioress claims her mind hadn't been clear for some time now."

"She spoke to you?"

"Yet, at that moment of death perhaps she was very clear. At first she was mumbling, praying. But then ... Sometimes as one draws near death, there exists a profound clarity. Do you ever feel that, Giovanni?" he asked. "When you sit with someone at the last moment, when they take in and then exhale that last breath, do you ever feel that presence, the presence of our dear Lord, when you hold the hand of a dying soul? Do you ever feel as if you are handing them over to the Lord?"

Giovanni knew other priests who had described a sense of God's physical presence in claiming a soul.

Both men were silent for a long moment. Giovanni knew from experience it was sometimes more fruitful to refrain from interference or suggestion that might alter one's perception and memory, though he was getting impatient.

"She told you something?" he finally asked.

"Yes."

"Then we must start from there." Again, Giovanni Borelli forced himself to be still.

"After the initial mumblings," Beppe said, starting in once more, "her words were very clear, but the reliability, the proper interpretation, I'm not sure." He looked at Giovanni, deep into his eyes.

Dark circles hung beneath Beppe's warm brown eyes, and myriad wrinkles fanned out from the corners, something Giovanni hadn't noticed until that very moment, as if his friend had aged during the short time they'd sat in the garden.

"She told you what she saw?" Giovanni asked.

Father Ruffino shook his head. "Sister Claire had been completely blind for the past ten years."

Ornate Bohemian palaces and sturdy Renaissance homes lined the avenues of the Malá Strana. Tall, slender structures in a variety of pastel confectionery colors, topped with red tiles, stood shoulder to shoulder along the narrow streets. A group of tourists gathered before a wheeled cart, eating mustard-slathered *klobásy* cradled in buns not quite long enough to fully embrace the sausages. Dana was tempted by the spicy, warm aroma, but she would wait for lunch at the convent. She was meeting Caroline at noon.

Emerging from a narrow street into an area clogged with foot traffic, she gazed up toward a wide stone path already bulging with visitors making their way up to the castle. She turned in the opposite direction and strolled down toward the river and onto the Charles Bridge, the Karlův most. A walking-only bridge, it overflowed with artists, vendors, musicians, and tourists. Baroque statues of saints perched on the balustrades of each side. She stopped to look at the miniature paintings displayed by a young artist with a mop of blond hair, an untrimmed beard, a colorful tie-dyed shirt. Little fairy-tale scenes of the city. She lingered for a moment, joining the crowd gathered to listen to a quartet of musicians. A fellow wearing a baseball cap sat on a stool playing a guitar, a man plunked a bass, one played a flute, another slid a trombone. The bass player smiled at Dana flirtatiously. She smiled back. After listening several more minutes, she placed a euro, left over from Italy, in the instrument case propped open for the listeners' offerings. The bass player nodded a thank-you. Dana moved on to the far side of the bridge and watched a skeleton marionette, dressed as a sad-faced clown, play a guitar orchestrated by an enthusiastic puppet master. A group of tourists knotted in a circle around the performance.

How different the city had been those many years ago when she'd visited. No holiday crowds gathered in a carnival-like atmosphere. Those congregating then had been protesters, dissenters, mostly young people demanding democratic reform. When she and Caroline arrived, they found themselves in a city in which the students had already set the stage. On November 17, 1989, the two girls joined a peaceful, officially sanctioned march to commemorate International Student Day, though everyone knew it was more than that; the true intent was to protest the oppressive Communist regime. The marchers wound down the hill from the cemetery at Vyšehrad, where they had visited the gravesite of a student who'd been killed fifty years before during a similar march protesting the Nazi occupation of Czechoslovakia.

Fifteen thousand strong, Caroline and Dana numbered among them, they moved along the bank of the River Vltava and up Národní Street, where they were met by antiterrorist squads in red berets and police in white helmets with shields and nightsticks. The students chanted and sang songs of freedom—*Svobodu!* Some carried flowers, and others placed candles along the streets and sidewalks. Now, Dana could hardly believe that she had been there.

After that November seventeenth demonstration, in which it was reported that several were beaten and one killed—though this death turned out to be a false account—the students were joined by actors, musicians, and eventually workers. By November twenty-third, the day before Dana left for home, four days before a national strike, the throngs had swelled to over a million. The red berets and helmeted police had disappeared, though plainclothes officers, easily identified in their polyester raincoats, observed without interfering, overwhelmed or simply understanding the inevitable. It had already happened in Poland, Hungary, and East Germany.

The Velvet Revolution, Dana thought now as she continued toward Václavské náměsti, where the original march had been destined to end. Today the streets were lined with holiday shoppers, along with businessmen and -women who worked in this busy, vibrant commercial section of Prague. She lingered several moments near the statue of St. Wenceslas, recalling how the area had once been carpeted with flowers, candles, and handmade signs, overlaid with peaceful, hopeful young voices.

Just before noon, she set off to have lunch with Caroline.

Again she crossed the bridge and pulled out the map she'd picked up at the hotel. Finding the street where the convent was located, she dug her address book out of her bag, checking numbers as she walked.

She approached a building, enclosed within an iron fence, set in a quaint little square with chestnut trees and stone benches, which was identified with brass numerals, though nothing announced it as a convent. Healthy green vines climbed the gray stone, sprouting small violet-colored buds reaching toward the midday sun. Dana unlatched the gate and walked up to the door, finding a handwritten notice tacked beneath a small peephole. A series of Czech words, which she could not decipher, appeared along with numbers that Dana guessed from the configuration must be dates.

She knocked. Nothing. She checked her watch. Her lunch date with Caroline was scheduled for noon and she was a few minutes early. She knocked again. Still, nothing.

For the first time since she'd left home, Dana felt ill prepared without her lifeline—her cell phone. She had a number for the convent, but no way to call. After another quick knock, a wait, she wondered if she should go back to the hotel to use the phone. She could slip a note under the door, but saying what? Didn't they have a lunch date? She felt a trickle of irritation.

Sensing a shuffling of footsteps on the cobblestones, Dana turned. An elderly man made his way toward the convent gate, his steps, oddly, both quick and labored. He wore a tweed cap and a heavy wool sweater that hung at an odd angle as if he'd mismatched the buttons with the buttonholes. As he approached she noticed patches of whiskers, spots of chin missed in shaving due to the deep crevices in his lined face. His eyebrows, thick wisps of white hair sticking up here and there, had taken on a life of their own.

"Ne, Ne," he said, annoyance lacing over his voice. His brows pinched together, wisps of hair from one mingling with the other.

He rattled off a series of words as he unlatched the gate.

She didn't understand, though the word for *no* had pretty much the same tone and inflection in any language. When he jabbed his finger at the sign posted on the door, she raised her shoulders, arms extended, palms flat, in the international gesture of *I don't understand.*

His eyes flashed, then softened. "English?" he asked.

She nodded, realizing he was asking about her language, not nationality.

"American English," he said knowingly.

"Yes," she replied with what she hoped was a friendly tone.

Again he jabbed at the sign. *"Ne, ne."* He ran his finger under the dates—written in the European style: day first, month second. *"Ne, ne,"* he said again, hands flying, head jerking as if looking for help. "Maria," he called out to a trio of girls passing on the opposite side of the square.

The tallest skipped over, unlatched the gate, and greeted the old man. They carried on an animated conversation and then she turned to Dana.

"You wish me read the . . ." She hesitated, searching for the words, and then, like the old man, she pointed to the sign on the door.

"Prosím," Dana replied. *Please.* "The sign," she said, offering the word in English. "Yes, please read the sign."

The child smiled. "Yes, I read the sign." She was a beautiful girl—blond curls and bright blue eyes—made even sweeter by her friendly smile. Dana guessed her to be about ten.

"The womans," the girl said slowly, pausing to point at the convent door. "The good womans . . ." She pressed her hands together as if to indicate the nuns. "They is no here for you today. They is prayer for the good old woman. The very old woman." She smiled an apologetic smile. "My English no good. I learn in school, but some words . . ."

"You're doing fine," Dana said.

"The good old, yes, very, very old, she . . . she . . ." The girl turned back to her friends across the square. Three more children had stopped alongside the two who had accompanied her. The girl—Maria, according to the old man—threw a quick succession of Czech words toward the youngsters, who exchanged glances before all eyes landed on the smallest boy.

"Jan," Maria called to him. He appeared to be about seven or eight, with the same blond curls. Perhaps they were brother and sister.

He called back, "She dead."

The girl grinned now, pleased that he'd supplied the correct word, unaffected, it seemed, by this grim news. "Yes, she dead," Maria announced proudly.

"The old nun?" Dana asked.

"Yes, *nun*." The girl nodded, her smile still intact.

The dates, Dana realized now—covering a full week from last Friday to this coming Saturday—indicated a period of mourning in which the nuns would not be available. She wondered why Caroline hadn't left a message for her at the hotel.

The girl said, "Very, very old nun." Her smile faded slowly as if she realized it might be misinterpreted. "Very sad she dead." The corners of her mouth turned down in an exaggerated, artificial way. "Very old. She go to . . ." She pointed up.

"Thank you for your help," Dana said. *"Děkuji."*

"Yes, I very happy help you. The good womans, the nuns, they be here for you after this day." Again she pointed to the sign.

Sunday, the day before her scheduled departure, Dana thought.

After thanking the children and the old man for their help, Dana returned to the hotel and called the convent, leaving a message for Caroline, expressing her condolences for the nuns' loss and suggesting they get together Sunday for lunch. Again, she left the hotel, found a street vendor, and ordered a grilled sausage, which she smothered with golden mustard and ate sitting on the edge of a large concrete flower box. Then she set out to explore.

Later that evening, after visiting the Mucha Museum, as well as the National Museum, she returned to her hotel to find a message for her at the reception desk. Sealed in an envelope, DANA PIERSON was hand-printed in familiar large block letters on the front. Immediately,

Dana tore it open. The brevity, the large caps, the lack of punctuation—all Caroline's style. It read:

MEET OUR LADY VICTORIOUS 11 AM
THURSDAY VOTIVE CANDLES URGENT

It was signed simply *C*.

· 8 ·

Dal Damek sat, along with a half dozen officers, as he had each morning for the past two and a half weeks, going over photographs, crime scene mock-ups, charts, graphs, autopsy and ballistic reports, studying information that had been gathered during the previous day, anything relating to the murder of Senator Jaroslav Zajic. Some days there was little new, and they found themselves stepping back to move forward, attempting to see something new revealed in what they'd already discovered. Each day there was little of value to report to the chief of criminal investigations.

They'd had numerous calls and tips, some from the usual suspects, among them a couple of well-known crazies who had theories on just about any crime that had taken place in the city. They'd interviewed shopkeepers, restaurant workers, the doormen at the Grand Hotel Praha. A mime who worked the square had come in voluntarily in full costume, whiteface, white hat, white clown suit, to say he'd seen something suspicious several days before the murder—a man taking photos. Not of the clock tower, the Jan Hus monument, or the Kostel Panny Marie před Týnem, like the hundreds of tourists every day, but of rooftops of buildings, such as restaurants, shops, and hotels. A little unusual, for sure, but the description the mime gave of the man was vague and he'd not seen him again.

The number of possible suspects, as well as multiple motives to consider, along with the difficulty in obtaining financial, phone, and e-mail records, made the case all the more difficult. It seemed there were as many willing to protect the senator—from what, Dal wasn't sure—as those with reason to wish him dead.

The senator's wife had to be considered a suspect, and this had not been completely dismissed. Senator Zajic met once a week, same time, same place—the Hotel Rott Praha—with a woman who was not his wife. The hotel, located in the center of the tourist district frequented by foreigners, provided a perfect place to go unnoticed.

Then, on schedule, as the senator was a man who kept to a regular routine, he walked to his office, passing through the Old Town Square, always walking directly on the cobblestone path below the astronomical clock. If there was one thing the senator could be counted on, it was keeping his schedule and routine. And the murderer knew this routine.

The wife, aware of the affair, possibly past affairs, seemed to accept this as part of the deal. If she was involved, she'd hired a professional. The shot had indeed come from the roof, and the wife, a large woman in her sixties, had surely not made this ascent. During her first interview she'd said if she was going to kill her husband she would have done it long ago.

The mistress, too, a buxom amber-haired stage actress, had to be considered, though Dal sensed that she was perfectly content with the present arrangement, desiring no further entanglement. She had no known motive.

The press, which tended toward high drama, had already decided the murder was politically motivated. With the volatility in the ever-evolving democracy of the Czech Republic, it had to be considered. In

March, the government had collapsed under a no-confidence vote. The prime minister, a supporter of the EU Lisbon Treaty, had resigned, though he would continue in office until a replacement was designated. Senator Jaroslav Zajic, an ally of the president, who opposed the treaty and often clashed with the PM, was rumored to be on the verge of a shift in alliances. Those against ratification of the treaty claimed it would diminish the country's financial freedom and autonomy won through the revolution years ago. Political motivation had to be considered.

The senator's early-morning incoming phone call had been traced, though not without difficulty, Dal having gone to the top of the chain, all the way to the office of the minister of the interior to have the information released. The call to the dead man, with the official government block, had been made by a fellow senator of the Czech Parliament, Senator Viktor Vlasák, a man getting on in years who had served so long that this in itself might account for the demanding tone of his voice. It was unlikely he'd been directly involved in the murder and was calling to determine if the feat had been accomplished. Yet his sudden hang-up puzzled Dal. The senator had explained he was in a hurry and the continuing discussion he referred to in the call had concerned a matter of Parliament that he was not yet at liberty to discuss. Senator Vlasák was known to be in opposition to the Lisbon Treaty.

Detective Kristof Sokol was in the process of following up on information from Senator Zajic's recently obtained phone records, now thoroughly picked over by a unit technician. With the number of blocked calls, the resistance, jumping through hoops, and wending through red tape, this had proved to be an arduous, frustrating task.

The financial forensics expert, recently transferred from the commercial crime unit, was attempting to decipher the senator's complicated financial records. Bo Doubek, like Kristof, was one of the new breed, well educated, tech savvy, analytical. He could crack just about any bank account and trace a money trail like a squirrel picking up peanuts. But this one, even he admitted, was rough going, with enough holes and blackouts it was like analyzing a string of ruptured DNA.

"I'm still working on it," he told the group. "One path leads to another, but so far, nothing that might indicate a motive for murder." Doubek scratched his face nervously. Though now in his early thirties, he still had a bad case of acne. He looked like a kid who holed up in his mother's apartment, spending his entire day sitting at a computer, having no emotional or social contact with anyone in the real world. Dal knew him to be shy, but he was a true wiz with a computer and an asset to the department.

Branislov Černý sat silently, shaking his head now and then. He was of the old school: Crimes were solved in the field, not sitting at a desk all day in front of a computer. Černý operated the old-fashioned way—gut instinct, and perhaps at times too much force. Often it seemed he fell back on the old ways. A favorite quote: "Take a wrench to justice and get the job done." He'd served as an officer in the SNB, the National Security Corps, the police force of Czechoslovakia, before the country was divided into the Czech Republic and Slovakia. Officers coming into the police force had been thoroughly vetted, attempting to purge any remnants of the Communist ideology.

"I'm still checking out several recurring calls," Kristof said. "One in particular that popped up several days in a row, then disappeared about three weeks before the senator's murder. We've traced it to a Hugo Hutka, but unfortunately the man was killed in an auto accident in early March."

Eyes popped wide around the table; papers shuffled. Černý took a slow, thoughtful drink of coffee, then got up to refill his cup.

"Anything suspicious about the accident?" Dal asked.

"The body was badly burned, but nothing indicates, at least from the report, that it was anything but an accident. Detective Černý and I are headed over to talk with the widow this morning."

Dal nodded, considering this new information. Someone who had been communicating with Zajic on a regular basis, passing away just before the senator himself, certainly warranted another look.

Dal opened a second file and withdrew a photo of a thin man, facedown, red seeping into the sparkling snow like a macabre version of a kid's cherry ice treat. A man in shabby clothes lying dead at the foot of the statue of St. Wenceslas on Václavské náměsti.

"You're looking at the Filip Kula murder again?" Černý grunted as he maneuvered himself back into his chair, straightening his back, planting his coffee mug on the table.

"You believe the two homicides are related?" Detective Sokol asked his superior. From the photo, comparing this man to the well-dressed, well-fed senator, it would seem unlikely the two men had anything in common or had met in social circles. Dal, who'd had no part in the Kula investigation, did not intend to officially reopen it, yet he doubted the person responsible for this earlier homicide had been put away. The fact that the lead detective had retired along with the prior chief, Tomáš Malý, concerned Dal. There had been a major shake-up in the department in the past few months.

The case of Filip Kula would not have made headlines—an addict out to score some drugs—had the victim not been a once-popular film star. His murder had dredged up history as well as headlines. Twenty years ago he'd been active as a dissenter during the Velvet Revolution, one of the popular voices of the movement. Within years, his health and fame declined, ravaged by an expensive drug habit. Many younger citizens of Prague, Kristof among them, had not initially recognized

the name Filip Kula. Those who knew of the star would not have recognized the man. He'd once been the heartthrob of many a Czech girl,
but he'd died a vagabond in frayed trousers and ripped overcoat. His
identity had not been known for several days, as he carried no ID. No
one was looking for him. His family had disowned him. The first
reports assumed he was involved in either prostitution or drugs, since
the area was frequented in the early morning by those seeking either.
Days later, during a separate investigation, an ID had been found in
the hotel room of a man well-known for being part of a petty theft
ring, and it had been matched to the murder victim. Being Romany,
the accused was considered expendable.

Dal had not seriously considered these two cases related except
for the fact that they were far from the norm in Prague, if murder
could in any way be considered normal. Prague was a relatively safe
city. When a murder occurred it was generally domestic or gang
related. And very few murders remained unsolved. Yet he continued
to think of Josef Kovář's taunting words concerning the Kula investigation as he and Detective Sokol had left the professor's study in
Kutná Hora.

Dal had gone personally to question Ludovit Holomek, the
Romany man in jail accused of the Filip Kula murder. The man swore
he had nothing to do with the actor's death, that he didn't even know
who Filip Kula was, that he'd come across the body and simply taken
advantage of the situation and removed his wallet. He'd admitted
that much—the evidence was right there. He'd complained that, for
all his trouble, he'd discovered but a few tattered bills. Dal's inclina-
tion was to believe him on all counts. The Romany were known as
petty thieves, preying mostly on tourists. Dal had investigated one
murder during his entire career in homicide involving a Romany as
the perpetrator—an angry wife who had stabbed and killed her hus-

band for no reason other than his complaints about a meal she'd prepared for him.

Across the table, Detective Branislov Černý seemed to ponder this, though *ponder* was generally not a word associated with the man. Once a virile, athletic man, Černý had been worn down to a hard core of resentment, if not apathy, passed over time and time again for promotion. Perhaps he should have retired years ago, but he was hanging on three more months for full retirement. Dal liked the man, if not always his methods.

"You're not buying this Gypsy's confession?" the old detective asked.

The record showed the man had confessed, but that wasn't the song he was singing when Dal visited him in jail.

Silence all around the room as the photo of the deceased Filip Kula made its way around the table. Dal attempted to catch the reaction of Detective Karel Beneš, a chunky, round-cheeked redhead. His first case in homicide as a junior detective had been the Kula case. Several weeks ago, after the detective assigned to the case had retired, Dal had asked Beneš to come in. Dal sensed the young man had concerns regarding the murder of Filip Kula as he sat nervously in the office of his newly appointed chief, though he was reluctant to criticize the former chief investigator or lead detective. He'd told Dal the case had received little attention; a true investigation hadn't even been initiated. Then came the discovery of the man's identity and the headlines praising the chief investigator for closing the case. Now, Beneš twitched again, his pale redhead's complexion burning with what might have been either embarrassment or anger.

"One shot in the head," Černý mused. "One stabbed in the heart. A fallen film star meets his demise while attempting to score some drugs? How does this relate to a philandering senator?" Dal had implied in no way that the two were related. Černý shot a look toward Beneš, then Detective Sokol, realizing it was he who was attempting to make the connection.

"Political motivation?" Kristof asked. "The common link between the two? Filip Kula was a dissenter during the Velvet Revolution. Those engaged in the arts—actors, playwrights, musicians—were particularly involved in promoting political reform and the end of Communist censorship."

Dal realized the young detective had studied the case. He liked his initiative. Had Kristof, too, sitting silently in the professor's study with his superior, then following him in his exit like an obedient puppy, caught something in the man's speaking of this case? Neither Dal nor Kristof had mentioned a possible connection on the drive back to Prague.

As Dal's eyes darted around the table, he realized, not for the first time, that, other than Černý and Detective Zik Reznik, the latter with whom Beneš was now partnered, he was working with a bunch of inexperienced investigators. Tadpoles, he mused.

"Any evidence he'd become involved in politics in recent years?" Reznik stared down at the photo of a man who had obviously fallen on hard times.

"Senator Zajic joined the Civic Forum in late 1989," Kristof replied. A fact that Dal was well aware of since the investigation had been initiated. "Kula had been active since its inception. A Charter 77 advocate."

Černý shook his head. "The Civic Forum, catchall for post-Communist Czechoslovakia. Anyone who wanted to be involved in the new republic joined. Any recent connection between the two men?"

"No connection." Kristof glanced sideways at Beneš, whose nostrils flared as he looked down at the table. "Yet," Kristof added.

"If there is, I'd certainly like to know," Dal said, waving a hand over the file, then the table of officers. "I'd like to take a look at Kula's activities in the weeks preceding his murder." Damek handed the file to Reznik, glancing at Beneš, who nodded as if ready to get moving on the case, to prove himself. "Every detail. Places frequented, acquaintances. Financial"—he indicated Doubek—"I want to know if he had any income. How he was supporting his drug habit."

"You're reopening the case?" Reznik asked. Detective Reznik had joined the force at the same time as Dal. They'd gone through the academy together. He was movie-star handsome, with thick, dark hair and five o'clock shadow, and could have been cast as a cinema detective who always got his man as well as the girl. In reality he was lazy, often taking credit for the efforts of others. He hadn't celebrated when Dal was named chief.

"You want us off Zajic?" Reznik asked. "Work the Kula case?"

"Not officially," Dal replied as he scanned the table of officers. He didn't want the press getting hold of this and he was sure his officers understood. Old Branislov Černý once told Dal that before the republic, nothing got out to the press. The government *was* the press. A cop could do his job. "Nowadays it's the damn reporters who seem to think they're going to solve all the crimes," Černý had said. Dal knew of several instances, one in particular, when they had set up a sting—then in came the reporters and blew the whole damn thing.

He had little use for snoopy reporters.

Just like the city of Prague, the Church of Our Lady Victorious, Kostel Panny Marie Vítězné, had experienced many incarnations. Originally built between 1611 and 1613 and dedicated to the Holy Trinity as a Lutheran church, the Catholic emperor gifted it to the Carmelites after the defeat of the Protestants in the Battle of White Mountain in 1620. It was rededicated to Our Lady of Victory. The Carmelites were forced to flee in 1784 when their monastery was closed by Emperor Joseph II. The administration of the church was turned over to the Maltese Order. More than two hundred years later, in 1993, the Carmelites were allowed to return and reclaim the church.

A broad stone staircase led up to the structure of pale ocher stone, a Baroque facade topped with onion domes and spires. With its architectural swirls and curves, recessed carvings and medallions, it had the look of a multilayered, decorated cake, though compared to many European churches it was relatively small. Perhaps it would have gone unnoticed, without visitors other than a handful of devout members of the Czech congregation, had it not been the home of one of the most famous religious icons of the world. The Holy Infant of Prague.

The statue had come to Prague as a gift from a Spanish princess. In Córdoba on the eve of her marriage to Lord Vratislav of Pernštejn in 1556, Princess Maria was presented the little statue by her mother, Dona Isabella Manrique de Lara y Mendoza. The princess would soon travel with her new husband to his home in Bohemia, and her mother wished to send her off with a personal protector in the form of the Infant King.

Later, Maria passed the statue on to her own daughter, the beautiful princess Polyxena, when she married a Czech nobleman. After two marriages, twice widowed, in 1628 Polyxena presented the Little King to the Barefoot Carmelite community in Prague. In 1631 Prague was invaded by the Saxons. The conquerors, according to the traditional story, discarded the Infant. Several years later a young priest, recently returned to the city, found the statue, hands missing, in a pile of rubbish. One day while in prayer, Father Cyril heard the Infant speak. "Have pity on me and I will have pity on you," the Infant said. "Give me my hands and I will give you peace. The more you honor me, the more I will bless you."

Father Cyril prayed for funds to repair the statue. Miraculously, benefactors appeared. The statue was restored and many blessings were bestowed upon the monastery and the people of Prague. These blessings, as well as miracles, were said to continue to this day.

As Dana climbed the steps, she was well aware of these facts, this history. The myths. She had read the books and pamphlets Caroline had sent her before the trip, the guidebooks purchased in anticipation of her visit. She had come to regard churches in general as historical, architectural monuments rather than houses of prayer. She had forgotten how to pray. She had given up on prayer.

She entered. Gilt on the high altar, the six side altars, and an ornate pulpit sparkled, giving the impression everything had been dipped in gold. A grand assortment of carved angels and saints, paintings, sculptures, and spiraled columns adorned each altar. Carved stone communion rails, several with decorative iron gates, separated the altars from the aisles. An abundance of Easter lilies festooned the entire church, bringing to Dana's mind the expression *gilding the lily*.

No sign of Caroline, or any other nuns, though Dana was a good thirty minutes early. She glanced around, locating the votive candles in the back of the church, and then she sat in a pew. A few people milled about in addition to those gathered around the main altar, where a Mass was being celebrated. Dana knew this was not the official 9:00 A.M. Czech Mass listed in the brochures, but guessed masses were offered throughout the day for visiting pilgrims. Two women chatted quietly behind her. Dana scanned the right side of the church, her eyes finally resting on the middle altar. A glass box stood above the golden tabernacle, so high it was difficult to see what was inside, though she knew it was the Infant. The brightness of the lights in the church, as well as the natural light coming from skylights in the vaulted ceiling, created a glare on the glass. Dana pulled her book from her bag and flipped to the page with a photo of the little statue. Not really an infant, the child appeared much older, a young boy with cherubic face, pale complexion, and blond curls. Though Dana herself had enticed Caroline on that first visit to Prague by suggesting they could see the world-famous figure, they'd become swept up in events enveloping the city and did not step foot inside the church. Dana had never seen the Infant of Prague.

Book in hand, she rose, walked, and knelt at the communion rail before the altar where she could get a better view. Protected under glass, the Infant's features were difficult to make out, though she assumed they were the same as those pictured in her book. She glanced from photograph to authentic Infant. The Infant of Prague, approximately forty-seven centimeters tall, was described as being constructed of carved wood, covered with a thin coat of wax molded into a simple white tunic. His wardrobe consisted of over one hundred garments, donated by royalty as well as wealthy patrons. The Carmelite nuns of the Malá Strana were honored with the duty of dressing the Infant.

The little figure in the box wore a white gown made of what appeared to be silk brocade with ornate gold trim. A jeweled crown perched on his head. In his left hand, he held a small orb—surely the world. His right hand rose in a gesture with two fingers pressed together, offering a blessing. Dana noticed, along the walls on either side of the Infant's altar, plaques with words and names and dates, though they were at such a distance that she could not make them out. They were said to be gifts, accompanied, she guessed, by monetary offerings from those who had been blessed. With miracles? she wondered. She had once prayed for a miracle, though she had never believed in miracles. In desperation, she had prayed. Suddenly and unexpectedly she felt a twitch in her eye, a rush of heat across her face. She was about to cry, something she seldom did. But these were not tears of sadness. They were tears of anger. She turned and returned to the pew and sat, attempting to rid herself of these emotions, to create a void, a blank to dismiss these feelings. She remained sitting, breathing heavily.

Mass finished, the tourists gathered around the altar with the priest. All shifted and settled into a group pose with picture-ready smiles. Various members took turns snapping away with their cameras. Several held replicas of the Infant King to be captured in their photographs.

Dana glanced at her watch. A mere five minutes had passed. Time creeping. She shouldn't have come so early. Twenty-five minutes to go—if Caroline appeared on time. Dana thumbed through her book, trying to read, to concentrate. She needed to get out of this place. This church, where the faithful came to pray for miracles, to pray to an Infant who was said to be God. Suddenly she sensed someone standing beside her.

She turned and faced the priest who'd just said Mass.

"Welcome to the Church of Our Lady Victorious," he said in a soft voice in perfect English, though Dana could hear the traces of an accent. Italian? He was a handsome man, with silver hair, a lovely smile, and warm, kind eyes. "What brings you here today?"

Dana felt a prick of nerves move like an itchy insect across her arm. Had he noticed her approach the Infant's altar? Had he sensed her discomfort?

What was *she doing here?* Meeting her cousin, possibly a clandestine meeting with a nun who should be sequestered in mourning.

"When I was a child in my school," she began, her voice cracking, "we had this little statue in the classroom, the Infant of Prague."

"Yes, yes," he replied with an inviting smile. "I hear that from many, particularly the Americans. Keep him always close to your heart, and he will bring you many blessings."

Again her eyes darted around the church, resting once more on the Infant King. The priest stood as though waiting for something. Dana wondered if such a virtuous person could see right through to the darkness of her soul. She felt near tears again, her face burning, a compression in her chest.

"May I include special intentions in my prayers?" he asked, his words, the texture of his voice touching her in a strange, unexpected way.

She knew what he was asking. She shook her head.

He waited, saying no more.

Several moments passed. The silence seemed to shout, *I know there is something. Please let me help you.* Finally he said, "Bless you, my daughter." He did not touch her, but she felt the lightest weight press down upon her, as if he had placed a gentle hand on her shoulder. The priest stood another long moment, and then he turned and walked away.

Dana sat for one minute, two, five. Minutes that seemed to stretch on and on, as she attempted to push her mind into blankness. She needed to get up and move around, yet she felt a heaviness within, as if her own body would not release her.

Finally, she rose and made her way to the front of the church and around to the right. She climbed the stairs toward the museum. Along the spiral staircase, large photographs of the Holy Infant hung, pictures showing a variety of robes and garments presented over the centuries, some from royalty, others from religious groups and devotees. Robes and gowns and jeweled crowns and winding steps.

Upstairs in the museum she found more little robes displayed under glass on headless, limbless forms, along with an explanation of where each gift had come from, what particular colors were used for the various liturgical seasons. Nuns dressing the Infant projected on a screen, accompanied by soft music. To protect the statue the sisters enclosed it from the waist down in a metal cone. Dana watched in silence for several minutes, wondering if Sister Agnes would appear in the film, but she did not.

Winding back down the stairs, Dana found the gift shop with books, statues, rosaries, postcards, and religious paraphernalia. She continued on to another room behind the altar, through the sacristy, where she gazed into a glass case filled with little statues, replicas of the original Infant of Prague in a variety of sizes and attire, some plastic, others porcelain. Another display presented pamphlets and literature describing the African mission the church supported. She glanced at her watch. Ten minutes. She should return just in case Caroline arrived early.

Back in the church, the tourists from the Mass had left, though the priest stood conversing in whispers with two other visitors. Surely this was the prior, Father Giuseppe, whom Caroline had written about in her letters, describing him as a gifted linguist, able to say Mass in a dozen languages. According to Caroline the man was a saint. Maybe he was—he had the voice and demeanor of a saint.

Dana sat and waited, but Caroline did not appear. She walked to the back of the church and positioned herself in a pew, glancing around, searching the area near the votive candles. It was five past eleven. The minutes crept as Dana's eyes flickered from her watch to the votive candles. She waited five more minutes, ten minutes. Caroline wasn't going to show. She was about to leave when she saw, coming through the sacristy door, genuflecting before the high altar, then making her way along the side aisle on the right, small cardboard box held in front of her in both hands, head dipped in reflection, a tall woman dressed in the black and brown of the Carmelites. With the veil and wimple framing and shadowing her face, it was difficult to make out her features.

The woman stopped at the three altars along the side of the church, genuflecting at each. Dana felt herself overcome with a sense of excitement as she studied the figure gliding toward the back of the church, eyes now fixed on something at a great distance. Dana could see now—it was Caroline. She looked older, fleshier, her face a little plumper. Still beautiful. Pale blue eyes, dark, perfectly formed brows. And yet a sadness enveloped her, and Dana realized her fine features were touched with grief that, in turn, touched Dana. This was a woman in mourning.

Dana genuflected and sat in a pew near the votive stand. Caroline continued, eyes downcast once more, making her way to the little stand holding the candles. She glanced up, no acknowledgment other than a slight tilt of the head. Dana smiled.

Placing the box on the floor, she pulled a key from a voluminous fold of her habit, opened the offering box, removed the coins, extracted a small velvet purse from another pocket, and quietly emptied the coins into the little pouch. She began removing spent candles, replacing them with new ones lifted from small corrugated slots in the box.

Dana stood and stepped closer, fishing around in her own bag for coins. Caroline turned and her taut, white face suddenly but slowly tipped up, the slightest smile lifting her lips.

"Can I give you a hug?" Dana whispered, feeling foolish. This was her cousin, her childhood best friend. Why should she even ask?

With a quick movement of her head, Caroline indicated no.

Dana reached out and touched Caroline's hand.

"I need your help." Caroline spoke softly as she slowly withdrew her hand. Quickly her eyes rose up to the altar. The priest, the kind, sweet priest, stood with one remaining tourist, the two conversing in hushed tones.

"Something terrible, here at the church," Caroline whispered. "Our oldest nun, Sister Claire . . ." She stopped, her eyes darting to and then quickly away from Dana. "I need your help to . . ." She gazed up toward the altar of the Infant as her voice faded. "I can't do it myself. Someone must find . . ."

Caroline's hand trembled as she placed a fresh candle in the cup holder. She glanced back and forth from candles to the high altar, where the priest and tourist now stood just outside the communion rail, heads bowed as if in prayer. Dana dropped the coins into the votive box. Metal on metal as they hit the bottom of the now empty container reverberated through the small church. The priest looked back, seemed to find nothing amiss, and then continued his praying.

"Caroline," Dana said softly, her eyes set on the candles, "what is it you want me to do?"

"Please, we might be watched."

"By whom?" She picked up the lighter set in a holder on the stand, flicked it, raised the flame, and lit the candle.

"We need your help."

"We?" Dana asked.

Another worshipper, a small, elderly woman in a dark coat, approached the votives, inserted coins, lit a candle, and knelt on the kneeler in front of the stand. Dana swallowed a deep breath as she lowered her head, feigning prayer. The woman crossed herself, rose, and left.

Caroline placed a final candle in a holder and eyed it carefully. Her gaze flashed toward Dana, then back to the votive stand. Dana could see she had slipped a small paper under the candle cup.

"Sunday?" Dana whispered. "Noon?"

Sister Agnes nodded yes. "Bless you." She folded the flaps on the cardboard box and backed away, and then, taking the same path by which she had made her way down the side aisle, she moved to the front of the church and disappeared.

Dana looked around. The priest had vanished. Several tourists remained in pews, heads bowed. When they got up and started toward the museum door, Dana lifted the cup, removed the paper, and slipped it into her pocket. She stepped back, about to turn and leave.

"We meet again," a familiar low, rough voice said, startling her. "You, too, Ms. Pierson, have made your way to the Church of Our Lady Victorious."

· 10 ·

They sat at an outdoor café on the Staroměstské námĕsti waiting for delivery of a bottle of Czech wine—produced in Southern Moravia, according to Father Borelli—and going over menus, he offering commentaries as if a food critic for the *New York Times*.

After their second unexpected meeting, this one in the Church of Our Lady Victorious, Father Borelli had glanced at his watch and said, "Do you have plans for lunch?"

Startled, at a loss for words, Dana had replied, "No."

And so, just thirty minutes later, here they sat. It was quarter past noon and the priest informed her that they had missed the twelve o'clock tolling of the fifteenth-century astronomical clock on the tower of Staromĕtská radnice, the old town hall, reigning impressively over the south side of the square.

"Perhaps we'll catch the one o'clock show," he suggested.

In addition to providing the time, the clock presented the signs of the zodiac, astronomical data in the movement of the sun and moon, and an hourly show performed by four animated statues. In the upper tier of the tower's face, two windows opened to reveal the twelve apostles, turning and gliding past. Father Borelli explained the figures did not properly represent the twelve apostles. The traitor Judas had been excluded, St. Paul thrown in for an even dozen.

A good crowd gathered, many waiting to get into the restaurant, some lingering after the performance, many strolling among the Easter market's colorful booths overflowing with pink and purple tulips, yellow daffodils, decorated eggs, and intricate handmade toys and puppets. Even without the seasonal market, the square would have been a noisy, active spot in the city, a hub flanked by a collage of Gothic, Renaissance, and Baroque structures. The dark, spiky, double-spired Kostel Panny Marie před Týnem rose up from behind a row of houses, looking more like the abode of a medieval dragon than a church. Painted facades, Renaissance figures, and saintly kings adorned several of the buildings. The bronze statue of Jan Hus, with its green patina, stood as a monument to a revered Protestant preacher who'd defied the Catholic Church.

After arriving at the restaurant, Dana and Father Borelli had waited in line but a few minutes when a gentleman—the one counting heads—approached the priest, spoke to him, and immediately escorted them to the best available table in a patch of warm sunshine along the outer edge of the outdoor seating, front-row accommodations to watch the activity.

"What did he say?" she asked.

"Who?" the priest replied.

"The gentleman who seated us. What did he say to you?"

"He said, 'Your table is ready.'"

"You made a reservation?"

He shook his head.

"It's the collar," she said, running her finger along her neck. Today he wore a priestly cassock and collar.

"I eat here often when I visit. No, it isn't the collar. I tip very well, very generously."

"I thought you priests were required to take a vow of poverty. How do you come up with the big tips?" She knew she shouldn't have said this, but his reply came in such a puffed-up way, she couldn't help herself.

He laughed that deep, deep laugh, then casually ran his hand over the top of his balding head. "There's some confusion among you lay-people," he said. The way he slid in the word *you*, Dana had no doubt that he included her with those who sat far below the clergy. There was, in general, something irritating in the way he spoke, as if because he said it you had to listen and believe it was true. This was a man comfortable in a pulpit.

"Poverty is a vow often taken by certain orders," he explained, "religious communities. But no, I do not belong to a community that professes poverty. I am not a wealthy man, but I've learned if you want to feel appreciated, you must show appreciation for others."

"Thus," she replied, motioning toward the line of people waiting to be seated, a line that seemed even longer than when they arrived, "we get the best seat in the house."

"Correct."

"Certain orders?" she queried. "Like the Carmelites? A vow of poverty?"

He nodded.

"Like your friend Father Giuseppe Ruffino, the prior of Our Lady Victorious?"

He nodded again, more a tip of the head, a sign of acknowledgment, which she could see held a hint of admiration. "Yes, my friend at the Church of Our Lady Victorious."

On the walk from the church, Dana had gathered the facts together and drawn her conclusion. From their conversation on the plane she knew that Father Giovanni Borelli—he had formally introduced himself as they walked—was here to visit a childhood friend. From her reading and Caroline's letters, she knew the Carmelites came from Italy to care for the Church of Our Lady Victorious. Father Borelli was Italian, as was Father Ruffino. They were approximately the same age. Finding the two men in the church at about the same time, she easily put this together. He'd just acknowledged she'd guessed correctly.

The waiter delivered their wine, poured a glass for Father Borelli, which he tasted and approved, then a glass for Dana. She took a sip. She was no expert, she seldom drank, but it had a nice flavor, not too strong, but nice and smooth. The *man* had good taste, at least in the wine department.

He held his glass up to the light and gave it a little swirl, then took a drink. "I feel I owe you an apology," he said and paused.

She said nothing, waiting for him to continue.

"For our conversation on the flight," he added.

"For that little game you were playing?"

He nodded. "You knew who I was?"

"The priest sent from the Vatican to Boston."

He took a slow sip of wine and let it linger in his mouth for a moment. "You did a nice job on the investigation. The articles."

She knew he was speaking of the articles she'd written about the priests in Boston. "Because I arrived at the same conclusion as you," she said. "Even though I was given little cooperation or access." *Guilty as sin,* she wanted to say, but refrained.

He set his wineglass on the table and ran his finger along the base. "Such men give the priesthood a bad name. The Church is served poorly by such—" He shook his head. "It is unjust to judge many on the actions of a few. There are some very good, decent men in the priesthood."

"I know that."

"Some good, holy men," he said. "Devout men, some even saintly."

"Saintly? Like your friend Father Ruffino," she replied.

"I'm certainly not referring to myself." His tone, the shift of his shoulders, his hands raised in an open gesture, dripped with self-deprecation. Very dramatic, Dana thought.

The waiter delivered a basket of bread. He poured more wine for the priest. Dana had taken but a few sips. She asked for a bottle of water. They placed their orders, Father Borelli requesting lamb with rosemary and garlic, Dana a bowl of soup.

"Your friend, an Italian Carmelite," she said. "Assigned by the Holy Father to care for Our Lady Victorious after the new government took control."

"You're an informed traveler," he said.

"Comes with the job," she replied, taking a piece of bread as he offered the basket, "doing the research."

"I thought you were on holiday." He placed a piece of bread on his plate. "Visiting a friend. You've had an opportunity to get together with your friend?" There was a smugness wrapped over his words and she knew he'd figured it out, too. He knew Sister Agnes was the friend she'd referred to on their flight. She wondered how long he had been standing behind them as they conversed in whispers before the votive candles. He couldn't possibly have heard their words, but he'd conceivably seen Caroline place the note under the candle cup, and Dana retrieve it. She'd yet to have the opportunity to read it, but had fingered the small paper nervously and protectively in her pocket as they walked to the restaurant. She wanted desperately to read Caroline's note, but with Borelli sitting across from her at the small round table, it would be impossible without his noticing.

Dana thought of Borelli's taunting her on the flight, the hint of an important summons to Prague.

The priest lathered his bread with butter and said, "You've had an opportunity to visit some of the sights in the city?" He took a large bite.

The waiter delivered their lunches. Dana's large bowl of soup, which the menu's translation had described as broth with meat and vegetables, looked more like a stew with chunky meat, potatoes, and carrots in thick gravy. The savory scent of rosemary and garlic wafted up from Father Borelli's plate. He lifted his fork, nodding, obviously pleased with his selection.

They spent the remainder of the meal speaking of the various places to visit in the city, Borelli giving her a rundown on the best restaurants, going so far as to write them down for her on a napkin. They talked about their work. Borelli explained that over the years he'd held a variety of positions, reporting directly to the Vatican. He'd served as Promoter of the Faith, an office in the Sacred Congregation of Rites.

"More commonly known as the Devil's Advocate?" she asked. "You argued against canonization and beatification of saints."

"Well," he said with a sly grin, "there are very few saints."

He went on to explain how the position had been abolished by Pope John Paul II in 1983, though he considered this a mistake, that the process of beatification and eventual sainthood should never have been streamlined. He told her that since that time he had used his investigative skills in various capacities. Educated in canon law, he'd taught classes in Rome for several years to young seminarians from around the world. He was fluent in seven languages, he told her, barely attempting to contain the arrogance as his chin tilted upward.

"A dry academic, I'm afraid," he said, and she sensed now a hint of apology. "I suppose that's why I found such satisfaction in the position of Protector of the Faith. It gave me the opportunity to talk to real people, to take depositions, to experience the world of the common people."

"Your investigations were successful?" she asked, controlling her urge to ask if he enjoyed working with "common people."

He smiled. "Yes, in the sense that I prevented several possible canonizations."

He seemed to take pride in this pronouncement and she wondered how this could give one satisfaction. Wasn't the Catholic Church all about saints?

Borelli ordered dessert, a Bohemian torte, for both of them. He was a man who obviously enjoyed a good meal. When the waiter delivered coffee, the priest took out a cigarette holder, flashed it at Dana, and asked her permission. As he took his first drag, his shaky hand told her it had been an effort to get through the meal without lighting up.

When they finished their substantial lunch, he insisted on paying the bill, telling her again he owed her an apology. Was he attempting to gain her trust? She was sure he'd seen Sister Agnes place the note under the candle cup.

Father Borelli told her he was taking a cab back to his hotel for a little nap and offered to get one for Dana.

"I have shopping to do. Gifts to take home for family," she said. "I'll walk back to the hotel. But thanks for your offer, and for lunch."

As they stepped out into the square, he extended his hand and said, "Perhaps we will meet again," with a smile that informed her that he was not unhappy about such a prospect.

After he'd waved down a cab, climbed in, and disappeared around the corner, the clock on the square began to toll as Dana pulled the note from her pocket, opened it, and read Caroline's words. She gazed across the square up toward the figures on the clock tower as the performance began. Yes, she thought, her pulse increasing, her heart thumping against her rib cage, she would definitely see Borelli again.

Though he'd told Dana Pierson he intended to return to his hotel for a nap, as soon as Giovanni Borelli settled down in the backseat of the cab he ordered the driver to take him to the Czech Republic Police headquarters. He had an appointment with Investigator Dal Damek.

Giovanni knew that the Czech police force was notoriously corrupt, and he guessed Beppe had asked him to conduct a separate investigation for this very reason. It wasn't a secret that bribes and unofficial, personally pocketed fines were common in Prague. Just a few years back, as Giovanni walked down the street, he'd been issued a ticket by an officer for an infraction he still didn't fully understand. No court summons or invitation to explain himself came attached to this citation. He'd paid the designated fine right there on the spot and watched the officer stuff it in his pocket.

Father Borelli hadn't shared with Father Ruffino his plan to visit the Czech investigator, but he felt this was the best place to start. He knew enough to tread carefully.

Giovanni replayed over and over again the details of what Beppe had told him, the words the old nun had shared before she died. But Giovanni wondered if they had any meaning. The woman obviously suffered from dementia, if not full-blown Alzheimer's. She exhibited all the symptoms—night wanderings, confusion, loss of short-term memory, perhaps even imaginary voices. Was the nun pointing to the killer with her words or was this all a grand delusion?

Giovanni had an uneasy feeling, a suspicion that there was more to what had happened at the church that morning than his fellow priest had shared. It had been Good Friday. This thought turned with near audible agitation in Giovanni's mind, like a rock tumbling in a clothes dryer, adding to his suspicion that Beppe had not been completely honest. Father Ruffino claimed he came early each morning, before his server, to open the church. But Good Friday was the one day in the liturgical calendar in which Mass was *not* offered. Servers would not have been scheduled that morning. Why had the priest come to the church early that morning?

This perplexed and disturbed Giovanni. He did not want to push his friend or suggest he doubted him. Not right away. Eventually he'd have to confront Beppe about this discrepancy. He would do this later, after he talked to the police investigator.

Investigator Damek, wearing an open-collar shirt, which Borelli immediately decided could benefit from a good once-over with a hot iron, invited the priest into his office and offered him coffee. Feeling bloated from his enormous lunch, Father Borelli declined. He'd eaten nearly an entire loaf of bread himself, that dainty Ms. Pierson barely touching it. And she wasn't much of a drinker. He'd finished the bottle of wine with little help. He'd had a cup of coffee with dessert, a sugary concoction that was much too rich. His stomach turned at the thought of anything more.

"Father Ruffino has asked for my assistance in checking on the progress of the investigation concerning Sister Claire's death," Father Borelli told the investigator. A lie. Beppe had not asked him to come and would not be happy to know that he had. "It has disturbed him terribly and I want to do what I can to help."

"You've come from Italy?" the investigator asked.

"Father Ruffino and I have been friends for many years." Giovanni explained how they had grown up together, and maintained their close friendship through the years, though he had been assigned various duties in Rome, while his friend had joined the Carmelites, working in Italy, at an African mission, then in Prague.

Investigator Damek listened affably, nodding as the priest carried on longer than was probably necessary to establish his credibility as a true confidant of the prior of Our Lady Victorious.

"I spoke with Father Ruffino just moments ago," Investigator Damek said, "to let him know the autopsy report should be available sometime this afternoon or tomorrow morning. I thought perhaps he had called you to let you know."

Borelli's heart jumped. If the investigator had called Father Ruffino, had he mentioned Father Borelli setting up this appointment?

"I was lunching with a friend," Borelli explained. "I'm afraid I'm rather old-fashioned in that I do not carry a mobile phone. He had no way of contacting me."

"I see," the investigator said slowly, thoughtfully. He turned, opened an overstuffed glass-fronted file cabinet, one of many along a faded green wall, and pulled out a file. Boxes were stacked about the room as if someone had just moved in or was preparing to move out.

"As soon as the report comes in," Damek said, "we should be able to release the body. At the present time there is no reason to believe there was any criminal wrongdoing."

"Nothing suspicious discovered in the church?" Father Borelli asked, trying to calm his voice, attempting to get a closer look at the file. Upside down, he could not read the report, other than the date and time. Early the morning of Good Friday, just as Beppe had told him. He could see the file contained several pages.

"Nothing missing, no damage," Investigator Damek replied. "I myself, along with Father Ruffino, did a thorough search of the building." His fingers combed quickly through his thick brown hair, which Borelli observed could use a trim. "As I told Father Ruffino when I came to the church, I suspected Sister Claire died of natural causes."

Beppe had said nothing of this, Giovanni was sure. He had most definitely led Giovanni to believe the nun had been murdered. Yet, was the investigator now telling Father Borelli that he suspected from the beginning there was no murder?

Investigator Damek unceremoniously unbuttoned one cuff, then the other, and pushed his sleeves up to reveal muscular arms, which he rested casually on his desk. "It is my understanding that the prioress would like the funeral services and burial to take place Saturday." He glanced at a calendar on his desk. "This request shouldn't present a problem." He closed the folder. The finality of this action seemed to say, *Case closed.* "May I help you with anything else?"

Giovanni wondered if Beppe had shared with the police *anything* about Sister Claire's speaking to him. She was dead by the time the investigator arrived at the church.

"I'll be staying several days. I'd originally scheduled this visit to the city as a holiday, but this . . . unfortunate loss of Sister Claire . . . has come up unexpectedly. I just want to be here to assist Father in any way that I can."

"Everything has been taken care of," the investigator said as he rose and reached across the desk for Father Borelli's hand. He towered at least four inches over the priest. "I'll make sure the body is released. This should give Father some peace. As well as the nuns." He walked around the desk to escort his visitor out.

Giovanni wasn't sure now if the inspector was lying to him, if Beppe had lied to him, or . . . "I'd hoped to reconnect with a friend during my stay," he said as they approached the door, "but I'm having some difficulty locating him. Do you know a person named Pavel Novák?"

"Pavel," Investigator Damek said slowly, thoughtfully. "Novák. Both common Czech names." He shook his head. He glanced back at the file on his desk. "Do you have other concerns about Sister Claire's death?"

Giovanni had a very clear feeling now that Beppe had not shared the name Pavel Novák with the investigator. A name Sister Claire had spoken just before she died. But why had Beppe withheld this information? Was it because he did not trust the police? It almost seemed as if Father Ruffino was playing the two men, one against the other. Sharing and withholding information as he saw fit.

"Do you have reason to believe," the police investigator asked cautiously, "that it was anything other than an accident?"

"I'm confident you did a thorough job," Father Borelli replied, wondering why the man referred to it as an accident when he had just said that he told Father Ruffino he believed the nun had died of natural causes.

The investigator opened the door.

"I have some free time in the city," the priest added, turning back to Investigator Damek. "As I said, my original reason for this visit, a little holiday, though this unfortunate turn of events, Sister Claire's passing . . . certainly sad news."

"It's kind of you to avail yourself to your friend. Perhaps you will still have time to enjoy your holiday. You weren't personally acquainted with Sister Claire?"

"I never met her," Father Borelli said. "I understand she had been a member of the order for many years."

"Very elderly." The investigator nodded and stared down at the floor. A line of small ants moved across the worn linoleum. Investigator Damek squished one, then another, with a casual rotation of his foot. "No reason not to enjoy a little holiday." His eyes rose, as did Borelli's. For a moment they locked. "Please, let Father Ruffino know that arrangements will be made to release Sister Claire's body."

"Thank you."

"Yes, surely not a problem."

"Is there anything you would personally recommend in the city?" Father Borelli asked, lingering just inside the doorway, the bulk of his body preventing the investigator from closing the door without giving the priest a shove. "For a visitor on holiday?"

"The usual," the investigator replied, showing little interest, as if he had other business to attend to. "The castle, the museums, and churches."

"I've heard the performance at the Laterna Magika is quite good."

Investigator Damek smiled. "We, my wife and I, have never been, but, yes, I've heard that it's a wonderful performance. Living here in Prague . . ." He laughed. "We tend not to take advantage of what the city has to offer. You know how it is."

"Yes, yes," the priest replied lightheartedly. "I've lived in Rome for over thirty years, and, you know, I've never toured the Colosseum."

"We do have to make time for such things in our lives, now don't we." The investigator glanced back at the file on his desk again as if about to say, *Before we run out of time.*

· 12 ·

Dana sat at an outdoor café sipping a lemonade, an order placed simply to have somewhere to sit. Caroline's note lay open in front of her on the table.

SISTER CLAIRE MURDERED IN
CHURCH INFANT MISSING
POLICE NOT DOING PROPER INVESTIGATION
NEED YOUR HELP

She had read the note a dozen times now, but her heart still jumped at every word. *Need your help*? Dana's help? Who needed her help? The nuns? Were they in danger? Or the police? Did *they* need her help?

Why did Caroline believe Sister Claire—obviously the old nun being buried this week—had been murdered? Her words concerning the Infant puzzled Dana, as she'd seen the small statue in the church that very morning. It appeared to be authentic, though the glass box sat on such a high perch it was difficult to know for sure.

She took a swallow of lemonade. Looking out to the square, she attempted to remain calm, trying to determine what to do now. Hundreds of tourists strolled about the Easter market. Carved wooden Easter eggs hung on pastel ribbons from the booths. Real eggs, hollowed out and painted with intricate designs, filled wicker baskets. A pair of live, fluffy ducklings nuzzled inside a wire fence.

Again she stared down at the note. Why couldn't Caroline, or the prioress, or Father Ruffino, do something? Dana envisioned Caroline's nervous, guarded glances toward the main altar and wondered if the priest was somehow involved, if he posed a threat to the nuns. The same priest who had spoken so kindly to Dana.

She needed to go back to the convent and speak with Caroline again, yet Dana wondered if she could even get inside. She'd received no confirmation to reschedule their lunch for Sunday, other than a guarded nod from Caroline when Dana whispered, "Sunday?" as they stood at the votive candles.

She considered returning to the church. Because of her uneasiness about the priest, she should probably stay away from the church until she knew more.

The note contained very little useful information; most likely Caroline had written it in a hurry. Perhaps someone inside the convent was watching over the nuns' every move.

Surely, if the Infant of Prague had been taken this information would have gone out to crime units around the world. An Interpol report would have—*should have*—shot out of that office. Maybe no one would care about an old nun's passing, but there would be serious concern if one of the most famous religious icons of the Catholic Church had been stolen. She hadn't read a newspaper, and had barely glanced at an English-language newscast in her hotel since leaving home, but surely a nun's murder, the theft of a valuable religious icon, would have been reported in the press.

Maybe she *should* go to the police. She wasn't sure what Caroline meant by her accusation that the police were not doing a proper investigation. Did this refer to corruption or incompetence?

She stood, made her way around the other tables, and walked out into the square, threading her way through the crowd. Hand-carved puppets—trolls and fairies—perhaps too sinister for children, hung from lines strung along the front of one of the booths. The vendor, who appeared to have been created by the same artist as his trolls, grinned at Dana. "Is the missy in need of a little magic?" Returning his smile, she shook her head and moved along. She skirted the outside of the market and stopped at a newsstand to pick up an English-language Czech paper. Standing in front of the news kiosk, she skimmed over the headlines on the front page. An article about the European Union, the tug-of-war going on between the prime minister and Senate in adopting the Lisbon Treaty. A story on the worldwide banking crisis, another on the global financial markets. The newspaper appeared to be printed weekly and was dated just the previous day, so anything that had taken place over the weekend would likely be covered in this edition.

On the second page, she found an article about the influx of visitors to Prague during the Easter holidays, which were generally considered the beginning of spring and the tourist season. The gist of the article appeared to be that Prague was a very safe city with little crime, though the story offered a number of statistics pointing out that minor crimes such as pickpocketing had increased since the city had become a popular tourist destination. A sidebar suggested ways to avoid such unpleasantness.

According to the article, more serious offenses occurred infrequently, and the percentage of these solved was impressive. The recently appointed chief investigator of the homicide department, Dal Damek, was quoted as saying that most serious crimes, such as murder, generally involved domestic disputes and organized gangs. The story referred to a recent unsolved murder at the Old Town Square just before Easter, the victim a member of the Czech Parliament. Dana gazed around, realizing she was standing near that very spot. Investigator Damek was again quoted as saying all resources were being used to solve the crime and the investigation was moving forward. The article did not mention the murder of a nun, and Dana discovered nothing concerning an incident or theft from the church elsewhere in the paper. She thought of the children she'd met near the convent, of Maria's reference to the *very, very* old nun. Perhaps the death of an elderly member of a religious order would be less than a headliner. Unless foul play was suspected, which didn't appear to be the case.

She stuffed the paper in her bag and walked resolutely across the square. Suddenly an idea came to her.

"Coffee?" Investigator Damek asked Dana as she sat in front of his desk at police headquarters.

"Please."

He picked up the phone, said a few words, asked Dana if she needed milk or sugar. She shook her head, and he replaced the receiver.

"You have come all the way from Boston," he asked, the words spoken carefully and precisely, his heavily accented English easily understood, "to interview me?" He leaned back in his chair, a slow, smug grin spreading over his face. He was about her age—early forties, she guessed. His demeanor, his voice, reminded her of her older brother, Jeff. He looked nothing like Jeff, and he certainly wasn't as tidy as her big brother. He wore a wrinkled, white, long-sleeved, button-down shirt rolled up to his elbows. No tie.

Slightly disheveled, she'd thought when he introduced himself and invited her to sit. With broad shoulders and thick brown hair, he wasn't a bad-looking fellow. Married? If he had a wife, surely she wouldn't have let him out the door like this.

"I'm also on holiday," she said.

He nodded thoughtfully as if he wished her to continue.

She'd been amazed that he'd agreed to talk to her without an appointment. She'd explained she was an American reporter doing a story comparing crime rates in the Eastern European bloc before and after the fall of Communism. She'd come armed with few facts or statistics, which wasn't her style. She always did her homework. But she knew she had to work quickly. She'd quoted some of the facts she'd just read in the article, to give the impression she wasn't a flake, but she now had the feeling he could see right through her, that he knew exactly where that information came from, that she'd picked it up on the fly.

"You join business to pleasure?" he asked, examining the card she'd given him, which identified her as a reporter for the *Boston Globe*. He studied it for a moment and then placed it faceup on his desk.

"Yes, taking the opportunity to see the sights." She glanced around quickly. Certificates and landscape photos hung on the walls. There was something about the room that made her think the occupant hadn't fully settled in yet. Several boxes were stacked on the floor.

"First visit to Prague?" he asked.

"I was here in the late eighties, just as the change in the government was about to take place. I suppose that's why I'm interested in what this has meant in the area of crime." The room was very stuffy and smelled of bug spray. No windows to let in fresh air, she observed. File cabinets lined the wall, one pulled partway open, filled with old manila files, papers sticking out like lettuce in a sandwich.

He turned, the wheels on his chair rolling, so he could reach one
of the glass-fronted cabinets. As he rummaged around, Dana noticed
a stack of files on his desk. A surprisingly neat, organized stack. She
straightened her back, craned her neck to get a peek, attempting not
to appear too obvious, in case he suddenly turned around. She could
make out some of the typed letters on the top folder, first line of the
file label—P-A-N-N-Y . . . *Panny Marie Vítězné?* Her heart jumped.
She knew this was the Czech name for the Church of Our Lady Victorious! Could this possibly be Sister Claire's file? Right on top of his
pile. Had he been studying the file before she arrived? She wondered
if someone had been here just a short time ago inquiring about this
very case.

Borelli?

Investigator Damek swiveled around and placed a sheet of paper
on the table. From the columns of numbers, the dates—all in the
1990s and after—Dana guessed it listed crime statistics, but it was
useless to her because she couldn't translate the words.

"I go to check on the coffee." Damek stood.

After he was out of the room, she reached over and, hand shaking
with nerves, grabbed the top file off the pile. A photograph slipped
out and floated to the floor. Dana gasped and took a deep breath. A
woman, obviously a Carmelite, evidenced by the dark habit spread
about her legs, the sandals sticking out below at an odd angle. A gash
slashed her face, and dark red streaks flared from the side of her head
on the floor like rays of a half-lit halo. Dana knew this was no halo. It
was blood.

She picked up the photo and opened the file. The first page, a
printed report. Dated April tenth. Dana couldn't decipher the Czech.
Quickly she examined a second photo. A garden shears. The murder
weapon? Then a third photo, taken from a distance. The nun on the

floor, inside the communion rail in front of the altar. The Infant's altar. A glare on the glass box, a barely discernible figure inside. She replaced the photos in the file, praying they were in the correct order, guessing the photo that had slipped out was right behind the written report. She heard a movement in the hall. Just as she closed the file, the last line of the report came into focus.

Laterna Magika. These words she knew!

File replaced, she glanced back as Damek closed the door with one hand, holding two cups of coffee in the other.

"You read Czech?" he asked as he set one cup in front of her.

She forced herself to keep her eyes from sliding to the side of the desk, the pile of files. For a moment she felt light-headed, then her entire body felt on fire, but then she realized, of course, he was asking if she was able to read the report he'd left on the desk for her to examine.

He stepped to the opposite side of the desk, gulping a drink from his coffee as he sat.

She took a deep breath, trying to remain calm, to collect her thoughts. She picked up her cup, but set it back down quickly, hoping he didn't notice the tremor of her hand. "I wasn't really here long enough to learn the language, but I'm sure I can get some help with that."

"You have friends in Prague?"

"Yes, well . . ." She didn't want to mention Caroline and realized with this thought that she probably wouldn't be able to rely on her cousin for help anyway, not that she had any true interest in these statistics, unless they included Sister Claire's. "Do you have additional statistics from back before the late eighties?" She could hear a nervous twitter in her voice. Her head throbbed with the vision of what she'd just seen in the file, and she wasn't sure how long she could maintain this charade.

"Such statistics," he said, "more difficult to . . ." He stopped for a moment as if searching for the correct word. Though his English was good, now and then she detected a hesitation as if he were thinking in Czech, translating in his mind. "The Communist police were not particularly . . . how to say . . . when one sees easily and clearly?"

"Transparent?" she offered.

"Yes, transparent." He nodded and took another swallow of coffee.

"And now?" she asked.

"Much improved."

"From what I understand, your rate of closure on murder cases is admirable."

He smiled, but the smugness had returned, and she got the impression he suspected she was playing a flattery game.

"I understand there's an open case," she said, steadying her voice, "regarding a murder of a senator at the Old Town Square."

"It will be solved." His voice betrayed some irritation.

She proceeded carefully. "Are there other unsolved recent murders, or unexplained deaths?"

He paused for a long moment. "Nothing notable." He leaned in, folding his arms on the desk, and then picked up her business card, tapping the edge, slowly, rhythmically on his desk. His fingers were thick, his nails clean and trimmed to the quick. He stared at her. His eyes were very blue. "I will ask for one of my staff to search for these statistics. Such records are not readily available. You stay with friends here in Prague?"

"No, I'm on my own. Could I call later this week?"

"Yes, please."

Dana shifted in her chair, trying to come up with something to move the conversation forward.

"You are more interested," he asked after several strained moments, "in unsolved crimes, than solved?" Did she just imagine a quick sideways glance, brief as a blink, toward the pile of files on his desk? Her heart stopped for a moment. Did he notice a shift in the stack? Had she replaced the folder a centimeter off? Were the photos in the proper order? A person trained as an investigator might notice such small details.

"Well, as a journalist . . ." She laughed nervously. "Those unsolved crimes do make better stories."

"Yes." He laughed, too. "Solved crimes are no longer stories."

· 13 ·

Minutes after the American reporter left Dal's office, Kristof and Černý entered, the younger man with a wide grin slapped on his face that made him look like he was ten years old. He carried a briefcase. The older detective was shaking his head.

"The answer's right here," Kristof said, tapping the briefcase, which Dal now realized was a laptop computer case. "Hugo Hutka's," he said.

Dal was aware that the two detectives' trip the previous morning to visit the widow of the man whose phone number had appeared several times on Senator Zajic's phone records had turned up nothing, the woman having moved out several weeks earlier.

"We followed some leads, found the widow living with her brother's family. She told us she'd reported her husband's accident to the police as suspicious, but they'd basically brushed her off." Dal thought it interesting the way Kristof referred to "they," when the "they" was actually "we," including the detectives presently standing in the office of the chief investigator of homicide.

Not on my watch, Dal thought, though this just didn't work. He had inherited everything that had come before him, which he was learning day by day was a lot of crap. He'd recently heard, just rumors at this time, that his predecessor was being considered for a position heading the security of a large Czech media conglomerate, earning, Dal would guess, substantially more than chief investigator. One hell of a reward for incompetence. Or was it corruption?

"You checked?" he asked. "Did she file a report?"

"No record," Kristof replied, "but I believe her."

Dal glanced at Černý, who nodded. "You think there's something suspicious about her husband's death?" Dal asked, directing his question to both detectives. Dal had reviewed the death certificate himself. Nothing seemed amiss. An accident. Yet, if that was the assumption from the beginning, if something was being covered up . . . Dal had investigated "accidents" before.

The old detective motioned toward Kristof as he unzipped the case, pulled out the laptop, set it on Dal's desk, turned in on, signed in, and typed in a code. A list of files appeared on the screen.

"Explain," Dal said impatiently.

"The widow said her husband had been working on this for the past six months, spending all his spare time in state archives, going over records kept by the Communist secret police prior to 1989. . . ." Kristof's fingers pecked at the keyboard, a two-finger technique. When nothing on the screen changed, he shook his head. "It might take a while to get through it—we still need to come up with some passwords—but basically what he was doing was cross-referencing records, attempting to set up an online index where anyone could type in a name and access the relevant files." Dal scanned the list, everything apparently coded or abbreviated. None of it made any sense to him.

"Files in archives, dating back to the forties," Černý said, his voice skeptical, "said to contain somewhere in the vicinity of three hundred million pages."

"Isn't a similar system being compiled by the USTR?" Dal asked.

"Institute for the Study of Totalitarian Regimes," Černý replied, "government agency, which many believe won't truly make this information available to the public."

Dal sensed that Kristof's excitement over this discovery could be valid. The senator had chaired a committee set up by the Civic Forum to investigate possible connections and collaborations with the Communist regime and StB, the era's secret police. Public officials and others in government positions, such as Professor Kovář, had been removed when such connections were revealed even years after the revolution. If Hugo Hutka had been trying to construct an index that could be helpful in uncovering such information, did Senator Zajic's recent communications with Hutka point to a possible motive for his murder, as well as Hutka's suspicious death? Was a clue hidden somewhere in thousands of files spanning a period of over forty years?

"Without some type of index," Kristof said, "opening the records has little value unless you want to sift through millions of pages. Without a key, if someone was looking for something, say, a particular name, it might take months. . . ." He glanced back at the two older detectives.

"Or years," Černý added.

As Dana sat on the bus after leaving police headquarters, an irregular pulse throbbed behind her rib cage, and then it felt as if her heart were jumping about in her body, unattached, moving from chest to throat, then sliding back down to her gut. She had to talk to Caroline as soon as possible.

She walked from the closest stop to the convent. After several attempts to get someone to respond to her vigorous knocks—nothing.

As she turned to leave, thinking maybe she *should* go back to the church, a group of noisy children appeared on the opposite side of the small square. They must be just getting out of school, Dana thought, realizing these children probably passed by the convent several times a day. Morning, noon—yes, this was when she had seen them before—and now, late afternoon.

She spotted the pretty little blonde, the girl she had spoken to just the day before.

"Maria," Dana called out.

The girl twirled around gracefully, giggling over something one of the boys had just said to her. Eyes wide with recognition, she called back, "I help you?"

"I spoke to you yesterday," Dana said as the girl made her way across the square. The others stood silently, watching.

"Yes," Maria said, smiling, "I remember you."

Dana stepped outside the gate and extended her hand. "My name is Dana Pierson."

"You the American stay at hotel on Nerudova!" Maria said proudly.

How would the child know this? Dana wondered. "Yes, how did you—"

"I take to you the . . ." The girl squinted and pursed her lips as if this might help in finding the correct word. "The sign!" Her eyes flashed brightly.

"The sign?" Dana glanced back at the handwritten sign on the door below the peephole. "The sign?" She motioned.

"No. Different sign."

How did the child know her name? Then Dana realized the girl was talking about the message that had come from Caroline, delivered to her hotel. It was sealed, Dana's name on the outside of the envelope. Maria had delivered it.

"The note from Sister Agnes?"

"Yes, yes, Sister Agnes," she replied excitedly. "Yes, the very pretty *nun*." She pronounced the word *nun* clearly, as if demonstrating she remembered the word Dana had taught her the day before. "Yes, the *note*."

"She gave it to you?" Dana asked, motioning as if handing the girl another note.

"Yes, she gave to me."

"Do you see the nuns often?"

"Yes, they come out. They go back in."

The sisters operated on a very strict schedule, much of their time spent in the convent in prayer and meditation. But Dana knew their work took place outside, mostly caring for the Church of Our Lady Victorious. If she just waited, maybe Caroline would leave the convent.

"They come out here?" She pointed to the door, then tapped her watch. "What time?"

"Many time," the girl replied. "Different nun, different time. But, no, they come that door." Maria made a wide half-circle motion with her hand.

"Back door?" Dana repeated the same motion.

"Yes."

A girl shouted from across the square. The others had already moved on.

"Your friend is waiting for you," Dana said.

"Yes, I go now." She backed away with a little bow, turned, and ran toward her friend. "Bye-bye," she said, glancing back with a wave.

"Thank you, Maria," Dana called out as she watched the two girls disappear at the corner. She made her way to the back of the large stone structure and found a single door, most likely the one the girl was referring to, and waited, hoping Caroline might come out.

About fifteen minutes later, Dana realized this was a waste of time. Even if they stuck to a schedule, the terrible loss of Sister Claire had most likely rearranged everything. Caroline hadn't exactly been on time for their date at the votive candles.

Were the nuns in chapel right now, observing extended hours to pray for one of their own? "May she rest in peace," Dana whispered, as a vision of the blood-soaked scene from the photograph flashed in her mind.

She walked up to the door and knocked. She waited. No one answered, and she knocked again, knowing instinctively there would be no reply. A knot tightened in her stomach, a mixture of frustration and fear for Caroline and the other nuns. What would it be like to have so little control over your own life? She'd never understood how Caroline, once a free spirit, could live under such restrictions. Dana gave the door one more forceful knock. Nothing. Reaching for the door handle, she gave it a twist, having no plan as to what she'd do if she found it unlocked. She was not forced to make that decision.

She couldn't wait around at the convent any longer; there was something else she had to do. After a quick sandwich, eaten outdoors as clouds gathered and the sky darkened toward evening, Dana ran back to her hotel to freshen up, change, and pick up her raincoat, before taking off for the theater.

The Laterna Magika was a well-known attraction in Prague. The performances, presented without dialogue, mostly dance and music and black lights, appealed particularly to tourists as there were no words to decipher. A modern-looking glass edifice near the National Theater, the structure contrasted so drastically with the traditional style of the surrounding buildings that it looked like an adopted child in a family of look-alikes.

Back in the late eighties, as the revolution began, the basement rooms provided a gathering place for students, artists, and theater people, active members of the movement. The leader and later president of the new Czech Republic, Václav Havel, was a playwright, the stage they were setting replete with drama and emotion.

Dana wondered why the words *Laterna Magika* had been entered in Sister Claire's file. And she wondered if Damek was aware she had opened it.

A half dozen people stood at the will call booth, while the line waiting to purchase tickets was at least double that. Dana feared it might be difficult getting in without having already purchased a ticket. As she waited, she admitted she had no idea what she was looking for, what she might possibly find relating to Sister Claire's death. A nun who'd been in a convent for the better part of a century would have no idea about the cultural life of the city.

The woman at the box office held up one finger and pronounced clearly and, Dana thought, almost apologetically, "Just one?"

"Yes, one," Dana answered.

"You have luck tonight," the woman replied.

The woman told her it was in the back, but with the show sold out she was fortunate to get this one remaining seat.

Inside, an usher directed her to the last row on the right. Dana was early, many of the seats throughout the theater still empty. In keeping with the modern design, the interior of the building was rather stark, lacking the architectural embellishments of many of the older theaters throughout Europe. A few people sat scattered about, chatting quietly, perusing programs. Sitting in the back she had a good view of those arriving. She watched as patrons strolled in, some dressed in evening wear, others in jeans and sneakers. As the hall filled, Dana studied the program, searching for an unknown, looking for a hint as to why she was here.

With just a few seats empty, the show about to start, she saw him. Sashaying down the aisle, conversing with the pretty blond usher, he moved with that sense of entitlement up to a row just a few back from the stage, where he would enjoy a perfect view of the performers. Not too close, but close enough to see the expressions on the faces of the actors, the sheen and sparkle of their costumes. She wondered what kind of tip he'd offered for this. The others seated in his row had arrived in a timely fashion, which necessitated several having to get up and out of their seats to make way for the bulk of the priest, who, Dana noted, wore a suit and collar tonight.

His presence here was more than a coincidence. She wondered now if that last entry in the police investigator's file had something to do with Borelli, who had, without doubt, paid a visit to Police Central just before Dana.

The lights dimmed as the music started up. A large three-screened background with pulsing kaleidoscope splashes of color appeared, along with gliding, dancing figures that seemed to step in and out from stage to film, from reality to fantasy and illusion. Large clown faces, wild beasts—a tiger, a lion, a giraffe—one ringmaster, then another, flashed and faded on the screen, keeping time to an untamed beat, then to a tune that rose and fell with the false merriment of a carnival calliope. Acrobats tumbled across the stage, unattached body parts twisting and turning to the rhythmic beat of bright lights. The performance was both beautiful and disturbing. As she sat alone, enthralled with the trickery of light and color, enjoying the performance, a wordless tale of reality and dream told through movement and music, Dana saw nothing that connected in any way to the church, the convent, Sister Claire,

Father Ruffino, or the Infant of Prague. The only connection seemed to be Borelli.

She remained in her seat during intermission, peering over her program until the priest made his way to the lobby. Then she rose and followed, keeping a discreet distance. He disappeared into the men's room, and then came out, purchased a drink, which he downed quickly, and returned to the theater, Dana watching behind a lobby column. Nothing unusual in his behavior. She went back to her seat.

As soon as the performance ended she left the theater and stood out front, away from the crowd waiting for cabs. The air was balmy and damp. It felt like rain. She put on her raincoat as she watched for Borelli, concluding after about ten minutes that he must have taken a side exit that she was unaware of, or perhaps he had a backstage pass and was chumming around with the performers right now. Searching for a cab, she saw none. Most of the theatergoers had already left. She walked down the block, past the National Theater, which appeared to be just letting out, patrons emptying onto the street. She walked another block. The crowd was thinning. It had started to sprinkle. She shouldn't get too far out of the area where the after-theater crowd gathered at restaurants. As the rain continued to fall, showing no sign of letting up, she thought about going into one of the coffee shops, but instead stood under the eaves of a building, watching for a cab.

Finally one appeared down the street and she stepped out and waved. Slipping into the backseat, she gave the driver the address of the hotel. Tired and drained, Dana knew she'd accomplished very little over a very long day. The thought was accompanied by a quick moment of panic, which she attempted to suppress with some line of logic. A plan, she needed a plan, and she had to talk to Caroline again, or someone who had more information, anything to make sense of Caroline's note, the photos from the police file.

She gazed out the cab window. It was raining like crazy now, pelting the windshield and roof. The cab came to a halt. The construction on the street in front of her hotel had made little headway over the two and a half days she'd been in the city. "Damn," she said under her breath. She knew the driver could go no farther, and her hotel was still over a block away.

"I am sorry," he apologized, "I can no go to hotel."

She paid him and got out, pulling the hood of her raincoat up over her head. The rain poured down in an ever-increasing abundance. A half block from her hotel, big globs seemed to be bouncing off the street like water balloons bursting as they smacked the cobblestones. Water ran in torrents; cascading waterfalls flowed into the ditch the length of Nerudova Street. She walked quickly, staying on the boards that had been placed around the ditch, crisscrossing in strategic places to allow her to keep out of the mud where the stones, stacked in piles, had been pulled up to make way for the ditch. Uneven boards knocked one on another as she stepped. Plastic sheets draped along the side of a building flapped in the wind.

She saw no one else on the street. Then she heard the slosh and splash of footsteps behind her. She turned, pulling her hood back from her face to get a better view. A figure ducked into the recessed entrance of a building. Probably just trying to get out of the rain.

Her soles were now covered with mud and the boards felt as slick as slabs of ice. Again she heard something, someone following her. Yanking off her hood, she glanced back. Rain-soaked light from buildings and distant streetlamps provided little help, but she could make out a tall, broad-shouldered figure in a dark jacket.

She sensed the man behind her getting closer. The beat of her heart increased with the rhythm of her steps. She felt the squish of moisture seeping into her shoes. Her hair was drenched. Again she glanced back and saw the figure move into the shadows. Suddenly, her feet slid from under her, her body twisting, glasses flying as she hit her head on something hard. She was on the ground, her hand slipping on mud. Stunned, she attempted to push herself up, reaching, searching for her glasses, aware now that she'd hit her head on a pile of stones.

Someone stood over her, and then he bent down to within a foot of her face. Without her glasses, the rain still falling, everything was blurred. He handed her the glasses. She attempted to put them on, with difficulty as the side stem was bent out of shape. The left lens was streaked with mud. She rubbed it on the sleeve of her coat. "God damn it," she said fiercely, finally propping herself up in a sitting position.

"Not a good end to the evening," the man said, the words slow and precise, as he reached down to help her up. Then, in his smug big-brother voice, which carried a familiar Czech accent, he added, "You enjoyed the performance tonight?"

· 14 ·

Dana sat shivering in the hotel bar, staring across the table at a blurry Investigator Damek. He'd insisted on walking her to the hotel and she hadn't protested. Once inside he'd flashed his badge at the desk clerk, instructed him to bring two coffees, and motioned Dana to a small table in the bar tucked away behind the stairwell. Still stunned from her fall, she complied.

He asked for her glasses. She took them out of her coat pocket as he pulled something out of his jacket, opened it up like a pocket knife, flipped out a mini screwdriver. He tightened a loose screw on the glasses and then attempted to straighten the bent stem. With a perfectly pressed white cloth handkerchief, unfolded from another pocket, he cleaned off the muddy lenses. Without a word, he handed them back to her.

She slipped on the glasses and fixed her eyes on him to test them out. His hair, like hers, was damp and the moisture had created a mass of curls softening his squarish features. He returned her stare as if waiting for her to say thank you.

She said nothing. If he hadn't been chasing her down the street, she wouldn't have fallen and broken her glasses. She'd offer no gratitude.

The bar area consisted of little more than just that—a small bar and two tiny tables. Dana and Damek were the only patrons. Their coffee arrived. Dana cradled it in her hands, attempting to draw some warmth. Her head throbbed. She reached up and pushed a wet strand of hair behind her ear.

"Why were you following me?" she asked. "Ducking into recesses and doorways like some crime novel detective."

"I am a detective," he said dryly. He took a drink of coffee, looking directly at her from above the rim of his cup as if she might up and leave if he took his eyes off her. "But that was not the reason I was ducking, as you say, into doorways. It is raining."

"Yes, that's why I brought my raincoat."

He smiled, an almost human smile. "Better prepared than I."

Yet here she was—wet hair, filthy coat, broken glasses. Glasses purchased just a week before she'd left home. Practically new, now ruined. "You want to talk about Sister Claire's murder?" she asked, wondering instantly if this was wise, if she ought to just continue with her original ploy. Yet she was sure he knew she'd looked at the file.

His face registered no surprise. "Sister Claire died of natural causes," he said.

They sat for several long moments without words.

"I saw the photos," she admitted.

"Is there anything you might share with me?" His voice remained calm, not accusatory.

"Not a particularly natural-looking death." She continued to glare at him, wondering if she should just shut up, yet knowing she'd already said too much. Was she being a fool? Could he arrest her for interfering in an investigation? She felt another shiver come over her, little bumps rising along her arms. She took a slow sip of coffee, the warm liquid sliding down her throat, doing little to warm the rest of her body. "The case is closed, right?"

He nodded.

"Natural death?" she asked, then added, "With all that blood?"

"You are aware the Carmelite nuns tend the altars at the Church of Our Lady Victorious."

"This explains the blood?"

He remained silent, and she guessed he was the type who weighed everything before he spoke. She liked that about him.

"She cared for the altar flowers," he finally said, "unfortunately with recently sharpened shears. She suffered a heart attack—the woman was over ninety—she fell."

"On the shears?"

Again, he nodded.

"That's the official report?"

"At the moment."

"But you're having doubts?"

"When two people come to my office within an hour of one another, both with interest in the same case—"

"Two?" she asked. "Borelli?"

"You know this man?"

"Not well."

"But you know him," he came back.

"Laterna Magika?" she replied. "This has something to do with your case?"

He smiled, part smirk, part admiration, she thought, for her nerve in having examined his file. "This is why you attend tonight?"

"A popular place for tourists," she said, "which both Borelli and I just happen to be." Her head throbbed. She reached up and touched the tender spot where she'd hit it. "You do know he was there tonight?"

The investigator didn't answer. Of course he knew. Obviously Damek had seen the priest. They each took another long, slow sip of coffee.

"It was Borelli," she said, "who mentioned the Laterna Magika as having some relevance?" She knew it wasn't part of the original report. Hand-printed, it had been added later.

"We had a rather odd conversation. He was, perhaps, attempting to tell me something. Or testing to see how much I knew."

"What did Borelli tell you?"

"*Father* Borelli," he corrected her, as if to say the priest deserved some respect.

At the desk, out in the hallway, someone was chatting with the clerk, papers rustling, and then they were climbing the stairs, footsteps thumping overhead.

"If you know anything that might have relevance," Damek said as the muffled noise subsided, "if you believe there is more to . . ." He didn't finish his statement, but paused again as if searching for a word.

Dana wondered if this was just a method he used to encourage someone else to do the talking, if he'd be doing the very same thing if they were conversing in Czech. She also wondered if he'd interviewed any of the nuns, if he'd spoken with Sister Agnes. Protective of Caroline, as well as afraid for her, Dana didn't want to tell the investigator about the note, the accusation that he wasn't doing a proper job. Until she had a better feel for just what Damek was up to, she wouldn't bring her cousin into this conversation. Her glasses were slipping, and she could imagine how lopsided they must look. How lopsided *she* must look. Her head throbbed. She guessed a knot was swelling up before Damek's eyes. Removing her glasses, she gave the bent stem a little twist.

He held out his hand as if to have another go at the glasses. She handed them to him.

Again she reached up to rub her head.

"Do you need a doctor?" he asked. He studied the glasses as if they were an intricate mechanical device.

"I'm fine," she said. She was sure he, as well as Borelli, knew something she didn't. She sensed the investigator was attempting to gauge how much he could trust her, determine if she held information that he did not. As far as she knew, there had been no mention of any of this in the press. In the States, reporters would have been all over it—*old nun discovered in pool of blood at altar of ancient icon.*

Dana realized that neither priest nor detective had made even a casual reference to the Holy Infant of Prague.

"You can trust me," he said. His voice sounded so sincere she was tempted. He didn't look up from his work at hand—fixing the glasses. She would prefer he look her in the eyes while declaring his trustworthiness.

"How did you get a ticket?" she asked. "The woman at the box office said the performance was sold out." She hadn't seen him and guessed maybe he hadn't sat in the theater in a regular seat, having gained entry by flashing an official police ID.

"Single tickets . . ." he said, his voice even, almost uninterested now, as if this conversation were beginning to bore him. "Not difficult."

"No date?" she asked, fully aware of her rudeness, but feeling too tired and beat up to care.

"I'm married—"

"You don't take your wife on dates?" *Stop,* she told herself, knowing she'd already gone too far. She could hear something in her voice she didn't like at all—defiance mixed with a casual flirtiness.

"You travel alone?" He looked up at her now. "No husband?" He gave the stem another twist and handed her glasses across the table.

She'd hit him in a tender spot and he'd sent it right back at her. Bad marriage, she thought. She adjusted the glasses on her nose. They were still off, the lenses not lined up just right.

"I apologize," he said sincerely with a hint of exhaustion. He folded his arms on the table. "Why did you come to my office?"

She was still weighing this out, trying to determine if she could trust him.

"Why did you come to my office?" he asked again.

She drained her cup and pushed away from the table. "Are you arresting me?" she asked. "Or am I free to go?"

"Do I have reason to arrest you?" He reached out and touched her hand as if to prevent her from leaving. His touch was light, nothing threatening about it, yet suddenly Dana felt very warm, her chills turning within an instant to an intense heat. When he asked, "Do you know Pavel Novák?" the heat burned hotter, shooting up along her arm, her neck, moving about her face, on to her ears.

He released her hand.

She wondered if Damek could sense her discomfort, if her face was turning red. How could she be shivering one moment, burning up the next?

"Novák? Pavel?" She tried to steady her voice. "Aren't those both fairly common Czech names?"

"Yes, common," he said. "Exactly what I told Father Borelli this afternoon."

Dana sat in a warm tub. The heat invading her body had left the minute she'd started up the stairs, and she was shivering again as she entered her room.

She reached up and felt the bump swelling on her forehead. She needed to get her glasses fixed. When attempting to bend the stem back into shape after she got to the room, she'd broken it completely. She needed to find an optometrist's shop first thing in the morning.

Here she was—injured, eyesight impaired, barely able to speak the local language. At least she wasn't sitting in jail. If she was going to find out what had happened at Our Lady Victorious, she'd need some help. If she could just get into the convent to see Caroline. Yet she knew she needed someone outside. She understood this was precisely why Caroline had asked for her help—she couldn't gather the information she needed confined within the convent walls.

Borelli or Damek? She didn't know quite what to make of either of them. Borelli was a priest, but Dana knew that in itself did not guarantee a man's honesty or integrity. What about the police investigator? Did Caroline believe he was corrupt or just incompetent?

She got out of the tub, wrapped herself in a towel, and searched for a phone book, finding nothing, not even stationery or postcards. She needed to know if Caroline's Pavel Novák was involved in this in any way. The name, she was sure, had come from Borelli—had he offered this to Investigator Damek as some kind of . . . what? And the significance of the words *Laterna Magika* in the file? Obviously both the priest and the Czech investigator felt they had some meaning. She wished now that she'd brought along her laptop. She wanted to do some research. She grabbed her handbag and pulled out the rumpled program from the performance, but, even squinting, then holding it at arm's length, she couldn't read the small print. Holding the broken glasses up to her eyes, she scanned the list of performers, attempting to find a connection, a name relating to Novák, but discovered nothing.

She knew she needed help. Borelli or Damek?

Should she trust a pompous priest or a smug police investigator?

She slipped under the covers. Closing her eyes, she attempted to relax, to put together the bits of information she'd gathered from her conversations with both Borelli and Damek. The bloody photo of Sister Claire. The Laterna Magika. The name Pavel Novák. Damek insisting the case was closed while clearly still pursuing it.

Borelli's presence in the Church of Our Lady Victorious. His childhood friend Father Giuseppe Ruffino. This was especially puzzling. She remembered the priest's kind words, then Caroline's guarded glances toward the altar. If Father Ruffino was involved, why would he have contacted his friend for help? No one had mentioned the Holy Infant of Prague; no one had alluded to the fact that the little statue was stolen or missing. Other than Caroline.

Was the statue Dana had seen on the altar a fake?

She couldn't sleep. She rolled over, glanced at the digital clock. The numbers flipped over to a row of ones—1:11. Her head throbbed. She got up and went to the bathroom to get an ibuprofen. Finding the white plastic bottle in her small bag, she squinted in an attempt to line up the arrows to remove the childproof cap, finally resorting to searching with her fingers. When she thought she had it right, she popped the cap, sending tiny red pills all over the floor, still damp from her bath. As she stooped to pick them up, streaks of red smeared across the white tiles.

Sister Claire—the image came to her again. Blood on the floor around the nun's head. She grabbed two pills and swallowed them down with water and placed the others on a tissue set on the vanity to dry. She returned to bed.

"You should be here with us, with family." Ben's voice. Her brother. A familiar protest to her annual Easter trip. "Why do you think you can go away each year and block it all out? Don't you understand we're here for you?"

Ben's voice. But it was also her father's. Dad's gone. Her brother—in her father's voice—telling her that her father had died.

Suddenly Dana's mother appeared, standing over her daughter. Dana held a baby.

"Lovely," her mother said. "You were meant to be a mother."

Dana looked up and smiled at her mother. She knew this, too, the moment her son was placed in her arms. This had surprised her. She'd never thought of herself as maternal. When she gazed down, the baby was gone.

She felt wet, hot tears, the damp pillow. She sat up, rose shakily to her feet, crossed the room to the window, and stared down at the street. For a moment she thought about dressing and going out. The room felt terribly stuffy. She found the thermostat, but couldn't read the small numbers, so she just gave it a slight twist and returned to bed.

Sister Claire, the blood streaking about her. Then Father Borelli stood above her, Father Ruffino by his side, in the Church of Our Lady Victorious. Investigator Damek had joined them. Then a line of nuns stood in a row. Looking all the same. Dana couldn't make out the faces, couldn't tell which one was Caroline.

Everyone disappeared. Dana was alone in the church. She ran from altar to altar. Princess Polyxena appeared. She presented the little statue to a Carmelite priest, wearing a white cloak, sandals on his feet. Now Dana stood with Father Cyril. They were digging through a pile of rubble, side by side. The priest pulled a small bundle from the mound of garbage and held it up. Then, in a shrill, high-pitched voice, as he handed it to Dana, he screeched, "Your turn now." He slapped her shoulder. "You're it."

She was alone again, trembling, standing at the altar of St. Joachim and St. Anne. Her eyes darted, scanning paintings of angels and saints, then she moved toward the Infant's altar.

The little King stood above her in his protective glass box, though he wasn't an infant at all—he was a boy. He wore a white and gold embroidered gown and held an orb in his hand, a shape that slowly morphed into a lopsided sphere, the form of an egg. Reaching out, he opened the box and stepped onto the altar. Then he flew as if he had wings, down toward the floor. It was covered with a slippery, deep red blood. The Child King floated over the floor, not even touching it. Then he alighted in the wide central aisle. He marched toward the back. Others had joined him. A series of little kings, some large, some small. Dozens and hundreds and thousands of kings.

Dana sat up in bed, her head and chest damp with sweat, awake again but confused. She glanced at the digital bedside clock. Two hours had passed. She'd been dreaming. Recurring dreams—nightmares, again. But something new now. Marching down the aisle of Our Lady Victorious. Along with hundreds of imposters, like the figures she had seen in the gift shop, like the little replicas of the Holy Infant that graced churches and classrooms around the world, and she knew the statue she had seen in the church was not the authentic Infant gifted to the Carmelites in the seventeenth century by Princess Polyxena.

The statue she had seen on the altar of Our Lady Victorious was a replica, like so many all over the world. Just as Caroline had written in her note, the Holy Infant of Prague was missing.

· 15 ·

It wasn't yet 6:00 A.M. Investigator Dal Damek sat in his office. He'd left his apartment early, unable to sleep. The pull-out sofa in the room above the florist's shop he'd been renting for the past two and a half months, since he and Karla separated, was about as substantial and comfy as a piece of toast. Sometimes he ended up sleeping on the floor, though *sleeping* was an exaggeration. He didn't feel like he'd slept in weeks.

He missed his wife; his son, Petr; his home; his bed. Often when working a case he went without adequate sleep, but this morning he wondered if the emotional turmoil of this separation combined with his lack of sleep was affecting his work. He'd screwed up with the way he'd handled the situation at Our Lady Victorious. He realized this now, particularly after those two foreigners came inquiring. He knew the minute Dana Pierson sat down in his office that she wasn't being honest about her reason for the visit. He generally didn't invite reporters into his office, unless he initiated the meeting, but the unexpected appearance of this American both puzzled and concerned him. It wasn't until she left and he picked up the file to replace it in the cabinet that he suspected she'd come with the intention of learning more about Sister Claire's death. Her presence at the Laterna Magika confirmed it.

Now he wondered if he'd become so caught up in his "high-profile" case of Senator Zajic, his revisiting the murder of Filip Kula, as well as the accidental death of Hugo Hutka, that he had missed something. Overlooked an important piece of evidence in his investigation of the nun's death? Yet there was absolutely nothing to point toward murder.

When he'd arrived at the church, summoned by a personal call from Father Ruffino, Dal's first thought was that the nun's death had to be considered suspicious. But he could see as he examined the gash on her cheek that it hadn't come from someone stabbing her—a person would have had to be less than two feet tall to inflict that wound. She'd obviously tripped or suffered a stroke or heart attack and fallen on those shears. He could tell from the angle, the thrust, and the depth of the wound. And he could see it wasn't the gash that had killed her. His theory had been substantiated by the autopsy. She hadn't been murdered.

He and Father Ruffino had done a thorough search of the church, going through the sacristy, altars, museum, and gift shop, finding nothing missing, nothing out of order. At Father's request, he'd come alone, then called in a scaled-down team, using his latitude as chief investigator. No fingerprints were found on the shears, other than the old nun's. The postmortem verified what he believed had happened. She'd suffered cardiac arrest and fallen on her shears. Father Ruffino had requested no media alert, a request that wasn't difficult to grant. The press hadn't even come inquiring. The death certificate, a public record, listed cardiac arrest, and the demise of a very old woman generated no interest. But now, Dal wondered if he'd let his emotions, his sense of gratitude, get in his way.

He would always be indebted to Father Ruffino. A debt he would in no way be able to repay. And, years ago, Father Ruffino had granted Dal the same request—no media alert.

Dal glanced at his watch. He probably didn't need to rush over to her hotel, but he wanted to be nearby, within viewing distance, when Dana Pierson stepped out. She'd most likely eat at the hotel buffet, giving him plenty of time, even if she was an early riser. He'd be more discreet than he had been the night before. This time he didn't want her aware. He guessed she'd be contacting this Pavel Novák. When Dal had mentioned the name he saw the tension in her eyes, the flush of her face. Dana Pierson knew this man, and Dal suspected he had something to do with Sister Claire's death. After doing a search that morning, checking out a number of possibilities, he'd determined the most likely person to be involved in any wrongdoing—if that was what he was looking at—and who might also be an acquaintance of Dana Pierson, had been a student dissenter back in the 1980s. But that Pavel Novák had disappeared over fifteen years ago.

Dal envisioned her rushing down Nerudova the previous night, the street a muddy mess from the evening's storm. It had been torn up for several months and the inconvenience couldn't be good for business, especially this time of year. The city was jumping with tourists.

A dead nun in a church couldn't be great for business, either. Particularly during Holy Week. This thought fused with another, something else he couldn't shake from his mind, a concern that had been stirring inside him since he'd knelt beside the lifeless body of Sister Claire.

Though Father Ruffino had told him she was still alive when he found her, according to the autopsy report, and Dal's own observations, he was sure the old nun had died several hours before the priest had bothered to place that call.

Shortly after eight, as Dal was about to leave, he heard a knock on the door and Detectives Reznik and Beneš appeared, the younger man with file in hand.

"I believe," Reznik announced, "I've found something of interest in the Filip Kula case."

The two detectives had already obtained phone records, finding nothing of interest other than calls to his dealer. So far, no motive for his murder related to his drug usage, though his bank account might indicate he was dealing, rather than using. Doubek had located an account, the source untraceable. A regular deposit went into Filip Kula's account each month. But a deposit scheduled, if the pattern was to continue, for the morning he died was never made. Whoever had orchestrated these deposits knew Kula would not live to spend it. None of this had been considered in the very short investigation leading up to the Romany's arrest for Kula's murder.

Dal motioned Reznik to sit as Beneš pulled up another chair. "We visited Kula's apartment and a coffee shop where he often hung out," Reznik explained. "Rather shady neighborhood. Seems he was meeting someone there, a couple times over the week before his murder. The owner said it was a woman, not the type he generally served, not a woman who might hang out with a drug addict. He said she wore a plain gray suit, rather dour. He pegged her as government right away. Did a little research, on a hunch." Reznik smiled. "Determined there were only three women on Senator Zajic's staff. And here we go." He placed a photo of a thin, middle-aged woman with a pinched look about her on the table. "Fiala Nedomová."

Dal knew that members of the senator's staff had been interviewed, but this was not a name that had come up in any of the information passed on to him. He'd never heard of Fiala Nedomová. Obviously something important had been missed.

"She's been on Senator Zajic's staff for the past seven years," Beneš explained. "Dedicated worker, never takes time off."

"Interestingly"—Reznik jumped back in for the final word—"Fiala Nedomová's been on holiday since before Easter. No one seems to know where she's gone."

Dana held her broken glasses up to her eyes as she nibbled a fresh croissant and studied a pamphlet from the Church of Our Lady Victorious spread out on the table before her. She'd come down to the breakfast room early, starving, unable to sleep. According to the pamphlet, the gift shop closed just two days a year, Christmas and Good Friday. Mass was celebrated at least once each day. Except on Good Friday, when there was no Mass.

The report on Sister Claire's death in the police file was dated two days before Easter—Good Friday. This was also the first date listed on the note attached to the convent door, which meant Sister Claire probably died early that day. Whoever had taken the statue came in early Friday morning—they knew the priest would not be in for the 9:00 A.M. Mass. With the gift shop closed all day, the thief would have plenty of time. Good Friday would be the perfect day. The one day of the year when there would be little if any activity in the church until late afternoon or evening. Damek had said Sister Claire was there to tend the altars. Dana wondered if the thieves would have been aware of this, and if she had been alone. Again Dana envisioned a frightened Caroline in the church at the votive candles, her eyes darting back and forth from her task to the priest at the altar.

Dana studied a photo of the Infant's altar. A person would need a ladder to remove the statue. And most likely a key. Surely the box must be locked. Shatterproof glass, she imagined. The box was intact when she saw it—no broken glass—and even if the glass had been broken it was likely custom-cut and could not have been replaced so quickly as to go unnoticed. The nuns changed the costumes on the Infant, she reasoned, so they would have access to the box. As would Father Ruffino.

The costume would have been scheduled for a change sometime Saturday, before the Holy Saturday services. If a replica had been substituted for the authentic statue, it would have been discovered then. Surely the nuns would recognize it as a fake. They would tell the priest.

An image came to Dana—the final photo in Sister Claire's police file. Though it was difficult to make out because of glare on the glass, she thought the Infant was in the altar box. And the box was intact. She'd had such a short time to look through the file, and now she wasn't even sure what she'd seen. Other than a dead nun.

Dana thought again of Damek's mention of Pavel Novák and wondered what this man could possibly have to do with all this. And was it the Pavel Novák she knew? Caroline's long-ago love, Pavel? She plucked red grapes, one by one, from a small bunch and slid them into her mouth as she considered her growing suspicion that somehow Father Ruffino was involved. Yet for some reason he had called on his friend Father Borelli for help? Or had he enlisted his fellow priest to aid him—in what?

Dana thought back to the events in Boston when the abuse of children by the Catholic clergy first came to light. Soon after Borelli's visit, new guidelines were set in place to protect children, to immediately remove offending priests from duty and report them to secular authorities. Classes were set up to increase awareness by training the laity as well as the clergy.

She sensed that Borelli was honest. He'd served as the Devil's

Advocate at one time. Denying sainthood to those found unworthy. He was a truth teller. Though unsure that she cared for the man, she felt she could trust him. She would find Borelli and confide in him. She would share what Caroline had told her and what she had written in the note slipped under the votive candle. Maybe Borelli could get into the convent to check on the nuns, to assure Dana of their safety.

Folding the single stem of her broken glasses, she slipped them, along with her pamphlets, into her bag and stood to leave the breakfast room. As she started up the narrow staircase, a large, bulky figure suddenly appeared at the top. Slowly the body descended, step by step. Without her glasses, she could not make out the details of his face, but the girth of the form, the way he moved, were becoming very familiar.

"I've arrived too late to buy you breakfast?" he said in his rough, smoky voice.

"I just finished," she replied. They both stopped in the middle of the staircase.

"You look different," he said. "New hairstyle?"

She grimaced. "I broke my glasses." She touched her head. She'd combed her hair a little differently, adjusted the part in an attempt to cover the bump. Maybe this was why he thought she had a new hairstyle. He was very observant for a man. "I fell," she said.

"I'm sorry," he replied sincerely. He wore a black suit with white shirt, no clerical collar, today. "Let me buy you coffee," he added sympathetically. "There's a place close by. You can tell me about your fall. I can commiserate."

· 16 ·

As they walked from her hotel to the restaurant, Dana Pierson and Father Giovanni Borelli agreed to share what they knew. They each admitted they'd gone to see the chief investigator, then to the Laterna Magika, that each had been asked by their respective friends to look into the circumstances of the old nun's death.

"Did you discover anything at the theater?" Borelli asked.

"Nothing. You *do* know Damek was there? He followed me back to the hotel. He told me Sister Claire died of natural causes, that she had a heart attack and fell on her shears."

"He implied something similar when I met with him. And, yes, I'm aware he was at the theater." He smiled knowingly.

"Do you believe him?"

Raised shoulders from Borelli.

Dana envisioned Caroline's troubled glances toward the altar, toward the priest who had approached Dana with such kindness just minutes before. She couldn't let go of the thought that Father Ruffino might be involved in whatever had happened at Our Lady Victorious. She'd said nothing of this to Borelli, aware that they were close friends with a relationship dating back many years. Neither Dana nor Borelli had yet mentioned the possibility that the Infant of Prague had been taken from the church and replaced with a fake.

They arrived at the coffee shop and Borelli suggested they sit out in the sunshine, though the sun was almost nonexistent and provided little warmth at this early hour. They were the only customers seated outdoors. Dana suspected he wanted to smoke, her suspicion confirmed as he pulled out his silver cigarette holder and lit one up. He requested that a double espresso and a coffee for Dana be brought right away.

"I think much better on a full stomach," he told her as he scanned the menu. When the waiter returned with their coffee, the priest ordered, and then added a generous scoop of sugar to his cup and stirred.

"Laterna Magika?" she asked as the waiter left. She shivered and wrapped her hands around her warm cup. "These words were handwritten at the bottom of Sister Claire's file."

"Investigator Damek showed you the file?" Father Borelli's nostrils quivered with the slightest agitation. He took a deep drag on his cigarette, balancing it in its elegant holder, one plump finger wedged awkwardly through the small espresso cup handle. He exhaled slowly, then tipped the tiny cup, draining the thick liquid.

"No, he didn't show me. I took a quick glance when he left the room for a moment."

Borelli wiped his mouth with a napkin, his lips lifting into a smile, his agitation replaced with a hint of admiration.

"Then last night," Dana added, "when he followed me to my hotel he asked if I knew a Pavel Novák. Do you?"

"No, but . . ."

"But?" She sensed that Father Borelli was still reluctant, still not sure about *her*.

"Laterna Magika and Pavel Novák." Borelli looked directly at her as he spoke. "This is what Sister Claire told Father Ruffino just before she passed."

"With no further explanation?"

"Not as far as I know."

"What do you think Sister Claire meant by these words?"

"I believe this is what we are attempting to discover."

"She was still alive when Father Ruffino arrived at the church?"

Borelli nodded.

"She told him someone was in the church? Pavel Novák? She saw someone?"

"Sister Claire was blind," he said as if reminding her of something she already knew.

Well, that's important, Dana considered, too surprised to even comment aloud. She added this to her mental file of facts. "Father Ruffino told Investigator Damek what Sister Claire said?" she asked Borelli.

"I don't believe so," the priest replied. "I believe I was the original source of that information, though Investigator Damek is not aware these words came from a dying nun. As I said, I do not believe Father Ruffino trusts the man."

"Do you?" Dana asked.

"I'm not sure what or who to believe." She guessed he was referring to his friend Father Ruffino as well as the police investigator.

The waiter arrived with Father Borelli's breakfast rolls, a plate of cheese, another with fruit. They sat silently for several moments as Borelli broke a roll, lathered it with butter, and stuffed a piece in his mouth.

"I'm inclined to believe the investigator," she said. "How difficult would it be to kill an elderly, blind nun? One with the intent to murder would certainly find a more vital spot to place the shears. The heart? The gut? Not the face. And I don't believe a woman of Sister Claire's years would put up much of a fight. If someone intended to kill her, they would have finished the job."

Borelli seemed to consider this. "There was something else in the missive Sister Agnes slipped under the votive candle?" he asked, as if testing their agreement to share.

She knew she should reveal the entire contents of Caroline's note if they were to work together, yet a trace of doubt still tapped along her spine. She glanced around, everything fuzzy without her glasses. The scent of strong coffee as well as smoke grabbed the air. Dana sensed the movement of a man who'd arrived shortly after they were seated, the rustle of his newspaper. It seemed, without her glasses, her other senses were on alert. She thought of the old blind nun, how senses dimmed often increased the power of others. Had Sister Claire *heard* something in the church that morning?

Finally, after a long silence, she said, "Sister Agnes believes the Infant of Prague is missing."

Borelli remained very still and then, under his breath, he muttered something in Italian. A curse, she thought. Or maybe a prayer.

"This belief is expressed in the note?" he asked and Dana nodded. Obviously neither Father Ruffino nor Investigator Damek had mentioned the possibility that the Infant had been stolen. "The statue on the altar is a fake?" Borelli took another deep drag on his cigarette, a slow exhale. He pinched his bottom lip in a nervous, agitated gesture as if removing a speck of tobacco.

"Is there any way," she asked, "we could get a closer look at the Infant, the one now standing on the altar? The statue consists of a wooden core covered in a layer of wax. If the one in the box is fake, I don't imagine the body is wax."

Again Borelli appeared as if he were thinking this all over, still stunned by what she'd just told him. He ran his fingers along the top of his balding head, then scratched his crown.

"It doesn't make sense," he finally said. "And I'm not sure if, at this point, we should ask to examine the Infant."

"Well, someone certainly should," she replied.

Nothing from Borelli.

"What else did Father Ruffino tell you?" Dana asked. "He didn't mention the missing statue?"

Borelli ground the cigarette stub in the ashtray with very deliberate force as if he were attempting to smash the life out of it, pulled another from the pack he'd set on the table, inserted it into his holder, and lit up. He shifted his bulk in the chair and gazed out across the outdoor seating toward a man in a business suit hurrying by.

"Maybe he's involved," Dana said.

"No, no, no," Borelli came back quickly. "That's impossible."

"Maybe he doesn't know." But the nuns knew, she thought. Surely they would have shared this discovery with their priest. "Or maybe—"

"Why would he have asked for my help," Borelli broke in, "and why would he lead me to believe it was murder, when the police report clearly indicates it was not?" She realized Borelli was leaning toward the police investigator and away from his friend.

"Because he wants you to locate this Pavel Novák, who he believes took the statue. I'm not sure why he didn't share this with the police." She paused. "Or you."

Borelli forked a piece of melon and stuffed it in his mouth.

"*When* did he call you?" Dana asked. "Maybe he wasn't aware at the time that the statue on the altar was not the original. It's up so high and the features are difficult to make out. It wouldn't have been noticed until . . . when? Late Friday or early Saturday when the nuns took it down to dress it?"

"But he would have shared this with me when we met here in Prague."

"Maybe a demand for ransom came after that initial call and he was told not to tell or—"

"Or what?" Borelli's eyes flashed—with fear or anger, Dana wasn't sure.

"Would the Church be willing to pay for its return?" she asked.

Borelli spread a second roll with butter and took a bite, though Dana sensed he was losing enthusiasm for his breakfast. "The Vatican?"

She nodded.

"The statue is owned by the Carmelite community and they would have little to offer in the way of ransom," he told her. "Father Ruffino has mentioned several times how in need of repair much of the church is, the attic, the lower crypt. The tourists have certainly helped with the upkeep, but Our Lady Victorious also supports an African mission. No, not a ransom. And, if later, after his initial call to me, it was discovered that the Infant was missing, surely Father Ruffino would have shared this with me."

Dana could see that Borelli was having a difficult time grasping the possibility that his friend wasn't telling him the truth, or at least not the whole truth.

"Ransom," the priest said, with a dismissive wave, again muttering something in Italian. "More likely it's out on the black market now, possibly stolen to order. This is happening more often than one might expect. Religious icons, artwork, disappearing from churches. What a godless world we live in." His voice was growing louder. "Thieves going right into a church. Museums have increased the security, but churches..." He paused for a moment as if to collect himself. "Churches, with equally precious treasures in the form of paintings, sculptures, religious manuscripts, golden chalices, and ciboriums, seem to think the only security necessary to discourage a thief is the fear of stealing from God. No one fears God anymore." Borelli worked over a crease in the tablecloth with his thumb.

"I know—or knew"—she corrected herself—"a man named Pavel Novák."

Father Borelli's eyes rose up—startled again. "Why didn't you tell me this?" he said in a demanding voice. "I told you what I know." A tone of childish petulance wrapped his words.

"He was a friend of Caroline's. More than a friend, actually. Years ago, during the revolution. We were very young and became involved with the students, the artists, the actors, who took part in the demonstrations. We met Pavel at one of the rallies. He was a handsome young man, tall, athletic. Dark curly hair, piercing black eyes. The big romance really started after I left for home."

"You went home before your cousin?" Borelli asked. "Well, yes," he added thoughtfully, "of course. She stayed."

"Yes, which is rather ironic. It was my idea to visit Prague. I thought maybe I'd get a great story to launch my career. As it turned out I had a job offer back home, one I couldn't pass up. By then, Caroline was caught up in the cause and she decided to stay. She's a good person, though it surprised me when she joined the convent." Dana thought back to those days after she left Prague, and then later, learning that Caroline had entered the convent. Dana didn't understand, and even now, years later, she suspected Caroline had not revealed her true reason for becoming a nun. It seemed some type of wall had been placed between the two women. Was it merely a religious conversion that Dana would never understand? "It's difficult to envision my beautiful, adventurous cousin cooped up in a convent," she told Father Borelli.

"There is great need for those who lead a life of prayer, contemplation, and simple acts of service," the priest replied. "St. Teresa founded the Order of the Discalced Carmelites on this very principle, a simple and total dedication to Christ."

There was a sweetness, a reverence and sincerity, in the way the man spoke, a side of him Dana had not seen until now.

"This Novák and your cousin," Borelli asked, his voice business-like again, "they were romantically involved? What happened? She became a nun. Unrequited love?"

"No, not that at all. Pavel adored her. Simply adored her, and she was madly in love. But then she discovered that his girlfriend—a woman he was with before Caroline entered the picture—was pregnant. He didn't bother to tell her himself. It broke Caroline's heart, this lack of honesty. She called it off. The relationship ended."

"She went to the convent? This sounds almost medieval."

"No, not right away." Dana thought this reaction a little odd, coming from a celibate priest. "But she felt he had an obligation to the girlfriend. I think her name was Lenka. Caroline said she couldn't be with a man who would abandon his own child, his responsibility to the child's mother. She was a performer, an actress or dancer or something, although I don't really know much about her."

"Lenka?"

"Yes, and Pavel was a musician. He composed and performed a number of pieces about the revolution and the fight for freedom."

"Did Novák marry the woman?" Borelli shifted a piece of cheese around on the plate with his fork.

"I don't know."

"She wasn't one of the players in the performance at the Laterna Magika?" he asked.

"I don't think so. I looked over the program this morning, and—"

"But maybe this is the connection," Father Borelli said, his voice again growing in volume, "with what Sister Claire told Father Ruffino."

"It might be," Dana commented pensively, "but there *is*, or at least there might be, another tie-in with Pavel Novák and the Laterna Magika."

"You *did* discover something at the theater?"

"I hadn't yet heard his name when I went to the theater, so I wasn't looking for a connection. Even later last night, after the performance, when Damek asked me if I knew a Pavel Novák, I didn't put it together just then, either. But now I wonder if there is a connection somewhere. The gatherings of students, actors, dissenters— many of them took place in meeting rooms in the basement of the theater."

"The Laterna Magika?" Borelli asked. "Ah, yes, I recall now. The president of the new republic, a playwright, Václav Havel. Perhaps we need to revisit that time . . . the Velvet Revolution."

"Perhaps," Dana said without much enthusiasm. How would the death of an old nun and the possible theft from the church have any connection to a political event that had taken place almost twenty years ago? They should start by finding Pavel Novák.

"We must begin by locating this Novák," he said, echoing her thought, then pushed aside his plate and reached for his cigarette balanced on the edge of the ashtray.

"Caroline wrote that he left Prague years ago."

They sat without words. When the waiter appeared to inquire if they wanted anything more, Borelli gestured for him to remove the plates.

"Could we get a key?" Dana asked. "To the church? To the box on the altar?"

"You want to examine the statue?" he asked with a dismissive grunt, a wave of his hand that sent ash from his cigarette flying to the ground.

"We could get the keys, go in after the church closes, open the box. See if it's real or fake. At least then we'd know what we're dealing with."

"I'm sure Father Ruffino has keys, but I'm hesitant to ask, until I know how he . . ."

She understood how difficult it was for him to believe that his friend might be involved in any way. She could see this was the major source of his frustration, and she could also see that Borelli suspected his friend had deceived him.

"If I request the keys," the priest said, "I might as well ask if he knows who took the Infant and why he didn't bother to mention it."

"Why don't you?" she replied.

They sat silently for many moments.

"You could 'borrow' the keys," she said. "You are staying with him?"

"Oh, no, of course not. I'm staying at a hotel. He lives in a monastery with a bunch of Carmelites. Not much fun."

"All those vows. Poverty, chastity, and obedience."

"Yes." He grinned despite himself. "Perhaps this evening . . . I'm going to the monastery; I could attempt to find—no, I don't believe I would have time. What about the nuns? They must have keys. You could ask Sister Agnes."

"She already told me the Infant is missing. Of course I'd like to talk with her again, but I can't even get in to see her. The whole convent is in lockdown until Sunday. And I'm concerned. She seemed so . . . well, nervous and scared. One of their own has just died under very strange circumstances."

"I'm sure they have keys; they work at the church," he said slowly, as if thinking it through. "The funeral Mass and burial are scheduled for tomorrow morning at ten. Father Ruffino is saying the Mass. All the priests and nuns will attend. He's asked me to serve as a concele- brant. Everyone will be in chapel for at least an hour, possibly two."

"You would be inside the convent and you could search for the keys."

"It might indeed be a perfect opportunity to borrow the keys."

"Do you think you can break away from the services?"

"Not long enough to search for the keys, but possibly long enough to check the door. I could probably find a moment to unlock it. Then someone else could come in and take a look around while everyone is occupied in the chapel."

"Someone else?" she asked. "Who did you have in mind?"

· 17 ·

Dal Damek stood between two buildings across the street from her hotel where he had a good view of anyone leaving, out of the way enough that he wouldn't be seen. After about twenty minutes, wondering if he'd arrived too late, he started across Nerudova, around the muddy ditch, and stepped inside the hotel and up to the desk. "Has Dana Pierson left this morning?" Dal pulled out his badge.

"She left about a half hour ago," the clerk said.

Early riser, Damek thought. He'd misjudged on that one. It seemed he was making a number of errors in judgment lately.

"Which direction?"

The clerk glanced outside as though trying to recall. "I'm not sure. They went . . ." He pointed right. "I think they went that way."

"They?"

"She left with a large man." He held his arms out to his sides, allowing substantial air between his own slender body and the curve of his lanky limbs.

"A priest?"

"He wasn't dressed like a priest," the clerk said, then added, "They asked where they could get her glasses fixed."

Of course, Dal thought, as blind as the woman seemed to be, she'd find a place to have her glasses repaired.

Within ten minutes he stood across the street from the address the clerk had given him for the optometrist's shop, watching for someone to come in or out, wondering again if he'd arrived too late. After waiting ten more minutes, sure enough, they strolled down the street and entered the building, a rather odd couple—the enormous priest and that dainty Dana Pierson. If the two were associates, Dal wondered why they'd come separately to his office, then each solo to the theater the previous night. Yet, from the way she'd reacted to his mention of the name Pavel Novák, he was sure she hadn't heard the name earlier from Father Borelli. Dal couldn't quite see the connection between the two. He'd already run a background check on each and she was indeed a reporter from Boston—an award-winning journalist at that—and he a priest from Rome.

"I no can fix these," the clerk told them. "You buy new glasses."

"How long will that take?" Father Borelli asked with impatience.

"I have them in one week," the man said. His voice was high-pitched to the point of being irritating.

"She needs them now," Borelli insisted.

Dana looked down at the display case, amazed to see frames identical to her broken glasses. The styles of frames seemed to change every time she went to get a new pair, but she'd purchased these shortly before her trip. She wondered if they could possibly just switch the lenses. She pointed this out to Borelli, who asked to have them taken from the display case, then asked for her broken glasses.

The priest and man now conversed in Czech, having switched over from the English they'd spoken to accommodate Dana. The shopkeeper's shrill voice rose and fell, his thin shoulders bobbing up and down, his head shaking in disagreement. After several more moments of intense verbal exchange, Borelli reached in his pocket, yanked out a credit card, and slapped it on the counter. Then, rattling off a string of angry words, he grabbed the display frames and snapped them against the counter, breaking them in two.

Dana's hand went to her mouth in amazement as the two men continued, words flying. The shopkeeper's brows rose, as did Borelli's voice, and then, abruptly—silence. With a grand gesture the shop-keeper slid the credit card through the register. He stared at Borelli, then Dana, his mouth so tight it could have snapped his head in two. Glaring at Borelli, he slid pen and credit card voucher toward the priest, who signed. The man stuffed it into the register and then took out a pliers and miniature screwdriver and proceeded to dismantle one side of the broken glasses, a magnifier affixed to one eye like a jeweler. His mouth twitched as his hands and tools moved quickly, attaching the stem from the new frame to Dana's original frame. After several more minutes, in which no words were exchanged, the man held the glasses up and handed them to her. Carefully she tried them on, glancing around the showroom. Perfect! She smiled and nodded an okay. "They're great," she told the two men. She just wanted to get out of there.

As soon as they completed the transaction and exited, she said, "You got him riled up."

"I told him emphatically that I would pay the full price for the frames, plus labor, and he went on and on, how these were for display only, that he would order you a new pair. And I said, 'The poor girl cannot see; she does not wish to wait a week. Just remove one stem from this frame, attach it to her glasses. I offered to pay him double the price for the frames and he still refused." Borelli pulled out his cigarette, fumbled for a smoke, and lit it up. Dana could see he was still irritated. She wondered how much he'd paid for fixing her glasses.

"That's when you snapped them in two?" she asked.

"Yes," he replied with a guilty grin. "That's when he really began raving. *'Now what am I going to do with these broken frames?'* " Borelli laughed. "I explained what he could do with them."

"Which was . . . ?"

"Stuff them up his ass."

For two people attempting to solve what they had evidently decided was a murder, Dal thought they were having an unusually good time. He watched as Dana Pierson and Father Giovanni Borelli left the optometrist's shop. At first they were involved in what appeared to be a serious discussion. Within seconds, the woman stopped, stared at the priest, and broke into hysterical laughter. The priest joined her.

Dal noticed she was wearing glasses, so she must have gotten hers replaced or fixed. As they walked down the street, they were so engaged with one another, they didn't even notice him. He could have followed a mere two steps behind.

They continued for several blocks, stopping a couple of times to rest—Dal thought for the benefit of the large priest, as the woman seemed to be in good physical shape. Father Borelli enjoyed a cigarette as they strolled. They spoke to no one.

They arrived at a hotel in the Malá Strana and went inside. Had they set up a rendezvous with Novák here? Or were they on holiday, just as they'd both informed him, enjoying the city? Were they now about to enjoy a midmorning tryst? *No,* that was ridiculous, Dal thought. The man was twice her age, bald, and fat.

He waited a few moments, then slipped inside, discreetly checked out the lobby—empty—and then approached the front desk, showed his badge, asked the clerk if a Dana Pierson, Giovanni Borelli, or Pavel Novák were registered at the hotel. Informed that Borelli was on the third floor, Dal hopped on the elevator and went up.

He waited several minutes, and then quietly, feeling more like an amateur detective in a goofy film than a chief homicide investigator, he approached the room and put his ear to the door. He heard voices inside. Just two—the priest and the American reporter. Conversing, he judged from the cadence, not grunting and rolling around in bed. The priest did most of the talking, but Dal couldn't make out the words. He watched the room for some time. No one went in or came out. Finally he left, heading directly to his office to pick up Kristof. They had an appointment later that morning with the director of the Archives of Security Forces, then they were headed back to Kutná Hora to visit with the professor once more. Dal needed to let go of Sister Claire and Our Lady Victorious, a case that most likely wasn't a homicide case, though he wasn't sure what it was. He needed to let go of this, but for some reason he could not.

Stanislav Buzek looked and smelled as musty and bloated as the three million pages stuffed into the ancient faded files that had been entrusted to his care. His thinning hair, a dull gray, appeared as if it had not been washed or combed in weeks, and the wool vest he wore under his tweed jacket, straining against a protruding belly, was spotted with what might have been his breakfast porridge or last week's goulash.

Though the records were now open to the public, the archives' hours were limited and a special appointment was required to gain access.

"You know this man?" Dal asked, handing a photo of Hugo Hutka to the director.

Buzek pushed his reading glasses, lined bifocals, up on his nose and studied the photo. "Quite a nuisance, this man."

"A nuisance?"

"In here night and day, requesting this file, then another." The man's arm circled in the air with agitation. "He wanted to bring in his computer," he added, as if this were some destructive device that might blow up his precious files.

Dal understood that Stanislav Buzek made the rules, that he presided inflexibly over his domain. There didn't appear to be any stated or written guidelines as to how many files a person might request, but the director had made it clear that a written form was required for each. Notes could be taken, using pencils only, not pens, and on small notepads, both supplied by the archives. A strong whiff of Communist control still permeated the air.

Kristof had meticulously filled out the forms, requesting a number of files, which, according to the information obtained from Hugo Hutka's computer notes, contained references to the actor and Communist dissenter Filip Kula. The young detective had contacted Hutka's widow to ask if there might be handwritten notes, but she had cleaned out the apartment when she moved and believed everything had been transferred to the laptop. As it turned out, the files in Hutka's computer were not as easily understood as they had hoped, and they were still attempting to open several protected by unknown passwords. But when Kristof had discovered the name Filip Kula, along with reference numbers to state archived files, he knew he was onto something. Dal, too, was eager to take a look. It appeared that Hutka had begun to gather information for his index but, as far as they could tell, no complete index yet existed.

Director Buzek had sent his assistant off to retrieve the requested files, as the two police officers would not be allowed direct access to the rows and rows of shelves bulging with the archived materials.

With a stack of files cradled in her arms, the assistant appeared, as young and fresh as the director was old and musty. She wore a short skirt, a curve-enhancing sweater. And smelled of a strong, musky-floral mix of perfume, as if she had doused herself to combat musty with musky. She smiled flirtatiously at the younger detective, then at Dal as she handed the files over, flipping her long blond hair back as she did. "Let me know if I can help you with anything else," she said sweetly, before turning and leaving.

Kristof's brows rose as he watched her shapely butt sway back into the rows of shelves. He glanced at his superior with an embarrassed shake of the head as if to indicate, *Let's not get distracted here.* Dal placed the files on the table, separating them into two piles, pushing one toward Detective Sokol as they sat.

Dal scanned the first few pages, finally finding a reference to Filip Kula, the actor, identified as a government dissenter, outlining his involvement in setting up some of the initial protests. He flipped over to the next page, which included a photo, a head shot of the handsome young man. Filip Kula in his prime, such a contrast to the photos in the official crime report. Then a snapshot of a meeting with a half dozen others. Dal recognized the leader and future president of the Czech Republic, Václav Havel. Others he did not know. As he sifted through several additional files, it seemed as if he were looking at history itself. He scanned a list of dissenters. Scheduled meetings. Locations, times, names of those involved in leadership roles, surely supplied by someone on the inside, one of the dissenters. As he studied the next couple of files, Dal realized that Kula had begun sharing information with the StB, the Communist secret police. An informer as well as a dissenter. A famous actor, doing what he did best—acting—set in the thick of it all, gathering information for the enemy. Dal knew many had played such roles, some because of ideology, others seeking monetary rewards, many keeping options open if the Communists prevailed. But they had not. Thousands of these people had faded back into society. Others, such as Professor Kovář, had been outed and removed from prestigious positions.

He slid the file toward Kristof, who read, a look of amazement spreading over his face. "Kula was an informant, an StB collaborator, working for the Communists even as he marched with the protesters, demanding reform and overthrow of the regime."

"But motive for his murder?"

"Revenge?"

"Possibly."

"But . . ." Kristof spoke slowly, thoughtfully. "Kula's bank account? Where was that money coming from? The deposit scheduled for the morning he died was never made, which surely indicates—"

"The person paying him was also the person who killed him," Dal said.

"He was blackmailing someone? Someone who decided murder would be a better way to handle the problem?"

"He definitely wasn't the one being blackmailed." Dal considered what he'd just read. "Information he shared with the Communists concerning dissidents would have no value to a present-day possible blackmailer. These protesters are still considered heroes."

Kristof nodded. "But information regarding another informant? Someone who aided the Communists? Someone determined that this information remain hidden?"

Dal rolled this thought around and around in his head. The value of the information in these files lay in the possibility of finding information on those who had been Communist informants or collaborators. Since Communism had been overthrown back in the late eighties, the dissenters had become the new leaders, the heroes. Those who had aided the Communists were the "bad guys." Some, whose true roles in the revolution had not been revealed, had become part of the new democratic society. Intuition now told Dal that Filip Kula's death was related to ancient politics, but did any of this relate to the senator's murder? Hugo Hutka's accident? If the murderer was the same, he . . . or she . . . had taken care to use a different means of doing away with each. Kula stabbed, the senator shot, Hutka suspiciously meeting his demise in a car accident. As Dal gazed down an aisle between rows of dusty files, bulging with the weight of tons of yellowing papers, he realized what a momentous task they had before them and wondered if they were even on the right track. Something tied these three deaths together. Was the answer hidden here in these ancient archives?

· 18 ·

Dana wandered around the Hradčany, looking for an Internet café after eating an early dinner alone. She had invited Borelli—her treat this time, she'd insisted—but he had reminded her he was having dinner at the monastery.

They'd spent a long afternoon sitting in his hotel room, going through the list of Nováks in the city, the priest attempting to find Pavel by calling every one of them. She'd listened with admiration as he spoke, his voice taking on an engaging, friendly tone, though she didn't understand the words. She sensed if there was information to be had, Borelli could get it. They ordered lunch, delivered from a restaurant near the hotel, Borelli tipping generously, then continued. They discovered little, other than finding a distant cousin who said Pavel was no longer in Prague and he had no idea how to contact him.

Dana found an Internet café and checked in with the clerk at the counter, a man in his late twenties with greasy black hair and an untidy mustache that seemed to dip into his mouth every time he spoke.

"Děkuji," she said as she sat down at the computer, glancing up at the clerk as he hovered over her in the pretense of helping. "Thank

you. I'm fine from here." She waited until he ran a finger over his mustache, smiled, and moved on.

Dana signed in and got on the Internet. She typed in *Pavel Novák* and came up with almost a half million results. Sorting through the first few pages, scanning articles about a professor, a composer, and even an art forger, she concluded none was the Pavel Novák she was looking for. Attempting to narrow down her search, she typed in *Velvet Revolution*, then skimmed several articles that contained the name Novák, but found no mention of a Pavel in this context. She added the word *musician* to *Velvet Revolution*.

Finally, she found a black-and-white photo, a group of four young musicians who had been involved in the Velvet Revolution. The only person identified in the photo was a long-haired fellow named Marek Cermak who'd evidently made a name for himself after the revolution as a rock musician and passed away a few years after. One of the men, holding a guitar, looked very much like Pavel Novák. Slender with dark curly hair. Yes, this was Pavel Novák—a very young Pavel from twenty years ago.

Then she noticed the man standing in the middle of the group as if this was exactly where he belonged. At the center of the universe. She felt her face grow warm, her heart palpitate as a memory returned of a long-ago evening after a demonstration, a meeting of students in an old deserted theater. Not the Laterna Magika, she was sure, though she could not recall the name or even the exact location. Then a gathering, a party of sorts, in a small, run-down apartment nearby. They were drinking. Emotions and adrenaline high, mixed with fatigue. And something else, though she could not name it at the time—youth combined with the aphrodisiac of risk. They were in the middle of a revolution, and she wanted to be part of this, to be part of something more than herself. He'd stared at her from across the room, then approached. He had a beautiful, though dangerous, smile. His hair, his beard, wild, the color of fire. They were talking, drinking, then making out. Someone passed a smoke, hand rolled. He took a drag, pressed it to her lips. She pulled the smoke deep into her lungs, exhaled. He led her out of the room, down a narrow hall, past others, some conversing, others engaged in more intimate discourse. Alone somehow, in the narrow confines of a stairwell. He kissed her again, the pressure of his body lowering her to the stairs. His tongue, probing. He tasted of beer, cigarettes, rebellion. His beard rough as sandpaper against her face. Fingers fumbling with the hooks on her bra, touching her breasts, sending a shock wave through her. He was working his way along the waistband of her jeans, touching, moving, the snap undone, the zipper, his hardness pressing into her. The angle of the uncarpeted rough wooden stairs digging into her back. A loose nail, jabbing. This discomfort of her surroundings, the position she'd willingly placed herself into. She didn't even know him.

"No," she said. "Please, no. Stop." The weight of his body crushing her. She pushed, elbows against the stairs, trying to escape, then her hand against his broad chest. He resisted. She dug her fingers into his arm, feeling the tightness, the strength of his muscles. He grabbed her wrist. She shoved him again, her knee into his groin. He let out an angry shriek. Finally, freeing herself, she sat up, pulled her shirt down over her unsnapped bra, brushed her hair away from her eyes. She could hardly breathe.

She hit print and glanced over at the printer. It whirred out a copy.

She sat for a moment, attempting to push thoughts of this man out of her head. Caroline and Pavel had been there that night, too, but they had been falling in love. Caroline chirped all the way back to the youth hostel. Dana, overcome with guilt, said nothing of Branko. She never described what had happened that evening.

Branko—yes, she remembered his name. *Bronco, like a wild horse?* she'd asked earlier in the evening and he'd smiled and explained it was spelled B-r-a-n-k-o.

The attendant had picked up her copy from the printer and was studying it. As long as she was here, Dana thought, she'd check her own e-mail. She signed on to her office account—nothing important. Her professional life appeared to be on hold. Then she signed on to her personal account, which she hadn't checked for a week and a half. She cleaned out the spam, deleted a dozen e-mails from places she shopped back home—a bookstore, a bath and body shop. No messages from friends or family. Of course not—they all knew she'd be gone for two weeks, that she hadn't brought her laptop. She typed in her brother Ben's e-mail address and wrote:

I miss you. Have been thinking about you. Enjoyed Rome. Now in Prague. Will see Cousin Caroline on Sunday. I've become involved in quite an adventure here in this magical little medieval city. Mystery and intrigue abound! Tell you all about it when I get home. Love to Mom, Jeff, Pammie, and the kids.

She reread it, thinking it sounded much too light and amusing to reflect what she'd become involved in. But she didn't want to alarm them or tell them anything about the events that had possibly taken place at Our Lady Victorious. And she didn't want to share her fears for Caroline.

She hit send and logged off.

The attendant gave her a once-over and took her money for the copy. When she stepped out of the Internet café the sun had set and the sky was spinning a tapestry with the most incredible threads of deep fuchsia and gold and orange. She walked through the square, then down the hill toward the hotel, realizing she didn't want to go back to her room just yet. She continued on to the Karlův most, the streets still clogged with groups of young people, students on spring break, families on holiday. The vendors had closed shop, packed away their portable kiosks. The music of a handful of performing groups floated along the bridge. Several people were taking photographs. She stopped for a moment to admire the lovely scene of the spires silhouetted against the sky, now softened to pink and lavender.

Strolling over to the Staroměstské námĕsti, where she'd eaten lunch with Borelli the previous day, she found the stalls for the Easter market shuttered for the evening. She still hadn't done any shopping and had no gifts to take home. Her musings turned again to family— her mother; her brothers, Ben and Jeff; Jeff's wife, Pammie; the little ones, Zac and Quinn and Olivia.

As she turned and headed back toward her hotel, Dana thought of how much fun she'd had with Borelli and felt a touch of guilt that she was enjoying this. Spending the morning and much of the afternoon with him, between going to the optometrist's shop and searching for Novák, making the calls, he'd unobtrusively asked about her life back home, and she'd revealed that her dad was gone and her mother still lived just outside Boston. She'd told him about her brothers, niece, and nephews. He shared that he had but one sister, and together they owned a small vineyard in Tuscany, which his only nephew managed. The nephew and his wife had an eight-year-old daughter named Mia.

Borelli did not inquire about husband or children, perhaps aware this might be a sensitive topic for a woman her age, and Dana shared nothing of this part of her life.

She wished he could have joined her for dinner. She now anticipated, with a mixture of excitement and horror, what might happen the following evening after the church closed. She'd done a few questionable things in her life as a journalist, but she'd never sneaked into a convent, then illicitly entered a church and climbed up on an altar to examine a religious icon. She realized she was much more nervous about their plan for the morning—Borelli unlocking the convent door, Dana entering and searching during the old nun's funeral. The building was large and ancient and, she imagined, divided into a number of small rooms, nooks and crannies, and secret places, and she wondered if she could even find the keys.

She crossed back over the bridge. The musicians were gone, save for a lone young man with a sonorous voice, sitting cross-legged near the statue of the queen's confessor, John of Nepomuk. The crowds had diminished, yet dozens still idled on the bridge. Many huddled in groups as a slight chill now hung in the evening air. Young people leaned up against the balustrade, laughing and passing bottles of wine among themselves or sipping from beers. Lovers stood holding one another, oblivious to those making their way over to the Malá Strana. Others stopped to admire the view. Again Dana lingered. The colors were fading. The sky slowly darkening.

She thought of Drew, Joel's dad, how much like these lovers they'd once been. She hadn't seen or heard from him in over three years. Perhaps the pain and memories were too much for both of them. Grief bound some couples closer, while others were pulled apart. Maybe she and Drew had not loved each other enough to make it through their loss. She'd had two brief and, in retrospect, meaningless affairs since, but there was no one in her life now.

Again she thought of Branko, that night long ago. After she'd told him no, he called her a bitch, a tease, then angry Czech words she did not understand. "First you say yes, then no. A man goes after

what he wants. Women," he snorted. His nostrils flared and for a
moment she thought he was about to strike her, but instead he placed
his hand under her chin, lovingly at first, then moving slowly to her
throat, fingers tightening. She began to cry. He released his grip and
laughed. "Go home, little girl," he said. "You are not woman enough
for all this. Go home and grow up, you little American bitch." Then
he stood and walked back down the hall.

The following morning she told Caroline she was ready to go
home. Caroline wanted to stay.

As Dana continued across the bridge, strangely, she now thought
of Investigator Damek, their meeting at headquarters, their encounter the previous evening. His hair, curling wildly from the rain. He
didn't appear to spend much time primping, but she'd never liked
that in a man. His looks were natural, unassuming. Yet he carried a
perfectly pressed white cloth handkerchief in his pocket. A man of
contradictions. But also—what was it? His quiet consideration before
he spoke? She realized she was smiling. He was married. She knew
that. She'd as much as asked him, though she wasn't sure why. Sometimes her mouth took off before her brain. She was well aware of this.

She headed toward the Malostranské náměstí. A block from her
hotel, she had another thought. Maybe they could find Pavel by finding Lenka. If they'd had a child together, even if they never married,
wouldn't they maintain some kind of contact? Or Branko? Had they
remained friends? She couldn't remember his last name, though she
was sure he'd told her. As if someday this would be important, as if
he would become a major figure in the new Czechoslovakia.

She headed back toward the Internet café, guessing it stayed open
late, maybe all night. Just as she turned the corner, a half block from
the café, she stopped abruptly. Investigator Damek stepped out the
door and started down the street in the opposite direction. Had he

been following her? Dana watched as Damek walked away briskly, but in her mind she pictured him entering the café, flashing his badge, and sitting down at her computer, the seat perhaps still warm, insisting the shifty-eyed clerk retrace her steps on the computer, maybe even passing him a handful of korunas. But what would Damek discover? That they were all looking for Novák? She wondered if he could hack into her personal e-mail. She'd mentioned to her brother that she'd become caught up in an adventure in Prague. But Damek could learn nothing from that. The only thing he might discover from her e-mail to her brother was that she missed her family. That she was lonely.

Dal Damek woke as her soft, sweet-smelling body faded away. He sat up, realizing the woman in his dream was the American reporter, puzzled by this erotic presence of a woman he found more irritating than attractive. He slipped out of bed, made his way to the shower, turned it on full blast, not bothering to let it warm up as he relieved himself of the throbbing ache in his groin, as the spray of freezing water pelted his chest.

Out of the shower, wrapped in a towel, he opened the fridge in the kitchen, little more than an extension of his living room, which was also his bedroom. He grabbed a bottle of water and sat on a stool at the small, raised counter that created a divider between the two areas. Staring down at the copy of the Internet photo he'd left there the night before, he could smell her again. She didn't seem to be the type to wear perfume—she was almost boyish—yet she smelled lovely, like a wildflower he couldn't quite place. Sweet and erotic. He had been aware of this as he sat across from her at her hotel, then in the seat at the computer café where she'd been just a short time ago. He did not understand this strange appeal. She was as skinny as could be, and he preferred a curvy girl like Karla. But she wasn't ugly—she had a pretty face, nice eyes—he'd noticed her eyes as she'd stared across his desk, then the table at the hotel bar, blinking nervously without her glasses. Full lips. Straight American teeth. She was perhaps most attractive when she smiled, which he guessed she didn't often do.

He tried to shake this image, this sensation, her scent from his head. Yet he could not let go of Dana Pierson because he had to determine why she, as well as the Italian priest, had taken such an interest in the death of an old nun.

After spending over an hour the previous morning following the two foreigners, then again trailing Dana Pierson that evening, he'd accomplished little other than confirm they were looking for a man named Pavel Novák. The clerk at the Internet café had guided Dal through the websites the woman had visited, and it seemed he'd been correct—the man they were searching for was the Novák who'd been active in the late 1980s during the *sametová revoluce*.

The photo, a group of four young musicians, was dated 1989. Dal guessed Novák was among them, but couldn't identify him. He'd found no photos in his earlier search, but he had yet to delve into the archives—thousands, if not millions, of files in the basement of headquarters in such disarray it might take weeks. He had no time for this.

He took a sip of water, the cool liquid sliding down his dry throat, and then picked up the magnifying glass sitting on the counter. Again he examined the details of the blurry picture. The tall blond man in the front he easily recognized as a once-famous Czech rock star, Marek Cermak, though he'd passed away years ago, possibly of a drug overdose. A stocky fellow standing in the center, hands clasped together, feet set wide, wearing an open-collared shirt and jeans, sporting a scruffy beard, displayed a confident smile. Dal sensed this man oversaw the whole production. He looked familiar. Maybe someone he'd known years ago, or maybe a younger version of someone he'd encountered recently?

According to what Dal had discovered at the Internet café, Dana Pierson had also looked at some e-mail accounts. It appeared, just as she said, that she was on holiday. Dal took another swallow of water. He was tired, and the thought of jumping back in bed tempted him, but his mind was too full, and he knew he couldn't sleep.

An image came to him—the old nun's feet, tattered leather sandals, wool socks so worn he could see through to the flesh of her heels. A threadbare habit and tattered knit shawl. Then another recurring image pushed it aside: finely polished black leather shoes, fur-trimmed winter coat fit for a king, a hundred tiny, shiny mink having given their lives to warm a rich, plump Czech senator. The unsolved murder that should now be receiving Dal's full attention. This along with the murder of Filip Kula.

Dal had accomplished little with his visit to Kutná Hora the previous afternoon. The professor was in the hospital, having suffered another stroke. He'd spoken with the niece, but gained no further information. Dal's instinct told him there was something in Hugo Hutka's files, and he and Kristof had indeed made some progress with their trip to the state archives. There was something there . . . something buried somewhere in three hundred million pages of material. Did the senator's contact with Hutka, as well as the actor, Filip Kula, through his aide, Fiala Nedomová, indicate he was attempting to dig up something from the past, a possible connection to the Communist secret police to discredit someone now in a position of political power?

Detectives Reznik and Beneš continued in their attempts to learn more about Fiala Nedomová, but she had no family, a spinster without husband or children. If she was dead, like the senator, Kula, and Hutka, no one cared.

The previous afternoon, Friday, Dal had received an e-mail from the chief of criminal investigations. *Report to my office Monday morning at 9:00 a.m. Progress, in my opinion, is much too slow.* Dal had no doubt he was speaking of Senator Zajic's case.

Taking another swallow of water, he went to the window and stared down. A man across the street was filling a newspaper stand. Dal's thoughts turned again to the American reporter. He had no use for reporters—Czech, American, or otherwise.

He let out a dry hacking cough and sensed he was catching a cold or his allergies were acting up. Spring did this to him every year. Everyone loved spring, but Dal preferred the cold, hard winter. He ate better. He breathed better. He slept better.

Draining the bottle of water, he stepped into the kitchen, tossed the bottle in the trash, and then wandered back to the foldout sofa and sat among the rumpled blankets, staring at the photo of Karla and Petr on the end table.

"You are a spineless coward," Father Giovanni Borelli chastised himself as he sat, nursing a whiskey, unable to sleep. He'd slumbered restlessly through the night and awakened early.

He had yet to confront Beppe. He had not, if he were to defend himself, even had the opportunity. They had taken their dinner along with the entire community of the Carmelite monastery, Brother Gabriele hovering attentively. Giovanni was always suspicious of those who appeared most innocent and caring. A monk who looked like an angel. A priest overly fond of children. An attorney who went out of his way to visit an ailing widow who'd lost touch with reality as well as family.

Perhaps he should have called Father Ruffino aside and spoken to him or shared his concerns as his friend walked him to the monastery door and bade him farewell for the evening. But Giovanni had said nothing.

He'd always admired Beppe, always trusted him. They had been best friends so long Giovanni often felt they understood one another without words. He couldn't imagine the man lying to him. Was this the reason he could not confront him? Because he felt a very personal betrayal? Would the friendship they had shared for so many years fall apart, unravel, if he learned that Beppe had deceived him? Maybe Dana was right in thinking a ransom had been demanded, that the man feared for his life if he revealed any of this. Giovanni considered that his presence in Prague might even be a threat to his friend.

He would wait until after he and Dana examined the statue on the altar to further question Beppe. If it proved to be a fake, then he would have to speak to him. He would not throw out accusations, but if the statue was missing, Dana was right. The nuns would know, and they would have run to the prior of Our Lady Victorious with this terrible news. He would speak to Father Ruffino then—if and when they confirmed the statue a fake.

Father Borelli was beginning to doubt that he even possessed the necessary skills to conduct a proper investigation. Dana had told him she was going to do some online research. Giovanni himself had limited computer skills. His nephew, Leo, had attempted to teach him, had even taken him to one of those computer stores to make a purchase. The place was confusing, with so many choices, so many parts, electronic devices Giovanni couldn't even put a name to. They'd taken the computer home, set it up, and Leo had started in, explaining this, then that. He'd attempted to show him how to use the Internet for research. After three days of trying, Father Borelli had become so frustrated he considered returning the computer and demanding a refund. Yet it still sat in his office at home, barely used other than for a game of solitaire now and then.

At one time, Giovanni had been known for his investigative skills—he knew who to call, he had a feel for how to phrase a question, and he could generally tell when someone was lying to him. Wasn't that where the real information came from—an interview with a real live person, not some electronic box supposedly attached to the world? Or from authentic correspondence, official documents, and historical archives. But everyone—investigators, reporters, the police force—relied on computers now. Maybe Giovanni Borelli was too far behind the times. Maybe he should just leave this to the young folks. He took another gulp of whiskey, feeling it slide down his throat with a surge of anger.

He had an acquaintance who might be able to help. Several years ago—no, decades actually—Father Borelli had been called upon to investigate the black market selling of religious icons taken from Catholic churches. The man who had helped him with this investigation had at one time been engaged in the trade. He'd reformed and confessed, though Father Borelli had doubts there had been any true reformation. As a priest he knew he should believe in repentance and forgiveness, but human nature was such that at times it was difficult. He taxed his memory, but could not recall the man's name. Maybe he'd been out of the trade so long he'd be no help. What was his name? He was Italian. Giovanni had the information in his file at home. He glanced at the clock on his nightstand. He would call his housekeeper. He knew right where the file was.

· 20 ·

Banik. The name came to her as she brushed her teeth, though it had been playing around the periphery of her troubled sleep all through the night. She had awakened several times, and it felt like he was right there beside her, on top of her, pushing himself into her. When finally she slept deeply, then woke, it was almost nine.

Yes, his name was Branko Banik. If she could find him, maybe she could find Pavel. Sister Claire's services, according to Borelli, were scheduled to begin at ten, so time wouldn't allow for a run up to the Internet café for research. Because of Damek's following her last night this probably wasn't a good idea anyway. Surely the hotel had a computer for guests to check on travel plans and flights.

She stopped at the front desk to inquire and was led to a room no bigger than a closet. A boxy, ancient-looking computer sat on a desk. A sign taped to the wall requested guests limit use to checking flight information. If she had any problems, the clerk told her, please come back to the desk.

Without difficulty she found numerous references to Branko Banik, most in Czech. The computer froze up every minute or two and it took forever to open the sites listed. She could have read a book during the time it took to translate. Branko Banik was well-known in the Czech Republic for his business dealings—primarily music and entertainment production. Several photos revealed he had not lost his swagger, though the rebellious beard had been shaved, the longish rocker hair neatly trimmed. But it was the same man. His image, the memories, sent a quick shiver through Dana. She'd never shared the events of that evening with anyone. She was jotting down a business address and number when the system crashed. Glancing at her watch, she realized she'd have to leave soon. She thanked the clerk on her way out and took off for the convent.

Finding a bench at the far side of the square, she had a perfect view of the front of the building. She didn't want to linger too close to the convent entrance in case others were attending the funeral, though she guessed it unlikely that a childless, ninety-plus-year-old woman who'd spent nearly her entire life as a nun would have many friends or family left. Perched on the bench, gripping the edge to calm and anchor herself, Dana gazed down the street, then up into windows, checking for Damek.

At the far end of the square she noticed the old man who'd helped her the first day she came to the convent. He sat conversing with two other elderly men. One sucked on a pipe, blowing circles of smoke into the air. Dana envisioned Caroline, along with the other nuns, heads bowed in prayer, solemnly filing into the chapel. She checked her watch. It was now ten. No one had entered the convent through the front door. If anyone else had come for the services, they were now inside the building. Just to play it safe, she waited until five after, then looked around again, making sure no one was watching or had followed her. She glanced toward the opposite side of the square. One of the old men stood and left; the two others sat for several more minutes before they rose, crossed the square, and shuffled down the street. It was eight minutes after ten. She guessed she still had at least an hour. She stood and walked up to the iron gate, and when everything looked clear, she unlatched it, hurried to the door, turned the knob, pushed, and walked inside just as easy as that. Borelli had come through for her.

A long, dark hall stretched out before her. A worn, gray rubber mat covered the stone floor at the entry. Scents of ancient stone and incense mingled in the musty air. Vaguely she heard chanting—sweet, melodic voices drifting from the chapel, which sounded like it was located at the other end of the building on this lower level. She crept as quietly as possible, noticing a faint squeak from her rubber-soled shoes as she proceeded along the bare stone. Adjusting her step, careful to lift each foot, she continued on. Maybe she should remove her shoes. Barefoot Order of the Carmelites, Dana thought with a nervous inner chuckle. God, she felt jittery. What was she doing here? She moved quietly down the hall, peering in the first open door to the right, which appeared to be an office. She stepped in, glanced around. A crucifix on the wall, three arched windows, all frosted glass. A movement outside caused her to jump, but she quickly realized it was just the branch of a tree.

She went to the desk and pulled out the narrow top drawer, searching for a key. Finding one, hidden among a pile of paper clips in a divided tray, she decided it was too small for a building key. She was sure it wasn't the church key. Could it be the lock to the altar box? No—it appeared to be for the lock on the file cabinet built into the desk. She slid it in, turned it, and opened the upper drawer, finding it full of files. Lifting one out she guessed—from what appeared to be a name, along with several dates—it was one of the nun's personal files. With shaky fingers she flipped through several sheets that seemed to contain medical information, including prescriptions. She opened the file labeled CLAIRE. The last entry was made several months back. Though Dana could not make out most of the Czech words, she knew Aricept was a drug used in the treatment of Alzheimer's patients. This seemed to confirm the nun had some memory loss, just as Borelli had suggested, and Dana wondered if searching for Pavel Novák based on the old nun's words was a waste of time.

She opened the second drawer and found several hanging file folders. She really needed to get on with her intended task—finding the keys to the church and altar box, which surely wouldn't be stashed here in a file cabinet. Yet, curious, thinking she might possibly find something inside the convent to point them in the right direction, something that might be more valuable than the words of an old nun with dementia, she opened the first file. Filled with bills. A few of them had business logos. From the hammer and saw images on one, she guessed it had come from a carpenter or repair person. Another, with wrench and pipe, a plumber? It seemed the nuns' quiet contemplative life required physical upkeep just like everyone else's.

Suddenly she had a thought. Father Borelli had suggested that someone outside the convent or monastery might have somehow gotten a key. Of course, entry could be gained into the convent by a person coming to do repairs or maintenance. She checked the dates on the top receipts. The only one within the past two weeks was a generic-looking bill without printed logo. Then she found another, dated a day later, same type of receipt, same scratchy handwriting. She needed copies. Her eyes darted around the room and landed on a copy machine. No quill-penned manuscripts in this convent. But if she turned on the copy machine, it might be noisy, and it might take forever to warm up. She slipped the two small receipts in her pocket, closed the drawer, relocked the upper file drawer, and placed the key back where she'd found it.

She left the room and walked down the hall, coming upon what appeared to be a library. She stepped in and surveyed the shelves of books, which she guessed to be religious tomes. No desks, no drawers, nowhere she might look for a key. She returned to the hall.

She came to the cloister, an open area surrounded by a columned, arched, covered walkway. Sounds of the city filtered through the cloudy sky hovering above the grassy square. Traffic on the street, a man calling out, words unclear. Continuing on, creeping along the open corridor, at the far side she found a staircase. From the music, the chanting, she knew she was very close to the chapel. She glanced at her watch. Ten twenty-seven. Borelli said the services would last at least an hour, probably an hour and a half. She started up the stairs. Hard, cold stone, no creaking loose boards here. When she got to the top, she found another small desk in an open corridor, much like the one in the office. The drawer was locked but a box sat on top. She opened it to find an assortment of tangled headsets and CDs. From the labels, affixed with small stickers, she gathered they contained sacred music—many titles in Latin, among them "Ave Maria." Lenten and Christmas songs, church music.

Quietly she continued down the hall; it was lined with doors. She peered into one. A small bed, covered with a plain gray blanket, stood against one wall. A door on the other—maybe a closet? A small bureau with three drawers. She stepped in, opened the closet to find a nun's habit and a simple faded white tunic. A nun's entire wardrobe. A spare habit and a nightie. She was touched with guilt at this invasion. These were women who had chosen a simple, private life, and Dana was an intruder.

Yet she knew she had to keep up her search. She'd made an irrevocable decision as soon as she opened the convent door. She went to the bureau and pulled out the top drawer. A rosary and prayer book. Writing paper and envelopes, neatly stacked. A small container of pens and pencils. The second drawer contained undergarments, the last some shampoo, toothpaste, a wrapped bar of soap—all the things a woman would need for minimal care. She moved down the hall, past a bathroom. Then past another room, and another. The nuns' chanting voices were low and quiet, and she imagined she was above the chapel, the notes muffled by the layer of stone between the two levels. She wondered which room was Caroline's, Sister Agnes's. No nameplates on the doors, no telltale posters or photos on the walls—this wasn't exactly a college dorm. She stepped into the last on the left and opened the small bureau. The most recent letter she had sent to Sister Agnes sat on the top. More letters underneath, some from her aunt, Caroline's mother. The next drawer was filled with personal items—toothpaste, shampoo, soap, deodorant. Sanitary pads. Caroline—Agnes—a woman still, though a woman who had chosen to give up the possibility of children. Dana remembered how she and her cousin used to share their secrets as girls during those weekend sleepovers, reading naughty romance books with a flashlight under the covers, talking about boys, about love, about how babies were made, how they would grow up to be mothers. Caroline had voluntarily given this up. Dana had not.

The lower drawer contained underwear, white cotton bras and panties, then, hidden in the bottom, a half-empty box of red licorice, Caroline's favorite. Her cousin's secret stash? Dana smiled. The girl still had a bit of the rebel in her.

And underneath, a CD with most of the label scratched off. A corner of color remained, the pale green strangely familiar. Dana flipped it over. Her heart nearly jumped out of her chest. Caroline had sent her a copy of this CD years before, recordings of musicians who'd been active during the revolution. Dana had listened to it then, but it had been long ago and she hadn't understood the Czech lyrics. Song titles and artists were listed. She felt her breathing deepen as she scanned the list. Then everything stopped abruptly: her breathing, her heartbeat. The title, *Laterna Magika*. The artist, Pavel Novák. Dana knew she could not dismiss the old nun's words. This was it—the connection; the musician's name, the title, the exact words spoken by Sister Claire. She tucked the CD into the waist of her jeans, fingers shaking, and then put everything else back in order and crept out into the hall.

She arrived at the kitchen, which smelled of the previous night's dinner—fish, she guessed. Not a pleasant smell, though she could also detect the scent of toast. Large aluminum pots sat on shelves above a stove. Dishes were arranged in the cupboards, visible behind glass panels. The refrigerator hummed. She could no longer hear the nuns' voices. Again she glanced at her watch. If Borelli had calculated correctly, she still had time. They were probably only halfway through the Mass now. She pictured the nuns taking Communion, palms pressed together, fingers pointed heavenward, heads bowed in prayer.

Off to the right of the stove, she noticed a door, then another at a right angle to that, which she guessed led to the staircase that led to the hallway that led to the back door, which, according to the young girl, Maria, the nuns used in their daily comings and goings. Dana walked over to the stove and glanced through the first door into a small narrow room, the pantry. Cans and boxes, bottles of oil and syrup, napkins, and paper towels sat on the shelves. She turned and noted a small table next to the second door. A small dove-shaped water font hung to the right of the door. She walked over. The nuns' voices started up again, and Dana could imagine the priests gathered around, reciting the final prayers, sprinkling the old nun's casket with holy water. A large, round, ceramic container filled with black umbrellas sat on the floor next to the small table. Stacked on the bottom were several books and magazines. The top held additional books, a box of paper and pencils, and a phone book, though she could see no phone.

She heard a sound, a door lightly hitting a wall. Her heart jumped! She turned. A cat, up on the counter, arched its back, pushing against the cupboard door.

"Shh . . . shh," she whispered. The animal leaped down and sauntered over on padded feet along the carpet runner on the stone floor. It rubbed up against her leg, creating a spark of electricity. She gave the cat a little pat. It was black, brown, and white—the colors of the Carmelites' habits, which she found rather amusing. It moved gracefully along the floor, finding a bowl next to the table filled with a lump of wet food that Dana now guessed was the source of that awful fishy smell. The cat started in on the food.

Dana glanced back at the small table. A tiny box was partially hidden behind the phone book. She moved closer and peered down into the open box. Inside she saw two keys held together on a key ring with a medal of the Virgin Mary staring up at her. She studied the keys for a moment, her heart pounding. The larger was big enough to be a key to the church, the other small enough to fit the Infant's altar box. A second medal was attached to the smaller key. She was about to reach in when she felt a movement against her leg. The cat had finished the food and was now purring like a little motor of fur, attempting to lick her leg just above her sock under her jeans. Thirsty, she thought, and she glanced down at the floor, searching for a water dish. A second bowl stuck out from under the stove. A dead fly floated in the water. She glanced at the cat and could almost imagine it saying, "You don't expect me to drink out of *that*, do you?" Dana smiled despite herself, stooped, feeling the CD still secure in her waistband press against her stomach, and picked up the bowl.

Quickly she carried it to the sink and carefully, quietly poured the water, fly and all, down the drain. She turned on a dribble of water. What was she doing? The nuns could probably hear the water moving through the ancient pipes right now. No, the music would drown it out. She placed the bowl with a small amount of water on the floor. Taking a deep breath, she walked back to the table, stared down at the keys, then turned the second, small medal over to examine it. The Infant of Prague! She lifted the key chain and keys out of the box. She could hear the cat lapping at the water without so much as a thank-you. The music had ceased. Then the cat was silent, the room so quiet she could have heard a pin drop. Or a key. The cat had curled up in a ball on the carpet runner. Dana stuck the keys in her pocket.

She took a step toward the door, sure that it was the exit down to the stairs, then the hall that led to the door and out of the building. She dipped her hand into the holy water font and crossed herself, leaving a cool damp spot on her warm forehead. Taking in a deep breath, slowly she opened the door, then hurried quietly down the stairs and through the hall and out into the fresh air, where she finally exhaled and lifted her face triumphantly to the late-morning sky, barely noticing the gathering clouds.

· 21 ·

Dana placed the purloined items in the hotel safe, showered, and put on a clean shirt. She hadn't realized until she was on her way back from the convent that she was covered with sweat. Now, refreshed, she left the hotel, going through a shopping list in her head as she walked. The thought of shopping for her church break-in escapade with Borelli made her laugh nervously, aware this wasn't funny at all. She couldn't believe they were going to do this. But it was too late to turn back now. She'd just stolen a set of keys from a convent, along with a couple of receipts and a CD.

Making her way through knots of tourists on the bridge, wending through the crowds toward the Náměstí Republiky, Dana looked up, checking the dark, cloud-filled sky. Her chest compressed at the words on the building above her: PRAHA INTERNATIONAL. She glanced at the street sign and realized this was the name and address of the headquarters she had seen during her Internet search.

Should she?

She stepped into the building, her eyes darting from the high glass ceiling back to the marble floors, a traditional look meshed with the modern. Following arrows and signs, she took the escalator up to the second floor. A large round table, displaying a human-sized arrangement of live flowers, stood in the center of the lobby. Several photographs—corporate executives, she guessed—hung on one wall. There he was, Branko Banik. A flattering photo, one she'd seen on the Internet.

A young, attractive receptionist sat at a large curved glass and metal desk. Dana approached. "Is Mr. Banik in?"

The woman gave her a look as if to say, *Mr. Banik doesn't speak to just anyone off the street,* but then she asked her name.

"Dana Pierson," Dana said, guessing he most likely wouldn't remember her, though she'd kept her family name after she married. She honestly couldn't recall if he'd even asked her name.

The woman spoke into the phone. She hung up. "Would you care to arrange an appointment or leave a message?"

Dana fumbled in her bag for a business card as the woman presented a pen and pad with the company logo emblazoned across the top.

Dana wrote:

We met years ago here in Prague. I'm trying to contact a mutual friend, Pavel Novák. Would appreciate any help you might give me.

She scribbled her hotel name and phone number, then handed the note to the woman along with her business card. Without even looking at it, the woman paper-clipped the two together and smiled at Dana. *"Děkuji."*

Dana nodded and turned and walked across the cavernous lobby, down the escalator, and back onto the street, only slightly stunned at what she had just done. She guessed she would not hear back from

Branko, who, it appeared, had done quite well since last they'd met. Why had she bothered to stop, and why had she left her card? Perhaps to say, *See, I've not done so bad myself.*

She arrived at the Kotva department store and found it had taken on a new glow since the late eighties, as if touched by the magic hand of free enterprise. After passing through the lower level, the assault of perfectly coiffed and made-up perfume girls, offering to spray or dab, Dana took the escalator up to the men's department, where she found a black sweatshirt—with a hood, no less. In the electronics department she found a flashlight and CD player. Eager to listen to Pavel Novák's song on Caroline's CD, she grabbed a quick lunch—chicken sandwich to go—at the market on the first level of the store and started back to her hotel. As she walked, Dana wondered if Sister Claire had heard the CD, if her speaking the name Pavel Novák and Laterna Magika, the title of one of his songs, had some connection to the music on the CD.

As she passed the front desk, the clerk, a young man with spiky hair, handed her a note. With a thank-you, she glanced at it. Borelli had insisted they have dinner before going to the church and had called to let her know he'd made a reservation and would pick her up at seven.

As she arrived at her room she wondered if she should dress for dinner. She knew Borelli enjoyed a good meal and guessed it was probably a nice place if it required a reservation. Maybe her jeans and black hoodie wouldn't be appropriate attire. Of course, the priest could wear his black uniform, the same outfit to break into the church. She decided she'd wear her skirt for dinner, then come back to change.

She put the CD in the player and forwarded immediately to the song "Laterna Magika" as she sat on her bed. Pavel's voice sounded so familiar, strong, yet gravelly, taking her instantly back in time. He had a very distinct and easily recognizable voice. She envisioned the young man, handsome with his dark hair, his alluring smile. The music had a strong, thumping beat, not the folk songs of the American protests of the sixties, but a loud, rebellious, sexy rock. Her heart thumped to the beat, the thought of a true revolution in which she'd played a small role. Several other voices joined in on the chorus, lyrics indistinct. Borelli would have to translate the Czech. Was there something hidden in the words?

Dana ejected the CD, placed it on the nightstand, and collapsed on the bed, exhausted. She'd had a big day and, in a sense, it had just begun.

She woke several hours later, confused and rummy the way she always felt when she took a daytime nap. She stood, went to the window, and glanced out. The sky still appeared overcast. She looked at her watch. Already 6:30. She washed her face, put on some makeup, and then slipped on her skirt and blouse, her flats. They still felt damp from getting caught in the storm on Thursday night. She'd not heard from Damek since, though she knew he'd followed her again—to the Internet café.

Before she left, she looked in the safe. Should she take the keys with her now or come back for them? She had to come back to change anyway. She hesitated a moment and then picked up the keys and ran her fingers over the small medal of the Holy Infant. She slid it off the key chain and stuck it in the pocket of her cardigan, and then stuffed the two receipts in her purse, along with the photo of the group of musicians she'd printed out at the Internet café. She placed the keys in the safe.

Borelli was early, waiting in the lobby for her.

"I'd planned on picking you up in a cab," he said, "but then I remembered that damn ditch in the middle of the street. I've got a driver waiting down the street," he added with a touch of ill temper.

"I appreciate your coming by. I could have met you at the restaurant."

He started out, as if he expected her to follow, and she did. They walked around the construction single file, past a road crew now beginning to cover the ditch, and then side by side up the hill.

"Well?" he asked. "You have the keys?"

She pulled the little Infant of Prague medal out of her pocket.

"I hope there is more to it than that," he said with a grunt.

"Yes. Two keys. This was attached. I brought it along now for good luck."

"It's a religious medal, not a rabbit's foot."

"I know that," she said apologetically.

"You plan on coming back to the hotel after dinner?" Borelli asked.

"Yes, of course. I didn't want to wear my church-break-in outfit to dinner." She laughed nervously. He laughed, too, but it soon turned into a cough. He breathed heavily as they walked and she sensed this would be a long walk to the end of the street, to the waiting cab.

She was about to tell him about the CD when he asked, "How's your head?"

"Still on, still functioning," she replied. She knew he was referring to the knot she'd received in her fall. Actually she was doing fine. The black and blue was barely noticeable with the adjusted hairstyle, and tonight she'd added a little makeup.

"The glasses?"

"Perfect," she said with a smile. "Thank you." She still wondered how much he'd paid to have them fixed. He'd waved her off earlier when she said she'd like to pay him back.

"Was Sister Agnes okay?" Dana asked. "The other nuns?"

"It was a funeral, but yes, the nuns' conduct seemed appropriate for a group of women who had lost a good friend. I saw nothing strange, no calls for help. I don't believe you should worry about their safety."

"Good," Dana replied, but she was thinking—now, how could you tell if they were being held hostage or not? It wasn't like they had a lot of freedom before all this transpired. "I just want to talk to her. Being unable to is frustrating, if not frightening."

"Yes," he agreed, though she heard little sympathy in his voice.

"I found a CD at the convent," Dana said. "A recording by several musicians from the revolution. There's a song entitled 'Laterna Magika,' the artist, Novák."

Borelli's eyes nearly popped out of his head as he turned and stared at her. "Do you have it?"

"At the hotel."

"Very good."

"I couldn't understand the Czech lyrics."

"This could be very interesting, possibly some meaning..." He grinned as if quite excited about her discovery. "I'll listen to it. Later." They'd arrived at the cab. He opened the back door and she got in.

"I've put a call in to my acquaintance," he told her as he wedged into the backseat from the opposite side, "but I have not heard from him. If the Infant has been offered on the black market, he might know, or he might be able to point me in the proper direction."

"What did Father Ruffino have to say today?" she asked. "And last night?"

"I thought it best that we wait until we know for sure—"

"That it's missing?" She felt a little jump of anticipation and excitement at the thought of what they had planned for later in the evening.

He nodded.

Everyone seemed to be tiptoeing around Father Ruffino as if he'd been granted a special dispensation. Dana didn't understand this at all. Father Ruffino, she was sure, knew more than he had shared, yet Borelli seemed unable, or unwilling, to accept this possibility. She wasn't sure about Damek. Did Father Ruffino have some hold over him, too?

They arrived at the restaurant and were greeted warmly by the maitre d', who appeared to know Borelli and showed them to the best table in the house, with a lovely view of an outdoor garden, it being too chilly to actually sit outside. She liked this treatment that went along with taking a meal with Borelli. He went over the menu with her, suggesting dishes he'd enjoyed on previous visits. She decided on the tournedos of beef béarnaise and he on roast leg of venison with pears and millet gnocchi. Borelli ordered a bottle of wine.

She told him about going to the Internet café the previous night, then returning to find Investigator Damek just stepping out.

"Well," the priest replied, "I'm certainly glad Investigator Damek has decided to take this seriously."

She pulled the copy of the photo of the four musicians out of her bag, then presented the receipts she'd taken from the convent. When she told Borelli her theory and explained where they'd come from, his expression held a hint of respect and admiration. He seemed impressed that she'd stolen not only the keys, but a pair of receipts as well as a CD.

The sommelier appeared with their wine, Borelli tasted and nodded, then Dana's glass was filled.

"Do you think this is a good idea?" she asked when they were alone again. "Indulging in alcohol when we might be handling a priceless, delicate little religious icon later tonight?"

"You're so convinced it's a fake, it shouldn't matter," he came back with a chuckle. She laughed, too, but she could hear that nervous twitter, which seemed to be lacking in Borelli's. She wondered if he'd done something like this before.

The priest inspected the first receipt. "This is hard to make out," he said. "The handwriting is terrible. But I believe it says . . . sharpen three scissors, fifteen . . . knives. . . . Yes, I believe that's what it says."

"A knife sharpener?"

"It appears to be. Now, this," he said, picking up the second receipt, "same atrocious handwriting, same type of receipt, sequential numbering. It appears this one was for a . . . a garden shears."

"The shears from the church," she said. "This is the person who took the keys. A sharpener—is there a word for that, a name to describe such an occupation?"

"L'arrotino," Borelli said, and then he sang, *"Donne, è arrivato l'arrotino."* He grinned. "A little ditty from my childhood—*l'arrotino* used to drive through the countryside on a bike and sing to let the villagers know he had arrived. It's funny—I haven't thought of that in years." He shook his head. "But I don't know the word in English. Or in Czech."

She pointed at the signature line on the receipt. "This fellow—*l'arrotino* . . ." She liked the sound of the word in Italian. It was almost musical. "He arrived one day at the convent, sharpened scissors, knives, then asked if they had anything else. One of the nuns said, 'Why, yes, the shears that we use at the church. Why don't you come by tomorrow.' So he stole the keys—that first day—made a copy, came back the next day to sharpen the shears, returned the keys."

Borelli sat silently, adding nothing to Dana's theory.

"It wouldn't make sense if it was someone the nuns had called themselves," she continued, "like, say, to fix the toilet or repair a leaky pipe. In such a case the nuns would have initiated the service call, but if it were an itinerant *arrotino*, he would come to them. They hadn't called him or asked him to come. He just dropped by."

"To sharpen scissors, knives, shears, and to steal the key to get into the church?" Borelli snorted dismissively, then took a drink of wine. "There's no identification on this receipt, no address, no phone, only an unreadable signature." His admiration for her thievery seemed to have soured.

She looked down at the receipt. The signature was little more than a scribble.

Other diners had come in and the restaurant was nearly filled, quiet chatter drifting through the room. Their meals were delivered. Borelli's wineglass was refilled. Dana shook her head. One was plenty.

"Even if we could read the signature," Borelli said, "it would most likely be an alias. If your premise is correct. You believe it was this Pavel Novák?"

"Maybe," she replied. "We could show this photo of the musicians to people who live around the convent." She thought of the school-children, the old men who hung out around the square.

"Do you believe Novák looks the same after twenty years?" Borelli worked away at the leg of venison with knife and fork. Dana returned photo and receipts to her purse. The priest sat quietly for a moment, then ran his hand over his bald spot and she could tell he was at least mulling this over. "It seems we have a very busy evening ahead of us," he said.

After dinner they engaged in a small disagreement over who would pay the bill—the bullheaded Borelli insisted, and Dana finally caved in. He seemed to enjoy picking up the tab. A means of control?

she wondered. They took a cab back toward the hotel, again walking the last block under overhead clouds threatening rain. She went up to her room to change and get the keys. They'd decided to listen to the CD later, after going to the church.

When she stepped into the room, she glanced toward the closet and noticed the door slightly ajar, though she thought she'd closed it when she'd checked the safe. She hurried over to look inside.

· 22 ·

The safe was unlocked, though the keys were still there. Had she been so careless she hadn't even bothered to lock it? Taking in a deep breath, Dana exhaled slowly to calm herself, knowing she had to maintain control, to be more alert to what was going on around her.

She slipped out of her skirt and blouse, pulled on her jeans and T-shirt, worked her new hoodie over her head. Sliding into her sneakers, she put the keys in her jeans pocket, her recently acquired flashlight in the roomy front pocket of her sweatshirt, and returned to the lobby to find Borelli asleep in a large leather chair.

"Father Borelli," she whispered, giving his shoulder a little nudge.

His eyes popped open. He glanced around, seemingly confused.

"Time to go," she said after a moment.

The leather squeaked as he braced himself and rose from the chair. He straightened the crease in his pant leg and started out the front door. Dana followed. His breathing was labored by the time they'd progressed a half block down the street, past the crew, just finishing up covering the ditch. She suggested they slow down, though if they didn't hurry they might get caught in a rainstorm, clouds hovering heavy above. Fearing he might collapse on the street, she considered stopping to search for a cab, but decided it would be unwise to have someone witness their being dropped off at, or near, the church. They walked down Nerudova Street, turned right at the Malostranské náměstí, and then on to Karmelitská. Dana's heart beat wildly, and then seemed to flutter like a trapped moth inside her chest, finally escaping and settling in her throat. When she turned to Borelli and asked, "Are we really going to do this?" it came out as a froggy croak.

He smiled and nodded. Now he seemed almost energized.

A streak of lightning illuminated the sky, followed by a clap of thunder. Dana, who had never believed in signs or messages, wondered if they were being warned. She and Borelli exchanged glances, his eyes flashing in the dark. She knew what he was thinking: *No turning back*. She nodded as a second clap of thunder sounded.

The church stood like a dark shadow, reaching up, appearing much larger and foreboding than it had during the day. As they approached the side door, Dana took the keys from her pocket and inserted the larger into the keyhole. A perfect fit. She glanced back at Borelli with a grin, then turned the key and pushed the door, and they walked inside, locking the door behind them.

The overpowering, pungent scent of the almost-week-old Easter lilies filled the air, and Dana wondered if the altar flowers had gone without the nuns' careful tending since Sister Claire's death. They smelled as if they had begun to rot.

Quietly they moved through the church and on toward the sacristy, Dana with flashlight in hand. Borelli had assured her there was a ladder in the closet, and behind a broom, dustpan, and vacuum cleaner, they found it. He flicked off the altar alarm. Earlier they'd talked about security and he'd told her the surveillance cameras were nonfunctional. He lifted the far end of the ladder, Dana hoisted the other, and they proceeded back through the church. Gripping the increasingly heavy ladder, they crept past the altar of St. Joseph and on to the Infant's altar, Dana shining the flashlight ahead, a small path of light leading them. Thinking of the small Infant of Prague medal in her pocket, she whispered, *Protect us tonight,* so softly it was more a thought, though she felt her lips tremble as she formed the words. Another clap of thunder sounded.

In the glow of the flashlight, Father Borelli unfolded the ladder and secured it, performing these tasks with surprising precision and quiet. Together they positioned it to the left of the altar. Then the priest turned to Dana with a grand inviting gesture.

"*I'm* going up?" she whispered. Oddly, they hadn't talked about this—who would climb the ladder to examine the statue. Yet, even in the dim church, she could make out an eye roll, and she realized Borelli had no intention of making the ascent. It had started to rain. Dana heard the low hum of a car, muted by the pelting rain.

She handed him the flashlight and stepped on the first rung, aware that her entire body, every limb, every bone, was shaking. Rain slapped with vigor against the church windows. Inside, everything but her body was still. She took a second, then a third, then a fourth step, slowly, cautiously, until she was level with the top of the altar, the base of the large ornate box containing the little statue. Pots of lilies covered the altar, surrounding the base of the altar box. She would have to reach the statue from the ladder unless they removed some of the pots. The overripe scent filled her nostrils.

Suddenly she sneezed.

"God bless you," Borelli called up with irritation.

"We should move some of these lilies," she called down, though she wasn't sure he could hear, as rain continued to assault the window.

"You're fine," he reassured her.

From the top of the marble altar, Dana reasoned, it would be much easier and safer to reach the glass box and statue. If she could just stand on the hard stone, it would provide better support than the ladder. "We should remove the lilies," she said again. Louder.

"No. You're fine."

Easy for him to say, she thought, rubbing her nose, attempting to hold back another sneeze. She shivered as rain drummed against the window.

Borelli shone the flashlight up on the altar box, centered on the Infant's face, though it quivered and Dana felt her heart jump, overcome with an eerie sensation that it was the little Infant who had moved, not the beam. As if he were alive. So much for that bottle of wine, she thought. She'd had but one glass, Borelli finishing off the rest. He seemed to hold his alcohol well, but he probably wouldn't have been her number one choice to help with this particular task, had she actually had a choice. A brief image of Damek flashed through her mind.

"Well?" she heard loud and clear from Borelli below, the single word conveying his impatience. The rain had stilled to a quiet pitter-patter, and she heard another motor out on the street, then fading into the distance.

"I can't make out where the lock is," she said. She breathed heavily through her mouth, not wanting to take in any more of the rancid scent, as she examined the box, realizing it was much larger than it appeared from below. With its ornate golden curls and scrolls, the interior stand with angels and rays of golden light, it stood at least five feet tall. It wouldn't be easy reaching the statue, and she envisioned herself stretching, losing her balance, tumbling forward, bringing down the entire box, it crashing on the floor, spilling out the Infant, his jeweled crown tumbling off his head, the tiny globe—the world—rolling about before the altar. Logic told her the box was well anchored to the altar, but she was shaking with nerves.

Borelli moved the flashlight along the outline of the glass case. "Try the back."

"There's no way I can reach the back," she cried. She wondered how the nuns did this. Maybe removing the statue required more than climbing up a ladder. Then boldly, without a word, she pushed one lily, then another, along the smooth marble, bunching them tighter together, providing just enough room to set one foot, and then the other, firmly on the altar. She didn't bother to look down for Borelli's approval, and he said nothing.

Slowly, starting from up as far as she could reach, she ran her hand along the side of the box. There it was, halfway down, an indentation, a hole. A keyhole! She reached into her pocket and pulled out the key chain and, as she did, she felt something slip from her grasp and drop to the floor with a tinny clink that echoed through the empty church. Damn, she'd forgotten to fasten the small Infant of Prague medal back on the key chain with the larger Virgin medal.

"What was that?" Borelli asked.

"I dropped the Infant medal."

He turned the flashlight toward the floor, moving it slowly from side to side.

"We'll get it later," she said resolutely. The smell was making her dizzy; she needed to get down. But not until she finished.

"Okay," he replied reluctantly as he shone the light back glaringly on her face. For a moment she closed her eyes, and then, taking a deep breath, grasping the edge of the altar box, she fit the key into the small keyhole and turned. She slipped her finger into the joint where the corners of the box met and carefully pulled it open. "It's unlocked!"

"Just touch it," Borelli advised her. "Touch the face. We should be able to tell if it's wax and then we won't have to take it out of the box."

Dana drew in another deep breath, exhaled, and then with her index finger she reached out. For a second she imagined the Infant moving, striking her, knocking her off her ladder. She steadied herself, extending her finger to within inches of the statue. But she couldn't, she just couldn't do it. What if this *was* real? She felt so nervous, so hot, she envisioned her touch melting wax. Her hand felt moist and sticky. She'd leave a fingerprint right there on the child's face. Why hadn't she thought to buy a pair of gloves?

"What if it's real?" she asked.

"What?" Borelli replied incredulously. "Does it *look* real?" He was attempting to center the light beam directly on the statue's face, but to Dana it seemed to vibrate.

"I don't know," she said, her voice as shaky as her legs, as Borelli's grip on the flashlight.

"Well, then, for heaven's sake," he bellowed, "take it out."

"Just give me a minute here," she snapped. The rain had started up again.

"Reach in with both hands and lift it out, then hand it down here to me."

A dreadful thought coursed through her. This was the real Infant of Prague and she, an accomplice, was helping Borelli steal it. *No, no, no,* she told herself. That didn't make any sense whatsoever. It had been *her* idea to break into the church and examine the statue. Her breathing was labored, her heart beating too rapidly. She stood for a long moment and then she reached in, placed her hands lovingly around the Infant as if he were a real child. The garment felt soft, rather than stiff as she had imagined it. She lifted him out, held him to her breast, one hand cupping his head and crown, the other on his lower back. Slowly she inched, one step on the altar, one more. Onto the ladder, leaning in, trembling, rung by rung by rung, she descended.

Borelli stood waiting. "Good girl," he said, reaching out. Dana clutched the little figure, unable to let go. She was shaking and feared if she released her tight grip she might drop it.

"Let's take it into the sacristy," she said. "We can turn on the light in the closet."

Borelli did not object and they quietly retraced their steps in the dark. She heard something—or did she just imagine it?—a crack or creak. She glanced at the priest. He'd heard it, too.

"Old building," he said calmly.

Just settling, she decided as they continued toward the sacristy, Dana holding the child carefully, cradling the head and golden bejeweled crown, which she didn't believe was secured to the head. The Infant was larger than she had realized. Forty-seven centimeters, she remembered, but in her mind she hadn't really been able to picture what that meant. Now it felt about the size of a newborn baby, though rigid, without any flexibility or softness to the body.

They walked slowly, cautiously, without words, Dana taking the smallest of steps, Borelli surprising her without protest or impatience. Another vehicle passed by slowly on the street—she could hear it splashing through puddles—but again she reassured herself that no one could see them in the dark interior.

Once in the sacristy she carried the Infant to the closet. Borelli switched on the light. Having been roaming about in the darkness, she found the light overwhelming, much too bright. She let her eyes adjust and then released her embrace of the little Infant and held him out in front of her. He had the same sweet face of the real little King she'd studied over and over again in the books and pamphlets. The small, doll-like mouth, the soft blond curls, the arched eyebrows as if he had been suddenly surprised. *Don't be afraid,* she wanted to say. *We won't harm you.* The crown tilted slightly on his head, but she had prevented it from falling off. For several moments, neither of them spoke. Dana wondered if Borelli were praying. Surely as a priest he had some respect for what this little statue represented. Christ, the child. Christ, the king. God, made man.

God, help us, she thought.

Suddenly, startling Dana with his abrupt gesture, Borelli reached out and touched the Infant's face. He gave it a little knock on the forehead, at the same time supporting the crown with his free hand. It had a hollow, porcelain sound. This was not a wooden statue covered with a protective layer of wax.

"You're right," he said. "It's a fake."

Again they were both silent, Dana wondering where the authentic Infant was at that very moment. *I hope they are treating you kindly,* she thought, and then she said, "Now what?" They were ready to move on to the next step, though she wasn't sure what that next step was.

"First of all, we replace it on the altar."

"Yes," she agreed. Again she wrapped it in her arms and they proceeded together as if in a religious procession to the altar of the Infant of Prague. Dana climbed back up the ladder as Borelli held it for her. She placed the porcelain child lovingly in the glass case, adjusted the crown, relocked the door, slid the keys in her jeans pocket, and rearranged the potted lilies.

"We'd better find that Infant medal," she told Borelli as she climbed down. She dropped to her hands and knees, feeling in the dark for the small medal. Borelli stood above her, moving the light along the parquet floor. In this position, Dana could not help but think of the old nun, lying in this very spot just a week ago. And she could not help but envision the photo in Damek's file. Suddenly a thought came to her. "I want to take a closer look at the ladder." She glanced up at Borelli.

"Okay," he said, puzzled. "There, right there!" he added. His flashlight shone on the little medal now visible near the base of the altar.

"Oh, thank God," Dana said with a brief thought of the irony in her words. She picked it up and secured it back on the key chain.

Borelli was already folding the ladder. Dana wondered what time it was. It had been almost eleven when they left the hotel for the church.

Dana led the way with a path of light, lifting the front end of the ladder, Borelli following with the back. They proceeded slowly, and she could tell he was very tired. As was she.

When they arrived at the sacristy, she opened the closet. Again they turned on the light. She asked Borelli to tilt the ladder so she could see the bottom. She got down on the floor, examining it carefully with the added light of the flashlight.

"What are you looking for?" Borelli asked.

"This," Dana replied, pointing. She glanced up at the priest, who hovered over her. A questioning look flashed in his eyes and across his brow.

"What is it?" he asked.

"Dried blood."

"Sister Claire's?"

She nodded and stood.

They replaced the ladder and she motioned him to follow as she flipped the closet light off. They started out of the sacristy, into the church and toward the side exit.

"What does this mean?" Father Borelli asked.

"If Sister Claire heard something—voices—I'm guessing there were two or more involved in the theft. Possibly they didn't even need a ladder. One might have hoisted the other up on his shoulders."

"Now, why didn't we think of that?" Borelli said dryly.

"The ladder wasn't there when the police arrived—at least, not in the photos. But it was moved after Sister Claire fell. I see several scenarios. If the thief, or thieves, killed the nun, which Damek claims didn't happen, would they have taken the time to remove the ladder, leaving the not-yet-dead nun bleeding on the floor? If she interrupted them, they most likely fled, leaving the ladder. Maybe they never even knew she was in the church."

"But if her words have meaning, she heard something."

"Exactly. But any way you look at it, it's likely someone else removed the ladder other than the thieves."

"You think it was Father Ruffino?"

"I'm thinking, not saying."

"I'm sure he would not have taken the statue. You believe he placed the fake in the altar box after the thieves took it? But why? Why would he cover for the thieves? It makes no sense that he would call for my help and then withhold such important information."

"I'm not sure," Dana said as she opened the door. They both stepped out, the air damp, though the rain had stopped completely. She took the keys from her pocket and relocked the door. As she turned back to Borelli, a dark figure stepped into their path.

"Good evening," he said. "I ask that you both come with me."

· 23 ·

Investigator Damek grabbed Dana by one arm, Borelli by the other, and escorted them down the street to a parked car. He had followed them, Dana was sure, but had known to park away from the church so they wouldn't hear the motor or notice as it came to an abrupt halt nearby.

The car was an older model, with a dent in the left fender, not an official car, not one of the silver, blue, and yellow she'd seen moving about the city. As an investigator, Damek wouldn't be driving a marked car anyway, Dana realized, but she didn't think he was on the clock now. There was something very personal in the way he was going about this investigation, in the way he gripped her arm. And he was alone. Detectives generally worked in pairs.

When he opened the back door and motioned them to get in, Dana said, "Where are you taking us?" Neither she nor Borelli had protested as they walked, both perhaps too stunned, but now neither of them budged, feet planted firmly on the sidewalk. "You have no right to take us anywhere," she said.

The generally loquacious Borelli said nothing, but he shot her a look that told her to shut up. They all stood outside the car for a moment before the priest closed the door with a slow, careful motion, letting the Czech investigator know they weren't getting in.

"Perhaps we could go somewhere, sit, and talk," Borelli said in a surprisingly congenial voice as he glanced down the street. "It seems we all have similar goals, and we are all attempting—independently, unfortunately—to solve the same puzzle." Now he shot Damek a look that seemed to say, *Let's all be reasonable here.* "As Ms. Pierson said, I don't believe you have valid legal reason to transport us anywhere."

Damek responded in Czech. Dana shivered. It was well after midnight now, and the spring evening air carried a sharp, damp chill.

"Breaking and entering?" Borelli replied in English, shaking his head dismissively.

Dana wrapped her arms around her quaking body. Even in her fleece hoodie she was freezing.

"We have a key to the church," Borelli said calmly. He motioned for Dana to show the inspector, which she did, pulling the keys from her jeans and dangling them in the air like a wind chime. Her hand trembled and she hoped the investigator took this as her being cold, not nervous or frightened, though she realized she was all three. She was a foreigner, a tourist, and she'd just entered a church in the middle of the night with keys she'd stolen from a convent. A church where a valuable religious icon had recently been stolen. She might have reason to be frightened. She studied Borelli, suddenly angry. They shouldn't even be here. He should have confronted his friend, insisted that Father Ruffino take him to the church to examine the Infant, to explain why he did not reveal the icon had been stolen and confess his part in the theft.

"Why are you in the church at this hour?" Damek demanded. "What do you look for?"

"Same as you—Pavel Novák," Borelli said, which shocked Dana, though she knew this was one of the two facts they were all working from—all three of them were searching for Pavel Novák.

"You are out of luck, as the Americans say," Damek shot back, glancing at Dana. "This man, he disappeared years ago, and I do not believe he would seek refuge in a church at this hour."

No one said anything, until finally Dana asked, "Disappeared? Is he dead?"

"Something was taken from the church?" Damek asked.

Her gaze shot from the investigator to Borelli. "Could we go somewhere warm?" she asked, burying her hands deeper in the fleece pocket of her hoodie.

Damek motioned down the street.

Within minutes, they were sitting in a café, hot cups of coffee before them. "I will not take you to headquarters," Damek said, "if you agree to surrender your passports."

"You can't . . ." Dana started in, then stopped herself. She suspected he could.

Damek's subtle smile let her know he was aware he had control. "Your choice. We have a jail cell where you can wait." His voice carried a heavy weariness, and his accent seemed more pronounced. *Ver* you can *vait.*

Dana wondered if this was nothing more than a scare tactic to get them to reveal what they knew, which she guessed wasn't much more than the investigator knew.

Borelli had been surprisingly quiet on the walk from church to coffee shop. No words had been exchanged between the two men, and Dana, too, had held her tongue, attempting to determine if Damek was serious, if he had any legal reason to confiscate their passports. Borelli was a priest, and for all the investigator knew, they *might* have obtained the keys legally.

"My passport is back at the hotel in the safe," Father Borelli said.

"Mine, too," Dana said. She usually carried it in her handbag, but she'd brought nothing but flashlight and keys along tonight.

"I will escort you," Damek said.

Borelli nodded, but Dana could see he was in no hurry to leave. He called to the server, a bored-looking young man who gave the impression he had better things to do. The priest spoke to him with his usual animation and enthusiasm as he placed his order. The waiter glanced from Dana to Damek, but they both shook their heads.

"It seems you've taken a special interest in this case," Borelli told Damek as the young man left. "We all know there is more to this than what Father Ruffino is sharing. Something happened in the church the morning Sister Claire died. Something which possibly frightened Father Ruffino. Frightened him to the point that he is withholding important information. You have a prior relationship with the priest?" he asked Damek. "A personal connection?" His voice had shifted and a roughness scratched about his tone, as if he were attempting to turn things around, trying to scare or threaten the police investigator.

Damek didn't answer. He looked down at the table, eluding both Dana's and Borelli's stares. When he looked up, his entire face had shifted; his features, his eyes, the line of his mouth had somehow become softer, almost vulnerable.

"Please, tell us about it," Borelli said. His voice, which could morph from harsh to kind in the blink of an eye, had taken on the timbre of a father confessor, a kind, helpful priest, perpetually ready to extend a hand of forgiveness.

No one said a word. Dana and Borelli sat quietly, waiting. Damek lifted his head, straightened his shoulders, but Dana could see he was not about to reveal anything, that in fact he was attempting to regain his composure. *What is going on?* she wondered, glancing from the investigator to the priest, then back again, waiting for someone to say something.

The waiter delivered a chocolate torte for Borelli and refilled coffees around the table. Dana guessed they were all here until the priest finished eating. Then, it seemed, they were going back to their respective hotels to give up their passports. She wasn't sure what was happening after that. But she knew one thing for sure. Someone had stolen the Infant of Prague.

They sat, Borelli enjoying his midnight snack, Dana's stomach twisting with nerves as her hands slid up and down her coffee cup in an attempt to warm herself, Damek studying the two of them while giving up nothing in response to Borelli's question about his connection to Father Ruffino.

"We all know," Borelli finally said slowly, as if he had thought this through, "that the Infant was stolen from the church that morning." His willingness to share this shocked Dana, and Damek seemed simultaneously surprised and calm. She didn't think he knew about the theft, though he was obviously attempting to give them the impression he did.

"Pavel Novák is involved?" the investigator asked coolly.

"According to what Father Ruffino said," the priest continued, lifting a piece of chocolate cake to his lips, chewing slowly, deliberately, then touching his napkin to his lips. "According to what Sister Claire told him before she died."

Again, Damek remained unruffled, but he paused for a moment as if adding this revelation—if that was what it was—to what he already knew. "The old nun spoke to Father Ruffino before she died?" Dana was certain now that the prior of Our Lady Victorious had not shared this with the Czech police investigator. "Pavel Novák?" Damek asked. "Laterna Magika?"

Borelli nodded, and Dana thought of Pavel Novák's CD, the receipts she'd found at the convent, her belief that someone had stolen a church key from the nuns. Now Damek claimed Pavel had disappeared years ago. Caroline had said he left Prague, and this had been confirmed by the cousin to whom Borelli had spoken, but this was quite different from claiming he had *disappeared*. She took a swallow of coffee, then another.

"Perhaps if we worked together," Borelli offered, "we might obtain better results." He stared directly at the investigator, who said nothing.

"You followed me to the Internet café last night?" Dana asked Damek, though she knew he had. *And you were in my hotel room tonight,* she realized. He'd opened the safe, but she'd come in before he could remove anything. Had he been hiding in her bathroom? Behind the drapes? Had he watched as she slipped off her skirt and blouse, pulled on her jeans, T-shirt, and hoodie, stuck the flashlight in her pocket?

He didn't deny it. Finally he asked, "What did you discover on the CD?"

She was sure he knew Pavel Novák was a musician, maybe from her Internet café research, or maybe he'd figured this out on his own—he was a police officer with access to information unavailable to her or Borelli. She guessed he'd seen Caroline's CD on her nightstand and wondered if it was still there.

The priest's scraping the frosting off the plate with his fork made an irritating grating sound. The man could simultaneously be refined and so terribly uncouth. "There was a woman connected with this Novák," he said.

Dana felt a tight compression in her chest. *No,* she wanted to scream, *don't bring Caroline into this.* But before she could get the words out, Borelli said, "She was a performer, a dancer, perhaps an actress." Dana felt the knot of tension relax. The priest was talking about Lenka. "If we can locate this woman, this Lenka," he explained, "with whom Novák had a child many years ago, she might lead us to Novák, to the missing Infant of Prague."

"You believe she is still in the city?" Damek asked, looking directly at Dana.

"I don't know," she replied.

"An actress?"

"A performer. Possibly a dancer," Dana said. "I'm not sure."

She could see Damek was thinking this over, and then, something in his eyes, in the shift of his body, changed, as if he'd just had a revealing thought pass through his mind. Yet he shared nothing.

Borelli wiped his mouth with his napkin, refolded it neatly into a triangle, placed it on the table, and shoved the empty plate aside. He leaned back, scratched his balding head thoughtfully, and said, "I'm visiting with Father Ruffino tomorrow after Mass. It is my intention to confront him with what we have discovered. I think it best that we get it out on the table, try to determine why information is being withheld, attempt to bring some calm and reason to this." He picked up the bill, set money on the table. "If you will please escort me back to my hotel," he said, rising, brushing crumbs off his slacks, "I will relinquish my passport."

They walked back to Damek's car, Dana hoping, since they all seemed to be getting along so well now, that he might reconsider confiscating their passports.

The priest and Dana sat in the backseat. Borelli gave the police investigator directions, though it seemed he was turning the steering wheel before any instructions were given. He knew where the priest was staying. When they arrived at the hotel Borelli went inside while they waited.

"You were in my hotel room tonight," she said to Damek.

He stared out to the street in front of them but said nothing for some time. "I believe, as Father Borelli does, that we should work together." He turned and looked directly at her. "You must trust me."

She remembered he'd told her something similar when he followed her home from the theater.

Father Borelli returned to the car. Damek rolled down the window and Borelli handed him the passport. "I'd like to accompany you to Ms. Pierson's hotel," the priest said.

"You have had a long night, Father," Damek replied kindly. "I promise to return Ms. Pierson safely to her hotel."

Borelli looked at Dana. She attempted to roll down the window, but Damek had evidently set the lock.

"I will return her safely," the investigator repeated. "But if you wish to accompany us, you may."

Surely she would be okay, Dana thought. If anything happened, Borelli knew she was with the police investigator. He'd hardly leave a witness if he intended to harm her.

Damek reached for the glove box and pulled something out, so small it fit in the knot of his fist. He handed it to Borelli. "Keep this until tomorrow. I will contact you."

Borelli looked into his hand and nodded, though Dana could not see what he held.

"Are you comfortable with this?" the priest asked Dana, his hand gripping the edge of the open driver's-side window.

"I'll see you tomorrow," she said, leaning forward. "After you speak with Father Ruffino."

He hesitated for a moment, considering, and then said, "Tomorrow." Standing back from the car he watched as they pulled out and headed to Dana's hotel.

Strangely, the nervousness she'd felt since she rose early that morning, which had escalated through the day in her search of the convent, the church break-in, and then Damek's unexpected arrival on the scene, had all but disappeared. She felt oddly calm as they drove on in silence. In her exhaustion, she wondered if she was too drained to be afraid. And maybe there was no reason to think that Damek was anything other than what Borelli had evidently determined he was—a good cop doing his job.

"What did you give him?" she asked.

"A religious medal."

"Oh," she said. "You're a religious person? You offered this to Borelli as a symbol of your spiritual bond?" She wasn't quite tired enough to lose the sarcasm.

"*Father* Borelli," the detective corrected her.

"Yes, *Father* Borelli, of course." She slumped back into the seat, let out a deep breath. "A miraculous medal? A good-luck charm?" She laughed, recalling her earlier conversation with Borelli. "Do you believe in miracles?"

"Yes," he replied without hesitation. She hadn't expected him to say that. Before she could reply, he added, "The ditch has been covered."

She glanced out the window. "Just this evening." They'd evidently finished it while she and Borelli prowled through the church, hopefully before the downpour. She was grateful for that as she wasn't up to walking down the street to the hotel, then back with her passport. She wondered if Damek would have insisted on going with her. He'd trusted the priest, but she wasn't sure he'd trust her.

Suddenly, and abruptly, he yanked the steering wheel and they were doing a U-turn right in front of the hotel.

"What the hell?" she shouted, bracing herself against the car door.

· 24 ·

"I have an idea," Investigator Damek said calmly, "and I need your help."

"What's going on?" Dana asked, her voice high-pitched, her mind reeling with confusion.

He didn't reply. They had arrived at the Malostranské náměsti and were headed toward the river. A lopsided Cheshire grin of a moon winked behind parting clouds.

"My help?" she asked, trying to calm her voice, attempting to stand up to Damek's composure. "Where are we going?"

"Three years ago." He gave the wheel another turn and she guessed they were headed south. "A murder in the theater district. An actress."

"This relates to what happened at Our Lady Victorious?"

He was slowing down now, but he didn't answer.

"Or something to do with this Lenka?" Dana asked. "She wasn't the victim?"

"No."

Dana glanced at her watch. "It's almost one A.M."

"Then they will just be starting."

"Who?"

They turned left, then a sharp veer to the right, passing a slow-moving car, a cab, vehicles parked bumper to bumper. Preoccupied now, it seemed, with finding a parking space, Damek slowed, glancing from side to side. Several people stood, conversing, others entering, some exiting buildings in what looked to be a mixed residential and business area. A group of young men huddled close, shadowed under the eaves of a building. Damek pulled into a space that Dana guessed might not qualify as legal, wedging between a motorcycle and compact minicar. He hopped out, unlocked the back door, opened it, and motioned her onto the street. They walked.

He had a long stride, and she stepped quickly to keep up, hands in the pocket of her hoodie, fingering her flashlight. They passed a couple looped arm-in-arm, walking slowly, another fellow in ratty jeans and a stocking cap, dragging nervously on a cigarette, calling to another young man across the street.

Through a narrow alleylike passageway, past a mismatched duo of bikes—one sleek and flashy, the other with wire basket and makeshift plywood box strapped on the fender, both chained onto a small rack—they arrived at a green lacquered door set into a brick building. Damek held the door and gestured for her to enter.

Lively chatter collided with jazz drifting out from an old-fashioned jukebox in the front of the room. The place smelled of greasy bar food and smoke. Photos and cartoons hung on the walls, like in restaurants back home where the proprietor wished to claim a distinguished, or perhaps just interesting, clientele. Dana guessed that performers hung out here after the theater closed.

At the table nearest the bar, three men and a woman sat engaged in conversation. The woman had long, dark hair, a tight tank top, a tattoo of a snake wrapped around her upper arm. She moved her ornamented limb in a strange, undulating way as if attempting to make the snake slither. One of the men reached out to feel the muscle on her firm and well-defined arm. The man sported spiky, unnaturally blond hair and wore a patterned paisley shirt. The other two seemed rather common, other than the fact that one was wearing a coonskin hat. The guy in the fancy shirt grabbed the hat off the man's head and passed it around the table to the other, who stood, took an exaggerated bow, then swung it around by the tail.

Damek stepped up to the bar. "You want something?" he asked her.

"Water," she replied, realizing how dry her throat was.

His eyes darted quickly around the room, and then, without even looking at Dana, he pulled a stool away from the bar and offered it to her. Holding up two fingers, he said something to the bartender.

"Which is Novák?" he asked Dana as he pulled a wrinkled paper from his jacket pocket.

She pointed to the young Pavel in the photo.

Toward the back of the room, two men and a woman shared a table with some kind of furry creature. It was difficult to make out, the room dim and smoky, but then Dana realized, from the long, thin appendages and agile movement, it was a monkey, outfitted in a diaper, red vest, and hat. Climbing up on the table, it draped itself around the neck of one of the men.

The bartender slid two bottles of water onto the counter along with two glasses set on cardboard pilsner coasters. Damek and the man spoke for several moments, the investigator showing him the photo, the man shaking his head. When the bartender left to help another customer at the end of the counter, Damek took a swig directly from the bottle. Dana poured her water into the glass.

Again Damek studied the crowd as if searching for someone he knew. Dana wondered if any of these people had been here in '89, during the late-autumn months of the revolution. The dissenters had been mostly young people, students, and theater people, actors, musicians, playwrights, people like those she saw all around her now, though she didn't recall this same freedom in dress and style back then. Almost twenty years ago—she probably wouldn't recognize anyone from that long ago. She spotted several people near her age, some even older—a fellow with a neatly trimmed silver goatee and frameless glasses, who looked like a college professor or poet. She wondered if any of them knew Lenka or Pavel. She understood this was why Damek had brought her along, though she wasn't sure she'd recognize an older Pavel, and she'd never met Lenka.

She noticed three men sitting at a table against the wall, the back of the bald head of the tallest reflecting a collage of light from one of the half dozen Tiffany-like lamps hanging about the room. Though slick as an egg on top, he sported a tuft of pale hair standing out above each ear in a comical fashion like a circus clown. As his head bobbed from side to side, these fluffy protrusions took on a kaleidoscope of spotted color, as did the smooth surface of his head. The man held a child slumped in his lap, dressed all in red, wearing a floppy hat. *At this hour in a bar?* Dana immediately thought, but realized within seconds that it wasn't a child but a marionette. The man jumped up and, maneuvering the attached strings, lifted the puppet in a well-orchestrated dance, limbs and large eyes coming to life, the lids fluttering with animation. The puppet wore a jester's costume: red velvet with a wide white ruffled collar, bells adorning the tunic, slippers curled like those of an elf. The mouth was set in a grin, opening and closing as if the marionette could speak. A cigarette dangled from the left side of the man's mouth. A large duffel bag sat on the floor near his chair and Dana wondered if his small friend would be stuffed inside at night's end. As she exchanged a quick glance with Damek, Dana could almost detect a smile, and then something in his eyes as if he were about to say, *See how we entertain our visitors in Prague? A performance on every corner.*

In a voice that sounded part command and part concern for her safety, Damek said, "Stay here." She watched as he worked his way around the room, stopping and speaking to the patrons, passing the picture around and then, after negative head shakes, moving on. He walked over to a table where two women sat, both about twenty, bleached blondes with too much makeup. They could have been twins, and Dana imagined them in a chorus line where every girl looked the same as the next. Damek returned to the bar. He said nothing, and she guessed he hadn't learned anything. He stood, taking another drink of water, still scoping out the room.

Finally Dana asked, "Was there a ladder in the church at the Infant's altar, when you were called that morning? It *was* Father Ruffino who called?" She spoke loudly over the music.

"Yes, it was Father Ruffino."

A woman with obviously dyed red hair, cropped short like a man's, a low-scooped turquoise velvet top, dangly gold earrings, and a long chain with a glass medallion settled just above her ample breasts approached from behind and threw her arms around Damek. Her fingernails were long, lacquered with polish the color of wet maraschino cherries. She said something to him in a slurred voice, then eyed Dana suspiciously and continued speaking to Damek in an intimate voice, very close to his ear. The investigator nodded agreeably, smiling as if they were exchanging bar stories.

He turned to Dana. "Lenka Horáčková?"

"Might be," she replied. "Ask her how old this Lenka Horáčková is."

The woman had repositioned herself and was leaning into Damek now, her large breasts pushed up against him. Dana couldn't tell if Damek was enjoying this or not. She'd have to give him credit for maintaining a professional demeanor. The woman said something as Damek raised his shoulders, took a step back. A weird techno rock now blasted from the jukebox.

Leaning in close, cupping his mouth with his hand, Damek said to Dana, "She tells me Lenka has a grown son, about twenty."

"That would be just about right for Pavel Novák's son," she said, more to herself than Damek, who she wasn't quite sure heard her anyway, as he was again speaking to the redhead. The woman held a beer glass, though it was near empty. She turned it upside down as if to test if there was any left. A dribble spilled on Damek, who didn't seem fazed, who spoke to the woman in a friendly, reassuring way, as if he were comfortable here in the bar with this odd assortment of people.

"Ask her if the woman is married," Dana said. "Ask her about Pavel Novák."

The woman, now resting her breasts on the ledge of the bar, flirted with the bartender. Unlike Damek, who had looked at the woman's face when he spoke to her, the bartender seemed to be focusing on the large orbs.

The bartender presented the redhead with another beer. She turned to Damek and smiled, then planted a little kiss on his forehead, leaving a red smear. Damek said something. The woman spilled another little dribble from the top of her full beer glass and then wiped it off Damek's lapel. Making a little smacking sound with her lips, as if offering another kiss, she turned and teetered slowly toward a table in the far corner of the bar.

Damek glanced at Dana and said, "She does not know Novák, but she said the young man, Lenka's son, he is a musician."

"Did she give you a name?" Dana motioned with her hand, touching her own forehead where the redhead had left a smack mark on

Damek's. "You've got a little smudge," she said, feeling almost embarrassed for the investigator.

"He goes by his mother's name," Damek said as he pulled a cloth
handkerchief from his pocket and wiped his forehead. "It is Václav
Horáček."

"I thought her name was Horáčková," Dana said. She nodded,
telling him he'd got the smudge. Damek replaced the handkerchief
in his pocket.

"We do it differently here."

"What do you mean?"

"Names," he said.

"Oh, right." She remembered now, the endings of Czech family
names were different for male and female. Even if Pavel and Lenka
had married, her name would not have been Novák. "His name's
Václav, after the famous playwright dissenter?" she asked. "The first
president of the Czech Republic?"

"Possibly. Again, a common name."

"Someone involved in the revolution might have chosen this
name in his honor."

Damek slid some bills onto the bar and motioned a thank-you to
the bartender, who had moved down to the far side of the counter.
The man saluted with one hand as he served something in a whiskey
glass to a fellow wearing a cowboy hat and a bolo tie.

Just as they were about to step out, the redheaded woman
approached, took Dal's arm, and slurred something into his ear.

They were out on the street before Damek explained. "The
woman told me her friend knows of this Lenka who once performed
at the Divadlo Archa. He believes she no longer . . . how to say . . . no
longer engaged in a profession."

"Unemployed?"

He shook his head. "Retired," he said after a moment.

Young retirement, Dana thought.

"Now I have the name," Damek said, "perhaps I will be able to gather information."

"Like an address?"

"It is possible." They walked without words as Dana considered if she should press on the issue of the ladder, when he said, "Why did you ask about the ladder?"

She told him what she and Borelli had discovered and shared her thought that Father Ruffino had moved the ladder after Sister Claire's death. He didn't respond, just listened as they approached the car.

"I find this most difficult to believe," he finally said. He shook his head.

She could tell he was considering this as he opened the passenger side for her. She guessed she was riding shotgun, not the backseat where he might put a prisoner.

"Father Ruffino is a kind, spiritual man," Damek said as he started the car. "The kindest, the most godly man I have known."

Borelli was right, Dana thought. This was personal. Investigator Damek had a very personal connection to Father Ruffino. Had this in some way compromised his investigation? Like Borelli, Dana thought; these two men believed anything and everything the priest told them, causing them to overlook what was so obvious to Dana: Father Ruffino was involved. She pictured Caroline, her fearful glances up toward the priest on the altar. Then she thought of how kindly the priest had spoken to Dana herself as she sat waiting.

"You were acquainted with Sister Claire?" Damek asked.

"No, I didn't . . ." Dana hesitated, questioning whether she should tell him about what she'd discovered at the convent, her thoughts about how someone else might have gained access to the church and Infant's altar box by taking the convent's keys. "No. I didn't know Sister Claire. Did you?"

"But, you *were* at the convent?" he asked.

Had he followed her to the convent? she wondered. She thought of the CD she'd taken from Caroline's room. Damek knew about the CD. He'd mentioned it as they sat with coffee earlier in the evening. Dana glanced at his dashboard and then, without bothering to ask, she hit play on the CD player. He made no attempt to stop her, but forwarded to the tract she instantly recognized as "Laterna Magika," the song she'd listened to just hours before at her hotel. She still had no idea what the lyrics meant. She wondered if this was his CD or hers. She guessed hers—Sister Agnes's—but made no accusations.

When the song came to the second refrain, he translated:

Under the wing of peace we march in gentle revolution
to claim our cherished life and freedom
The salvation of the world
to be found in the human heart

She liked the sound of Damek's voice, the cadence and tone as if he were reading poetry. It sounded different, softer, than his cop voice.

He hit eject. "You believe this has significance relating to Sister Claire's death? The theft of the Infant?"

"Not exactly church music," she said.

"These words, some from poetry of the first president of whom we spoke."

"You read poetry?"

"At times."

There were many sides to this man, Dana thought. "You think there are political implications?"

"In the music? Of course."

"I mean in the motive for the theft of the Infant."

"I do not know the motive." He glanced at Dana as if she should offer something more. They pulled onto Nerudova.

"You still believe Sister Claire's death was natural?" Dana asked.

"She suffered a heart attack. Yes, this *is* the official cause of death," he replied emphatically. "I have no doubt of that fact."

They were just a half block from her hotel, their car the only one on the street. "Are you going to check into this Lenka connection?" she asked.

"Tomorrow." He glanced at his watch.

Dana glanced at hers. It was now half past two in the morning— already tomorrow. "Could I go with you?"

"With me?"

"If you find her."

"What is your *personal* interest in what has taken place at Our Lady Victorious?"

"A friend," she said after the smallest hesitation.

"If the Infant is truly missing, as you and Father Borelli believe, there are few who would know. The thief. Or thieves. Father Ruffino. The nuns who dress the Infant. One of the nuns, American. About your age. Your friend, she is the American nun?"

No response required.

They'd come to a stop at her hotel.

"You still want my passport?"

He nodded.

"When we arrived at the bar, you referred to a murder three years ago. Did you solve that one?"

"Yes."

Suddenly she felt so tired she questioned if she even had the energy to go up to her room, get the passport, and return with it. She was about to get out of the car, wondering if he intended to escort her to the room, when she turned to face him. "You and Father Ruffino? You obviously know him. You speak so highly of him. As does Borelli. According to just about everyone, the man's a saint. Shouldn't you have called in someone to take over the case? Back home we'd call this conflict of interest." She thought this might make him angry, which at this point probably wasn't a good idea, as they seemed to be working together, but it was pretty obvious he'd done a terrible job. Even if the old nun had died of natural causes, something else had definitely taken place in the church that morning. The Infant of Prague was missing.

The look on his face was not one of anger; she couldn't read it at all. Then something shifted almost as if a mask had been removed, a softening, a vulnerability, something she'd had a brief glimpse of earlier in the evening.

Damek nodded, but for several moments he remained quiet. Finally he said, "My son." He stared out the car window at the deserted street. "Several years ago he became very ill." He spoke in a soft voice. "There were tumors, cancer. One tumor, then a second, then a third. The first, at the base of his skull, and then the second, it moved up closer to . . ." Damek ran his fingers slowly along the back of his head. "They remove these. But with the third—" He shook his head. "He is dying. The doctors say there is no hope. Though Karla . . ." He smiled, and Dana understood he was speaking of his wife. "She will not let go of hope. She told them—the doctors—that Petr will be saved. If we believe in God's power, he will be saved. I did not believe her. How could I? I stare down at this fragile boy, my son, so small his bones cracking the thin skin at the bends of his elbows, his bruised knees, his frail little shoulders." Investigator Damek paused for a long moment as if the image had taken away the words. "The doctors, they tell us the third, too close to his brain. Nothing more they can do. . . . Our son, so weak . . . he now goes into a coma." The dim glow of the streetlight revealed a glisten on Damek's cheek.

She could hear, in the quiet night, his taking in a breath, releasing it slowly. Then she could hear her own breathing and feel the tense beat of her heart. Did they share this—an unspeakable bond of loss?

Then Damek smiled and said, "He's doing very well now. He is nine and a healthier boy you would never see." He took in another deep breath as if attempting to regain his composure, and again Dana felt the thump of her own heart.

"Karla, my wife, is a spiritual person, very religious. She believes in the goodness of people, in the loving mercy of God. She wanted to take him to the church, Our Lady Victorious. We argued. Karla begged me to take Petr to the Christ child. They say the little statue can heal the sick, that the Infant is an instrument of miracles. I told her we could not take our son from the hospital, that he would die if we did. I knew the doctors would not allow it. I called Father Ruffino. He came immediately. When Karla told him what she wanted to do, he said . . ." Damek was again on the verge of tears. He sat quietly for a long moment before continuing. "Father Ruffino told us, 'It is not the statue that has the power to heal. It is God. The statue represents God's love for us, his sending his Son to become one of us, to die for our sins, but in itself, the statue has no power. We will pray together here with Petr to the Infant King.'"

Damek stared out on the street. A cab moved by, bumping on the slight mound where the ditch had recently been covered. It stopped in front of them. A couple got out and walked into the hotel.

"I did not believe in miracles," he said. "I did not have Karla's faith, but I prayed as I have never prayed in my life. I begged."

"But you do now?" Dana asked, remembering what he'd said earlier when she asked him about the religious medal he'd entrusted to Borelli. Her chest, as well as her throat, felt so tight and dry now, she could barely get the words out. "Now you believe in miracles?"

His shoulders heaved, and she thought he might be crying, and the mother in Dana wanted to reach out and hold him, and yet it was that same maternal feeling that burned like a stone in her chest, the heat fanning out as if her entire body had been placed into a fire.

"Yes, I believe in miracles," he said.

She had prayed. For a miracle. A miracle that had not come. Dana closed her eyes tightly to prevent her own tears from escaping. *Breathe,* she told herself, though she felt as if she were suffocating. *Breathe.* Slowly in, slowly out.

She was filled not with tenderness toward this man, not with joy for his miracle, but with anger that had been seething inside her for five long years. Finally, after a long, empty silence, she said, "I have a son." The words came as if from someone else, so oddly calm. She did not hear the anger in her voice. She could not bring herself to say the words, *I had a son.*

Their eyes met, and now it was Damek who waited for Dana to tell her story.

"He would be eight," she said.

He said nothing.

"Just a little younger than your son. It was five years ago." She paused, and considered leaving, just opening the door, going up to her room. She could do it. *He won't follow me,* she thought. "We had gone to visit my mother for Easter. It was a tradition. We'd go to my folks every year. When we were kids—myself, my two brothers—

when my dad was alive, he used to do the Easter egg hunt. He always said it was the Easter Bunny. My brothers, Jeff and Ben, do it now. Outdoors if the weather is nice. I have two nephews, Zac and Quinn, a little niece, Olivia. We just had Zac and Joel, my son, our son—I had a husband then, too. That year it was just the two boys. Quinn and Olivia don't even know Joel—Joseph Leon, but we always called him Joel. The kids were both excited and we expected them up early. Zac got his dad up, but he said Joel was gone. The two boys were sharing a room. He said a man came in the night and took him. Jeff thought Zac had just had a bad dream, but when he went in to check on Joel . . ."

Dana didn't think she could continue, but she knew she had to. Now that she had started, she had to finish. She had told it so many times, during those first days, so many times. But she hadn't spoken of that morning in years. She didn't think she could anymore. But she knew, tonight, she had to.

"We searched everywhere. Inside. Outside. We thought he was playing a trick. Hiding, like an Easter egg. He was gone. We called the police. Another search. Hours passed. I prayed. I prayed so hard. I begged God. *Please return my son safely.* A day passed. Another. Now it was a miracle I prayed for. I knew after those first twenty-four hours . . . if . . . I prayed for a miracle." Heat burned behind her eyes, invaded her brain, as if it could scorch every nerve, every fiber, heat to a boil, explode inside her head. She felt the warm, sticky moisture roll down her cheeks.

She stared at Damek through the blurriness. "Am *I* not worthy?" Her voice rose with each word. "Was *my* son not worthy? Why were *you* given a miracle? Why was *your* son chosen, not mine?" Her hand curled in a fist, against her leg, shaking. Everything trembling, as if her body, her limbs, were moving on their own, as if she had no control.

Their eyes met, and she saw a reflection of her pain in his eyes. She hated him at this moment.

She grabbed the car door, yanking at the handle. He reached for her, his hand on her arm, but she pulled away and was outside the car, sprinting toward the hotel, running on legs of rubber. She could sense him coming behind her, again reaching for her, spinning her around. Then she hit him in the chest. Before she realized what was happening she did it again. Hard. He grasped her wrists, but she jerked away. She slammed her fist against his chest again, feeling something hard and unyielding beneath his jacket. He held up his arms defensively and then again he clutched her wrist, her arm, then her whole body, holding tight to prevent her from hitting him again, to calm her. She shoved, pushed, pounded his chest, striking him with all the power her body possessed. He grabbed her again, held her tighter and tighter as if he could force the grief out of her, as if his grasp could destroy the pain still growing, tangling, snarling deep inside her.

She was sobbing, then her mouth was pressed to his chest, reaching with her hands to his face, pulling him to her, her lips soon on his, and she wanted nothing more than to consume him, to become part of this miracle, which in some strange, unexplainable way she knew was the only way she would be saved.

· 25 ·

Father Giovanni Borelli knew Dana Pierson was right, but he did not understand why Father Ruffino, his fellow priest and childhood best friend, was withholding information. Giovanni was certain Beppe could not be involved in the theft of the Holy Infant, but there had to be a reason for his deceit. Had he been threatened by someone?

Giovanni sat alone in the dark, nursing a whiskey, a growing concern for Dana Pierson stacking itself atop his worry for Beppe. He'd called her hotel a half hour after Investigator Damek dropped him off at his, to make sure she'd made it back safely. No answer. Maybe she'd gone to get her passport, then when he called had returned to the car to surrender it to the Czech officer. Father Borelli called fifteen minutes later, but still no answer. Maybe she was in the shower, he reasoned, or she'd turned the phone down to get some sleep. It was late when they left the restaurant. They were both tired. He guessed all three of them were tired. But Giovanni thought they had reached an agreement—that they would work together. He reached toward the nightstand where he'd placed the small medal Investigator Damek had given him earlier in the evening. He ran his fingers over the surface of the image of the Infant of Prague. Had he misjudged the man?

Giovanni realized he was developing a fondness for the young woman, clearly a paternal protectiveness that both surprised and puzzled him. Had he remained in a secular life, he might have had a daughter her age. There was something about her . . . he genuinely liked her. The Americans would say she had spunk. He liked a woman with some spirit, some determination.

Gia had been such a woman. He thought of her often. They had been engaged to be married—over forty-five years ago, which seemed impossible to Giovanni, as the memories were fresh and clear. Just three weeks before the wedding, she had come to him and told him she was in love with someone else. She had gone to Rome with her mother to pick out a wedding gown, and she had met someone. Just like that, she falls in love with someone else. She told Giovanni he was not a romantic, that he was too caught up in his books, his studies—at the time he was studying secular law—and that she had decided, after meeting this man in Rome, that she would end up leading a boring, uneventful life if she became the wife of Giovanni Borelli. That was what she said—he would bore her to death. There were worse ways to go, he thought now.

In his heart he knew it would not have worked. She and the man, according to Giovanni's aunt, had separated three years after the marriage, though at the time divorce was not an option in Italy. She'd run off with another man. No, it would never have worked. Giovanni Borelli was a man who believed in commitment.

He fixed himself another drink and sat, studying the pattern of morning light beginning to play against the wall of his room. Then he stared up at the wooden beams on the ceiling, hand-painted in a

Bohemian style. He would go to Dana's hotel to make sure she was okay. Then he would visit Giuseppe and have it out with his friend.

Dana, barely aware of how she had made it up to the third floor and into her bed, awoke as morning stripped the darkness from the room. She had collapsed on the street in front of her hotel, and it was coming back to her slowly as if she were watching the scene from outside her own body. Damek had carried her up to her room, taken off her shoes, washed her face with a cool cloth, and put her to bed. She was still dressed in her jeans and hoodie. The flashlight, her glasses sat on the bedside table next to the convent's keys.

She looked over at the chair near the window. He sat, body slouched, staring out.

"I'm sorry," she whispered. She guessed he'd been afraid to leave her alone. She had been hysterical. An insane, uncontrollable madwoman. Strangely, now, as night turned to morning, she felt calmed. She was grateful that he had stayed, that he hadn't left her alone.

"You are okay?" he asked.

"Okay?" There was a tone in her voice—she could hear it herself. She might as well have said, *I will never be okay.*

"I know," he said, and Dana felt that this was as close as she'd get to true understanding from another human being.

"Thanks for . . . for getting me up here, for not leaving." She knew he could have left her on the street in front of the hotel or taken her down to police headquarters, thrown her into that jail cell he'd talked about earlier in the evening, arrested her for assaulting a police officer, for interfering with an investigation. She remembered how she had pounded on his chest, beating with all her strength, how she'd pressed her lips to his, how he had resisted. Should she just curl up, pull the blanket over her head, and die from shame now? Yet somehow she felt that he did understand.

"You can go now." She could think of nothing else to say.

He stood. "My number." He tapped the top of the table next to the chair and she could make out a small piece of paper, along with a pen. "I will run a check on Lenka Horáčková." He lifted his jacket, then handgun and holster, from the back of the chair. "Father Ruffino will have to file a report. I will do nothing official until I hear from him."

Dana knew he believed what she and Father Borelli had told him the night before, yet he still waited for a confession from Father Ruffino. Now she understood why. She watched, saying nothing as he repositioned his holster, put on his jacket, and started toward the door.

He turned. "There was no ladder at the altar when I arrived."

Father Borelli had the cab stop in front of the hotel. Just as he was digging in his pocket, pulling out his money clip for the fee and tip, he looked up and saw Investigator Damek come out. Instinctively, Giovanni dipped his head, glanced at his watch, realizing how early it was. What the hell was going on here? His first thought was that the Czech investigator had done something to harm her and Borelli should never have left them alone. He had trusted the man. Was he losing his ability to judge others? But then he realized that if that were the case— if the Czech investigator had harmed her—Damek would have been out of the hotel hours ago or would never have even come to the hotel.

Then, slowly, he realized that Dana Pierson and Chief Investigator Damek had just spent the night together, and Giovanni Borelli felt an unprecedented jolt of paternal concern. These feelings were ridiculous, he realized, attempting to brush them aside. She was an adult, as was Damek. If they wanted to screw around, that was their business.

He waited until the police investigator was out of sight before he got out of the cab and walked up the steps to the hotel. At the desk he was greeted by a perky young woman, freshly scrubbed and well rested, as if she'd just come on duty. Father Borelli himself was exhausted. He was hungry and tired, and he could feel the sweat staining his fresh shirt, which he'd just put on that morning. He'd showered and made coffee in his room, but he hardly felt ready to welcome a new day and had yet to say his Office, which he generally tended to first thing in the morning.

He knew it was too early to ring her room and wondered what he was thinking, coming here at this hour in the first place. She was probably still asleep, dreaming of romance and adventure.

Yes, adventure, and hadn't he gotten himself into this one. The statue of the authentic Infant of Prague was missing, and no one—Dal Damek, Czech police investigator; Dana Pierson, award-winning American reporter; nor Father Giovanni Borelli, canon lawyer, Vatican investigator, Devil's Advocate—seemed to be making much progress in finding it.

Borelli felt a heaviness press down upon him. The devil had them all by the balls this morning.

He stepped out of the hotel, onto the street, and found an open restaurant, where he ordered coffee, a basket of bread with butter, a plate of cheese, a plate of sausage, and a plate of fresh fruit. He pulled out a cigarette, then sat alone, trying to put the words together for his meeting with Father Giuseppe Ruffino later at the Church of Our Lady Victorious after the 9:00 A.M. Mass.

After leaving Dana Pierson's hotel, Investigator Damek headed directly to his office. He'd slept little—dropping off for a moment or two as he sat gazing out the window—and he felt the familiar fatigue invading his body and spirit once more. *Why?* she had asked.

He couldn't answer, because he didn't know. He did not understand why he and Karla had been blessed with this miracle—a son who was dying one day, healthy and thriving the next. It was a gift from God, he knew that. But he did not understand why *he* had been given such a gift. He had been determined to make himself worthy, to be a better man. Each day he got down on his knees and prayed a prayer of thanksgiving.

After his son's miraculous cure—and he knew that was what it was—he and Karla asked that Father Ruffino not make this known, as they did not want a spotlight shining upon their son. He knew the priest could have taken advantage, released this to the public. The doctors could not explain the boy's instant cure. Father Ruffino could have advertised that a miracle had occurred through the Holy Infant, could have plastered it on the wall, along with the list of other miracles attributed to the Infant. But he did not.

Those first years after were the best of Dal's life as he watched his little son grow. He had never loved his wife with such passion and tenderness.

But still he never felt worthy of this miracle. He often wondered, *why?* Why had they been chosen?

And now, had he and Karla squandered this gift? Should life not be perfect for a miracle family? In those last weeks before their separation they'd argued, it seemed, every day. Mostly over their son— their gift, their miracle. He was a normal, healthy boy, and wasn't that exactly what they had prayed for? The child did not wear a halo. He wanted to do what boys do. He wanted to play football. He wanted to skateboard and learn to snowboard. He wanted to go with his cousins—all rowdy, undisciplined boys, according to Karla—to visit his grandfather in the country and swing out over the river on a rope knotted to a tree.

Karla treated him as if he were as fragile as a little statue made of porcelain. Entrusted with his care, she felt she should shield him from anything that might harm him. She wrapped him in warm woolen hats and scarves, outfitting him with gloves and boots before sending him out on a winter's day. She lathered him with sunscreen and insisted on sunglasses and hats to shield him from the summer sun. If he caught the slightest cold, she rushed him off to the doctor. She would not allow him to play rough games in the neighborhood with the other boys, and she forbade him to join any teams at school. The boy had begun to resent this. He spoke back harshly to his mother, which his father did not allow. And yet, Dal understood.

Dal and Karla fought, continually, continuously. "You've got to allow him some freedom, some fun," Dal would tell her, starting out calmly, but soon they were screaming at one another.

"What if he hurts himself?" she would come back. "What if he is injured?"

Dal had no one to talk to. He didn't know anyone who had been gifted with a miracle. He and Karla went to a priest, their own parish priest, not Father Ruffino; neither of them could face him. How had this happened, how had they come to this?

He was going by this morning to take Petr on an outing. Soon he would be back with his family. And yet, again, Dana Pierson pushed herself into his mind. He had never met such a woman. Strong and yet so fragile. The image of her changing in her hotel room, before she and Borelli went to the church, kept coming to him. Though thin, she was curvy and feminine, something not evident from the way she dressed. When she leaned over to pull up her jeans, he could see her breasts spilling out of her bra, round and firm and tempting.

As he parked at headquarters, he thought again of her screaming, her pounding on his chest. *Why?* He could not answer, because he did not know. And then, her lips on his, forcing herself on him, as if begging him to make love to her, to take her, when he knew all she really wanted was for him to take away the pain. Which he knew he could not.

It would have been a betrayal in so many ways. No, he would never take advantage of a woman filled with such unyielding grief. And he would not betray his vow to his wife. He had been tempted many times, but now perhaps it was this loneliness, the pressure of his work that made him feel so vulnerable. But why this American woman?

It was early Sunday morning and the officers and administrative staff at the police headquarters went quietly about their work, no one aware that he was at this moment scheduled to take some personal time, his first in several weeks, perhaps accustomed to the fact that he was always working. Officially on his high-profile murder case, unofficially on the officially solved murder of Filip Kula, the "accidental" death of Hugo Hutka. And, then, of course . . . Sister Claire and Our Lady Victorious. He went to his office, sat at his desk, signed on to his computer, and began checking out several of his databases, attempting to find Lenka Horáčková and her son, Václav.

· 26 ·

Dal's mind jumped from one thought to another as he scrolled down the computer screen. He was scheduled to fetch Petr at quarter to nine. He also knew he must confront Father Ruffino. Soon. He couldn't believe the priest had taken the Infant, and he found it impossible to believe he knew of this theft and had remained silent.

The ladder had not been at the altar when Dal arrived at the church. He realized that Father Ruffino had knelt beside the nun, his cassock grazing the floor, possibly sweeping away ladder tracks in the blood that would have alerted Dal. He would go to the church before the early Mass and speak to the priest, ask to examine the statue now on the altar and also the ladder he'd seen in the sacristy closet. Dal thought back to the lapse in time between the old nun's death and the priest's call.

His cell phone rang. Branislov Černý, who probably had no idea Dal was sitting in his office now.

"There's been a theft," Černý said, then paused. Through the fogginess in his mind, Dal wondered why Černý was reporting a theft to him, and then again why he himself was spending his valuable time on another theft, something that should immediately be assigned to another unit.

"He's loaded it on his hard drive," Černý explained tentatively as if expanding on something he'd already shared, "but someone broke into Kristof's apartment and took the laptop."

"He's okay?" Dal didn't bother to ask why the young detective had taken the laptop home and didn't bother to ask Černý if they were speaking of Hugo Hutka's laptop.

"He's fine, though he said you'd be pissed he took it home. Went out for coffee and came back, locks broken, laptop gone. Officers doing a crime scene investigation now. I know you're taking some time off, but I figured you'd want to know."

"He loaded it on his hard drive?" Dal asked, at the same time thinking, *Kristof doesn't drink coffee.*

"Yes," Černý said defensively, "the information isn't lost. The building has a surveillance camera, but someone had tampered with it. Nothing there."

"I'm here. In my office. For a while," Dal clarified. "Then later this afternoon." He wasn't going to let Petr down. His officers could go over any evidence uncovered at Kristof's apartment. "Get another technician on those files." Dal knew many were still locked, but the theft surely indicated there was something important in Hugo Hutka's files. "Have Detective Sokol give me a call."

"I will," Černý came back. "As soon as I figure out where the hell he's taken off to."

"You'll have him back home for dinner?" Karla asked. Dal stood just inside the living room. He smelled sausage and the comforting aroma of fresh bread coming from the kitchen. Karla's floral-scented body lotion. She wore her silk robe over her nightgown, and he caught a glimpse of her breasts as she bent to kiss their son on the forehead then adjust the collar of his shirt. A thick blond strand of hair curled along her neck just above a familiar mole below her clavicle.

"Yes, I'll have him home for dinner." It hurt Dal to say *home*. It seemed strange, picking up his son at his own house. He realized how little time he'd spent alone with his boy prior to this separation. When they were all living together, he seldom took Petr out; he couldn't even remember when he'd spent a day with his son, just Petr and himself, without Karla. It seemed unnecessary when they were living together, and when he was off duty, he liked to just hang around home.

In addition to their fights over the boy, Karla had accused him of not paying much attention to either of them. He knew she was right. Sometimes he'd be sitting at home at the dining table with his family, on one of the rare times they could actually schedule a meal together, not even aware of what his wife had prepared, something Karla might later point out she'd put some effort into, and she'd say, "Would you like to join us for dinner?" He'd pull himself back, try to be more engaged, talk to his wife and son. She'd known what she was signing on for, even when they were young and he'd told her he wanted to join the Czech police force, but lately, she'd told him, it seemed as if he'd disappeared completely.

"What would you like to do today?" he asked Petr as they hopped in the car, Dal checking to make sure the boy was strapped in his seat belt.

"I don't know."

"Are you hungry?"

"Mama made breakfast."

Yes, of course; he'd smelled the remnants of the meal as he'd stood waiting to collect his son. He knew Karla would not send the boy out into the world hungry. A scent hovered about Petr even now, the warm aroma of breakfast, but also of his mother, her natural perfume.

Dal had a sudden urge to bend over and kiss him on the forehead in the exact place where his mother's lips had brushed his face, to taste his wife, his son, to be a family again.

"You've gone to Mass?" Dal asked, realizing it was Sunday, this reflection accompanied by a fleeting thought of Father Ruffino. That would all have to wait.

"Mama took me yesterday evening."

Yes, of course she'd make sure his obligation was fulfilled, aware that Dal didn't always make it to Mass.

"What should we do today?" Dal asked again. "Where do you want to go?"

"Could we go to the arcade?" Petr asked. He liked to play video games and he liked to watch movies, none of which Dal had at his apartment. They went to the arcade last time Dal had picked him up. Maybe a movie? But it was not a day to spend indoors. Finally, after several days of cloudy skies and rain, the sun had come out. A youngster his age needed more physical exercise; even the priest they'd met with told Karla this. He suggested they introduce the child to activities that both parents could agree on, that the boy had expressed an interest in. Karla had suggested swimming, something Petr had always loved when he was small. Before the cancer. He'd really taken to the water. *As long as it's in a pool,* she'd said. No lakes. No rivers.

"Would you like to go swimming?" The gym where Dal worked out had a pool.

"Mother and I went Friday afternoon."

Dal noticed how the boy went back and forth—referring to Karla as Mama one moment, Mother the next. He was growing, changing. Within a few years he'd be into his teens, perhaps defying both his parents. Doing whatever he pleased when he was away from them. Dal had been such a boy. He'd had little parental supervision as a child and he swore when he and Karla married he would be a good father. Now he often doubted he'd kept this promise.

Soon Petr would make his own decisions, and they would have little control. Dal knew this. He didn't think Karla realized she could not shelter the boy under her wing for the rest of his life.

"I don't have my swimming suit, anyway," Petr said, reminding Dal he'd have to plan things better. But it wasn't like he had an abundance of time to set out a recreational schedule, having spent the better part of the night chasing after Father Borelli and Dana Pierson, then the morning attempting to get a lead on Pavel Novák, followed by his call from Černý, a new twist in his murder case. Where the hell was Kristof? The thought was laced with both anger and concern.

Dal hadn't made it over to visit Father Ruffino, but he'd found some basic information on Lenka Horáčková and her son, Václav, before Černý's call. He now knew she lived in an apartment near the Havlíčkovy sady in an upscale residential neighborhood. He wondered how an unemployed actress, or dancer, or whatever she was, could afford such a place. She had a son named Václav Horáček, just as he and Dana had learned the previous night. He didn't appear to have a current driver's license. He was a musician who'd once been issued a citation for performing on the bridge without a permit. Last year he'd had a legitimate permit as part of a group, but Dal was unable to access the most current information to see if he'd renewed it.

Dal couldn't find any evidence that the woman had ever used a name other than Lenka Horáčková. He glanced at Petr, who grinned up at his father with undeserved admiration. Dal attempted to push all these thoughts aside.

"How about renting a boat?" Dal suggested.

The way the child's face lit up, Dal wondered if this was something his mother had forbidden. With a life jacket it would be perfectly safe.

He patted the boy on the head. The way the river was dammed up there weren't any strong currents. They could paddle around the island. It would be fun. But his mind was reeling again, with what he'd learned from Černý, what he'd learned from Dana and the priest, then what Dana had shared with him in front of her hotel. He could, maybe *should*, take Petr home—*home*, he thought again with a stab to his gut.

"Do you have to go back to work?" Petr asked and Dal realized the kid could sense his dad's inattention.

"Nope," he said, patting the boy's head again, ruffling his hair, mussing the neatly combed curls. "Let's go get that boat."

· 27 ·

"May I buy you breakfast this morning?" Father Borelli asked his friend as he removed his vestments.

"A splendid idea," Father Ruffino replied.

Giovanni didn't want to confront Beppe here in his own church, and Father Borelli himself would feel much better out in the sunshine, the fresh air. He could have a cigarette. He couldn't light one up here in the sacristy. He thought about his being in this very room behind the high altar just last night with Dana Pierson, examining the bottom of the ladder in the adjacent supply closet. He knew he had to confront Beppe, to know if he was involved in the disappearance of the Infant of Prague.

Earlier that morning, just before leaving to meet Father Ruffino, he'd heard back from his acquaintance in Rome, who said he'd poke around and see what he could discover. "A valuable, well-known icon would most likely be stolen for a specific buyer. It would be almost impossible to sell on the open market," he'd told Father Borelli. "Years ago I had some dealings with a . . . well, let's just say a Russian living in Prague, his specialty religious icons, not always legitimately obtained. If something is being offered, he would know."

Again Father Borelli thought, *No fear of God*.

"How wonderful," Father Ruffino said as he hung his chasuble neatly in the vestment wardrobe, "that we've been blessed with this wonderful sunny weather after last evening's big storm."

The big storm, Father Borelli mused. The big storm was yet to come. They headed toward the side door, the very door he had entered under cover of darkness just hours earlier.

"I have a group coming in at eleven thirty," Beppe told him, and Giovanni guessed he spoke of one of his troupes of tourists lured by their devotion to the Infant of Prague. What would they think if they knew they were paying homage to a little fake?

"That should give us plenty of time," Father Ruffino added. He smiled as if neither priest had anything to do but sit, drink coffee, and eat pastries. It was almost as if Beppe had blocked out the reason he'd asked his friend to rush to Prague, perhaps thinking he'd passed off the imitation for the real Infant, and he could relax now. Giovanni wondered if he now regretted his initial call, obviously in a state of panic, if he wished that Father Giovanni Borelli would simply go home.

The two men started out, Giovanni stuffing a cigarette in his holder within the first three steps, lighting it within the next two.

"I'm very fond of the spring," Beppe said, "this time of renewal."

"Yes, particularly after a harsh winter. With each year, it seems I have less tolerance for the cold."

"Yes, so true. How did we get so old?" Beppe laughed.

"By not dying," Giovanni replied dryly.

They continued on in silence. Though the sun was out, they had to step over several puddles, evidence of the recent rain.

Finally Father Borelli said, "We've made little progress in determining if there was someone in the church that morning." If he was going to have it out with Beppe, he would tell him about Dana Pierson, about working with the Czech police officer. Yet, now, in addition to feeling betrayal from his oldest and dearest friend, Father Borelli wondered if he had been betrayed by his new friends, Dana Pierson and Investigator Damek.

"I'm afraid I might need additional information to solve this . . ." Father Borelli hesitated, trying to bring up the words he had rehearsed. He knew he should just come right out and say *theft*. He didn't think they were dealing with a murder. Sister Claire was not a victim, but perhaps a witness. "We've made an additional discovery," he continued, taking a long, comforting drag on his cigarette. He waited, fully expecting Beppe to catch on to the fact that he'd said *we*.

Silently they walked along Karmelitská, past an elderly couple out for a Sunday morning stroll. Both nodded and offered respectful smiles, the two cassock-wearing priests easily identified as clergy.

Finally Beppe replied, "You've enlisted help?" His voice remained steady.

"I'm working with an American woman who has considerable investigative skills."

"I thought you understood this should be kept in the greatest confidence," he said, and Giovanni recognized the calm as pretense. Fake, just like the statue. There was now an unmistakable tentative tone in Beppe's voice, a quiver in the word *confidence*. After a long pause, he said, "An American?"

"She has a close relationship with one of the nuns."

"Sister Agnes."

Of course, Giovanni thought, *Father Ruffino is aware that Sister Agnes is American.*

"We believe the Infant of Prague has been stolen." He would not accuse, but he would open this up for Beppe to admit his part, if indeed he had a role in the statue's disappearance or replacement.

Father Borelli stopped walking, as did Father Ruffino. Giovanni turned toward his friend. They had reached a major intersection, though traffic was light and there were few pedestrians out, none within hearing distance.

"It would be much easier to find the Infant," Giovanni said, staring directly into Beppe's eyes, then placing a reassuring hand on his shoulder, "if you shared with me everything you know."

Beppe did not reply; he wasn't surprised at Giovanni's words.

"Has there been a demand for ransom?" Giovanni asked, his voice tight.

"No," Beppe replied, lowering his eyes.

"It's been over a week now, substantially reducing the possibility of return. Why did you not share the truth with me?" Giovanni fought to keep his voice calm. "Have threats been made to anyone—you, the other priests or brothers? The nuns?"

Beppe hesitated before speaking, his voice subdued as the halting words came forth. "I . . . I often tell those who come to the Lord in my confessional that a lie can take on a life of its own. That it can grow and expand. I . . . I . . ." They had started to walk again, crossing the street with the pedestrian light. Father Borelli could tell that his friend did not wish to look him in the eye.

They had arrived at the café and entered, distancing themselves as far away from other patrons as possible. They ordered coffee.

"I'm sorry, Gianni," Father Ruffino said, calling him by his childhood name. His voice trembled and he seemed on the verge of tears. "Now, something else . . ." He stopped as if afraid to continue. He glanced around. A mother, who was attempting to settle her two small children at a nearby table, appeared too busy folding a stroller, encouraging her children to sit, to take notice of the two priests.

"Do you know what happened to the Infant?" Father Borelli asked in a low voice.

Beppe shook his head. "I hoped you might find Pavel Novák, that the Infant might be returned quietly."

Father Borelli was so angry now, he could barely speak. Beppe had lied to him. He had not believed the man capable of such deception. *Thou shalt not bear false witness.* Strangely, he had often seen Beppe as an extension of himself—the better half. The good Italian boy who had answered God's call and become a saintly priest. Perhaps this was one of the reasons Giovanni Borelli had feared this confrontation. His entire world was about to shatter. Beppe was no better than he himself. The man was a liar.

"You told me you come to the church each morning before your servers," Giovanni finally said, "but this was Good Friday, and there was no Mass that morning."

The mother was attempting to order, balancing the smallest child on her lap, the other fussing.

"It is true, there was no Mass," Father Ruffino said. "But I did come to the church early. After the services on Holy Thursday, I meditated on the Passion of our Lord. I thought about his praying in the garden. How Peter promised he would not betray him. And here I was, preparing for the Friday services, the day our Lord died, thinking about Easter Sunday, about the altars, the festivities, counting in my head how many tourists were in the city now, how we could draw them to the church. How the offerings would swell. I was counting the silver in my mind." Father Ruffino breathed heavily, rubbing his eyes. "I was ashamed at these feelings. Good Friday, and I felt that I, like Peter, had denied our Lord. Or perhaps, like Judas, given him up for a handful of silver. I was thinking about drawing the crowds. Like a huckster, I was trying to entice them to come to my church. *My church.*" He looked away, again unable to meet Father Borelli's gaze. "Yes, I went early to the church. I went to pray, to sit with our Lord that night, the night he was handed over to be crucified." Again, Beppe took in a deep, ragged breath.

Giovanni waited for him to go on.

"When I arrived at the church, I found the door unlocked. I entered cautiously and glanced about the church. I heard a murmur, a child, I thought. When I came to the altar of the Holy Infant, I found Sister Claire. I knelt down beside her, taking her hand in mine. There was a gash across her face. She lay shivering. She told me to look up. The altar box was opened, empty." Father Ruffino rubbed his head. His hand jerked fitfully. "Blood on the floor. When I asked Sister Claire who had done this, she pressed her hand to her heart. She told me someone had been there, but they were unaware of her presence. It was not an intruder who had hurt her; she had fallen. Again she touched her heart, and I noticed the garden shears on the floor. She told me she had heard him speaking... near the exit. She uttered words I could not understand. I told her I was going for help, and she said, 'No, stay with me.' I said I would go to the sacristy for the holy oils, but she begged me to stay. I knew she was dying. We prayed. She asked for a final confession. We prayed again. Then her mumblings became more clear, though the words she spoke made no sense."

"Pavel Novák?" Father Borelli asked. "Laterna Magika?"

Beppe nodded. "I held her until she was gone. Then I went to the sacristy and got the oils to anoint her." Father Ruffino fell silent. Father Borelli suspected he was praying.

"But it was not the thief," Giovanni asked, "or thieves, who replaced the authentic Infant with a fake?"

"No." Beppe lowered his head, hands trembling as they rose to cover his eyes. "I didn't want to leave her, but she had passed already into the good Lord's hands. I knelt and prayed for guidance, but I heard nothing."

"Perhaps you were not listening," Giovanni said, his voice cutting as deeply as his anger.

"I knew what would happen if the world became aware of the Infant's disappearance. It represents the Lord, who died for our sins. But it is not our Lord. Our Savior, who should be the focus of all on Good Friday. Easter Sunday . . . it was . . . I was . . ." The priest was blubbering now, his shoulders shaking with shame as tears fell.

Giovanni waited, too angry for words.

"I climbed the stairs to the museum," Father Ruffino continued, "and I unlocked the Infant's wardrobe case, took out one of the garments in the colors of Lent, similar to what the Infant had been wearing that day. Do you know that we have over eighty now, all gifts, dating back centuries, presented by royalty, by believers, good devout men and women. We've a very nice little museum. We have many visitors each year. We've attempted to do it tastefully, to encourage a devotion to the Infant."

Beppe was rambling, and Giovanni wanted to get to the point, to the truth. "You took one of the statues?" The word *fake* stuck in Father Borelli's mind but he didn't say it. "From the museum, or the gift shop?"

"I knew then what I was doing was not right, but in part of my mind I—now, it makes no sense, but I knew what would happen in my church." He stopped and corrected himself. "God's church. The people's church. On this most holy of days . . . the police, the press, the disruption—which would have been the result had the theft been reported. I thought, later when my friend Giovanni arrives, he will . . ."

"You took it to the Infant's altar?" Father Borelli encouraged him.

"Yes, I got the ladder, went back to the altar, placed the replica in the Infant's box, and locked it. I returned the ladder to the sacristy, and I used the phone in the office to call Investigator Damek. Then I called you."

Father Borelli remembered now, the sound of Beppe's voice. Shaky, fearful. He would not tell Giovanni exactly what he wanted at that time, but asked that he come immediately. Giovanni had come as soon as he could—no, it had taken him four days—it was the Easter weekend and he had obligations, visitors, his sister and nephew with his family, and there were festivities in Rome for the holidays. He had to make arrangements, to book a flight, which hadn't been that easily done. To arrange for his . . . the thought of his concern for his freshly laundered garments now made him feel petty and vain. Perhaps he— Giovanni Borelli, professed friend—did not deserve the truth. Beppe had called him, and Giovanni had taken his time in getting here. Why should he have expected his friend to trust him, when he could not drop everything and come immediately?

"When the investigator arrived, you said nothing about the missing—"

"No."

"Why didn't you tell Investigator Damek?"

"I . . . I . . ." He breathed with a heaving rhythm, like a small child who had just had a fit of weeping, unable to control his emotions.

"You don't trust him?"

"No, he is a good man. I knew if I told him the truth about the Infant's theft, he would be obligated to involve those who investigate such matters. I didn't feel the police needed to get involved. I knew he—"

"But Investigator Damek is chief of homicide. You obviously reported this as a possible murder."

"No, no." Beppe shook his head.

"You called him because he is a personal friend?" Father Borelli remembered Investigator Damek's odd reaction to the mention of the priest.

"Yes."

"And you knew he would not suspect you of such deception?"

Beppe nodded. "I imagined the press, reporters flooding into the church, the circus, the carnival. It was Good Friday, and I had just promised our Lord that I would maintain the sanctity of the church. I told myself, unrealistically, the Infant would return. Miraculously the Infant would find his way home. At first, I thought, after Easter Sunday . . . then I will speak again with Investigator Damek, I will tell the truth . . . by then my friend Giovanni Borelli, the solver of puzzles, will be here and . . ."

"Does anyone else know the truth?"

"The nuns came in to dress the Infant for the Holy Saturday services, and then, yes, of course they knew. They know the little Infant as if he were their own child. I've spoken with them, explained what I did and why."

Father Borelli attempted to put all this together, to determine if finally Father Ruffino was telling him the truth. "But why, Beppe, when I arrived, did you not share this with me? Do you think I'm so stupid that—"

"How did you know? The replica is quite authentic, particularly looking up from in front of the altar."

Father Borelli sighed. "That's a complicated story in itself; let's just say it involved a small theft, then an unauthorized visit to Our Lady Victorious."

He detected a small smile lifting the corners of Beppe's mouth. "I'm sorry, Gianni, that you had to go through this. I know I should have told you, but once I began the lies, the first led to another, then another. In my insanity, I thought you would locate the thief—it is this Pavel Novák?—you would tell me where to find him, I would go and speak to him, the Infant would come home. I know . . . I know . . . I wasn't thinking right. And now . . . something else."

"Something else?" Giovanni asked.

"I received a note."

"Concerning the Infant?"

Beppe nodded.

"A threat?"

"Possibly." Again Beppe buried his head in his hands.

"What did it say?"

Father Ruffino closed his eyes, and, reluctantly, yet as if he had memorized the words, he recited the message. "'Remain silent and it will be returned and no one will suffer. Otherwise it will be destroyed.'"

"The Infant?"

"There could be no other possible explanation."

"How did this note come to you?"

Beppe glanced around, more customers having arrived. But the chatter among those at the other tables would have made it difficult for anyone else to hear the priests' conversation.

"We have a website," he said, and Giovanni nodded, aware of this. "One of our brothers, Brother Marcello, maintains the site, but he checks it infrequently, perhaps a couple of times each week. With the Easter holidays, I don't believe he had looked at it for several days. Not knowing the significance, he brought this e-mail to me."

"These things, I believe, can be traced. We need to find out where it came from. When was it sent?"

"Early Friday morning. But I did not read it until . . . it was Wednesday."

"The day we met at the church, had our discussion in the garden?"

"Yes, early that morning Brother Marcello brought me the message."

"So you decided to continue your lies? The note warned you to remain silent?" Father Borelli saw that as a threat in itself.

"Perhaps I should have told Investigator Damek everything in the beginning, allowed the Easter services to be performed as a sideshow. Or perhaps not at all." He rubbed his damp forehead nervously, and then lowered his eyes. He looked up at his friend. "Will you hear my confession?"

"Not yet," Giovanni replied. "None of this will be protected under the seal. We must share with the police everything you have told me." He placed his hand firmly on his friend's shoulder, and then in the forgiving voice he used in his confessional, he said, "Let me tell you what we have discovered so far. Then we will proceed from there."

· 28 ·

Dana woke for the second time that morning. Glancing at the bed-side clock, she couldn't believe she'd slept so late. It had been an exhausting several days, but she still had much to do before she could return home. She showered and dressed, then grabbed the convent keys on the nightstand and went to the closet to get her handbag. She opened the safe to gather what she'd need for the day. When she reached in she could see, along with her wallet, her passport. Damek had left without it.

Her face burned, her chest compressed at the thought of him. What a fool she'd made of herself. She'd hit him, grabbed him, kissed him. He'd resisted. But he'd taken her to her room with such tender-ness. She'd fallen asleep, exhausted. What did he think of her now? And yet, she knew they had shared with each other emotions they each guarded closely. His son, a miracle. Hers, lost.

Attempting to dismiss these thoughts, she left the room, grabbed a cup of coffee in a disposable cup from the breakfast room, and stepped out of the hotel. Sunday—lunch with Caroline at the convent? Sip-ping as she walked, she headed down Nerudova. She wanted to talk to the old men who hung out at the square before meeting with her cousin. And the children—no, it was Sunday, and they wouldn't be passing by on their way to or from school. She wanted to know if anyone in the neighborhood had seen the man who'd come to sharpen knives and scissors. Though Borelli didn't think much of her theory, and she'd not even mentioned it to Damek, Dana thought it worth checking out. *L'arrotino*—could he possibly have a connection to Pavel Novák?

Just as she'd hoped, they sat lounging on their bench in the morning sunshine. Recognizing the old man with the dancing eyebrows, wearing the same sweater, same tweed cap, she waved and approached with a friendly smile.

"Dobrý den," she said.

He returned her greeting, but Dana wasn't sure he recognized her.

"There was a man," she began, though she recalled he didn't speak English.

All three listened intently. The youngest, who she guessed was in his early seventies, nodded, his eyes narrowing. The fellow sitting on the end of the bench smoked a pipe. He took in a deep suck, then blew out a circle of smoke.

"He was here to sharpen scissors and knives . . . ?" she added.

"English? American?" the oldest said as if he didn't recall their earlier conversation. She wished the children were there to help her.

Dana made a motion with her hand, like a scissors—which reminded her of that old scissors, rock, paper game she used to play with her brothers—then a knife cutting motion, then sharpening as if using a whetstone.

The men chatted with one another, each possibly offering his own interpretation of what she'd said. The pipe smoker laughed, slapping the oldest man on the back in an affable way. She could see now, none of them spoke English. English English or American English.

"Maria?" she asked, and then, "Jan?" Dana guessed the children lived close, and maybe they could help.

The man smoking the pipe, the one she had decided was the most friendly and likely the most helpful, nodded and smiled. He pointed to himself with two open hands. *"Dědeček."*

She didn't understand.

"Maria, Jan." He extended a hand, palm down, then lowered it a couple of inches as if to indicate the children's sizes. Then, tapping his heart, he said, *"Jsem dědeček."*

"Dědeček?" she questioned, and then she realized this must be the word for grandfather.

"Maria and Jan?" she repeated, glancing around. *"Kde?"* Where?

The man stood and motioned her to follow. The other two remained on the bench.

They passed through the small square, toward the largest building on the opposite side, circled around, down a narrow street. A boy on a blue bicycle passed by. A black dog ran out in front of them and jumped playfully up on the old man, who gave it an affectionate pat. They walked slowly, he drawing on his pipe, puffing out circles of smoke. They turned another corner, then down a tiny street that dead-ended. The old man stepped up on the concrete porch in front of the last door. He set his pipe on the ledge that ran under the window as if it had been placed there just for this purpose. He knocked, calling out in a loud voice, "Maria, Jan," as he gazed up at the second-floor windows, lined with planters filled with early spring blooms—tulips and daffodils. He knocked again with the rhythm of more words.

A plain-looking woman about Dana's age opened the door and stepped out. A half-eaten apple in one hand, she gave the old man a hug. "Papa," she said. Then her eyes slid toward Dana, her brow furrowed with confusion. Father and daughter exchanged several words, and the woman turned back and called out, "Maria. Jan."

Within seconds the boy stood at the door, tucked protectively under his mother's arm. "Good morning, Jan," Dana said. "I need your help."

"Yes, I help," he said brightly.

"There was a man"—Dana started in slowly—"he came to the convent, to the nuns."

"Yes," he said, leaning in toward Dana, his mother's arm still wrapped around his shoulder.

"He came to sharpen the knives and scissors."

She could see by his puzzled look he did not understand.

The old man said something rapidly to the boy, along with the pantomime Dana had enacted just minutes before—cutting scissors, slicing knife. The child nodded as if he understood.

"Yes, a man," the boy said, then looked up at his mother for reassurance. The woman nodded encouragingly. "I see this man."

"Dana Pierson." Another small voice came from the doorway, and now Maria stood by her mother's side. The woman looked surprised that the girl knew Dana's name.

As they exchanged quick words, the mother looked at Dana, offered a smile as if her mind had been set at ease. Maybe the girl had explained that Dana was a friend of Sister Agnes. She imagined the nuns were well respected and trusted, and some of this might transfer to Dana. Little Jan spoke to his mother, then the grandfather. Then, again, Maria to her mother. Czech words flew right over Dana's head.

"What did this man look like?" she asked the boy.

"The man," Jan said, "he tall, like this." He raised his arm to a half foot above Dana's head, which might have been a stretch for the boy

had he not stood one step above her in the doorway. "He not fat." He
held out his arms, then pulled them in. "He thin."

Dana remembered the copy of the Internet photo she had in her
bag—Pavel Novák. She pulled it out. "This man?" she asked, pointing.

"No," the boy replied without hesitation.

Dana felt a weighty disappointment settle over her. But, of course,
Pavel Novák would be much older now; maybe he looked nothing
like this—a photo from twenty years ago.

"Like this, but older?" she asked with encouragement.

The boy shook his head. "No. The man have some big hair. It not
black color like this man," he said with confidence. "More like white
color. He wear hat with big hair, like this." The boy cupped his hands
just above his ears.

The grandfather studied the photo now. "Karlův most," he said,
pointing at the image of Pavel.

"You saw him?" Dana asked. "On the bridge?"

The man nodded.

Dana turned to the boy. "Your grandfather saw this man on Karlův
most?"

The boy spoke to the old man, whose head bobbed up and down
enthusiastically.

"But older?" Dana asked. "This man, but older?"

"No, *not* older," the boy said emphatically. "This man just like this
man. The same."

The grandfather was continuing the little game of charades as he
played an invisible flute, a bass, trombone, finishing with an air guitar. The children watched, Maria's eyes wide, Jan covering his giggles
with spread fingers.

Was the grandfather telling her that this man in her photo was
one of the musicians on the bridge? Dana wondered. She'd walked

over it so many times over the past few days. Was Pavel Novák right before her eyes, under her nose, entertaining the visitors in Prague?

The old man poked an assertive finger at Pavel in the photo, as the boy said, "Young man, same like this in photo. He play..." Jan couldn't come up with the word, but imitated the grandfather, strumming a guitar.

According to Damek, Pavel had disappeared years ago, and Caroline had written that he'd left the city.

Young man? Dana wondered.

Suddenly, she realized that the man the grandfather had seen on the bridge could have been Pavel's son, Václav. He would now be near the age his father had been in the photo. The woman at the bar the previous night had told Dal the boy was a musician.

Maria said something to her brother, who in turn said to Dana, "My sister see other man. Man who come to sharpen."

"Yes, I see the man." Maria joined in now. "The man who come to... to..." She made a cutting motion with her fingers.

"At the convent?" Dana asked.

Maria nodded. "I see other place also."

Dana realized they were speaking of two different men. The young musician on the bridge—possibly Pavel's son, Václav—and a second person, the man who had come to the convent to sharpen the knives and scissors.

"Where did you see him?" Dana asked.

Maria consulted her brother, the two children carrying on an animated conversation. Then the mother joined in.

Finally Jan said, "Near the Staroměstské náměsti. It is a shop for..." He held up his hand, wiggling his fingers as if something dangled below, attached to them. "Marionettes!" he exclaimed.

"Maria saw this man in a shop near the Staroměstské náměsti?"

"Yes."

Attempting to calm her voice and slow the pace of her questions, Dana asked for a description, some directions. After much discussion among the four—grandfather, mother, and children—Jan described where the shop was located, tracing a map on his hand. No one seemed to know the exact street or the name of the store, but with this general information, Dana thought she could find it, though there were numerous such shops in the city.

After thanking them all for their help, Dana returned to the convent square, attempting to put all of it together and decide what to do next. It appeared that Pavel Novák's son was a performer on the bridge, the sharpener also a shopkeeper near the Staroměstské náměsti. But did either have any connection with the Infant's disappearance?

Was it possible that Václav looked like his father had twenty years ago? As she walked, Dana thought of how much her younger brother looked like their dad, and then a thought came to her—his voice was identical to her father's. Had Sister Claire heard Václav speaking in the church and recognized this voice, thinking it was Pavel? Had she merely recognized a voice identical to one she'd heard on a recording entitled "Laterna Magika"?

Dana glanced at her watch, then in the direction of the river. She had time. If she hurried, she could make it to the bridge and back again by noon.

· 29 ·

Dal studied his young son, strapped into his life jacket, rowing the boat with vigor, glowing in the warmth of the April sunshine, smiling proudly as if there were nothing finer than spending the day with his father. Petr had asked to row and Dal agreed, instructing the boy how to hold the oars, strike a steady rhythm, and keep the boat on course. With everything in him he tried to focus on his son. He'd asked about school, about his friends, but Dal's mind drifted, his thoughts invaded over and over by a dead senator, a dead actor, a dead nun, a missing Infant, and a missing laptop, whose owner was dead, too.

"Do you have to go back to work?" Petr asked.

"No." Dal dipped a hand into the water and playfully splashed his son, who ducked and giggled. Leaning back in the boat, Dal attempted to relax.

"You could take me home, if you do." The boy sounded so grown-up.

"I want to spend the day with you," Dal told him.

"I could go with you," Petr said with a grin. "I could help you solve the murder."

Murder? Petr knew that his father worked homicide, that he'd recently been promoted to chief. The boy knew what his father's work involved. This was what he did—solve murders.

"Could I go with you?" The boy stopped rowing for a moment and stared at his father, a serious expression fixed on his face. Like Karla, he had a pale sprinkle of freckles across his nose that seemed to all but disappear during the dark winter months, then explode with the first touch of sunshine.

"Look at that," Dal said, pointing to a couple of swans gliding along the far bank of the river. "Remember when you were little and we rented a boat shaped like a swan?"

"I think I want to be a police detective when I grow up."

"You'd make a good detective," Dal said. "You're a clever boy. But, you know, you'll have many choices." He thought back to when he doubted his son would grow up, to when he and Karla both thought they would lose him. Dal didn't consider that possibility anymore, but he knew Karla did. Perhaps Dal, who never saw his faith as equal to Karla's, had been the one to truly accept the miracle they had been given. He would never expose his son to harm, yet he felt the child had an extra layer of protection, as if permanently and safely wrapped in the arms of God, whether it be the Father or the Infant Christ.

The doctor had pronounced it spontaneous remission, but Dal had witnessed the mixture of astonishment and puzzlement on the normally unemotional man's face, the tears he could not contain. They all knew it was more than that. A tumor, growing larger each day . . . and then totally vanished!

"You hungry?" he asked Petr.

"A little."

"After we return the boat we'll find something to eat. Then we could—"

"Can we go to Stalinska?"

Everyone called it "the Stalin," though the enormous statue of the Russian leader, erected in the mid-1950s, had been destroyed in '62. The park, officially known as the Letná, stood on an embankment overlooking the meandering Vltava River and offered a lovely view of the city. Dal remembered how he and Karla used to go there when they were young, then with Petr to ride the carousel when he was a toddler. The boy had outgrown the kids' stuff now, and Dal knew very well why his son wanted to go to the Letná. The concrete slab, along with the marble stairs and metal rails left over from Stalin, made a perfect skateboard park.

"Stalinska, huh?" Dal asked with a grin, and Petr flashed back with a hint of father-and-son conspiratorial bonding.

What harm would it do to go and let the boy watch? Dal thought. He knew his mother would never take him there. Dal wouldn't allow him to go alone or with a group of boys, either, though most of the kids who hung out at the park were just having fun. Yet Dal knew a certain element could be found in sections of the Letná.

"Maybe after we get some lunch, we can go to the park," Dal offered.

The cell phone rang, though when he pulled it out of his pocket he didn't recognize the number on the screen.

"Damek."

"Father Borelli."

Dal knew the priest didn't have his cell number. It had to have come from Father Ruffino. Or Dana.

"Father Ruffino wishes to meet as soon as possible. He's ready to—"

"It would have to be later this afternoon," Dal cut in. *Good and fine,* he thought, Father Ruffino, finally ready to talk. A little late, and Dal wasn't adjusting his schedule. "Five," he said. "My office."

"I hoped we might meet sooner," Father Borelli said, almost apologetically. "Perhaps somewhere other than your office." He suggested a restaurant in the Malá Strana.

"I have obligations." Again Dal glanced at his son. How could he use the word *obligations*? This was a privilege, spending time with his son.

"He's not involved in the theft," Father Borelli said, "but he—"

"We'll talk at five."

"Yes, yes, of course." Borelli cleared his throat. "Yes. I understand." He paused for a long moment and then added, "Yes, I understand you've had a very busy day." The tone of his words carried a hint of contention that Dal couldn't quite read. "At this point perhaps there is no urgency."

"Five, then." He'd promised Karla he'd have Petr home for dinner. He wanted to talk to Kristof, go over the crime scene report from the theft at his apartment. He'd asked Černý to keep him informed, but he'd heard nothing. He wondered if he'd even have time for a trip to the park.

Dana's eyes darted from side to side as she hurried across the bridge. She could hear music at the far end, the familiar beat she'd heard her first morning in Prague. The quartet, she was sure. She pushed her way through the crowd and stopped abruptly. Not a quartet at all. A trombone player. Another musician on a flute. A third man on bass, the man who'd smiled at her with a flirty grin. Hadn't there been another? A guitar player? And wasn't this the exact group the grandfather had described? The now missing musician being the man who looked exactly like a young Pavel Novák. His son, Václav Horáček? She recalled the young guitar player had sat on a stool, wearing a baseball cap, head tilted. She didn't think she'd even noticed his face. She studied the three remaining players. The bass player looked up at her with a smile. She guessed he flirted with all the tourists and probably didn't remember her. She waited for them to break, but after several minutes realized she was running out of time. She stepped closer.

"Václav isn't playing today?" she asked the bassist.

An eyebrow rose, but he didn't miss a beat as their eyes met.

"Václav Horáček?" she asked, testing.

He nodded, but said nothing.

Her heart skipped a beat, then thumped to the tempo of the bass. "I'm an old friend of the family," she said.

He leaned in, still playing. "If you are friend," he whispered in a hoarse voice, "you know where he is today."

Just as Dal asked Petr if he was getting tired, if he'd like his dad to take the oars, the phone rang again. Dal grabbed it, thinking it might be Černý or Kristof.

"Investigator Damek, it's Dana." She sounded out of breath, her words hurried. "It's Václav, his son, not Pavel, we're looking for. He's a musician on the bridge."

She went on, explaining how she thought there were two people in the church that morning, one a man who had come to the neighborhood offering to sharpen scissors and knives, the same man who had been seen at a marionette store near the Staroměstské náměsti. She spoke so fast, Dal could hardly follow.

"Why do you believe it was Pavel's son and how are these two men related?"

"I talked to some locals who live near the convent, showed them the copy of the Internet photo. A man who looks exactly like Pavel in this very old photo is a musician who plays with a quartet on the bridge. *Young*, not *old*. It couldn't be Pavel Novák. Has to be his son." She took in a deep, exhausted breath. "I went over to the bridge and I think I found him . . . well, not him, but the group he plays with, and—"

"I'm with my son today."

"Oh, I apologize." Her voice had softened, slowed down. She sounded sincere, almost sweet, and he couldn't help but think of what she'd revealed to him early that morning in front of her hotel. "It's a beautiful day. I hope you're enjoying the outdoors."

"Yes, we are."

"That's wonderful." She paused for another moment, as if considering leaving him to continue this time with his son uninterrupted, but he sensed she wasn't finished.

"I am meeting with Father Borelli and Father Ruffino at five." He caught his son's eye and knew the boy was listening closely, though he wasn't sure how much English he understood.

Dana said nothing, as if waiting for an invitation to the meeting, which Dal had already decided wasn't going to happen. In fact, he would speak first with Father Ruffino alone, without his friend Father Borelli holding his hand.

"I'm having lunch with Sister Agnes—Caroline—my cousin," she said, then added something too fast for him to understand—he wasn't even sure she was still talking to him.

Again his eyes rested on his son. He should take the boy home, go back to headquarters, go over any information uncovered at Kristof's apartment. Surely Karla would understand. Now, a meeting with the priests. He thought of Father Ruffino's deception. He'd better have a damned good reason why he hadn't shared any of this with Dal when he called him to the church last Friday morning.

"I could meet you somewhere after lunch," Dana persisted. She was like an ornery old dog fighting for a bone, he thought, wondering again why he found her so attractive.

He said nothing and neither did she, but he could hear the tempo of her breathing increase, then a rat-tat-tat as if she were tapping on a counter or desk.

"I will call you later," he finally replied. Dal nodded at Petr reassuringly. He hoped the boy couldn't hear the frustration in his father's voice. He might think it had something to do with him, that his dad would rather work than spend time with his son.

"I'm concerned about my cousin." Her voice had shifted again, the tone fretful and motherly.

"The theft of the Infant implies no danger to the nuns. Have lunch with your cousin, tell her the police are meeting with Father Ruffino. An official investigation will take place. Please assure your cousin that we are doing everything possible to find the Infant."

"I will. Thank you."

He'd checked both Father Borelli's and Dana Pierson's flight itineraries. He knew Dana was scheduled to fly out the following morning, and Father Borelli was leaving Wednesday afternoon. He still had Giovanni Borelli's passport. He never did get Dana's. After her emotional collapse in front of the hotel, he somehow couldn't ask for it. He wondered if she'd cancel her flight, decide she couldn't leave until the Infant of Prague was back on the altar.

"Enjoy this lovely day with your son," she said again.

"I will." Dal motioned, gesturing back toward the rental shop.

"Where are we going?" Petr asked, squinting up at his dad against the glare of the midday sun.

"Stalinska." Dal flipped his phone shut.

· 30 ·

Dana arrived at the convent out of breath, having sprinted the last block from her hotel, where she'd returned to use the phone. Unlatching the gate, rushing to the front door, she saw immediately that the handwritten sign announcing Sister Claire's death and informing visitors of the mourning period had been removed.

Her knock was answered by a short plump nun, who greeted Dana with a *"Dobrý den,"* introduced herself as Sister Eurosia, and then silently led her down the long hall and up the stairs, through the kitchen, and into the dining room.

Caroline, Sister Agnes, sat at a long wooden table. An older nun, the prioress, Dana guessed, sat beside her, both women's heads bowed. Caroline's eyes jumped up, a relieved expression quickly flickering across her face as she rose and crossed the room to embrace Dana.

"Oh, it is so good to see you, Dana. Thank you so much for coming." She planted a kiss on each cheek then placed her hands on Dana's shoulders and looked into her eyes, studying her, taking in what she'd not had time or courage for when they met at the church. "I was worried. I thought you weren't coming." She smiled.

"I'm sorry," Dana said, realizing Caroline had been concerned for her, too. "I'm fine. You?"

Caroline nodded, but seemed unable to let go, her hands moving down Dana's shoulders, then her arms, clasping her hands. Finally she turned and spoke to the older nun and introduced her to Dana as Sister Thereza. The nun smiled warmly. Caroline led Dana to the table and motioned her to sit.

Another nun, tall and thin, glided in like a character from a Madeline book and placed a basket of bread on the table. Caroline introduced her as Sister Ludmila.

"You're all right?" Dana asked again as Sister Ludmila retreated to the kitchen.

"Yes, fine," she answered with a tentative smile. "We've been told to cooperate fully with you. To answer any questions you might have."

"By whom?" Dana asked, surprised.

"Our prior at Our Lady Victorious."

"Father Ruffino? The Italian priest?"

The tall nun returned with a tray on which she carried three large bowls of soup. She placed a serving in front of each of the three women and again left the room.

The prioress cleared her throat, and she and Caroline bowed heads and together recited a prayer. Then, reaching under the table, Caroline gave Dana's hand another reassuring squeeze. The prioress passed the bread. Dana took a slice, nodding a thank-you. It was warm, fresh from the oven. Sister Thereza said something to Sister Agnes and offered a cautious smile to Dana.

"She wants to thank you," Caroline said, "for the help you are giving us to return the Holy Infant to his home at Our Lady Victorious."

"Father Ruffino admitted it had been stolen?" Dana asked.

"We already knew that," Caroline replied, glancing at her superior. Dana didn't know if Sister Thereza understood what they were saying; she didn't join in the conversation. "We were told not to speak of it. Or what happened to Sister Claire."

Dana detected an uncertain tone in her voice. "What *did* happen to Sister Claire?" she asked. It appeared nothing in the conversation was being censored. Borelli had obviously met with his friend that morning. Dana wanted to know exactly what Ruffino had told the nuns after the two priests spoke.

"Father Ruffino says the police confirmed she suffered a heart attack," Caroline said, "that she fell on the clipping shears, though it was heart failure that killed her." She closed her eyes for a moment.

"You knew the statue had been taken and replaced with a replica, because you dressed it for the Easter weekend services?"

A silent nod.

"You believe what Father Ruffino told you today?"

"Yes."

"What else did he tell you?"

"That an important investigator has been sent from the Vatican, that he is working along with the Czech police, as well as an investigative reporter sent from America—"

"That would be me?"

Caroline's tightly pinched lips lifted slightly.

"How did he explain that? A tad bit strange, isn't it? He said *I'd* been *sent*?"

"He said the Holy Infant had sent these people to help us find the—"

"Holy Infant?"

Caroline smiled now, and the smile moved to her eyes, fully aware of Dana's perceived irony in all this.

"Did he mention Pavel Novák?" Dana asked.

A line of confusion formed along Caroline's brow, and Dana noticed a fan of wrinkles along the corners of her still-beautiful blue eyes rimmed with thick, mascara-free lashes.

"He didn't?" Dana asked incredulously. "He didn't say anything about Pavel?"

"What does Pavel have to do with this?"

Dana explained what Borelli had told her about his first meeting with Father Ruffino, Sister Claire's dying words, information he obviously hadn't bothered to share with the nuns or Damek. If there hadn't been all this deception and lying, the Infant might be back on the altar already. As things were going now, it had been gone for more than a week and might never be returned.

"Remember, years ago," Dana said, "you sent me a CD produced around the time of the revolution? Pavel had a song on it entitled 'Laterna Magika'?"

"Yes, of course."

"Is there a chance," Dana asked, "that Sister Claire had heard it, that she recognized a voice?" *And could Václav have a voice identical to his father's?* Dana wondered.

"Yes, and yes." A finger rose to Caroline's mouth and she tapped nervously for a moment. "When Sister Claire lost her sight . . . it was difficult. She still enjoyed music, our liturgical music, of course. . . ." Caroline put both hands to her mouth now, but this time Dana saw an attempt to suppress a giggle. "The old girl loved her rock and roll. Yes, she listened to that CD. She enjoyed it. It was sort of our little thing."

Dana smiled, too, as she envisioned the old nun with a headset, bobbing and jiving to the lively beat of rock.

Sister Thereza sat, slowly lifting soup to mouth, wiping her lips now and then with her napkin, looking up at Sister Agnes, then glancing at Dana, as they conversed. She said something quickly to the younger nun, her tone that of a protective mother.

"She says we need to eat our soup before it gets cold," Caroline said, and Dana couldn't help but think of her own mother and Caroline's mother. Sisters. Obediently each took a sip.

"I understand," Dana said, "a couple of weeks ago"—she hesitated, deciding she wouldn't add *before Sister Claire's death*—"a man came to the neighborhood offering to sharpen knives and scissors. Did anyone notice a missing key after that?"

Caroline set her soup spoon down on the small bread plate. "Keys disappear around here all the time. We've several sets." Dana had a set in her bag right now, and was trying to decide how to return it gracefully.

"We were all aware," Caroline continued, "that Sister Claire was in and out of the convent at odd hours. We considered putting a lock on her door." She glanced at Dana, who knew instantly that her cousin could hear the unspoken thought sitting on the edge of Dana's mind—*Well, aren't you all prisoners?*

"We are free to leave if we wish," Caroline explained. "Our vows are voluntary."

"Are you happy?" Dana asked. Even now, Dana wondered if there were more to Caroline's decision to join the convent than a religious calling. They'd been so close through their childhood, but the convent walls had created not only a physical barrier but an emotional one, too.

"With my life here at the convent?"

Dana nodded quickly.

"Yes, I am, though Sister Claire's death and the disappearance of the Infant, not exactly the happiest moments of my convent life. She was very old . . . but, still, losing someone you love. But then, we all . . ." She stopped. "I'm sorry, Dana." She reached out and placed a gentle hand over her cousin's.

Dana knew what she was thinking. She felt a touch of that familiar intimacy again, a memory of how it had been with the two girls when they were younger, how, at times, she felt they could read each other's thoughts.

"It was five years last week," Caroline said quietly. "You are in my prayers each day, but especially during the Easter season."

They had exchanged sporadic letters after Dana left Prague, which all but halted when Caroline entered the convent. She'd written after Joel's disappearance, during the difficulties with Dana's marriage, the divorce, but it had been twenty years since they had seen one another.

"How are you doing?" Caroline asked.

Dana just shook her head, and Caroline stroked her hand with heartbreaking tenderness, but for many moments she offered no words.

"I still pray for a miracle," Caroline said softly. "It has happened."

Dana nodded. They had never found the body. Yes, sometimes she, too, prayed for a miracle, though it was more a thought sent out involuntarily into a great emptiness, and maybe there wasn't much difference.

"Thank you," she said.

The tall nun entered with a tray and three small bowls of berries with cream. Caroline spoke rapidly to Sister Ludmila, then turned to Dana. "She says the key for the Infant's altar was missing after the man came to sharpen the knives, but then it showed up a couple of days later, and she just figured Sister Claire had misplaced it again. As I said, we keep several sets."

"Did you see him?" she asked Caroline. "The man who came to sharpen the knives and scissors?"

She shook her head and exchanged more words with Sister Ludmila.

"She says he arrived on a bicycle."

Dana remembered Father Borelli talking about *l'arrotino*, who traveled through the countryside on a bike, but guessed it was a common mode of transportation. If the sharpening tools were attached to the bike, he most likely wouldn't have come inside, which might shoot down her theory that he'd taken the keys.

"An old-fashioned bike," Caroline said, "with a portable toolbox that he brought inside."

"So he did come inside?" Dana asked, and then she remembered the second receipt. "Did he come twice? The following day?" That was how he'd returned the keys, she reasoned, after making his own copies.

Again the two nuns spoke. "Yes," Caroline replied. "Sister Ludmila asked that he come again, because she wanted to bring the garden shears from the church."

The shears that slashed the old nun's face, Dana realized, and guessed Caroline was envisioning the same.

"What did he look like?" Dana asked.

"She says he was probably about fifty-five, sixty, bushy hair."

"What color?"

More words between the two nuns.

"White, maybe gray," Caroline said.

Just like little Jan and Maria had described him, Dana thought. "Was there anything about him, any other distinguishing characteristics? Anything else that might make him stand out? Had she ever seen him before?"

Again Caroline spoke with Sister Ludmila, who thought for a moment, then replied.

Caroline turned back to Dana. "He appeared to have an abundance of hair, but when he came inside, took the hat off, he was bald as a mushroom on top. Spotted like a mushroom, too." Caroline smiled at the image.

"Did he say anything unusual, make any special requests? Was he left alone?"

"Yes, for a moment or two, while he worked."

"But she didn't notice anything else unusual?"

Again Caroline conversed with the tall, thin nun, who shook her head toward Dana.

With no other questions, Dana thanked her. Sister Ludmila tipped her wimpled head and left as the two younger women dipped into their soup again, the prioress having already started in on the berries.

"Did Pavel and Lenka marry?" Dana asked.

"They lived together for a while. Little Václav was born. Later Lenka had a daughter. As I understand, she was not well."

"The daughter wasn't well?"

"As I understand."

"She had a second child with Pavel?"

"No," Caroline said quietly, glancing at the prioress, then back at Dana. "No, I'm sure it wasn't Pavel. By then, he was . . ." She didn't finish.

"He'd left Prague by then? He isn't here in the city anymore?" Dana already knew this, but just wanted a final confirmation from Caroline.

Caroline shook her head, pushed her soup bowl aside. Dana could tell she didn't really want to talk about it. Maybe Borelli was right. Maybe she had joined the convent because of a broken heart.

"Is Lenka still here in Prague?"

"I don't get out to the theater much," Caroline said with a laugh. "I don't know . . ." She stopped, forked a berry, stuck it in her mouth, chewed, pursed her lips, wincing as if she'd just ingested something very tart. "About a year ago . . . sometimes I think back and consider that I might have imagined this, but . . . I think I saw him."

"Pavel?" Dana asked incredulously.

Caroline shook her head. "At first I thought . . . I actually thought it was Pavel. He was too young, but he looked so much like Pavel."

"His son?"

"He didn't tell me his name." Caroline picked up her spoon, studied it for a moment. Set it back down. "I was in the sacristy, preparing the vestments for the following morning. Yes, about a year ago, because they were the vestments worn during the Easter season . . . white, I remember that clearly. I stepped out into the church to say a brief prayer before returning to the convent."

"You saw the boy?"

"He was kneeling before the Infant's altar. I could see he was crying by the way his shoulders heaved and his hands rose to cover his face. I walked over and asked if I could help. When he turned, I was startled—I was looking at Pavel." Caroline's lower lip trembled.

"A ghost?"

Caroline laughed. "Yes, sometimes I feel as if spirits move about this ancient building, but reason tells me . . . Of course, he had no idea who I was. He asked if I would pray for his sister."

"You said she was ill?"

"Her heart. Yes, that's what the boy said, she had a weak heart. And incidentally, his voice—identical to Pavel's. That gave me a second jolt. I thought maybe I was losing my mind, and maybe it *was*

Pavel. But no, no, it couldn't have been unless he'd discovered the fountain of youth."

Yes! Dana thought—a young man who had inherited his father's voice. It was Václav, not Pavel, who'd come to the church and taken the statue.

"I think maybe it was Václav," Dana said slowly, "who took the Infant."

"You think Václav," Caroline asked, words slow and measured, "was *casing* the joint, as they say? Well, I'm sure that isn't true. The tears were sincere. I have no doubt of that. Yet sometimes I think I imagined this whole scene, that it was a dream. I was alone in the church. No one else saw him."

"Have you ever seen him, Václav, playing with a group of musicians on the bridge?"

"My life is fairly confined to the Malá Strana," Caroline replied. Then her eyes widened. "You will find the Infant and return him?" she asked hopefully.

"We're working on it," Dana reassured her. "Did Lenka eventually marry?" she asked. "The father of her daughter?"

"She—no, I'm sure she didn't. Why? Why would someone take the Infant?"

"Father Borelli believes it might have been offered on the black market, or stolen to order. There's been no demand for ransom, so that's not a likely motive."

"It's very old. The exact origin is unknown, though it was given to the Carmelites here in Prague by the Princess Polyxena. There are many miraculous stories surrounding the Holy Infant. I imagine it is very valuable."

Dana had a thought, a thought that now seemed so obvious,

though she was not yet ready to share this with Caroline. "We'll get it back," she assured her cousin.

Both women glanced again at the prioress, who sat quietly. She'd finished her berries and folded her napkin neatly on the table. Dana wondered if Caroline would share everything with her superior after Dana left the convent. She was sure now the woman did not speak or understand English.

Dana rummaged through her handbag, pulled out the photo from the Internet, and placed it on the table. She wanted to confirm that Václav looked like this long-ago photo of his father.

Caroline's face turned as white as her wimple as she stared down at the images of these four young Czech men. For a long moment she said nothing. Dana wondered if she'd reopened a wound, showing her this photo of a man she'd once loved.

"Pavel." She pointed, then paused, her eyes darting from one figure to the next in the photo. "And Marek Cermak. He was the only one in the group who really made it with his music, though he's dead now. Drug overdose." Her eyes flickered up, then dropped, again. "Branko Banik," she said, a whisper. There was something in her voice now that Dana could only describe as fear. "He was in Pavel's band, early on. He went on to become a successful music producer." Caroline paused, took in a deep breath. "And this man, Jiří Jankovič," Caroline said. "Branko's goon." Her eyes blinked several times.

Dana waited, wishing Caroline would go on, sensing she had more to share. Again she glanced over at the prioress.

"You know how the economy took off for some," Caroline continued, "those willing to take chances, after the revolution, free enterprise and all. Branko got into all kinds of things. I'm not sure he was completely honest and upright in his dealings, but you know a lot of that went on. Perhaps still does. Money to be made without the oversight and restrictions of the Communist regime. Capitalism gone wild," she added with a wan smile. "He married into money. His father-in-law, some official in the newly formed government."

"So he's still around?" Of course, Dana knew this, too.

"Yes." Again her slow smile took on a hint of irony. "We're not completely isolated here. We do read and keep up on current events. It gives us some insight into where our prayers are most needed. I know he's had some political involvement, not necessarily directly, but where there's money, opportunity . . ." Her voice faded.

"Convicted of any crimes?"

"Oh, Branko is too shrewd for that."

Dana wondered if Caroline knew the man better than she was letting on.

"I imagine," Caroline offered slowly, cautiously, "he's done worse things. . . ."

"Worse? What do you mean?"

"After the revolution, drugs, prostitution, black market arms trading, all kinds of things that were controlled during the Communists, well . . . I'm quite sure Branko was making a quick buck. Pavel confronted him . . . and . . ."

"What?"

Caroline hesitated. "That's when he disappeared. Vanished. One day. Poof, he was gone."

"Pavel?"

She nodded.

"Murdered?"

"As far as I know an investigation never took place. No body found floating in the Vltava."

"Didn't you go to the police?"

"If there was corruption in the prerevolution police . . . well, once

the new government took over ... Post-Communist Prague police."
She seemed to wave it off. "Things don't happen overnight, and there
are always those ready to take advantage. President Václav Havel's general amnesty, some say it put the scum of the earth back on the streets."

"So nothing ever happened, I mean with Branko?"

"I never had any evidence. Nothing but instinct, or maybe intuition. Just a feeling." She paused and took a deep gulp. "Branko Banik
was ... well, what you'd call an opportunist. Even back then, playing
both sides."

"Both sides? What do you mean?"

"Any situation he found himself in ... it was always, *what's in it
for me.* ... A man without loyalties." Caroline paused, took a breath.
She exhaled, and Dana had no doubt that it was fear she now saw in
her cousin's eyes.

Years ago he'd assaulted Dana.

Caroline blinked nervously, then bit her lip as if regretting what
she'd shared. She glanced at the prioress, who said something quietly
to the younger nun, who nodded. Silently the women finished their
meal.

As Sister Ludmila cleared the dishes, Dana said, "I'm scheduled
to go home tomorrow."

"I know," Caroline said. "I'm sorry we didn't have more time.
Early?"

"About noon, but I suppose I'll need to get to the airport by ten at
the latest." Dana wondered if she could really leave with all this unre-
solved. Yet it appeared Father Ruffino was now willing to go to the
police. Shouldn't she just let them handle it? Damek had assured her
the nuns were safe.

"We're up at five, chapel at five thirty, breakfast at six, Mass at
eight. Generally it's part of our great silence, but"—Caroline turned

and smiled at the prioress—"I'm sure, since I've had so little time with you, Sister Thereza would allow another visit. Could you come by before you leave for the airport? Is six o'clock too early?"

"I'll be here."

"Perfect," Caroline replied cheerfully as if ready to dismiss the strange conversation the two women had just had. "We could have breakfast."

Dana left the convent and started back to the hotel, replaying in her head all Caroline had told her. About seeing a young man she thought was Václav in the church a year before, a man praying for his ill sister. She thought of the grandfather's claim he'd seen a man who looked exactly like a young Pavel performing on Karlův most, and the children's description of another, much older man who'd come to the neighborhood to sharpen knives and scissors. Jan said this was the same man he'd seen at the marionette shop near the Staroměstské náměsti. Neither Maria nor Jan had described the man as being bald, but hadn't Jan said he wore a hat? It could be the same man Sister Ludmila had described.

Even as these thoughts turned in Dana's mind they were interrupted by Caroline's revelations about Branko Banik. Dana knew firsthand that Branko was a man set on having his way, controlling every situation. He was an opportunist, according to Caroline. But was he also a murderer?

· 31 ·

"I'd like to do that," Petr told his dad.

"I know," his father replied.

They'd had lunch and stood now before the remains of the Stalin monument, an unofficial skateboard park. Dozens of sneakers, tied in pairs, swung overhead from a power line. Watching the scruffy-looking bunch with baggy pants, kerchiefs tied around their heads, some with backward caps, all with attitude, Dal would have to admit it looked like they were having fun. It even sounded fun—the hard grate of wheels against stone, the shouts and whoops of boys letting loose, kids without a worry or concern.

"You'd have to wear a helmet and pads. You'd have to have your mother's permission."

"She treats me like a baby."

Dal gave his son's shoulder a gentle squeeze, but said nothing as they stood together, watching. The Letná Park, set high above the city and the meandering Vltava River, had always been a popular place, particularly on days like this—a lovely Sunday afternoon. Families strolled along the many tree-lined paths. Mothers pushed babies in strollers, toddlers grasped their fathers' hands, dogs tugged at leashes, eager to run. Others whizzed by on in-line skates, and some, like Dal and Petr, stopped to watch the kids on skateboards. The figure of Stalin, followed by familiar socialist symbols—a laborer, a farmer, a soldier—that had once stood on this base had been removed years ago, and the pedestal was now covered with graffiti. A bright red metronome, seventy-five feet high, had replaced the statue. The rhythmic beat clicked in tandem with wheels on stone.

"Investigator Damek," Dal heard a familiar voice call out. He turned, not particularly surprised to see Dana Pierson sprinting toward them, wearing that silly black sweatshirt that made her look more like a boy than a grown woman. She might have fit right in with these teenage skateboarders. And yet, as she approached he could smell her, that lovely womanly scent.

She stopped abruptly, glancing from father to son, as if she were surprised to see them, though Dal knew this was no chance meeting. Her eyes flashed.

"This is my son, Petr," he said, introducing the boy. "Dana Pierson."

She smiled, taking in a deep swallow of air as if attempting to regain her breath. She brushed her hair off her forehead, revealing a fading bruise, a trickle of sweat, and then ran her hand over the pocket of her sweatshirt. "Hi, Petr," she said, reaching for the child's hand, holding it for a long moment. Her hard edge softened before Dal's eyes. Not melted, or imploded like it had early that morning, but softened in a feminine, motherly way. *What is it about this woman?*

"*Těší mě,*" she said in awkwardly accented Czech.

"Very pleased to meet you," Petr replied in English.

"You speak English." Her smile expanded with warmth.

"I study in school."

"Very good," she commended, and she turned to Dal with approval. "He looks like you, miniature version."

"What are you doing here?" he asked, not completely surprising himself with the lack of harshness and exasperation in his own voice, realizing he was glad to see her. "How did you—"

"You were having two conversations when we spoke on the phone.... I apologize for intruding on this time with your son, but I—" She stopped, took in another breath. He knew she had no idea that this time was a precious allotment, that he was no longer living with his family, could no longer go home from work, sit down at the dinner table, and ask about their day.

"You were . . ." she said, "well, I overheard . . ."

"Yes," he said, remembering the conversation he was having with Petr as he spoke to her on the phone—more motions than words—and they'd been speaking Czech, but she must have heard Dal tell his son they'd come here to the park. Maybe he wasn't giving her due credit for her investigative skills, her abilities of deduction. She'd obviously found them.

"I discovered something important. It's Václav Horáček. He looks exactly like his father, Pavel Novák, and I'm guessing he inherited the vocal gene, too."

"And Sister Claire heard this familiar voice . . . from the recording . . ." Dal coughed and rubbed his nose. *Damn allergies.* Something in the park was irritating his sinuses, maybe all that skateboard dirt and dust.

"Yes, she heard him speaking," Dana said. "She was familiar with his father's music, particularly 'Laterna Magika,' but . . . I don't believe there's anything in the song itself. Sister Claire simply recognized the voice. I have another theory about the theft of the Infant. Václav has a younger sister with serious health problems. It's possible he took the Infant for its miraculous healing powers."

"A viable theory, perhaps." He nodded, but neither said anything for many moments, both thinking this through, watching the boys, one flying so gracefully he appeared to float on air. Dal remembered his own son lying in the hospital bed, near death, Karla's wish to take him to the church, as if proximity to the little Infant could in itself bring about a healing.

"Sister Agnes also told me she once saw Václav at the church."

Dal turned, his eyes meeting Dana's. "When?"

"About a year ago."

"Planning even then to take the Infant?"

"Caroline seemed to think he was sincere. He was there to pray."

Dal didn't know quite what to think of this information. He should probably visit the convent and speak to the nuns. No, no— once he met with the priests he would turn this over to the proper department. He would have no authority. And yet, he wondered if he could truly let go.

"You believe a second person was in the church with him?" Dal realized this was what she'd been telling him earlier on the phone. What had she said—a man from a marionette shop?

She explained about the man who'd come to the neighborhood sharpening knives and scissors, how the children had seen him and recognized him as the same man at a shop near the Staroměstské náměsti. Dana glanced protectively down at Petr as she spoke, but Dal guessed he wasn't that interested in their conversation. The boy's eyes were fixed on the antics of the kids on the skateboards.

Dal pulled a handkerchief out of his jacket and blew, folded it, stuffed it back in his pocket. "I found an address for Lenka and, according to what I have learned, her son lives at the same residence. I will pass this information to the assigned officer after my meeting with the priests."

"Damn it," she said, then glanced again at Dal's son, who kept inching closer to the boys on skateboards. "Can't we get something started here, drop by that address?"

"I am with my son this afternoon, then . . ." He didn't mention that he had a murder case opening wide.

"Doesn't he have a mother?"

Dal could see, as soon as she'd said this, she regretted it. He could tell by the way her eyes instantly dropped, then rose again toward the boy. One of the kids had stopped to talk to him, and it appeared the bigger kid was offering him a turn on the board. Petr glanced back at his father, eyes wide with excitement.

Dal shook his head.

"Too dangerous?" Dana asked.

"His mother would . . ." He searched for the appropriate English words. "Kill me," he said, thinking of no others.

"That I can understand," she said without hesitation. Then she smiled. So did he. "I'm sorry about, well . . ." Her words slowed. "That's none of my business."

He knew she was talking about his wife, Karla, his son's mother. He said nothing. Dana was right—it was none of her business.

As they stood watching the boys, Dal sensed she was thinking of her own son. She'd been a mother, too. And he knew she would have been protective like Karla. Yet she was much more aggressive and adventurous than Karla. He'd never liked that in a woman.

"They look like they are having fun," Dana finally said.

"Yes."

The sound of laughing, shouting boys, the grind of metal wheels on concrete filled the air. One of the boys, newly arrived, had brought a CD player, blasting an English-language rap, the rhythm pounding, throbbing.

"Go to any park in the world," Dana said. With her eyes, a

slight tilt of the head, she motioned over to a bench where a lone man sat.

Dal had noticed him, too. A middle-aged man with a paunch, wearing a ratty tweed sports jacket, a pair of dark glasses, he'd arrived shortly after Dana. The man wore high-topped athletic shoes, visible as he propped one leg over the other. Eyes darting around, he'd settled down on a bench with a newspaper as if he might become invisible. As Dal tended to do when he felt something wasn't quite right, he'd taken in every detail, even as he'd spoken with Dana and kept a vigilant eye on his son.

Most of the people in the park were families, couples, boys in bunches. But this man appeared to be alone. Perhaps here to observe the boys— these healthy, tempting, young preadolescents and teens. Now and then he'd look up, eyes darting, then suddenly back down, the newspaper a mere prop. One reason Karla might have legitimate concerns for her son hanging out here. That and the possibility of drugs. He'd never let him come without supervision. Again Dal considered what Dana had told him early that morning. She'd fallen apart before she'd finished and he didn't know . . . he wondered if the boy had been abducted by a . . . For a moment Dal felt like walking over, lifting the man from the bench, smashing his head against one of the concrete slabs. Dal didn't know what had happened to her son. Such thoughts were so painful, he couldn't even look her in the eye or comment on such men who hung around parks watching kids.

"I was here once before," she said, "here at the park for a demonstration during the revolution."

"Much history here. Kids still call this"—he pointed—"the Stalin, though the statue of Stalin was destroyed in 1962, and these young boys never even saw it. The marble makes a very good . . ." He searched for a word unsuccessfully. "For the skateboard."

"Might as well get some use out of it."

"The metronome, added in 1991." Again, Dal was aware of the rhythmic tempo that had almost faded into the background.

"Were you here?" Dana asked, a question Dal didn't understand. "In Prague," she explained. "During the revolution. Did you take part?"

"No," he answered. "I believed in the cause, but no."

One of the boys jumped into the air, grabbed the end of his board, and slid with ease along the concrete edge of a bench.

"I was at university that fall," he said. "My mother called me home. My father was ill. He died in November."

"The year of the revolution?"

"Yes." Dal did believe in the cause, but with his father dying, no, he had not participated.

"I'm sorry," she said. "My dad . . ." She didn't finish.

Neither added more but he could see she was thinking something over, that she wasn't done with him yet.

"My cousin . . ." She stopped for a moment as if considering whether she should go on. "There's another reason I felt I had to talk to you this afternoon." Dana stuffed her hands in the pocket of her sweatshirt. "Another man in the photo of the musicians. His name is Branko Banik."

That was who it was, Dal realized, the man in the photo who'd looked so familiar. The name was well-known in the entertainment and media business in the Czech Republic. He'd become somewhat of a philanthropist. Dal remembered reading about a big donation he'd made recently to a research hospital in Prague. "You believe he is involved in this theft?"

"No, no. It's just that she said this Banik—as I understand he is rather high profile in the Czech Republic, perhaps even involved in questionable business practices in the past."

"Your cousin suspects some corruption?" Dal said. This wasn't unusual—commercial corruption. The fall of Communism had opened up many opportunities, the lack of supervision and rules in the new republic providing fertile ground for questionable practices. "What does this nun know of Branko Banik?" He wasn't sure where Dana was going with this.

"My cousin thinks when Pavel Novák disappeared, Branko might have been involved."

"A murder?"

"Someone disappears? No trace to be found?"

"Yet she did not report this?"

"She had no evidence, and I don't think she trusted the police, particularly during that transition from—"

"Yes," he said, cutting her off. "To establish trust, this has been difficult, particularly with some of the older citizens. Your cousin believes Branko Banik had some part in Pavel's disappearance because he knew of Banik's illegal activities? A murder?"

"Possibly." She was quiet for a moment. "Murder. That *is* your department. Right?"

He didn't respond and she added nothing more. After several moments, he called out to Petr, who looked back at his dad and mouthed, *Just a few more minutes.* Again Dal glanced at Dana. She held his eyes, and he felt a touch of sadness. He knew what they'd shared early that morning had created a strange bond between them.

"You look like you haven't slept in weeks," she said. He could see she was studying him, too. She knew so much about him since his revelation that morning. "Sorry about..." Her tone was soft, almost a whisper. "That meltdown."

"I...I..." he started, wishing to say something more, knowing he could not.

"He's beautiful." She looked out toward Petr, who kept glancing back at his father as if Dal were about to relent and allow him to try out the skateboard.

"He is," Dal replied. They stood together silently for several moments, then he called to Petr, who started over. Dal motioned for Dana to come along.

· 32 ·

Investigator Damek left her with the boy at a café several blocks from Lenka and Václav's apartment. Dana wanted to go, but could see why Dal would hesitate to take his son along.

They ordered ice cream cones and found a table outdoors, then sat and talked about the boys at the park, Petr speaking slowly in English, throwing in some simple Czech now and then that Dana could understand. With the aid of animated gestures, accompanied by some giggles, they carried on a conversation.

She found him a delightful, intelligent child.

Suddenly he took on a serious tone and asked, "*Policie* . . . you . . . in USA?" She wondered if he thought she was a police officer like his dad.

When she told him she was a newspaper reporter, explained with pantomime and easy words, he smiled and replied, "My father, he does not like newspaper writer."

She couldn't help but smile.

"You write about . . . bad men?" he asked, eyes wide. "Killers?"

"I like to write about good guys like your dad. He would make a good hero for a story." She wondered if he thought this was why she was here—to write a heroic account of his father's adventures.

"Yes, superhero," he said with a grin, and Dana guessed the idea of superheroes was universal among little boys. "You have childs in USA?" he asked, running a finger along the side of the cone where the ice cream had started to drip.

"No," she said with a catch in her throat that she hoped he didn't notice. She studied the boy as he licked the ice cream off his fingers and thought about his being a little miracle, sitting right before her, enjoying one of the simple pleasures of life. She wondered how much he knew about his illness, his supposedly miraculous cure. She wondered if his dad shared anything about the murders he solved, about the missing Holy Infant of Prague. She guessed not. Perhaps his mother and father both protected him in their own ways.

She took a bite, a crunch of cone, and glanced down the street. Damek walked toward them with a brisk step, speeding up as he got closer.

"A nice apartment for a single woman," he said as he approached the table, "who once worked in the theater, now retired—"

"You saw Lenka? You got inside the apartment?"

"Unfortunately Lenka moved out last month. The landlord did not know where she now lives. He explained that she wished to be closer to the hospital. He confirmed there is another child, a daughter with poor health."

"Yes," Dana said with a nod and a tightening of her lips, determined she wouldn't add, *I told you that already.*

Damek pulled his cell from his pocket. Dana couldn't understand most of what he said, but she caught the names Lenka Horáčková and Václav Horáček. He flipped his phone shut, motioned them both toward his parked car. Dana had finished her cone and tossed her napkin in the trash. Petr was still working on his, more cone than ice cream now, which he was attempting to dig out with his tongue.

"An officer I work with, very good at tracking financial records," Damek explained to her as they walked. "I ask to find information on—"

"Lenka." She finished his sentence, understanding that Damek wanted to know how she could afford such a luxurious apartment when she had no known employment. "Do you think she's involved in some illegal activity, along with her son?"

"I am curious about the source of her income."

As they walked, Dana asked if he would give her a call that afternoon with an update and he nodded vaguely, a gesture that might have been interpreted as either a yes or a no. She told him she was going to find the marionette shop, to see if she could somehow tie these two men together—Václav and the man who'd come to the convent. Dal spoke only to Petr as they hopped in the car, motioning him to the back, Dana to the front. As they drove, the cadence and tone of the conversation was sweet and fatherly.

Just as they pulled onto her street Dal said, "Perhaps it best you leave this to the authorities. I will pass all information we have gathered to the officer assigned the case. You are scheduled to leave tomorrow. Please know that this theft will be treated seriously by the Czech Republic Police."

She took this to mean he most likely wouldn't call, that he was dismissing her. She obviously was not invited to the meeting that afternoon. He didn't have to tell her she had no value in this investigation. She had no firsthand knowledge of the crime. She'd witnessed nothing, hadn't even been in the city when it allegedly happened. Anything she knew could be passed on by Borelli or Damek.

She glanced into the backseat at Petr.

"A pleasure meeting you, Petr," she said with a smile, which he returned. Suddenly she was overcome with a deep, familiar sense of sadness and loss.

Before heading up to her room, she asked the clerk to look up the number of Borelli's hotel. Maybe the priest would go with her to search for the marionette store, and she wanted to share everything she'd learned over the past hours, before he and Father Ruffino met with Damek. No answer when she called from her room. She knew she couldn't sit still. She'd walk to his hotel and wait for him.

When she arrived she marched up to the desk and asked if they could ring Giovanni Borelli for her. Surprisingly, he answered the phone. His voice sounded groggy, as if she'd awoken him from a nap. Dana wondered if he'd been there all along.

"Can we talk?" she said.

"I was just napping," he replied. "Can we meet somewhere later this evening? I have an appointment at five with Father Ruffino and Investigator Damek. Perhaps I could drop by your hotel . . ." He paused as if checking the time.

"I'm here," she said. "And I know about the meeting." She attempted to keep the irritation out of her voice.

He was quiet. *"Here?"* he finally asked.

"Downstairs."

"Come up." He gave her the room number.

As soon as she arrived, he offered her a drink, which she refused. They sat. It was, as Dana suspected, a nice room with a little sitting area with sofa and chair. She told him she believed it was Václav, Pavel and Lenka's son, who had come to the church along with *l'arrotino*, who she now believed was a man who worked at a toy store near the Staroměstské náměsti. She told him about her conversation with Sister Agnes, then finding the police investigator at the park, his going to Lenka's apartment. When she asked Borelli if he'd heard from his friend the icon dealer, he told her no.

"So," she said, "Father Ruffino admitted the statue has been stolen."

The priest nodded, scratched his balding head. He went on to tell Dana what Father Ruffino had shared with him that morning, including the e-mail that stated the statue would be returned if he remained silent. If not, it would be destroyed.

"Too late for silence. Though the thief might not be aware that Father Ruffino didn't contact the authorities . . . until now." She shook her head. "The police might be able to trace an e-mail. Father Ruffino is willing to be completely honest?"

He nodded.

She told him her thought that the statue had been taken for its miraculous powers, and perhaps after the miracle—Václav's sister restored to good health—it *would* be returned.

"No miracle—then what?" Borelli replied with a grunt. "We wait for the miracle, which most likely will never come."

"You don't believe God grants miracles to thieves?"

Borelli laughed, cleared his throat, then said, "I dropped by your hotel early this morning." She noticed a certain tone in his voice that she couldn't quite read.

"Why didn't you call from the desk?"

"It seems you might have been preoccupied."

"What do you mean?" she asked, puzzled.

"I saw that you had another guest, perhaps an overnight guest?"

She stared at him, then realized what he was talking about. "You saw Investigator Damek?"

The priest didn't bother to reply, but it was obvious what he was thinking.

"It's not what you think."

"You're a grown woman. It's none of my business with whom you choose to spend the night."

"Maybe I'll have that drink after all," she said quietly. "A very small drink."

He asked if he should send for ice, a mixer, or add water, and when she declined he poured two glasses of whiskey, more than she wanted, Borelli's regular dose, she guessed. She took a sip and let it slide down her throat. She didn't like the taste at all, but it produced a nice, warm, numbing effect. She swallowed another gulp.

"Investigator Damek did spend the night," she said, "what was left of it after we went to the club."

Borelli raised an eyebrow. "A club?"

"He took me to a place where people who might know Lenka or Pavel hang out." She summarized what they had discovered. "When we got home I asked him why he was letting Father Ruffino get away with his deceit and lies, what kind of personal hold the priest had over him."

Borelli listened attentively as she told him the story about Damek's son, a story that had taken on new meaning for Dana since she'd met Petr that afternoon.

Then calmly, without tears, she repeated her own story of her son. He listened without interrupting.

"It triggered something in me," she said. "It brought back so many memories, so many questions, so much anger. Investigator Damek stayed, frankly, because I was hysterical, because he was afraid to leave. I was in no condition to participate in anything you might have imagined." She thought about how she had physically attacked Damek, how he could have so easily taken advantage of her bizarre behavior. But he hadn't.

"I'm sorry," Father Borelli said. He took a drink.

She took a sip.

"What do you do with such anger?" she asked sincerely. "Do I go to hell because I'm angry with God for taking my son?" She laughed harshly. "I'm already there. I know what hell is."

He nodded in agreement, ran his fingers over his head. His hand was shaking and she knew he wanted a cigarette, but he did not reach for the pack that sat on the table next to his chair. He took a serious gulp of his drink.

"When I was a boy"—he spoke thoughtfully, slowly—"we went to confession each week. It was, in a sense, a part of our school day, the curriculum...like math...geography...confession." He let out a small gruff sound that she thought might turn into a laugh. He rubbed his hand over his mouth. "The nuns would line us up and lead us over to the church, send us through the confessional one by one. But before confessing, as part of the ritual, the nuns assisted us in our examination of conscience. The good women, who surely themselves had nothing to confess—at least, this is what I assumed at that time, as a small child—they would orchestrate this with a review of the Ten Commandments, so we could count up all our sins silently to ourselves." He smiled as if it were not an unpleasant memory. He did not look at Dana. "Some of them, the commandments, I didn't understand, particularly 'Thou shalt not commit adultery.' They always seemed to skim over that one."

She wondered where he was going with this. Surely he understood that she and Damek hadn't slept together and, as he said, it was none of his business anyway.

"Later in life, as I became an adult, I realized it was much more effective, for me in particular, to use the seven cardinal sins for my examination of conscience—like a playbook for all my downfalls." His guarded smile turned now to a quiet laugh. "Pride. Covetousness. Lust. Gluttony." He pronounced the words clearly, pausing between each. "Envy. Anger. Sloth. Guilty of all." He threw up his arms, then settled back in his chair and took a slow drink of his whiskey. "Anger. That one I always ponder with some confusion. How can anger be a sin? Even Christ was angry."

"When he overturned the money changers' tables in the temple?" Father Borelli nodded.

"What do you do with the anger?" she asked.

"Hand it back to God."

"I think I've done that—thrown it right in his face. Over and over again."

"Then tell him to keep it, that you don't want it anymore, that you can't handle it. Move forward. Cherish the memories. Cherish those who are close to you. Family. Friends."

She said nothing.

"You know," he said after several moments, "I've always wondered why God allowed me to be a priest. I'm not very good at this." There was something in his tone, and she wondered if he, too, was plagued with doubt and uncertainty.

His vulnerability touched her, and she was filled with an unexpected tenderness toward this man. She took another sip of that awful-tasting liquid. "I hate to waste this," she said, "but it really is dreadful."

He smiled, reached over, and took it from her. Suddenly a shrill ring filled the room—the alarm clock, which he'd obviously set to rouse him from his nap. He walked over to the nightstand and turned it off. It was quarter past four, his meeting in forty-five minutes.

She stood. "I'm scheduled to leave tomorrow." They stood staring at one another. "It's been a pleasure, Father Borelli." She reached for his hand.

"Yes," he said, awkwardly. "I don't suppose I'll see you again before you leave."

"No," she said and bent over to kiss him on the cheek before she turned and left the room.

Tourists shuffled shoulder to shoulder, stopping now and then to admire the art, listen to a musical group, take a photo, lean against the balustrade to gaze out upon the city, the spiky steeples rising to meet the lovely blue of the late afternoon. The quartet, reduced to three that morning, no longer entertained on the bridge.

Dana wandered around the Staroměstské náměsti, looking for the street and the shop the children had told her about. Finally, after almost a half hour, she found what she believed was the one Jan had described. The sign in the window read CLOSED in both Czech and English, though the time posted on the door indicated it should be open until eight. Tourists, surely missed opportunities, still flowed thick as jam on the streets.

Gazing into the store window, Dana was reminded again that she still hadn't done any shopping and had nothing to take home to her niece and nephews. Along with a half dozen marionettes, wooden cars, trucks, and building blocks made for a colorful display.

A wide-eyed clown marionette stared out with open mouth, taunting. *What are you searching for?* he seemed to say. He looked familiar. As did the grinning troll and also the court jester, with pointy, elflike shoes. It seemed she'd seen them all during the past several days in the city. Thousands of marionettes entertained on the streets, the bridge, and at the Easter market. Clowns and jesters, witches, fairies, and goblins. Guidebooks touted puppet performances as one of the city's highlights. She turned and started back to her hotel.

As Dana began packing her bag, she questioned if she could really leave. She'd check in with Caroline the following morning as planned. If the nuns felt comfortable with the newly opened investigation, then Dana would head out to the airport.

She placed items she'd need in the morning on the bathroom vanity, a change of clothes on a chair next to the bed, then sat, going through items in her handbag. When she pulled out the twenty-year-old photo of Pavel and his band of musicians, again she studied the four figures.

Marek Cermak. Famous rock star. Dead from a drug overdose.

Pavel Novàk. Also dead?

Branko Banik. Still alive and thriving.

The fourth man had been identified by Caroline as Jiří Jankovič. Branko's goon. Still gooning?

Dana's gaze slid from the top of his head, down his body. His long hair hung loosely, the right side tucked behind his ear. He wore round, seventies-type sunglasses. He sat on a tall wooden stool, guitar on one knee, foot wedged on the stool's wooden rung. The position of his body and leg had hiked up his pants, making them appear too short. High-waters, she thought with an inner laugh. How cool was that for a rock star? He wore high-topped athletic shoes.

Something seemed familiar.

The man in the park—he'd worn the same kind of shoes. Nothing unusual there, she realized. How many millions of those were manufactured every year? Yet once a man, or a woman for that matter, found a well-fitting athletic shoe, he was more likely to trade out his spouse than change his shoe brand. She considered this as she studied the man in the photo—the goon. Did he look anything like the man watching the boys at the park? The man she and Damek had seen was heavier, but about the age this man in the photo would be now. He wore the same type of sunglasses. Could it possibly be the same person?

She dismissed this ridiculous thought. Realizing she was starving, she decided, since this was her last evening in Prague, she would have a proper Czech dinner.

After a half hour of wandering, she found a place she remembered reading about in a guidebook, a restaurant specializing in local food and beer, with rustic decor, hand-painted wooden beams and ceramic mugs hanging from the walls.

The waitress seated Dana on a bench at a large table by herself, though she could see the seating was family style and she wouldn't be eating alone. Soon, just after she placed her order, a lively foursome from Cleveland joined her. Immediately they requested the server bring a pitcher of beer, and by the time it arrived, they'd all exchanged the important facts, asking her where she was from, how long she'd been in Prague.

Her dinner—a traditional Czech goulash with dumplings—arrived. One of the men insisted that Dana have a beer and an additional mug was ordered and delivered with enough ceremony she felt compelled to accept. After another couple of pitchers, and the addition of two young Japanese students to their table, they were all the best of friends.

The waitress, plates stacked up her arm along the puffy sleeves of her costume, served the Americans—a variety of duck breast, pork loin, potatoes, cabbage, and dumplings—as one of the men filled up beer mugs so he could hand the pitcher back for a refill. He topped

Dana's mug and she knew if she was going to keep her place at the table, she should at least do a little sipping and join in the festivities.

"Bottoms up," one of her dinner companions sang with a click to her spouse's mug.

The Japanese students giggled and complied, beer dribbling down the chin of the one who looked too young to be drinking anything containing alcohol. The place was crowded now, a line starting to form at the door. Dana ordered dessert, an apple strudel.

Soon entertainers circled the tables—accordion music, men in colorful red pants, high black boots, embroidered vests, tall hats, women in dresses with lacy sleeves, intricately stitched aprons, twirling with partners, doing a Czech polka around the tables, grabbing a tourist now and then to join in the fun.

One of the Americans at Dana's table, a spry, elfish-looking lady, with inhibitions doused by several mugs of pilsner, jumped up to join in the polka.

An animated performer pranced from table to table, lifting his hat from his head, taking a bow, offering a grin, requesting a koruna or two. Though his hair appeared to be thick and dark, without the hat he was a different man—the crown of his head was smooth and shiny. And spotted. Bits and pieces, faces and forms, images from Dana's experiences over the past days in Prague crisscrossed and collided within her mind.

She stood, bid her new friends good-bye, paid for her dinner, and stepped outside. The air had cooled, yet she felt warm, perhaps from the beer, the heavy dinner. Her stomach turned. She walked, but too many thoughts circled through her head, too much food and drink doing the same in her stomach. She shouldn't have drunk so much beer. Added on top of the whiskey offered by Borelli that afternoon, the goulash and dumpling she'd tossed in over that, then a final layer of rich apple strudel, she felt like she might get sick.

She stopped, leaning up against a building, trying to put her thoughts in some kind of order. Sister Ludmila had said the man who'd come to the convent was bald—as a mushroom, she'd said! Was this the same man she and Damek had seen at the bar? The man whose slick head pulsed with the reflection of overhanging lights? The man with the marionette, a jester dressed in red, similar, if not identical, to the one she'd seen in the store window? As she walked again, she had another thought. Hadn't Sister Ludmila told her the man arrived on a bike with a detachable toolbox? Hadn't there been such a bike just outside the bar last night?

After finding a cab, requesting the driver open a window for some fresh air as she gave him directions, Dana returned to her hotel, hurried up to her room, sat on her bed, and called Borelli's hotel. No answer. She called Damek's number. No answer. She left a message telling him her thoughts about the man they'd seen at the bar. Just as she was about to end the call, Dana added, "Take another look at that photo of Pavel and his musician friends." She didn't want to mention the shoes or sunglasses; she wanted Damek to notice these without being prompted. She knew his trained cop eyes had taken in every detail of the man at the park.

She lay back, feeling exhausted and overtaken with nervous energy at the same time. Her stomach still turned, as did her mind.

Hearing a movement outside her room in the hall, she rose and stepped cautiously toward the door just as a piece of paper slid underneath with the slightest whisper. She bent over and picked it up. It was her final bill from the hotel. If she decided to stay, would she even have a room? It was tourist season. Rooms all booked.

She crossed back to her bed, swept up the handbag she'd thrown next to the nightstand, grabbed her sweatshirt off the chair, left the room, rushed down the stairs, darted past the desk, and stepped out onto the street, the cool evening air slapping her face as she walked, her steps quick, her mind buzzing.

· 34 ·

Her scent arrived before the door opened. But, when Dal looked up, Detective Sokol stood alone, enveloped in a cloud of that musky, overwhelming perfume Dal had smelled in the state archives as the young woman handed him the files on Filip Kula.

"Where the hell have you been?" Dal asked, though he wondered if the question was even necessary. He wouldn't say, *I was worried,* but he had been.

"This morning, before I left for coffee—I ran out for coffee, because I wanted to stay alert, and of course didn't have any in the apartment because I'm not a coffee drinker, as you know." It seemed important to the young detective to explain why he'd left his apartment with Hutka's laptop unguarded. Dal didn't interrupt. "Well, before...I unlocked a couple more of Hutka's files. They contained some names, and I wanted to get in to see those particular referenced files in the state archives, and then of course it being Sunday, the archives were closed, and then...I realized that...there's nothing illegal about examining the files. They are officially open to the public now."

Dal nodded, having a good idea how young Kristof had gotten access to those files on a Sunday morning.

"I've made copies. I didn't want to inconvenience anyone by hanging out in the archives on a Sunday."

Dal had no doubt the archives' director would not approve. But, if Kristof had simply made copies, the director might not even know the detective had come in that morning.

"Have you found anything of value?" Dal asked.

"I'm just starting," Kristof explained.

"Let me know if you find anything." Dal waved him out of the office.

No sooner than he was gone, Černý called. It was Dal's preference that his detectives trek down the hall to speak to him if it was important, but he made exceptions for the old detective whose leg didn't always cooperate.

"The mime came in," Černý said. "He was performing near the Karlův most and claims he saw the man again, the one taking photos of the rooftops in the square just days before the senator's murder. He had a more detailed description this time. The man was headed toward the bridge. Surveillance video's here for review. If we find anyone fitting that description, the mime's agreed to come in and see if he can identify him."

The bridge was laced with surveillance cameras, mainly to keep the tourists off the statues that lined the balustrades. Everyone seemed to want a photo involving one of the statues. It still amazed Dal what a drunk tourist would engage in with a stone statue for a little photo souvenir of his trip. But with the cameras on the bridge just about any activity was recorded. He wished he could say the same for the surveillance at Kristof's apartment or the nonexistent video from Our Lady Victorious. The apartment cameras had been tampered with and provided nothing. The cameras at the church weren't even functional.

"Call if you find anything," he told Černý.

Dal sat, rereading the notes he and Kristof had made after examining the Filip Kula files, studying the information Reznik and Beneš had gathered on Fiala Nedomová, Senator Zajic's assistant who'd had contact with Filip Kula then disappeared. Yet all the while he was thinking of Dana Pierson, her asking him to call after the meeting with the priests. Then he thought about his request of Bo Doubek to find more information on Lenka. He shouldn't be wasting his time and resources.

After Dal took Petr home, earlier than he'd originally anticipated to allow for his meeting with the two priests at the café in the Malá Strana, he'd spoken with each separately. He didn't completely understand Father Ruffino's reasoning, but Dal had determined before the meeting that after this, he was finished with any investigation concerning Our Lady Victorious. Father Ruffino had begged Dal to follow through on the possible connection with Lenka and Václav before turning this over to another investigative team. He feared that, if the Infant hadn't already been destroyed, an official report to Interpol would set off extensive media coverage, and the thieves would become aware that Father Ruffino had not followed their request.

Dal told Father Ruffino he'd give him one more day. He'd attempted to trace the e-mail source, but, just as he suspected, it proved untraceable, set up just for this purpose. He'd called the chief whose unit should be assigned the case, though, unlike the homicide chief, he kept surprisingly regular office hours. He'd left a message requesting a meeting with Father Ruffino for the following day, Monday. If they turned up nothing before, Dal was done.

He knew it was going to be a long night. He doubted he'd make it back to his apartment before his meeting with the chief of criminal investigations at nine the following morning. Gulping his coffee, he checked the messages on his cell, which he'd set on vibrate, determined he'd pick up nothing unless it related to the murder investigation. Dana had called and left a long rambling message about her belief that the man who'd come to the convent, taken the keys, stolen the Infant was indeed the man at the marionette store, but also the patron they'd seen in the bar, the bald fellow with the marionette. She'd given him the address of the marionette store. She'd also instructed him—yes, that was the way it came across—to reexamine the twenty-year-old photo of Pavel Novák and his music group.

Dal called her hotel room, but got no answer. Logging on to a business database, with the address she'd given him he found the name of the store, then the owner. Milos Horáček. Related to Lenka Horáčková? The only address listed for the man was the store itself.

This surely tied him, as Dana suspected, to Václav and possibly the theft of the Infant. He wondered if either Václav or Milos Horáček had sent the e-mail message and if they truly intended to return the Infant. Or if it had already been destroyed.

Dal grabbed his jacket, pulled the photo he'd examined time and time again out of the pocket. Immediately he saw why Dana had asked him to take another look at the photo. The only musician whose identity Dal did not know was the man sitting on the wooden stool, guitar on knee, leg bent, pants hiked up. He wore a high-topped athletic shoe, the same as the man they had seen in the park. Dal rubbed his forehead, attempting to bring up an image. The man they'd seen was heavier than the musician in the twenty-year-old photo. But people tended to put on weight as they aged.

The way the man sat in the photo, guitar on knee, was similar to the way the man had sat reading his newspaper. Dal was well versed in biometrics, the method of identifying humans based on intrinsic behavioral and physical traits. A person's basic facial structure, the symmetry or lack thereof, was a constant, and using computer technology for facial recognition was often beneficial in the modern age of terrorism. Exact measurements could be made to identify a face, either living or dead, something they had used on occasion to identify a homicide victim. Distance between eyes, space from nose to mouth. Shape of skull, measurement of eye sockets, angle of jaw and cheekbones. Many of these physical characteristics were obscured on the man in the photo because of his sunglasses. Round, like the type John Lennon wore. Exactly the style the man at the park had been wearing.

He heard a knock on the door, Kristof letting him know the surveillance video from the Karlův most was ready for viewing. As they left his office, Dal asked if he'd found anything yet in the files and Kristof just shook his head. "If I knew what I was looking for, I could probably find it," he said with a frustrated grin. They entered the room where the surveillance video had been set up.

"There are a couple of possibilities," Černý told Dal as they stared at the screen. The bridge was lined with a dozen cameras, and they'd sorted through the videos, pulling anything out that showed a man who might possibly fit the mime's description.

"This one," Černý said, "seems the most likely." Dal's eyes darted from frame to frame, trying to make sense of what he was seeing. It seemed impossible, but he was sure the individual Černý had singled out as the best match for the mime's description was the same person he and Dana had seen at the park. A man who might possibly be in a twenty-year-old photo with both Pavel Novák and Branko Banik. But the most disturbing and puzzling thing Dal saw was the woman whom neither Černý nor Kristof would recognize. A woman whose hurried, impatient pace had become very familiar to Dal over the past four days. And, if he was not mistaken, the man was just a few paces behind her.

Back in his office, Dal grabbed his holster and jacket. Just as he started out, Bo Doubek appeared, file in hand. "I've found some information for you on this Lenka Horáčková."

Dal motioned him in. Enthusiastically, the young man slapped a computer printout down on the desk. "If someone is trying to hide a payoff, a more sophisticated system of transfer would most likely be used. The woman is getting a nice deposit to her account each month. From a variety of sources."

"You've traced them?"

"Enough to provide some information."

Dal glanced down at the printout, noticing Doubek had also found an address for Lenka, as he'd requested. "Explain." He could hear the impatience in his voice; he didn't want to waste time looking over some printout. "Same amount each month?" Though he could see—four times what he took home as chief investigator of homicide. To an unemployed actress.

"But different sources. I wasn't able to trace all, but I can keep at it. Most are corporate accounts—see, here," he said, sliding a finger along a business name Dal didn't recognize, grinning as he flipped to a second page. This was a man who enjoyed his work, a man who loved the game, who relished explaining in detail every tiny aspect of his research.

Dal just wanted the bottom line. "A single corporation?"

"Subsidiaries of a large corporation. All interconnected."

"Publicly traded?"

"Private."

"Can you trace the major stockholders?"

"This appears to be a family-owned corporation," he said, "dating back to the midnineties."

"Primary stockholder?"

Dal glanced at the young man and saw a wide, satisfied grin tug at the kid's mouth.

"Branko Banik," he said, "but that's not even the good part."

Branko Banik? The very man Dana had said might have been involved in Pavel Novák's disappearance. A man who had possibly participated in illegal activities in the past. Banik was now considered a successful, legitimate businessman, a philanthropist. It was puzzling that Doubek had traced the source of Lenka's income in just a few hours. If a business mogul such as Banik wished to hide a money trail, he'd surely have done a better job than this.

"The good part?" Dal asked.

"This is a Swiss IBAN." Again, he pointed.

"Untraceable."

Doubek's grin grew wider. "The same number on the records I examined for Filip Kula."

"Same source?" Dal's voice jumped as he glanced back at Doubek.

But how, Dal wondered, did this all relate? Lenka...Branko Banik...Filip Kula? *Bribes? Blackmail payoffs? Shares of an illegal enterprise?* Dana had said Sister Agnes thought Branko Banik was involved in Pavel Novák's disappearance, along with questionable business practices. Somehow this all tied together. Lenka must have knowledge of something that could do great harm to Banik, and he'd been paying her off all these years. If he'd killed Pavel Novák, he might just do away with Lenka, too. Or possibly Lenka herself was involved in some type of illegal activity with Banik. Had Kula been blackmailing Banik? Dal sensed that his and Kristof's theory that the person paying Kula was also the person who murdered him was correct. Banik was involved, but Dal wasn't yet sure just how.

"Determine how far these payments go back," he told Doubek. "And if there are any further ties to Banik or Kula."

Doubek flashed a smile and gathered his printouts.

"When you were in commercial crime, ever do any investigations of Banik?"

"Nothing resulting in criminal charges. Most likely his wealth originated from illegal dealing decades ago, but no, nothing. The man is straight up now. A model citizen."

As soon as Doubek left, Dal entered Banik's name into his criminal database, quite sure he would find nothing. The man was as clean as they get. He entered the name in an Internet search engine. A quick glance at several articles in the *Prague Daily News* confirmed what Dal already knew. The man owned multiple businesses, was somewhat of a philanthropist; a recent article listed several contributions, one to the IKEM, a well-respected local hospital.

Then Dal did something he seldom did. He called the newspaper and asked for the reporter whose name was on the byline.

· 35 ·

Forgiveness.

It was essential to his identity as a priest, as a man entrusted by God and his Church to administer the sacrament of penance and utter the words, *Your sins are forgiven.*

Yet it was Beppe, also a priest, who had lied to Giovanni, his purported best friend, and this made it particularly difficult to extend a hand of forgiveness. Father Borelli lay in bed, unable to sleep. His stomach rumbled so violently he wondered if his neighbors in the next room could hear it, or the burp that soon erupted, making him feel somewhat better. He'd had a late dinner, and he'd eaten too much.

Were some sins greater than others? As a theologian he knew the answer, and any Catholic child past the age of reason could recite the catechism. Mortal sin was a grievous offense . . . venial, only minor. Murder, of course, was a ticket to hell. Stealing—depending on the value of that which was stolen, though he realized that was more a legal than a theological interpretation.

Lying? Everyone lied, and there were certainly degrees, a sliding scale of sin here. Now even Saint Giuseppe Ruffino was a liar. Just like Giovanni himself, who was perhaps one of the world's greatest liars. And perhaps the lies one tells to oneself constitute the most severe. Giovanni Borelli lied to himself about his harmful habits. He promised himself to give up smoking, the promise a lie in itself. He lied about how much he ate, how often he ate, sometimes until he was truly miserable. He lied about how much he drank.

And he lied about his wealth. He had told Dana Pierson just days before that he was not a wealthy man. He *was* a very wealthy man. Along with his sister, he had inherited the vineyards and winery when his mother died. He always referred to it as a *small* vineyard, which was not true at all. He had no active part in running the business, but each quarter a sizable check was deposited to his account in Rome. He had a financial adviser who had greatly increased his wealth. He contributed to the Church, to the missions, to political and social causes he believed in strongly. But it was difficult for him to admit, particularly to a stranger, that he was a wealthy priest. Priests were assumed to live in a saintly state of self-denial and poverty. Yes, he lied in so many ways. But he had never expected that Beppe was a liar, too, that he would lie to Giovanni, who had always held his friend up as a much better man than himself.

Now Beppe had finally gone to the police. Giovanni questioned if there was anything else for him to do. Perhaps it was time to return home to Italy. He wondered if the Infant would ever return to its home at Our Lady Victorious and wondered if it even mattered. He knew the news of this theft would soon go out to the world. Interpol police would be called in. Perhaps this news would bring even more visitors, more pilgrims to the church, more money dumped into the collection plates. Maybe Beppe should have let all this happen sooner. On Good Friday this might have created an even greater stir, larger donations. Damn it all anyway!

Finally Giovanni drifted off to sleep.

The shrill ring of the phone awakened him. Slowly, with physical as well as mental irritation, a dream fading into a wakeful fogginess, he reached across the nightstand. *"Pronto,"* he said groggily, speaking Italian without giving it a thought.

The reply came back also in Italian. The caller did not identify himself, but Giovanni recognized the voice. "My source," the man explained, "has located a religious icon that fits the description you gave me. Sixteenth century. Spanish origin. The Christ child, about forty-seven centimeters."

Borelli sat up in bed, ran his hand over the top of his head, trying to shake the murkiness, the confusion from his mind. "I must examine the statue," he replied slowly. *Remain calm,* he told himself. "You have used the alias I gave you?"

"Sì."

"Has a price been discussed?"

"The dealer wants cash. Euros. Two million."

"How much?" Borelli asked, the shock of this suggestion jolting him to full alertness now. He glanced at the digital clock on his bedside table. It was 11:03 P.M. His bank in Italy wouldn't open for hours, though he could possibly initiate an electronic transfer.

"Sì, due."

Two million? He wasn't even sure if a transfer that large could be done in this manner without being reported to authorities. Could it really be authentic, or was he being played? "I most definitely want to examine it, to verify its authenticity. You will arrange a meeting?"

He heard the phone click.

Giovanni sat on the edge of his bed, his heart thumping, his stomach rumbling. He got up to use the bathroom, then returned to his bed, lit a cigarette. Again his stomach turned, more nerves than indigestion now. A flame burned in his chest.

"What the hell are you doing, Borelli?" he asked himself aloud. And what was the significance of the note Father Ruffino had received in his e-mail? Was he heading into a scam? Should he call Investigator Damek? In the darkened room, lit only by the flicker of his cigarette, not bothering to turn on a light, Giovanni reached for the glass on his nightstand, his bottle, fixed himself a drink. He needed to calm his nerves. His hands were shaking.

Dana had suggested the thief had taken the Infant for its miraculous powers. The statue in itself held no power, but he was fully aware that some believed this to be true. Magic. Superstition. Worshipping false gods. The Church had been accused of idolatry more than a time or two. How weak is man, he thought. How easily we place our hopes in false gods.

Had two men entered the church? One with the intention of finding the physical, tangible source of a miracle, the other merely a thief? Giovanni's mind would not calm as he considered the possibilities. A thief, preying on the devotion of another thief, the first with the sole intention of offering the Infant to the highest bidder? But why now? Why now, after more than a week?

Again the phone rang. He reached over and picked it up.

"Midnight," the familiar voice advised him. "Come alone. Tell no one. Josefov. The cemetery." A click.

Borelli took in one deep breath, then another, feeling again the heat in his chest, rising to his throat. Josefov—the Jewish Quarter. *How appropriate,* he thought. *Searching for the lost child Jesus among the Jews.*

· 36 ·

Damek swung into a parking spot, opened the door, jumped out, and motioned Kristof to follow.

Before leaving the office, he'd slapped the now well-worn photo of the musicians on Černý's desk and told him to identify the man in the dark glasses. If anyone could recognize a man in a photo from twenty years ago it was Černý. He'd grabbed Kristof and explained, as they drove, what was going on, though Dal himself was not sure just yet.

Communist informants. Commercial corruption. Theft. Murder. Just what were they dealing with? Did the murder of a senator, as well as a film star, and a man intent on revisiting old Communist-era files, have anything to do with the theft of a precious icon? And was Branko Banik involved? The reporter he'd called was not available. Dal had left his cell number. It was now just minutes before midnight, but Dal had no doubt he'd call if he got the message. Any ambitious reporter was unlikely to brush off the chief of homicide.

"If the payoffs to Kula and Lenka Horáčková are somehow connected, why would deposits to Lenka's account be so easily traced?" Kristof asked. "Yet all deposits to Filip Kula come from an untraceable Swiss account?"

Dal didn't know, but one thing he did know: Dana Pierson had worked her way into something much deeper and more dangerous than the disappearance of a religious icon. And he had a pretty good idea where she was right now.

They made their way through the narrow, alleylike passageway of the brick building, opened the green lacquered door, and stepped inside. Immediately, Dal saw Dana Pierson sitting on a bar stool speaking with the bartender. The place was relatively quiet. A quick glance around told him there was no one else in the bar he wished to question.

She turned, her expression registering surprise, then something he interpreted as relief.

Dal introduced Kristof, receiving a puzzled look from Dana.

"He says the man," she told Dal, gesturing toward the bartender, "in the bar the other night is named Milos Horáček. The male form of Lenka's family name? Same last name as Lenka and Pavel's son, Václav? He owns the marionette shop, once worked in a puppet theater here in Prague." Dal realized this man had been here all the while as he passed around the photo, inquiring if anyone knew an actress named Lenka.

Dal grabbed her arm, jerked her off the stool, led her outside, no one speaking until they stood several meters away from the building, under the eaves of another, Kristof's eyes darting from rooftop to rooftop.

"What are you doing here?" Dana asked. "I thought you'd given up on the case of the disappearing icon, passed it on." She glanced at Kristof as if she needed further explanation as to why Damek had brought along another detective. "He's the assigned officer?"

"No," Dal replied. "He is a homicide investigator." They walked, his arm still linked through hers. Damek glanced around, attempting to keep in the shadows of the building, staying away from any street or building lights. Kristof continued surveillance.

"Somehow the theft," Dal told her, "might be related to the murder of Senator Zajic, as well as two earlier homicides." He motioned down the street toward the car.

"Murder?" she said. "There's a big difference between a thief and a murderer." She glanced at Kristof.

"Lenka is either working for Banik," Dal said, "or she's blackmailing him."

"How do you know that?"

"A payment deposited to her account each month."

"You're trying to tie Lenka and Banik to these murders?"

They'd arrived at Dal's car. He could see she was shivering, stuffing her hands in her sweatshirt pocket. He motioned Dana in front as Kristof jumped in back.

Dal began reciting facts from the murder investigations, the recent surveillance film from the bridge that showed the man the mime had described as photographing the scene of the senator's murder days before it happened, the same man Dal and Dana had seen at the park, the man who was obviously following Dana, the man who was in a twenty-year-old photo with Pavel Novák and Branko Banik. Dal knew there was a link, some connection between the theft at the church and the murders. And, unknowingly, Dana was the key to discovering it.

Pavel. Lenka. Václav. Milos Horáček. Senator Zajic. Filip Kula. Hugo Hutka. Branko Banik. The man at the park whose name he did not yet know.

"You believe the man we saw at the park," Dal asked, "is the same as in the photo with Pavel's band? Branko's band? Do you know this man? When you came to Prague many years ago?"

"No, but Caroline, Sister Agnes, knew him.... *Goon,* she said. That's what she called him, Branko's goon."

"Goon? This word I do not know."

Dana thought for a moment. "A thug? Someone hired to intimidate or—"

"Murder?" Damek asked.

Dana shivered. "Jiří something. . . ." She pressed her fingers to her forehead as if trying to withdraw the information, the name. "Jankovič. Jiří Jankovič."

"How do you know this?"

"My cousin." Dana took in a deep swallow. "Caroline, Sister Agnes, told me his name."

"You did not notice someone following you?" Dal asked.

"Well, you," she said. "I've had the feeling someone has been following me since I arrived in Prague."

In Czech, Dal told Kristof to call Černý, give him the name and this information on Jankovič, and find a current address, anything else that might be helpful.

As soon as he hung up, Dana said slowly, words halting as if she were still thinking it through, "Something else Caroline said about Banik, she said he was an opportunist, that he had no loyalties, that he played both sides."

"Did she explain?"

"She clammed up at that point. I could see she didn't want to discuss it further, as if she was afraid. But I sensed she was referring to something that happened during the revolution or shortly after." Dana paused as if thinking. "Could he have been acting as both a dissenter and possibly a Communist informer? *Playing both sides*, those were her words."

"Both sides?" Dal repeated and glanced back at Kristof.

The cabdriver had dropped him off several blocks from the cemetery, as per Giovanni Borelli's request. He knew he must arrive alone, yet with each labored step, each intake of the cool night air, doubt circled around him like a pack of hyenas waiting to pounce on their prey.

In the short time between his informer's second call and stepping into the cab outside his hotel, Father Borelli had decided he would go alone, just as instructed, examine the Infant, and then, if he found it to be authentic, he would arrange a second meeting to transfer funds in exchange for the icon. He would share all this with Investigator Damek then, after he was assured the Infant was real.

His heart pumped furiously. Again his stomach rumbled, the heat in his chest refusing to cool, though the night air felt crisp and refreshing against his face. Giovanni stopped for a moment to rest, as if standing still might slow everything else down, too. He considered pulling out a cigarette, but, glancing down at his illuminated watch, he knew there was no time. He gazed up at a dark, star-filled sky. The half-moon, waning, hung like a lopsided, open-mouthed laugh, taunting him. *You old fool,* it seemed to say.

He inhaled deeply as he started again down the deserted street. The cemetery, he knew, was just a block away now, but it seemed he had already exerted as much energy as his ancient body possessed. He was too old for this. Trying to be a hero? Perhaps he should have alerted Investigator Damek, sent a much younger man, a police officer who knew how to do this. Was he, Giovanni Borelli, so intent on solving this mystery alone, without the sophisticated aids of technology or the Czech police, that he was about to let his pride destroy him? He thought of the conversation he and Dana had had that very afternoon, and the words of a familiar Bible verse played through his head. *Pride goes before disaster, and a haughty spirit before a fall.*

Yet he knew it was too late for a change of plans; he could not turn back. He continued along the street, the shadows and silhouettes of buildings hovering above him. As he approached the souvenir shops, closed and battened down for the night, he knew he was almost there. The small storefronts were recessed into the concrete walls surrounding the cemetery above, its layers and layers—twelve graves deep—holding the remains of almost three centuries' generations of Czech Jews.

The plot had served as the only approved location where Jews could be buried from the fifteenth to the eighteenth century and contained, if he remembered correctly, over twelve thousand headstones, bodies numbering near ten times that, grave piled upon grave, dirt hauled in periodically to add another layer. Again he stopped, glancing up above the shops. He could make out the iron fence, the shapes of tombstones, pressed together, some leaning at odd angles. Though he saw little from this perspective in the dark, he had visited this popular tourist site several times and had a clear picture of how it was laid out, appearing as if the entire area had been disrupted by an earthquake, the ground swelling and tossing the stones about, though still clinging to the earth, rooted and refusing to let go.

He heard a rustle and jumped, then realized it was a crumpled paper blowing along the street, though he'd detected no wind in the still, quiet air. A quick wordless prayer formed in his mind, and he realized once more, clearly now, what an irrational and dangerous mission he had embarked on. "Protect this old fool," he whispered, his prayer now taking on words.

He leaned up against the wall, the bulk and pressure of his body rattling the rolled-down front of a small shop. Then again, he stepped forward, inching along as he approached the Pinkas Synagogue, his body taking on such weight he felt he might collapse.

He recalled that the only authorized entry to the cemetery was through the courtyard of this building, though he knew the gates would be locked at night. How would he find the person he was to meet? He laughed nervously—he didn't imagine there would be a great number of people strolling about the synagogue courtyard or cemetery at this hour. Giovanni's eyes flashed, searching for any possible sign of life. Sensing a movement on the rooftop, something inside him jumped. Gazing up, he half expected to see a golem lurking and darting along the roof. He made out a small dark outline, realizing it was a bird as soon as it took flight and then landed in the tree directly in front of the entry to the synagogue.

A golem? Surely he was losing his grip on reality. Merely a legend. Ah, yes, the Jewish community of this city had its own myths— among them the golem, a creature created out of clay from the Vltava River by Rabbi Loew, who rested in this very cemetery. During the daytime a tourist could buy a replica of a golem at one of the many souvenir shops. A creation of good, as he was said to have protected the Jews, he soon turned to mischief, some might say evil. According to tradition, he'd taken up residence, perhaps involuntarily, in the attic of the nearby Old-New Synagogue.

Father Borelli's eyes darted about once again, searching, finding no one, and he realized he was seriously thinking of turning back. He'd left the cabdriver two blocks away, requesting the man wait for his return.

"How long?" the driver had asked.

"Daybreak," Borelli replied. Then he pressed a scrap of paper into the man's hand, along with a stack of euros to cover his waiting time. On the paper he'd written the name and number of Investigator Damek.

Borelli felt a sense of panic come over him, realizing he had no idea exactly where he was to meet this person or what kind of danger he might expose himself to if someone actually appeared. From where he stood, he could see the gate leading to the cemetery. He stepped closer. A sudden hiss, followed by a series of screeches and yowls, startled him. Within an instant he realized it was probably a couple of tomcats, though he saw no sign of such creatures. When he finally reached the gate and grasped the iron bars, it appeared, as he had suspected, locked. He touched the scrolling iron of the fence and then rattled it, as if to announce, *I'm here*. No answer.

He gazed inside, but, shrouded in darkness, the shadows of buildings folding in on the small entrance, he could make out nothing.

"Here," a low voice called to him. Borelli turned. Across the courtyard of the synagogue he saw a figure.

"Italian?" the man said, then uttered the fake name Father Borelli had given his source over the phone. "You have arrived on time. Good." The man spoke Czech, no accent, as Giovanni could tell from the few words. A native, he surmised. He made out the form of a tall, thin man. The outline of his figure revealed he wore a hat, though the shape struck Giovanni as odd and unusual. He himself wore no hat—and strangely now the thought came to him that a head covering was required to enter the cemetery, that during regular hours the tourist office would provide such. Slowly, the man moved forward, though the tilt and angle of his head, the lack of light, made it impossible to make out the details of his face. But Giovanni could see now that the strange-shaped hat was actually a combination of hair and hat, a bunched mat protruding from each side of his head. It was too dark to determine his age, but from his stance, the sound of his voice, Father Borelli guessed he was not a young man.

He carried a large duffel bag. The man glanced around to make sure they were alone, as did the priest.

"Come," the man said, turning, motioning with one hand, leading Borelli deeper into the recesses of the courtyard. Father Borelli's heart pumped even faster. His shoulder ached as if it was he who carried a heavy bag.

The man stopped, held out an arm to tell the priest to come no closer. He set the bag down on the cobbled surface beneath their feet and pushed it toward Father Borelli, then backed away several steps.

Borelli stood without words, feeling as if he had not enough strength to lift the bag. Then, with great effort, he knelt, feeling the crunch and creak of his knees. Carefully he unzipped the bag. He reached inside, ran his hand over a bundle wrapped in cloth. An Infant wrapped in swaddling clothes. Slowly, not removing it from the bag, he uncovered the figure, nestling it into the folds of soft cloth. Running his fingers over the crown, along the garment, he could feel it was the proper size. He sensed the man standing above him and felt something rise in his own chest. He heard a click as a light flicked on and centered inside the bag for the priest to better examine the figure. Father Borelli glanced up, but the man quickly moved the beam, boring directly into Giovanni's eyes, preventing him from having a clear view of the man's face. Father Borelli gazed back down at the Infant. Dark garment, revealed by the shaft of light. Which would have been correct had it been taken on Good Friday.

Father Borelli ran his fingers over the fabric. A fine cloth, smooth and silky, befitting a king. His hand shook with nerves. He'd noticed the man wore gloves. Borelli himself did not and he could feel the moisture of sweat on his own.

With an odd flash of a vision and memory—he was entering the church, he and Dana creeping to the altar in the dark, he holding the flashlight, she climbing up, quivering as she reached out to touch the Infant. It had been a fake, but Giovanni sensed that this was not—it was authentic. But, still, he must make sure. He lifted the robe to touch the core of the statue, feeling as if he were taking part in some sacrilege, violating the body of Christ, though these hands, Giovanni Borelli's hands, had often held the body of Christ. In the Consecration and Communion. He had distributed the body and blood of Christ to the faithful.

He had no lingering doubts as his fingers made contact with the body. The lower portion had the texture of a candle. Wax, like the authentic Infant. He removed his hand, slowly pulled the outer garment back over the Infant's body, carefully rewrapped the small statue. He zipped the bag.

"Yes," he said. "We must make arrangements."

The light flicked off. Darkness enveloped the two men.

"You have the money?"

"It can be arranged," Father Borelli said. He still knelt, the man hovering over him, and he realized, as he braced himself against the cobbled earth, that he could not stand. He felt a sudden deep compression around his heart, his shoulder, moving to his jaw. He knew something was terribly wrong.

· 37 ·

As they drove, Dal's phone rang. Though Dana didn't understand the quick words flying out of him, nor could she hear the responses, now and then she'd pick up a familiar name or word. Lenka Horáčková. Branko Banik. Václav Horáček. Jiří Jankovič.

Dal slid his phone back in his pocket. "Jiří Jankovič. Many years ago, before the revolution, he serves in the Czech military. Many young men, when the protests begin, they start to defect. They know they are to be overturned. The Communists. Many sympathies did not rest with the oppressors; now they join forces with the youth. They have become sympathetic to the cause."

"Turns in his gun for a guitar?" Dana asked. "Protest through song?"

"He serves . . . served on special sniper forces. Guns for guitar? Music had become part of the protest, a velvet revolution. Perhaps violence is never far from those who protest, even in a gentle revolution."

"And now, in Prague, a democracy, he enters the world of free enterprise, doing business as a paid assassin?"

They had dropped Kristof off at headquarters. His assignment: Find a connection, something to link Kula and Banik. Now they knew what they were looking for. Damek continued to fill Dana in on details of their investigation.

Dana asked, "You suspect Banik decided to permanently shut Filip Kula up, too? Like he possibly did with Pavel Novák?"

Dal nodded.

"And the senator?"

"The senator had sent a representative to meet with Filip Kula. He was corresponding with a man who was constructing an index for the Communist-era secret police files. Perhaps delving into Banik's past."

"But why now? Why not years ago?"

Dal didn't answer and Dana suspected he did not know.

"Lenka was, or is, receiving payments from Banik, as was Kula?" Dana asked.

"Yes, but there is something different about the payments. Our financial forensics officer uncovered many payments to Lenka quickly, while the source of Kula's was securely hidden." Dal explained how they made the connection. They were now in what appeared to be a high-end residential area. Dal swerved quickly into a parking spot, jumped out, and Dana followed. The apartment building was locked, the lobby dim. A guard sat at a desk inside, reading a newspaper. Dal pressed the buzzer, peering through the wide window, and then spoke rapidly into the speaker as the man hopped up and approached. Pulling identification from his pocket, Dal motioned. The man unlocked the door.

After a flurry of questions, the guard returned to the desk, waited for a woman in a similar uniform to arrive, then escorted Dal and Dana to the elevator and up several floors. She could see from the lobby, with plush carpet and chandeliers, then the hallway, as they exited the elevator, that it was a nice complex.

The man unlocked the door to one of the units, and the three of them entered the darkened room. Dana guessed that they were in Lenka's new apartment, though she sensed, as Dal flicked on the light without a word, that no one was home. She wondered if this intrusion was legal under Czech law, if Damek was cutting corners. Or would this be considered a life-and-death situation?

She and the security man followed him as he went through the living room, down a hall, and entered what looked like the master bedroom with a queen bed and large adjacent bathroom. Dal glanced around quickly before stepping back into the hall. The three entered a second room. A floral bedspread covered the bed; stuffed animals were propped inside a dormer window with cushioned settee. The jewelry and makeup scattered on the vanity announced that the occupant had moved on from toys to the interests of a young woman, and Dana imagined a fragile, infirm girl, sitting in bed, propped up by pillows, her mother at her side, gently applying blush to her pale cheeks, a dab of lip gloss. A bookcase revealed not children's books but paperback novels, romances and fantasies that a young woman might read, some in English, others in Czech. But what struck Dana most was the array of photographs scattered about the room—on the vanity, the bookcase, the nightstand. She could see Dal, too, took special interest in these, as he lifted one, speaking to the guard as he examined it. The photo, Dana determined, was the girl with her mother and brother, looking so much like a young Pavel, it was spooky. Lenka was blond, the daughter's hair a strawberry blond. Dal motioned toward another photo on the stand beside the bed. Though a candid shot, rather than the formal portrait she'd seen at the Praha International headquarters, Dana was sure it was the same man. Branko Banik.

Dana stared at Dal, a million thoughts circling through her head.

"The payments to Kula were untraceable?" Dana asked. "Yet those to Lenka were easily traced?"

"Perhaps not *easily* traced. We have a skillful team—"

"So, they are different?"

"Yes."

"He had no fear that the payments to Lenka would be labeled illegal?"

"Possibly."

Dana examined the photo of the young girl, then the image of Banik.

"The payments to Lenka are not from illegal activity or black-mail," she said. "The payments are to support his daughter. Branko Banik is the girl's father."

Dal could see the resemblance between the girl and Banik. It would make sense that these payments to Lenka were to support her daughter. *Their* daughter. These transfers had been too easily traced to be of an illegal nature. Branko Banik was too clever to leave such a trail. Hiding payments from a wife through a series of corporate and business accounts made perfect sense. And there was no crime in supporting your own child.

Branko Banik's wife—a woman with a father who had been a high-ranking official in the Czech government. A man whose connections and influence would be essential to Branko. A connection he would in no way wish to sever. No, Banik would not want his wife, or his father-in-law, to know he was supporting a child with another woman.

Dal picked up a photo from the bookcase and handed it to Dana. A laughing child, a beautiful, but thin, girl, standing beside her brother, both delightfully observing the antics of a man performing with a marionette.

Then Dana's eyes rested on something that seemed not to fit at all with the rest of the decor. Against the far wall, on the opposite side of the bed, what appeared to be a small altar with votive candles. Though unlit, they still perfumed the air with the familiar scent of devotion. A small lace doily sat in the middle of the altar. Empty. Investigator Damek examined the area as he spoke with the guard, then glanced back at Dana, as a lump formed in her throat.

"The girl has been removed," he said quietly. Again he spoke with the guard, then turned to Dana. "Her name is Lisabeta. She is just sixteen."

He motioned Dana out of the room.

"You believe the Infant was here?" she asked, her voice low. "He's been taken along with the girl to—" Dana gasped, wondering if the girl was dead. "You know where she is? She isn't . . ." Dana glanced from Dal to the guard.

"She has been taken to IKEM," Dal replied.

Dana raised her shoulders, needing more.

"The Institute for Clinical and Experimental Medicine."

· 38 ·

The man was on top of him, his thin, angular body, his strangely shaped head outlined against the faint light of the moon, and he was pounding, pounding, furiously on Giovanni Borelli's chest. *He's trying to kill me,* Father Borelli thought, but confusion swirled through every numb limb. Where was he? What was happening? Had he passed out? Who was this man? He felt as if something inside him had exploded and then as if something was fading away, even as the man pounded. The man was sweating, then pushing his hat from his head, rubbing moisture from the smooth surface, screaming in a language that puzzled Father Borelli before he realized it was Czech. "Don't go, old man, don't go."

He woke, still confused, unaware of how much time had passed, to the hiss of the cats he'd heard earlier in the night, recalling now he was at the Jewish cemetery in Prague, though he was not sure why. Then the sound of a siren pierced the night air. Closer and closer, until he could feel it on top of him. Then he remembered, and though he could not move, the weight of his body pinning him down, he knew the man was gone. He would never return the Infant. The man was gone, and the Infant, too.

"You old fool," he told himself, even as he felt himself vanishing again, as another man's voice shouted, "Over here. He's over here."

"The Institute for Clinical and Experimental Medicine?" Dana asked.

"Much less sinister than it sounds," Dal replied calmly. "Here in the Czech Republic we are as advanced as any country in the fields of medicine. At this center many transplants have been successfully performed. Recently, Branko Banik has made a substantial contribution to the hospital."

"To assure the donation of a heart for his daughter?"

Dana turned and stared at Damek, her eyes blinking furiously. She removed her glasses, rubbed her eyes, slipped them back on.

The apartment guard, who was just getting off duty, had told Dal he'd seen the man coming into and out of the apartment, generally in the evenings, though he did not know his identity. The guard also confirmed a brother, an uncle, the toy store owner, pictured in a photograph on her bookshelf with a younger Václav and his little sister, Lisabeta, taken several years before. Dal was sure Dana was right—these two had taken the Infant. According to the guard at the apartment complex, she was the sweetest young woman he'd ever known. As ill as she was, she always asked about his family. Dal was sure she had no idea that her brother and uncle had stolen the Infant from the church, hoping for a miracle. That her father, whom Dal guessed she could not acknowledge in public, may or may not have been involved in this theft, and had certainly used his money and influence to procure her a heart.

"When I spoke with the musician on the bridge," Dana said, "he told me if I was a family friend, I'd know where Václav was.... He meant the hospital. For his sister's surgery, a heart transplant."

Within minutes, they'd arrived at the hospital parking lot, and Dal glanced around again to make sure no one was following them. He was about to step out when, again, his phone rang.

"Investigator Damek."

"What can I do for you, Investigator Damek?" the reporter asked. "Must be important. You know it's past midnight?"

Dal didn't apologize. "What do you know about Branko Banik?"

"He's one of the wealthiest men in the Czech Republic."

"Common knowledge," he came back impatiently. "Anything that hasn't been published?"

"What's in it for me?" the reporter shot back.

"The biggest scoop of your life?"

"As?"

"Not yet, but you'll be first."

"You probably know this, but your predecessor, the one who came in big on the Kula murder, he's being considered for a top security position with one of Banik's companies."

One plus one plus one plus one. Rumors had been flying around headquarters, but a company had never been named. Pieces were being laid out on the table, but still others were missing. Dal's predecessor, who had so easily solved the murder of Filip Kula, was being paid off with a position in the private sector with a company owned by Branko Banik. "Anything else?"

"How big's the scoop?"

"Big."

"It's not confirmed, so we haven't printed it, but it's likely he's going to make a run for Parliament. His father-in-law, retired years ago, has been using Senator Viktor Vlasák as his puppet, but looks like he is about to retire. Rumors are flying that Banik's setting up a team to run."

Senator Vlasák, the very man who had called Senator Zajic the morning of his murder. He was possibly attempting to get Senator Zajic, who by all accounts was a respected politician, if not a particularly faithful spouse, behind Banik's run. Senator Zajic was doing a little vetting of his own, checking into the background of Branko Banik. His phone communications with Hugo Hutka, his aide's meeting with Filip Kula, might indicate such and provide a possible motive for several murders. If it was revealed that Banik was an StB informant, that would be more than enough to keep him out of office.

He thanked the reporter, said he'd be in touch.

As they drove, Dal explained what he'd just learned to Dana.

"I met him once," Dana said. There was a tremor in her voice.

"Jankovič?" Dal asked. Hadn't she just said she didn't know him?

"Branko Banik," she said.

Dal wondered why she'd waited until now to tell him. He got the feeling that this was an important piece of information. "You know him?" Was she about to place another piece of the puzzle on the board?

"Years ago, during the revolution . . ." She stopped, as if deciding whether or not to continue. "I went by his office, left him a note."

"His office? When?" Was her mind stepping back in time?

"Yesterday. No. Day before. I told him"—Dana paused again—"I was looking for Pavel Novák. I asked if he could help me find Pavel."

"He contacted you?"

"No," she said, "but—"

"Pavel Novák? You asked about the very man Sister Agnes believes Banik murdered many years ago?"

Dana nodded, but for many moments there were no words, as if she, too, were placing, piece by piece, jagged edges into a puzzle.

Dal turned the steering wheel, screeched out of the parking lot without another word. He'd been a fool to bring her along. Treating her as if she were some kind of detective, the two of them working side by side, like romantic leads on a movie set. He'd sensed she might be in danger and yet he'd let her hop in the vehicle as if they were off on some kind of adventure. If Banik had murdered Pavel Novák years ago, Dana's inquiry, seemingly out of nowhere, surely stirred up concerns in the man. If his "goon" had seen her hanging out with the chief homicide investigator in Prague . . . Dana had no idea what she had gotten herself into, and he needed to get her out of harm's way.

"I am returning you to your hotel," he said, attempting to remain calm, yet aware the words were rushing out before they'd firmly formed in his head. "Lock the door. An officer will be sent to your hotel. Stay there. We will provide an escort to the airport in the morning."

For several moments she did not object. Finally she said, "No, I want to see this through. And the officer, send him to the convent. If someone has been following me, they might have seen me go to visit Caroline. Put a guard at the convent."

"I will send someone to the convent, but please—"

"I'm involved now . . . I want to help."

Arriving in front of Dana's hotel, again he surveyed the surroundings. He told her to stay in the car. He stepped out, went around for her door, and opened it. She swung her leg to step out as Dal caught a metallic flash, something off to the right on the dimly lit street. He pushed her down just as it sounded. And then another shot as they fell onto unyielding stone, another blast, as he heard and felt it, mere centimeters from his head. Then another quick shot, an explosion, a spray, spattering into his eyes. He smelled the warmth of blood, entrails. He knew she'd been shot—in the gut. Praying, praying his mistakes would not cost Dana her life, even as he sensed they already had, he pulled his handgun and shot toward the fleeing figure. One leg, then the other. He wanted this man alive. The man twisted and turned, getting off one more well-placed shot. Dal pulled his cell, feeling a sharp pain in his chest, smelling his own blood, everything moving in slow motion, the man's gun slipping from his hand as his body slumped and dropped to the street. Then all went dark.

· 39 ·

Dana hovered above. Bright lights. Masked figures. Reflection of light. Under her. Over her. Tubes and wires. Blood. Stainless steel flashing, clinking delicately, fine silverware at a feast. Her body the offering. She floated, somewhere above, watching. She felt no pain.

Then she was turning softly as if wrapped in fresh, warm, white towels, gently spinning through a tunnel of light, feeling the flawless perfect texture, her body weightless. Moving toward something she could not name. Perfect. Good. Comforting. There were no words. And yet she felt the presence of everyone she had ever loved. Her father. Her grandparents. Her son? Everyone, both living and dead. No grief. No pain. Just something warm and wonderful. As if all of life had become one. United in perfection. Without beginning or end. As if she were looking not outside herself but within, a presence that encompassed all.

Then, something pulling her back. A voice? Her own? A man's? She recognized the voice, though strangely there were no words, as if language did not exist. Quiet, and then again a voice, a question, a call, a pull. An answer and she was sliding back.

Doctors scurried about. Hours had passed, yet time stood still.

The clock on the wall, ticking slowly. She could smell the raw content of her own stomach, her bowels, intestines, but also the clean antiseptic scent of healing, of safety. They were sewing her back up, stitching, stapling. The doctors, nurses, chatted casually, foreign words she could not understand, yet words she knew. "We almost lost her."

"We've got an officer posted at his door."

Dal realized he was in the hospital, that he'd been shot. He wasn't in pain. Groggy. He'd been sedated. Yet he knew Černý was speaking of Jankovič, the man who'd shot him, the man who'd shot Dana. "American woman?" He managed to get the words out.

Černý shook his head. "Doesn't look good."

"Alive?"

He nodded.

"Jankovič—"

"Not going anywhere. Obviously you wanted him alive. Kristof filled me in."

"The press?"

"There's a reporter outside your door, but so far we've been able to keep him out. We're still trying to piece it together, but looks like Banik is definitely involved." Černý smiled. "Detective Sokol, sharp young fellow."

"Time? Day?"

"Monday morning." Černý glanced at his watch and corrected himself. "Afternoon. You're just coming out from surgery. Little fuzzy?"

Dal knew he'd been out for several hours, a vague memory, being loaded onto the response van.

"Oh, there's a priest waiting outside, too," Černý said. "You're in high demand."

"Italian?"

Černý nodded.

"Bald?"

"Silver hair. Distinguished. Carrying on about some missing kid, how it was all his fault. His friend, another priest, suffered a heart attack. Just down the hall." Černý motioned. "Busy place, this hospital this morning."

"The priest," Dal moaned, "send him in."

"No need for last rites," Černý replied with a grin. "You're going to make it. Karla just left for a minute to get me a coffee. Fine girl. Nice girl. You're a lucky man, Chief Damek." He smiled again, and Dal wasn't sure if he meant to be alive or to have such a lovely wife.

· 40 ·

She wanted to get up and run, but she was tethered. Tubes and wires. Something had happened, but she did not know what. Or when. Or where.

Her mother was there. Sitting. Standing. Pacing. She looked old and worn, as if years had passed since Dana had last seen her. Speaking to her daughter as though she were a four-year-old child, as if her mother desired nothing more than to cradle her tenderly in her arms. Dana wanted, for her mother's sake, to tell her she was okay.

Then others, in and out. Speaking to one another in words she could not understand, touching, prodding, adjusting, refilling, lifting the shades on her window, then lowering them as if the light and sun might melt her. She wanted to look out, to see if she was still part of the world. She'd left it—she knew that.

Her mother. Then her brothers. Ben. Jeff. All speaking intimately when they were in the room alone with her. Then speaking as though she could not hear them when they gathered together.

"*This* is the *adventure* you got yourself into here in Prague?" Ben laughed as if making a joke, as if making light of all this would bring her back. His face near hers. She could smell his minty toothpaste, his aftershave. "You've outdone yourself this time."

She wanted to respond, *Yes, funny story I have to tell you, Ben.* But nothing could dislodge itself from inside.

He smiled, then brushed a hand across his damp cheek. "We're taking you home as soon as we can."

More figures, gliding, speaking. Czech? Yes. She was in Prague. In the hospital. Bits and clips of conversations. Everything shifting— night, then day, then back again, at once quickly, then slowly, as unhur- ried and cold as a glacier. Dark and then light, lingering without advancing, outside her window. Then everything moving, down a moun- tainside, sliding.

"A miracle," the doctor said, English, speaking to the woman. Her mother. "It's a miracle she survived."

Then Dana slipped away and when she woke it was Damek stand- ing at her side.

"The Infant has been returned," he said in his slow, thoughtful voice, speaking English, switching to Czech when a woman with lemon-colored hair entered, smiled, made some adjustment to the equipment to which Dana was connected. There was something in her throat and she thought, *Surely this is why I cannot speak.* A tube, like a vacuum hose. Sucking, she thought, sucking language, air, life out of her. No, not out of her, but back inside her. There was something in her stomach, more tubes, wires and lines of plastic everywhere.

"When Father Ruffino took the officers to the church that morn- ing . . ." Damek started in as the woman left the room, "the authentic Infant, it had been returned. Unharmed." A memory reeled through Dana's mind like an old-fashioned movie, film turning on a projec- tor, the screen inside her. She watched as a clear image appeared, she and Borelli inside the Church of Our Lady Victorious. She climbing on the altar, examining the Infant. A fake.

Where was Borelli? Had he returned to Italy? How much time had passed?

Then, another thought—it was Borelli, yes, his voice that had called her back.

"I visited Father Borelli," Damek said as if reading her mind, motioning with his hand as though the priest were just steps away. Then Damek told her a strange story: Father Borelli had received a call from his informant, a meeting was set, he met a man in the Jewish cemetery and was sure the small statue he had examined was the authentic Infant of Prague. He was about to make arrangements to ransom the icon. "A heart attack," Damek said. "I believe the man involved in the theft was surely Milos Horáček, from Father Borelli's description, along with Václav. The boy's intentions as pure as grace, the uncle's perhaps not so pure, a very human mixture of love and greed. After Father Borelli's fall in the Jewish cemetery, perhaps a realization came to this thief that he did not want to be involved in the death of an old man. As you have said, there is a big difference between a thief and a murderer. The Infant was there at the church on the altar early the following morning."

Damek stood and walked to the window. His gait was stiff, and he held one arm to his side. Dana could see and hear it: In front of her hotel. Dark. A loud blast. This was why she was here. Damek had been shot, too, she realized.

"I am sorry, Dana," he said as he turned from the window.

She realized this was the first time he'd called her anything other than Ms. Pierson.

"I am sorry that I let you become involved in all this."

As if you could have stopped me, she wanted to say.

Again Damek sat. "The man who shot you is Jiří Jankovič, just as we suspected. He, too, was injured outside your hotel. The weapon used in the murder of Senator Zajic has been found at his home. So far he does not implicate Branko Banik. But it is just a matter of time." Dal rubbed his forehead. He looked very tired. "The index Hugo Hutka was constructing... more files have been unlocked. It is true what you have said: Banik was acting as an StB informant, playing both sides. These facts, if discovered, would be enough to keep him from pursuing a run for Parliament. A woman on Senator Zajic's staff, missing for several weeks, now found. She confirms the senator was checking into Banik's past. Motive, though surely not convicting evidence. At times such as this, I truly wish we had a death penalty in the Czech Republic. The bargaining tools for a confession are somewhat limited. But justice will prevail. Perhaps justice must be wrenched into place." There was a harshness in his words, something Dana had yet to see in this normally controlled man. "Jiří Jankovič will provide the missing information and Banik will be convicted," he added.

"The girl," Damek said as he stood once more. "The daughter. She is fine." Damek turned again to Dana and looked directly into her eyes. "I'm sorry," he added, and then he was gone.

A woman touched Dana's forehead thoughtfully, kindly, brushing back a strand of hair. Jesus dangled from the chain on the woman's neck as she stroked Dana's forehead.

"Václav's sister, the girl, is doing well." Caroline sat. She lowered her head, silent for a moment. "No signs of rejection." Somehow Dana already knew this. Had Damek told her?

"A miracle, some might claim, a heart taken from one, given to another. Death coupled with life." Caroline wrapped her arms protectively around her upper body, shivering as if the room had suddenly chilled. Her voice was barely audible. "It was Pavel's son who took the Infant, I'm sure, though perhaps we will never know. His accomplice—the uncle. When the police went to the church—the authentic Infant stood on the altar. Another miracle?" Caroline laughed lightly.

For the next several days, Dana saw her mother and brothers, then Caroline, then Father Ruffino, with more apologies than Investigator Damek. Again she wanted to say, *Do you think I would not have become involved, even if you had been forthcoming from the beginning?*

He told her Father Borelli had returned to Italy, but had left a gift for Dana. He unwrapped three beautifully carved wooden Easter eggs, like those they'd seen at the Easter market. Each was marked with a name: Zac, Quinn, and Olivia, her nephews and niece. Dana had spoken of them only once and Father Borelli had remembered.

"He told me to tell you that they are for next Easter," Father Ruffino explained. "At home."

She woke to Caroline again, sitting, softly massaging Dana around the tubes, the wires, the tethers attached to her body. Sister Agnes. No, Caroline. Her hair cropped short, a faded blond, threaded with silver. Caroline swept a hand across the side of her head as if adjusting the wimple that was not there.

"I could go home now, you know." She wore a dark skirt, white blouse, not the habit of the Carmelites. A pretty, middle-aged woman with a boyish haircut, no makeup, a cross hanging from her neck. No habit, but obviously a nun.

Dana realized what Caroline was saying. She had gone into the convent in hiding. This was one place that Branko Banik would not look for her. She knew Branko had murdered Pavel and feared that her own life was in danger, too.

"Investigator Damek says there is no chance he will go free," Caroline told her. "With all his money, his power . . ." She put a fist to her mouth, coughed, then stared down at the floor. "The shooter, at first he was unwilling to implicate Banik." She leaned down close and whispered, "Something happened . . . to make him talk." She closed her eyes as if praying.

After a moment Caroline's eyes lifted to meet Dana's. "You'll be okay. God wouldn't allow you to come this far, then take you away."

"I know," Dana said, the words releasing themselves as a painful, forced, animal-like grunt, sounding nothing like she expected, horrifying her.

Caroline smiled. "Praise God," she said quietly.

"And thank you," Petr prayed, adding as he did each time they sat down to share a meal, "for bringing Papa back to us, for keeping him safe, for letting the bullet miss all his vitals."

"Amen," Karla added. "We are truly the family of miracles."

A family again. Dal knew the moment he saw Karla standing by his hospital bed that they would be together again. In a sense he had never doubted it. But, even for a family that had been gifted with a miracle, there was much to overcome, and both he and Karla were intent on making it work. Often, now, Dal wondered if God truly reached down and placed a hand upon a person's life to change the outcome. He had witnessed an unexplainable, unnatural event in his son. But wasn't life itself a complex and often unexplainable series of separate but interlocking links of good, evil, coincidence, appearance, occurrence, men and women acting upon free choice, chaining both chosen and involuntary actions, natural and unnatural one to another?

Was it necessary for a small child to become ill for a miracle to occur? Was it necessary for a child to die, to give the miracle of a new heart to another?

If the daughter, Lisabeta, had not been ill, if the Infant had not been taken, if Dana and Father Borelli had not been summoned, would Banik's role in the murders have gone undetected? If Banik, a man of evil, had not so loved his daughter?

He knew that neither he nor Dana would have been shot had Dal used better judgment. He should never have allowed her to become involved in his investigation . . . and yet, part of him did not regret that she had come into his life. He thought of the morning she'd told him of her unbearable loss, something he sensed she had shared with few. She would not be called back to Prague to testify. He would not see her again.

"Let's eat," he said, glancing from Petr to Karla, offering silently a prayer of thanksgiving and pledging once more to be a better man.

· 41 ·

Four years later

It is her first solo journey since Prague. She is on her way to Tuscany to visit Father Giovanni Borelli. He's insisted on a visit in the fall, when the throngs of tourists dwindle, when the celebration of harvest is about to begin. She will stay at the villa with his family.

Dana has not spoken to him since the evening she sat in his room in Prague, telling him of the loss of her son. For the past four years, beginning with her first attempt at writing—a thank-you note to Father Borelli for the three Easter eggs for her nephews and niece—they have corresponded. He shared with her the events of the night in Prague, his near fatal heart attack.

The same night she was shot. The night Dal was shot.

Now, as he approaches, accompanied by his nephew, at the Peretola Airport just a short distance from Florence, Dana sees he has aged. He is still too heavy, still walks with that sense of entitlement. He kisses her on one cheek, then the other, in greeting.

"Benvenuta in Italia," he says and steps back, studying her for a long moment. "You look well."

She is about to tell him he also looks well—and despite the obvious and inevitable aging, he does—when he turns to the man standing beside him. Several years younger than Dana, Leo Antonelli looks only vaguely like his uncle Giovanni, perhaps a little about the eyes. His brows are thick, his hair dark and wavy, though definitely thinning on top. His build, unlike his uncle's, is fit and slender. She reaches out as Giovanni introduces them. Leo takes her hand, not meeting her eyes but glancing about as if looking for something or someone. Though it is early afternoon, it appears that he could already use a second shave. He is dressed much too tidily to have skipped his morning shave. He wears jeans and a long-sleeved denim shirt—casual, though neatly pressed. She's always had suspicions about men with perfect creases in their jeans. She laughs to herself, glancing at Giovanni, his fastidiousness in personal appearance still apparent. The priest is dressed informally, too, no clerical collar—he is fully retired now—gray slacks, an expensive-looking short-sleeved white shirt. Neatly pressed.

Leo asks if she has checked luggage, and when she replies, "Just one," he offers to pick it up for her. He looks at her now. His eyes are very dark brown, but she sees something in them that she can't quite read. A distance? A disinterest? She hands him her luggage tag. She and Father Borelli sit as they wait.

"So generous of you and your family to invite me," she tells Father Borelli.

"Our pleasure," he says with a warm smile. He and the nephew, Leo's elderly mother—Giovanni Borelli's older sister—and Leo's thirteen-year-old daughter all live at the family villa in the Tuscan countryside. The girl's mother, Father Borelli's niece-in-law, died two years ago from breast cancer. The teen is a bit rebellious, but smart and kind to her elderly great-uncle. Dana knows all this through their frequent correspondence, all the old-fashioned way, at the mercy of the U.S. and Italian postal services. Borelli has given up the possibility of e-mail, ridding himself of his ancient and seldom used computer when he moved from his apartment in Rome three years ago. He has assured her that the business, the vineyards and winery, is all up-to-date, using the latest technology in growing, harvesting, wine making, and marketing. His nephew has greatly increased the business and extended their market. He writes fondly of Leo, and Dana expected someone much friendlier.

As they wait, Father Borelli inquires about her mother, brothers, nephews, and niece. "Your cousin, Sister Agnes?" he asks. "She's doing well?"

"Yes, well," Dana replies. "She's happy."

After Dana's release from the hospital in Prague, Caroline returned to the States with Dana and her mother, but stayed in Boston only six weeks. Prague was her home, the nuns her family. She had entered the convent in hiding, sure that Branko Banik would not look for her there. After his arrest she felt a new freedom. Branko is now serving a life sentence for murder.

Back home, through correspondence with Damek, Caroline, and Giovanni, Dana continued to arrange pieces of the puzzle, pulling up her own memories, watching closely as the case unfolded in the Czech Republic. For health reasons she was not called to testify in person. No one was prosecuted for the theft of the statue.

The nephew returns, empty-handed, and Dana senses an irritation as he tells her the bag has been delayed in Rome. After a short layover in Rome, she took a second flight to the small airport in Sesto Fiorentino. It seems her bag has not accompanied her. The nephew tells her he'll send someone the next day to retrieve it. Dana senses a continuing frustration in his voice.

She has a small carry-on, stuffed with as much as possible, but the checked luggage was necessary as she'll be away from home for three weeks. She and Borelli sit and wait once more as Leo leaves to get the car, the priest explaining he would have come on his own, but he no longer possesses a valid driver's license. She doesn't ask, though she is curious, as he emphasizes the word *possess* as if it were a priceless, precious commodity.

Minutes later, situated in the car, Dana and Father Borelli in the back, nephew Leo acting as chauffeur, Dana begins to relax though she feels the weariness of travel and, even as she and Giovanni converse, the gentle motion and soft hum of the auto—a Mercedes, no less—threaten to lull her to sleep. Yet she does not want to miss any of the scenery or conversation—Leo does not take part. Tall, thin cypresses reach up into a lovely autumn sky touched by slender fingers of the wispiest clouds. Silvery olive trees and grape arbors ribbon the hillsides, dotted with red-tiled roofs perched upon pale stucco buildings and dark Tuscan stone. As they drive, Dana's fatigue meshes with a surge of excitement at the lovely view.

They talk about Investigator Damek. Though he and Dana kept in touch for a time, there was a distance in his correspondence, businesslike, mostly e-mail, to keep her apprised of the case. She learned through Father Borelli that Damek and his wife now have a three-year-old daughter named Rosa.

When they arrive at the villa, the nephew seems to disappear, and Borelli explains it is a very busy time of year. He stops short of apologizing for Leo's rude behavior.

The home is enormous and in the traditional Tuscan style—red-tiled roof, interior beams, and rustic wooden floors. Inside, Dana finds the furnishings more formal than she would have expected. The floors are spread with expensive-looking Oriental rugs and the antique furniture is more of the style one might expect to find in a French château than in an Italian villa. She's shown to her room on the second level and Father Borelli suggests she might like to take a rest and settle in, though without her bag she has little to settle. He asks if she'd like something to eat and then offers to send up a snack before she can reply.

"That would be nice," she says. She grabbed a sandwich on her layover in Rome, but she realizes she is hungry and recalls that Italians eat fairly late.

He tells her dinner is at eight, but she's welcome to come down at any time.

"Thank you, Father Borelli," she says.

"Giovanni," he corrects her.

"*Grazie*, Giovanni."

Shortly after they began their post-Prague correspondence, he began signing his letters Giovanni, and, taking this as a cue, she addressed her letters likewise. It seems more difficult to do so in person.

A large canopy bed takes up a good portion of the room, spread with a heavy brocade cover, fringed pillows set against the headboard. She hangs her jacket in the closet and unpacks her few items from her carry-on—makeup and meds in the cabinet in the small bathroom with shower off the bedroom, her spare set of underwear and extra T-shirt in the bureau. She hears a knock at her door and opens it to a thin woman of about fifty, who offers her a tray, then comes into the room and sets it on a small table by the window. Dana sits and sips the wine—a Tuscan white—nibbles on the fresh fruit, picks a nut or two out of the bowl.

Weary, she makes a nest among the pillows and falls onto the bed and is asleep within minutes. Several hours later she awakens and glances at the bedside clock, relieved that she hasn't missed dinner.

She shakes the confusion from her head, the webs and layers of jet lag. She hears something just outside, as if someone is shouting.

She rises, steps toward the window, pushes the shear drapes aside, and peers out. Leo is speaking. Harshly, she can tell from the creased brow, the hands flying, though she cannot make out the words nor understand the Italian. She knows it is the girl standing before him who is doing the shouting. Her back to Dana, she has the lazy stance of a teen, her arms to her sides, her back arched, her head bobbing as she speaks. She wears jeans, high boots, the type so popular with young girls now, a short jacket. Dana guesses it is the daughter. The girl's hands, still hanging at her sides, clench. She turns abruptly. Her eyes are lined with dark kohl, but she has already begun to cry, smearing the black with her fist. Her head is hung, then she glances up at Dana, expressionless.

Dana turns, embarrassed. *Poor motherless child,* she thinks, and at the same time, *Childless mother.* She can't help this—upon seeing a child the age that Joel would be now. She wonders if she might be going through this herself . . . if. Since Prague, she knows the anger has subsided. Dana still misses him terribly, but she realizes the anger has receded. She knew this as she recovered in Prague. Was it because she had come so close to dying, fought herself back to life? Because she realized that life was indeed fragile? That it was worth fighting for? And yet it was not the end? That there was indeed something after? She had touched it, if only briefly.

She freshens up a bit, washes her face, does her makeup, puts on her fresh T-shirt, which shows the wrinkles from being folded in the small bag. She hopes they don't dress for dinner.

She carries the tray downstairs, finding the kitchen by following her nose. The woman who brought it up hours earlier is busy at the stove. She accepts the tray with a *"grazie"* and motions Dana toward the dining room.

Giovanni and an elderly woman Dana guesses is his sister have gathered for dinner and stand conversing. Giovanni introduces Estella, who kisses Dana on each cheek.

Giovanni's grandniece, Mia, arrives looking fresh faced but red eyed. She wears not a trace of makeup and looks several years younger than she did just minutes ago. Dana is struck by how tiny and fragile she seems. She's still dressed casually in jeans and boots, but has changed to a long-sleeved, dressier blouse.

They are about to sit for dinner, when Leo arrives. He, too, has freshened up for dinner, now wearing a sports jacket, though no tie, still jeans. Dana feels slightly embarrassed, but realizes they're all aware her bag did not arrive; when she greeted her, Estella mentioned it with an apology, asking if there was anything she could get for Dana until it arrived.

Giovanni's sister speaks little English. She is a matronly, distinguished woman, curious and gracious, and, using Giovanni and Leo as translators, she tells Dana that this is her favorite time of year, beautiful, busy, and celebratory, all the while glancing at her son affectionately. Dinner is a pasta dish with fresh autumn vegetables—zucchini, onions and peppers, and garlic—along with hearty Tuscan bread, salad in the Italian style with vinegar and oil, and several bottles of Borelli Vineyards Brunello. She notices that Giovanni drinks slowly, refilling just once. They talk about the festivities scheduled at the winery and in the village during the next several days. Giovanni says that they most certainly will take a trip to Florence and also Siena during her stay. He whispers something to the girl in Italian that makes her laugh. He's the buffer, Dana thinks. Mia, Dana realizes, speaks English, though she says little. And Dana also realizes Leo is making an effort. She thinks how difficult it must be, raising his daughter alone, though he does have the support of a doting grandmother and great-uncle. And she sees something else that is so obvious to her now—Leo is touched with anger and it is evident in every word, every move he makes.

She understands such grief.

Stepping lightly, they all seem to make it through dinner and dessert, which takes almost two and a half hours.

Leo excuses himself, saying he still has much to do. Mia vanishes.

Dana has coffee with Giovanni and Estella and then retires to her room, but she has difficulty getting back to sleep, finally drifting off, yet awakening several times during the night.

The next morning after breakfast, including Estella, Giovanni, and Dana only, Father Borelli asks if she'd like to go for a walk, and when she tells him she'd love to he says he will pick her up in front of the house in fifteen minutes. He suggests she grab her jacket.

He arrives in a beat-up, old rusty pickup truck, Giovanni himself at the wheel. The air is cool and cloud cover darkens the sky. It looks like rain.

She gets in and immediately says, "I thought you didn't have a license."

Giovanni laughs and tells her it is no problem. "We won't be driving on any public highways." As they take off, Giovanni pointing here and there, explaining when and how each section of property was acquired by the family through the past centuries, describing the soil, the growing season for particular grapes, the process and time of harvest, Dana realizes they could possibly drive for some time without leaving the estate. She also gets a hint of why Giovanni might have been divested of his license as they bump along, the gears of the old truck grinding and grating, his pointing and talking as if the driving itself requires little attention. Several times, especially as they turn onto a narrow dirt road rising precariously up a steep hillside, they almost veer off the road. Finally they stop.

"Let's walk," Giovanni says.

They stroll side by side and she remembers her concerns in Prague as he panted and wheezed as they walked.

"I've given up smoking," he says, as if aware of her thoughts. He seems to be in much better physical shape than he was four years ago. "Doctor's orders." He laughs. "Of course, he also suggested I give up eating and drinking."

She noticed last night at dinner he had but two glasses of wine. She didn't notice a great change in the way he ate.

"Exercise has become part of my daily routine." He gives off a little humph. "My healthy lifestyle," he says with a wave of the hand. "The move from Rome, clean country air, exercise, no smoking—that was the most difficult—healthy diet, fresh garden vegetables, fruits from the local market. I'll have to take you to the village, quite lovely." He points to a path that follows the curve of the hillside and she follows. "Most of the land is much too hilly for my walking, so I take a little drive." He points down to where they have parked the truck. "But no drinking! A vintner who does not drink!"

"I read an article several years ago about a butcher who was a vegetarian," Dana tells him. "Seems he had a bad heart and the doctor suggested he give up red meat. He continued to work in his butcher shop—I believe in Germany—but no longer ate meat."

"A butcher without meat? Perhaps no stranger than a vintner without wine. What is life if one cannot enjoy it?" He laughs.

Dana takes a deep inhale of the lovely country air and gazes at the sky. Still cloudy, but she doesn't believe it will rain. Giovanni points out a group down in one of the vineyards. "It's been difficult for him," he says, the words slow and thoughtful. "The loss of his wife."

He doesn't need to add more. Dana understands.

She knows what it is like—the loss, the anger. She understands that grief has many stages, that each who has suffered a loss will progress. Or not. That one is often stuck in anger. How well she knows this. Many say it is time that heals, but she doesn't know if that is true. For some it never heals; for others it takes another life-changing event.

"I think you could become friends," Borelli finally says, and she understands he is still speaking of his nephew. Dana remembers how, for years, she pushed others away. Opening up to friendship cannot be forced.

They stand together looking down, then walk again. The path narrows as it curves gently around the hillside. They walk single file, then finally arrive at a place where it widens and again walk side by side.

"How are you, Dana?" he asks. In his tone, she hears, *I really want to know. I'm not just asking to be polite.*

"Good," she replies. "Yes. Good." She is. She knows this. "Is it strange how one must see evil, how one must suffer, to acknowledge good?"

"Not at all."

"Something happened," she says. "After I was shot." She did not describe her experience in her letters to him. She feels what happened is impossible to describe in written words. "I believe I had what they call a near-death experience."

"Tell me," he says casually, as if he has had this discussion before. Perhaps he has. "Tell me what you saw."

"I didn't see Jesus," she says with a little tease in her voice. "It was more a feeling, a feeling of total peace, complete, all encompassing." She gazes over at him. "I don't know if words could describe it." She pauses. "Maybe love."

"Well, then, maybe you did," he replies.

He doesn't have to tell her that maybe this was Jesus, because in her own way she has come to this conclusion. If not Jesus, it was surely God.

"You were there . . ." she says cautiously, looking to her side, a glance into his eyes to catch his reaction. "You told me to come back."

"Back to earth?" he asks.

She nods and they both laugh. She realizes how strange this must sound . . . but she realizes that she wants him to say, *Yes, I remember, I was there.* She doesn't want to think this was a mere illusion, a dream. And she wants a witness.

"How did I look?" he asks. "How did I look when you saw me in heaven?"

"I didn't actually see you. . . . It was your voice."

"A voice?"

"Well, honestly, I'm not even sure it was a voice, more of a . . . a feeling, a presence. I don't believe there were actual words."

"A spirit? The immortal soul?"

"Maybe."

"I certainly hope if we're allowed a body in heaven this isn't the one I end up with." He pats his belly. "When I was in my prime, I was quite an athlete." Their pace has slowed and he turns to Dana. "Difficult to imagine?"

"Nothing about you is difficult to imagine." As they reach a plateau, they stop to look down. Clouds cast broken shadows along the valley below.

"It was very brief," she tells him, "yet it did give me some peace, some hope. I'm no longer angry with God. In a way I sense he is protecting me, just as he is protecting my son. Wherever he is. It seemed this sense of peace was a promise of sorts." She searches for more words, but they do not come. She looks at Borelli, expecting something, not sure what she wants from him.

He holds her gaze, and for a moment she thinks he is about to quote scripture, something she's never actually heard him do. He has never preached to her. Even in his letters. The night she told him about her son was one of the few times he's seemed like a priest.

Something hangs in the air between them. A silence. But even in this Dana finds comfort.

"Hope," Giovanni finally says, "yes, hope." He motions down the hillside, and they walk without further words. About halfway down, he stops and points. The clouds have parted and the morning sun casts a glow on the entire scene below. Everything—the vineyards, the cypresses, the structures scattered along the hills—appears to be wrapped in gold.

"Now, have you ever seen anything quite so lovely?" he asks her.

She turns to Giovanni and smiles, but says nothing.

"Heaven on earth," he muses, and they continue, walking side by side down the hillside.

LOST AND
FOUND
IN PRAGUE

DISCUSSION QUESTIONS

1. How does the title, *Lost and Found in Prague*, apply to some aspect of the lives of each of the three main characters?

2. Dana travels each year during the Easter season to block out the reality of a terrible loss. How do the events of the story and the people she meets in Prague help her to face and deal with this loss?

3. How does the history of the Czech Republic, as well as the novel's present-day setting in Prague, affect the plot, mood, and tone of the story? How do Dana's personal history and her past experiences in Prague play important roles in the book?

4. Dana describes Caroline, now Sister Agnes, as her childhood best friend, but feels the convent has created an emotional as well as physical wall between them. Does the resolution at the end of the book explain the reason for the break in their friendship? Do you think they would have naturally drifted apart? How would you compare this friendship to that of Father Borelli and Father

Ruffino? Are friendships of childhood different from those of adulthood? Do you have friends from your childhood with whom you have later reconnected? Do these relationships have different dynamics as adults?

5. Dana and Dal learn that they share a common bond, with very different outcomes for each. How do you think this affects their relationship?

6. Dana is forced to work with two people she does not completely trust. Do you believe trust eventually develops between Dana and Father Borelli? Between Dana and Investigator Damek? How and when?

7. Before and since the revolution, Prague has been plagued by political corruption. The Czech police system is described by both Father Borelli and Dana as having elements of corruption. How do you see Investigator Damek? How does he work within this system?

8. Father Borelli is devastated by the dishonesty of his friend Father Ruffino, yet each of the characters deals at some point in the story with personal questions of honesty. Do you think each eventually overcomes the challenges? Is a person ever completely honest with herself or himself? With others?

9. Dal describes his wife as "a spiritual person, very religious. She believes in the goodness of people, in the loving mercy of God." Do you believe being religious and being spiritual are the same? Of the three people in the story who have taken religious vows,

Father Borelli, Father Ruffino, and Sister Agnes, which do you think is the most religious? The most spiritual?

10. Miracles have been attributed to the Infant of Prague. Do you believe in miracles? Have you ever witnessed an unexplained event?

11. Branko Banik is an important character in the story, yet he appears only in descriptions of Dana's memories or in information revealed through Dal's investigation. How does this influence your perception of him?

12. At the end of the story, who has made the greatest change in his or her life? Where do you see each individual's life going from this point?

· Notes ·